"MIND SCRUBBING SOMETHING ELSE FOR ME?"

Chuckling at her stricken expression, Cutter never ceased unbuttoning his denims. "If there's anything needs washing, it's these."

He dropped his clothing into the pile of laundry, naked as the day he was born. As Elizabeth gaped, he waded into the river. "Need help?" he asked, his eyes smoldering with hunger. His hand moved to cup her face, and then he slowly dipped his head to her mouth.

"C-Cutter," Elizabeth stammered. "The laundry . . ." Reaching out instinctively, she threaded her fingers into the thick waves of his hair.

"It'll wait . . ."

Praise for
Tanya Anne Crosby's
SAGEBRUSH BRIDE

"Written wit[...]
and insight, *S[...]*
best books I'v[...]
so captured [...]
Whatever you [...]

Sherrilyn Kenyon, *Affaire de Coeur*

SAGEBRUSH BRIDE

TANYA ANNE CROSBY

AVON BOOKS ◆ NEW YORK

SAGEBRUSH BRIDE is an original publication of Avon Books. This
work has never before appeared in book form. This work is a novel. Any
similarity to actual persons or events is purely coincidental.

AVON BOOKS
A division of
The Hearst Corporation
1350 Avenue of the Americas
New York, New York 10019

Chapter 1

August 1865
Dakota Territory

"I need a man."

The quietly spoken words had near the same effect as if they had been shouted at the top of the woman's lungs, drawing every ear and eye within spitting distance. At least seven brows lifted in silent question, four hat brims rose in consideration, three card hands laid flat, and a disbelieving jaw dropped in stunned surprise.

The storm of voices abated completely, and the cessation of sound was punctuated by the noisy thumping of mugs as one by one they came down upon the wooden tables. In the ensuing silence even the flickering gas lanterns seemed to roar in Elizabeth Bowcock's tender ears.

The glass Josephine McKenzie had been wiping clean plummeted to the floor, shattering. She nearly leapt over the polished mahogany bar in her horror. "Are ya crazy?" she shrieked. Reaching over the counter, she slapped a hand over Elizabeth's mouth to halt her impetuous words. "What do you mean coming in here spoutin' off that hogwash?" Her eyes narrowed in censure.

With an exasperated sigh, Elizabeth smacked her friend's hand away from her face. "Well! Where else

1

would I expect to find one?'' She fought back the despairing urge to crawl over the bar and spend her tears upon Josephine's shoulder. Only the knowledge that everyone's eyes were suddenly fixed upon them kept her rooted to the spot. As if to calm herself, she removed her worn spectacles and blew at a nonexistent speck of dust. Replacing them haphazardly on the bridge of her softly freckled nose, she straightened her shoulders and tried to bolster her pride.

Elizabeth Bowcock had never been anything more than Doc Angus's spinster daughter. When the old man had just up and died last fall, it had seemed only natural that she take over his practice. Doc Liz, as she was now called, wasn't exactly the type to call men's attention, with her ugly specs, her baggy clothes, and her thick, dark blond braid of hair hanging like a donkey's tail behind her, but for the briefest moment, with those spectacles gone, she had seemed . . . well, passin' pretty.

Maybe it was simply the effect of those four little words: *I need a man.* But her appearance did suddenly attract unusual attention—especially since there was such a shortage of women in Sioux Falls these days, both marriageable and unmarriageable alike.

Ears perked.

Josephine's dark eyes blazed. The red plume in her auburn hair shook determinedly. ''Not in my place you won't—leastways not the kind I reckon you're looking for!'' With a glaring sidewise glance at their unwelcome audience, she came around the bar and seized hold of Elizabeth's arm. ''Now look what you've gone and done,'' she muttered, firing another anxious look over her shoulder. ''Good Lord, no—don't! Come on, we'll talk in the back. Quick,'' she urged. ''Looks like you've hatched yourself a mess o' trouble this time, sugar.''

With the sound of a chair being raked behind them, Elizabeth realized her blunder.

Too late.

"Now, now, Miss Josephine, where ya thinkin' ta take the gal off ta?" Dick Brady asked, keeping pace behind them.

Elizabeth could almost smell his liquor-charged breath as he slipped a hand over her shoulder and jerked her to a halt.

"Dadburn it all, I said ta wait a minute," he blustered.

Squaring her shoulders, Elizabeth swung about to confront the bristle-faced man.

"I believe, if I heard the gal right, Miss Josephine," Brady continued, "she said she was needin' herself a man. I don't rightly think ya ken help her out with that, now ken ya?" He scratched his heavily whiskered jaw, his face contorting with the brutish pleasure that skin scraping gave him. "Best you leave that little business to me," he crowed. "What ya got ta say 'bout that, Miss Lizzy?" He gazed at her lewdly. "You wantin' me to help ya out, sweet Miss Lizzy?"

Sweet Miss Lizzy? Elizabeth's stomach recoiled at his revolting proposition. And since when had she become sweet Miss Lizzy? "It's Doc Liz!" she snapped, forgetting her fear in her indignation. "You oughta be ashamed of yourself, Mr. Brady, and no! I surely don't need your help!" Turning from him, she shuddered with disgust and started away, refusing to allow him to intimidate her.

By most accounts, the man was a shiftless ranch hand, unable to find permanent work with decent folks. Mostly he just gambled with drifters, cheating for his money—and he didn't do that very well, from the rumors Elizabeth had heard. How he'd managed to hang around Sioux Falls so long, she really didn't know, burning bridges as freely as he did.

Taking her cue from Elizabeth, Josephine turned, too, her eyes lifting skyward in supplication. She hoped it would end there, prayed it would. Trouble was, she knew better.

Brady immediately moved in front of them, blocking their path. He leaned his elbows back much too casually upon the bar, all the while eyeing Elizabeth obscenely.

Darting a look across the room, Josephine found their one chance at deliverance fast asleep, hat on face and all, and she muttered an unintelligible curse. How dare Cutter sleep so placidly just now? For a moment, in her irritation, she considered screaming out for help, but then decided against it. How many times had she spouted off to Cutter that she could manage things well enough on her own? Besides, if she could keep from mopping up blood tonight, then that was the way to go. There was no telling how her brother would react if she roused him from his nap, particularly to the sound of her screaming.

Brady scratched his forehead. The sound of it sent another shudder down Elizabeth's spine. "Well now, I think ya do, Miss Lizzy," he said with a meaningful grin. He reached out and seized Elizabeth's dowdy spectacles from her face before she'd realized what he intended, looking the shiny lenses over, this way and that, finally raising a matted brow at her.

"Well, well, lookee here," he said finally. "Don't think I done suspected there were a *real* woman behind these things." He looked up at her meaningfully. "Shame on *you*, Miss Lizzy. Now . . . you gonna bother ta tell us what else yer hiding from us poor fellas?" With a dirty little self-satisfied chortle, he then glanced toward the table where he'd been playing cards with his friends. He winked, his face contorting hideously with the drunken effort. "Whattaya think, boys? Think Doc Liz's been keepin' anything else from us?"

A round of laughter answered his question as one man rose, swaying, from the table and headed their way.

The other rose, too, unceremoniously dumping a petite, dark-haired woman onto the dusty floor at his feet. "Wait right thar," he demanded, then stumbled forward after his comrades, unwilling to miss any of the evening's promising entertainment.

As the enormity of the situation finally registered, Elizabeth's heart thudded frantically. How very stupid she'd been. She could see that now. But she passed these same self-loving clods on the street every day. Never once had they given her a second glance. She'd honestly not considered this a possibility.

Actually, she'd expected to pay dearly for the services she required—had even considered blackmail, in fact. But though she was a physician, she was only a woman, and while no one hesitated to seek her out for medical aid, neither did they seem to value her overmuch either. Threatening to leave the town without a doctor would have done little good for her cause.

With a sigh, Josephine inched closer to her prey, darting another irritated look toward the figure sprawled comfortably in the corner. She forced a smile, and slid a hand sensuously down Dick Brady's arm to lessen the sting of her coming rebuke. "Now, Dickie," she said, looking reproachfully at his men. "Boys . . . iffen it's a woman you're after, then there's plenty of 'em here other'n Doc Liz. Why," she continued on a sweet high note, winking at them coyly, "Doc Liz here wouldn't know your heads from your hairy heinies!"

Riotous laughter exploded. Dick Brady's smile turned lascivious, but his gaze remained pasted to Elizabeth.

Her cheeks warming with a mixture of chagrin and outrage, Elizabeth shot Josephine a warning glare, but said nothing. She and Josephine were very unlikely friends—a physician's prudish daughter and a saloon madame—but friends they were. Josephine would never intentionally malign her, she knew. It was just that she'd very stupidly gotten herself into this mess, and Josephine was kindly trying to deliver her out of it.

Still, Elizabeth couldn't quite contain her indignation. Never had she been spoken to so rudely! And though there was no way they could know of her grief, Dick Brady's crudeness was inexcusable. She was the town's *only* physician, after all—no respectable man of medicine would even come near the place—and as such, she deserved to be treated with a modicum of respect.

"But they's costly," the tallest man whined. "And if Miss Lizzy's offerin' fer free . . ." He shrugged. "Well, then . . ." The statement was left hanging in the air as each man mulled it over.

In the darkest corner of the Oasis, a Stetson lifted. Eyes as black as midnight peered out to scrutinize the woman in question. With casual ease Cutter McKenzie removed his boots from the small bare-wood table and quietly set down the front two legs of his rickety chair. He'd heard every word, of course, and his curiosity had finally gotten the best of him. The woman, "Miss Lizzy," had said very little in her own defense. On the other hand, it seemed his sister was near to panicking on the gal's behalf. Likely the poor woman was frightened out of her gourd, and Jo, naturally good-hearted, just couldn't bear to let her be gobbled.

Squinting as his eyes adjusted to the shadows, Cutter focused, and he saw *her*, her eyes blazing in the dim light, her expression wrathful, and more than his curiosity was piqued. Never had he seen eyes so intensely gold. Without trepidation, she snatched her spectacles out of Dick Brady's churlish hands.

"*Doc Liz*," the woman spat, her face pale and pinched with anger, "is not offering anything at all!" She shot Josephine a withering glance, then turned back to glare at Brady. "And I sure enough would know a man's posterior from his head," she told him, her eyes flashing. "Especially yours, Mr. Brady, since it was *I* that had to stitch that miserable knife wound of yours." She gave him a tight little smile, advising him without words that she'd reached the end of her tether . . . that he might want to take himself off before she was forced to tip her hand.

Brady started visibly, almost as if he'd been physically smacked, turning a deep, mottled shade of red.

Miss Lizzy, on the other hand, Cutter thought with a touch of respect, looked right pleased with her little bit of extortion, and it roused a satisfied chuckle from him.

"Two years past, wasn't it?" Elizabeth persisted, further emboldened by Brady's silence.

"How in tarnation did ya get stuck there?" the tallest man asked suddenly, scratching his head.

Brady swallowed convulsively. He looked solicitously to Elizabeth, as if daring her to spill his secrets. Seeing the resolve there, he quickly averted his gaze, slapping the tallest man's shoulder in appeal. "Come on now, boys, Doc Liz says she ain't offerin' . . . and sure t'Betsy's she ain't offerin'. Let's just let her be."

"Uh-uh," the man refused. "I know I plainly heard her say she was needin' herself a man, and I reckon I'm more'n qualified to give her what she's itchin' fer." He leered at Elizabeth, speaking to Brady without turning in his direction. "What's she got on ya, anyhow, ta send ya scampering like a spooked squirrel? How'd ya happen to get a frogsticker in that mangy ol' butt o' yers, Brady?" Tension mounted as the man turned to pierce Brady with an accusing stare.

Chuckling over Brady's flustered expression, Cutter stood, stretching slowly. He was sure *Doc Liz* could handle herself; the little harridan didn't even seem to need his sister's help. Still, he was ready to step in if the need arose. In the meantime, he stood back, watching with an admiring grin on his face as she replaced those god-awful spectacles on her face.

And by damn, if he didn't suddenly have a hankering for her eternal gratitude.

She wasn't a looker, not in the usual way, but she *was* pretty, in spite of her obvious efforts to prove otherwise. And he had to hand it to her, she had more spirit than Cutter had ever witnessed in a woman—besides his sister, that was. Jo had come by hers the hard way, though. A lifetime of dealing with prejudice just did that to a body, it seemed. Some would say he wasn't the most agreeable sort himself. With good cause. Their father had been an Irish trapper, their mother Cheyenne, and that made them nothing more than *breeds*, with no place to hang a hat. Didn't fit in with the Cheyenne, didn't fit in with the Anglos, either. But it didn't matter. He preferred it that way. Life was safer when you played a lone hand.

Still, Jo never complained. She understood, without having to be told, how lucky she was to have the Oasis, and she gave it her best, knowing that money and their father's name had gotten her further than she could ever have expected to go in the white man's world. Aside from that, folks had a healthy fear of the business end of Cutter's Colt. Anyone who tangled with his sister, tangled with him. He'd made that very clear.

Despite the fact that Cutter was filled with fury at his brooding thoughts, his expression revealed none of it as he pushed the brim of his John B. up out of his eyes and made his way forward. The discussion being carried on was such a heated one that no one noticed him until Cutter had slipped his arm cozily about Liz's waist.

She stiffened.

He stifled a chuckle as he bent to conform her body to his. "Mmmm, mmm," he murmured, embracing her as if she were his long-lost kissin' coz. "You're looking better than ever, gal."

Elizabeth's heart started violently at the deep, unfamiliar voice. Warm lips kissed her cheek in a familiar way, taking just a fraction too long to leave her flushed skin, lingering at her lobe. She swallowed convulsively.

He chuckled softly. "Gotta loosen up, Doc, if you want this to look good . . . Come on now," he coaxed, forcing her weight against him.

His husky whisper set Elizabeth's pulse to pounding, and her body into sudden paralysis. Powerless to fight him, she let him adjust her at will. Her legs felt wobbly, her body no more than mush in his hands.

"That's it, bright eyes; now turn real slow like," he whispered for her ears alone, his lips scalding against her face, "and act like you're damned glad to see me."

Elizabeth repressed a helpless shudder as she worked up the courage to turn finally, fully intending to slap the britches off the fool who'd dared to be so intimate with her. But the chest that confronted her left her momentarily dazed, her throat too thick to speak.

He was big . . . and tall. She watched, her eyes widening, as he straightened to his full height. Good night, but he was tall! Her eyes refused to lower, but neither would they move up to his face. She forced them, and found dark hair flowing from beneath a dun-colored hat.

He cocked a brow at her, amusement flickering in his black eyes. Tiny lines crinkled the corners of his eyes as he winked at her, and she felt her knees go instantly weak . . . yet she couldn't tear her gaze away even as they buckled.

He reached out to steady her, but Elizabeth continued to gape, helpless to do anything but. The longer she looked, the more she swore he didn't have pupils, his eyes were so blessed dark . . . his face too tawny . . . his cheekbones too high! But it was those lips of his that unnerved her so: insolent, smug, kicked up only slightly at the corners, as if he couldn't quite stifle his humor at her expense. His gaze roved, lazily assessing her, sliding down over her body

slowly, seductively, then returning to her face to bore
into her with silent expectation.

He anticipated some reaction from her, Elizabeth
thought dimly, but couldn't think what—couldn't
think, period. Staring as if transfixed, she tried to de-
cipher his stony features but found her brain as useless as her limbs.

Still, it occurred to her in that muddled moment
that maybe he had appraised her with more than a
mild interest, and her pulse quickened at that pros-
pect. No one had ever looked at her in quite that way.
Not anyone.

Those dark eyes still piercing her, he raised two
fingers to his brim, tipping his hat in greeting as the
remnants of a smile turned the corners of his mouth.
"Howdy, Liz," he said huskily. "It's been a mighty
long time, gal."

Long time? Elizabeth's brain echoed. She shook her
head, denying it, for if she'd ever set eyes on the man
before now, she would have remembered. He wasn't
the type to be forgotten. Unconsciously she lifted a
finger to her cheek, to the spot where he'd kissed her.
Her throat constricted, seeming suddenly parched,
and she licked her lips desperately as they parted to
speak.

To her mortification, no words came.

For the first time in her life, Elizabeth Bowcock
found herself dumbstruck. In spite of the man's
amused expression, he wore an air of menace about
him like a second skin, and a tremor shook her as she
averted her gaze to his boots. Dangerous, she thought
abruptly. The man was dangerous. She hadn't missed
the fact that he had the most vicious-looking revolver
she'd ever spied jammed into his gun belt, but she'd
only just spotted the jet black knife hilt peeking over
his faded leather boots.

And those boots of his told a tale in themselves, for
they were unmistakably U.S. Cavalry, and ominously
inconsistent with his buckskin dress. There was little

comfort in that he didn't wear his weapons as Dick Brady did, like cheap jewelry. The fact that he kept his blade concealed and wore his gun casually, as if it were not there at all, told her all she needed to know. He was no gun-strutting cowpuncher. He was the real thing. As for the boots, she could think of a dozen reasons he should be outfitted so, not one of them reassuring.

A quick, wide-eyed glance to Josephine told her that she was in no immediate danger, however. Josephine's lips had lifted at the corners, and she, too, was on the verge of a smile, her kindly cinnamon eyes warm with humor.

Not really understanding why she felt compelled to, Elizabeth decided to play along. "Uh . . . um . . ." Mercy's sake, she didn't even know his name! How was she going to pretend to know him if she didn't know his blessed name? In panic, her gaze skidded again to Josephine's.

"Cutter!" Josephine supplied with a laugh, seeming to have read Elizabeth's thoughts. Her eyes gleamed with mischief. "I believe you have her tongue-tied, brother dear. Reckon she thought she'd never see you again." Seeing Elizabeth's comically confused expression, she laughed softly. "Isn't that right, Liz?"

"Right?" Elizabeth echoed weakly. *Josephine's brother*? She nodded woodenly. "Oh—oh, yes! That's right! I did think I'd never see you again," she repeated with a wan smile, nodding dutifully for the benefit of their inquisitive audience. All eyes reverted suspiciously to Cutter, leaving her somewhat doubtful of her performance. Her brow furrowed softly.

Despite the fact that they were perfect strangers, Elizabeth's bewildered expression was so endearing that Cutter felt suddenly like wrapping his arms around her. Warmth invaded his eyes as he gently chucked her under the chin, much as a brother would a cherished younger sister.

Elizabeth felt suddenly too warm, almost as though she were being roasted over a slow fire. And the heat of his fingers . . . it lingered upon her chin long after he'd withdrawn his hand. Mortified that he could affect her so, she averted her gaze to Brady. He was watching her with unflinching eyes.

His eyes narrowing to shadowy slits, Cutter turned to Brady and his men, sending them each an unspoken challenge. Brady fidgeted, flinging Elizabeth a doubtful look before turning away. The rest of his haywire outfit followed immediately, slapping one another consolingly on the shoulder.

Elizabeth's brows rose as she watched the exchange, astounded at the ease with which Cutter had handled Brady and his men. Taking in a fortifying breath, she chanced another look at Cutter, knowing that it wasn't likely to go unnoticed if she didn't thank him. She opened her mouth to speak, but the words stuck in her throat like a spoonful of dry sugar. The man was just too insolent-looking for his own good. And he'd had no right to be so familiar with her. Still, she did owe him her gratitude, no matter how reluctant it came. "I suppose I should thank you," she said, with a rush of breath.

Cutter grinned. "Anytime, Doc."

Elizabeth smiled through clenched teeth, nodding. His assurance sounded so self-satisfied. And the way he spoke the word *Doc*—as though he doubted her claim to the title—struck a chord of dissent. As did everything else about him.

Sensing the tension between the two, Josephine jerked Elizabeth by the hand suddenly, leading her into the back room. Without being asked, Cutter followed, his footsteps amazingly lithe behind them.

Like a thief on the prowl, Elizabeth thought grudgingly. She supposed it was his Indian heritage that gave him such stealth. She peered anxiously over her shoulder, thinking that he really didn't look much like an Indian, except for his dark coloring. But neither did Josephine, for that matter, yet she knew that they were. Josephine had told her so.

"Now," Josephine asked, once she'd closed the door to her office, "what in thunder do you need a man for, Liz?"

Elizabeth's gaze never left the other occupant of the sparsely furnished room. He sauntered over and sprawled backward into a large leather chair, dwarfing it beneath him. Hooking the curved toe of his boot about the leg of a nearby stool, he drew it closer, propping his scuffed leather boots upon it. The longer she watched him, the more his arrogant presence provoked her.

With a slow gesture, Cutter adjusted his hat so that it shaded his eyes—more out of habit than necessity, because the light in the room was too dim to be glaring. "Don't mind me," he said presently. Lifting a dark brow and one corner of his mouth, he returned Elizabeth's regard, his infuriating smile locked insolently in place.

Caught in the act of staring, Elizabeth felt her breath snag. What was it about him that she found so discomfiting? Musing over that, she fanned herself, not realizing what that gesture revealed. Her eyes narrowed as she faced Josephine. "He's *not really* your brother?" she asked skeptically.

Josephine nodded. Pursing her lips to keep from grinning, she watched as her brother and her best friend sparred without words. "My baby brother, actually," she conceded, cocking her head with unconcealed pride.

"Then why haven't I met him before now?" Elizabeth persisted.

Josephine's eyes fairly twinkled with mirth, and Elizabeth could suddenly see a clear and maddening resemblance between them.

"Why do you think you should have? You know I didn't happen into Sioux Falls until about two years ago. Cutter was only here long enough to help me open up the Oasis. Since then . . . well . . . there's been a war goin' on, you know." Josephine tilted a sly look toward her brother, conceding with a sigh, "Still, he has managed to steal in a time or two . . . to check up on me. Isn't that so, brother dear?"

Cutter lifted his hat brim just enough so that Elizabeth glimpsed the lack of compunction in his jet black gaze. He obviously didn't give a fig that anyone knew of his solicitousness, and didn't bother even to deny as much to his sister—who seemed to take offense over it, if Elizabeth read her tone right.

"Now, mind you, he won't admit that it's so," Josephine continued, frowning benevolently. "Claims he's only checking on the Oasis. You see, it's his place, really, and not mine, but he swears he hasn't the patience to run it and kindly leaves that burden to me." She gave her brother a conspiratorial wink. "Fact is, he's just too generous, even if he is a bit too protective." She sighed with resignation. "I keep tellin' him that I can take care of myself just fine without him, but he doesn't seem to want to believe it's so."

Cutter said nothing to his sister's allegations, but his smile turned crooked. Wry amusement played subtly upon his sensuous lips, and somehow that arrogant grin made Elizabeth feel as awkward as a kettle-bellied mule, especially so because it was still directed at her. More than anything, she wanted to strike it from his face. But she was supposed to be grateful, she reminded herself. Yet, in spite of his cocksure expression, she found she couldn't quite tear her gaze away.

"Enough about that!" Josephine exclaimed suddenly, startling her. "What I'd like to know just now, Liz girl, is what you think you need a man for?"

Elizabeth nodded subtly in Cutter's direction. It was just too difficult to remain coherent with the man staring at her so intently. "*He* doesn't really need to hear this, does he?"

Josephine regarded Elizabeth impishly. "Well,

sugar, I'll put it to you this way. He could go . . . that is, if you could persuade him to leave his own office. But even if he did, there aren't any secrets between us. He'd more'n likely find out anyhow. So you might as well tell us before I die of curiosity—why on earth would *you* need *a man?*''

The last two words were emphasized, as if it were a ridiculous notion. Elizabeth tried not to take exception.

''And what could be so bloomin' important,'' Josephine continued, ''that you would risk life and limb coming into the Oasis at this time o' the night? You know better'n that!'' she chided.

The warmth crept higher into Elizabeth's cheeks as she glanced again at Cutter. He was still watching her, his expression unreadable but for the mocking smile upon his lips. She felt suddenly so conspicuous that she longed for the floor to open up and suck her down into it—anything to escape his bold scrutiny.

To Elizabeth's dismay, that scoundrel's smile spread clear to his fathomless eyes. Swallowing, she took a deep breath and averted her face, feeling his gaze rake her still like a hot southern gust over a thirsting man in the middle of the desert; it was nearly her undoing. God grant her strength, she just knew that any moment she would burst into tears, and she refused to weep in front of the lecher.

She decided it was best to ignore him. If he wouldn't go . . . then she would just make believe he wasn't in the room with her—sitting little more than six feet away . . . give or take a few inches. Simple enough. She forced her attention to remain on Josephine.

''I—I received a letter today,'' Elizabeth began, her voice catching. She swallowed convulsively. ''From my sister's father-in-law. Katherine . . . K-Katherine,'' she tried again, but her voice failed her. The words were just too difficult to speak. ''She and her husband were . . . well, they were killed. He didn't say how." She tried to keep the emotion from her tone and merely recite the facts, but her lips trembled traitorously. "It seems they left their four-year-old daughter to my care."

Closing her eyes, Elizabeth tried to steady herself, feeling suddenly as if she would swoon. But she'd never fainted before, and now wasn't the time to begin.

Not in front of *him.*

But then, *he* wasn't really there, she reminded herself sternly.

Josephine immediately placed a reassuring arm about Elizabeth's waist, noticing her sudden pallor. "You poor thing! I'm so sorry!" she declared. "Here now, sit yourself down in my chair."

Elizabeth sank numbly into the buttery-soft leather chair behind the tiny desk, grateful for the barrier it provided between herself and Josephine's irritating brother. Only, now she was forced to face him. Her limbs felt weak at the realization. And the rest of her? *Peculiar* was the only word to describe it.

"You gonna be all right?" Josephine asked, concerned.

Elizabeth nodded, and her gaze was again drawn to Cutter's. Like a hapless moth to a killing flame, she thought petulantly.

His smile was gone now, replaced with what seemed a disapproving scowl. He probably thought her a blubbering idiot, she reflected grimly—and what was worse, she felt like one, too.

"So tell me about the man part," Josephine prompted, waving her hand impatiently.

Chapter 2

⌒◯◯⌒

The pain in Elizabeth's amber eyes was fierce. "I can't claim Katherine's child unless I'm married," she said bluntly. "Her grandfather loves her, you see, and he won't give her up unless he's certain she'll go to a decent home."

"I don't understand," Josephine interjected. "So why doesn't the kid just stay with him, if he loves her so darned much?"

"Because he claims he's too old to raise her," Elizabeth disclosed. "And he also wrote that if I can't take her, he'd be forced to give her to a God-fearing couple he knows who was never blessed with children." She bit into her lower lip to keep from crying out, and her eyes closed for the briefest instant as she fought to retain her composure. When she opened them again, they were luminous and misty. "Oh, Josephine! I have to get that child! Katie's all the family I've got left—I *need* to raise her, can't you see? I can't bear to think of her growing up all alone . . . and my not knowing her." Her eyes grew melancholy. "She's only four." Her voice was soft with pain. "Don't you understand?"

Josephine nodded. "I think I do, sugar. So what are you gonna do?"

Elizabeth cleared her throat, because the words she was about to speak seemed outrageous even to her own ears. "Well . . ." Knitting her brows, she began,

17

"I thought . . . I thought, maybe, I'd hire myself a husband."

A sudden choking sound diverted Elizabeth's attention, and her eyes widened, her gaze flying to Cutter's as if she suddenly recalled his presence. To her annoyance, that unwelcome heat stole back into her cheeks.

Watching Elizabeth's back straighten stoically, Cutter experienced a potent longing to console. It amazed him that she'd not so much as shed a single tear, and he admired her for that strength of character. Most gals he knew would be spouting liquid salt like a wrung sponge—justifiably—yet here she sat, eyes glassy with grief, and not a drop to behold. Still, her grief was a tangible thing, and something stirred deep down. She seemed to deal with anger well enough, and so he thought to give her another focus. "Quit pampering her, Jo. She's no idiot child!"

Her head snapping up, Josephine gave her brother an incredulous look. Silence overwhelmed the small room for an uncomfortable instant as she glared at him, and said finally, "How would you know what she needs, you insensitive cuss!"

Cutter lifted a brow in amused surprise. "I was 'too generous' only a scant moment ago," he reminded her, a sparkle returning to his eyes. Without giving his sister time to reply, he rose from the chair and went to the private bar. Tipping a few long-necked bottles to better read the labels, he found one to his liking, lifting it along with two glasses, setting them down upon the desk before Elizabeth.

Josephine glanced back at Elizabeth, but Elizabeth was still watching Cutter. "Look, Elizabeth, even if you can work this plan out somehow . . . I'm not sure this is the best time to be traveling."

Elizabeth's gaze returned to Josephine. "Oh, but you see . . . it's really a very good time! Word is sure to have spread about the war by now. And Elias says that with so many troops in the area, there shouldn't be any concern over . . . over . . . over . . ." She glanced away anxiously, and then back, and was chewing her lip in search of a word.

"Indians," Josephine provided for her with lifted brows. She shared an amused look with her brother. Elizabeth was always so careful not to say *that* word.

"Uh, yes." Elizabeth nodded in relief, and both of them turned to watch as Cutter lifted up the small stool that had propped his feet earlier and set it down with a clatter on the opposite side of the small desk. Without preamble, he took his seat upon the stool, and as short as it was, he still sat taller than Elizabeth did in her plush leather chair.

"This," he informed them both, though he kept his gaze fastened to Elizabeth's, winking audaciously at her, "is just what the woman needs right now."

Elizabeth's brows drew together in disapproval. Her hair was pulled back too tightly, making her face appear taut and gaunt, but Cutter's eyes overlooked that, focusing only on the thick black fringe of lashes magnified by her lenses, and those dark brows so at odds with her honey-colored hair and complexion.

"Sure it is!" exclaimed Josephine in disgust. "Ain't it always a man's answer to everything?" She shook her head reprovingly.

Elizabeth, on the other hand, remained speechless, finding it difficult even to think under Cutter's scrutiny.

When he tore his gaze away from Elizabeth, releasing her finally, he glanced up at his sister. "Don't you have a hookshop to run, or something?" he asked pointedly.

Josephine glowered at him. "Well, yes, but . . ." She couldn't argue with truth—and she didn't dare leave that mangy bunch o' men alone in her bar for too long. Like as not, they were sneaking sips from her bottles, and pinches from her girls, even now, she thought with a touch of resentment. Besides, she had a suspicion about her brother's interest in Liz and was curious to see where it would lead. Still, her hands went to her hips in warning. "Behave yourself, Cutter. If you dare say anything to hurt Elizabeth's feelings . . ."

A shadow of annoyance crossed Cutter's sharp features, but faded just as quickly as it appeared. "You know me better'n that, Jo. Fact is, I figure I can help. Now, get the hell out of here and back to work before you have nothing left to get back to." His eyes flashed a gentle but firm warning.

Elizabeth opened her mouth to object, but before she could utter a word, Josephine snorted inelegantly and left the room, closing the door firmly behind her.

Rising abruptly, Elizabeth gasped in frustration, staring wide-eyed at the door. How dare Josephine leave her! Alone . . . with her heller of a brother! She turned slowly to glare at Cutter, her expression wrathful. "I needed to talk to her, Mr. McKenzie!" Her eyes narrowed upon him accusingly. "I assume it is McKenzie?" she said through clenched teeth.

Cutter lifted the bottle before him, turned it appraisingly, then poured a small portion of amber fire into her glass. "That's right," he drawled. His dark, hawklike eyes bored into her own as he slid the glass toward her. "Drink up. Might help." The curve of his lips seemed to mock her, challenge her.

Settling back down upon the edge of the chair, Elizabeth slid the glass back toward him, straightening her shoulders resolutely. "No, thank you, Mr. McKenzie. I do not partake of spirits." Her eyes narrowed. "Not ever!"

Shrugging indifferently, Cutter proceeded to pour himself two fingers. As he placed the bottle back upon the desk, it "accidentally" clinked against Elizabeth's glass, nudging it back into her immediate reach. "Suit yourself," he said, adjusting his stool. He leaned upon the desk, stretching his long legs out lazily before him.

Beneath the desk, the toe of one boot managed to

find its way just under the hem of Elizabeth's skirt, brushing her ankle. She jerked away with a gasp. Though not quickly enough, because she experienced a fluttering deep down at the unexpected caress. It sent her pulses racing and her senses reeling.

Surely he'd not done so on purpose? Or had he? She had to wonder.

Inclining his head slightly, Cutter lifted his own glass in mock salute, his expression knowing. "Don't mind if I do," he said softly.

Too flustered to speak, Elizabeth simply shook her head in answer, thinking that she really ought to get up and leave. Yet she didn't. Something kept her rooted to the chair, and she couldn't even force her gaze away. She was aware of Cutter's smug smile even as he downed his whiskey.

Could he have read her thoughts and realized how much his presence disturbed her? Was he making fun of her then? Somehow that possibility thoroughly distressed her. "I really wish you wouldn't smile so darned much," she snapped.

Cutter studied the expression on her face over the rim of his glass. He was making her nervous, he could tell. But he really couldn't help himself. He itched to remove her specs, to reach out and run his finger across those long sable lashes, see if they were as soft as they appeared. He kept his hand occupied with his rotgut whiskey instead, a pulse quickening in his temple even as he thought of touching her. Swallowing, he slammed the tumbler down. "Why is that?" he asked, his tone somewhat strained.

"Just because!"

His gaze became heavy-lidded as he contemplated how those delicate lashes would feel against his lips. "Why?" he persisted, his tone a bit huskier than before.

It sent a chill down Elizabeth's spine. "Be—Because it annoys me!" she said sharply, and then wished she hadn't, because his smile deepened, displaying stark white teeth against his swarthy complexion.

Forcing a deep, fortifying breath through her lungs, she decided that Josephine's brother or not, she was really beginning not to like the man at all. And she wasn't going to let him bully her. Again, her eyes narrowed. "All right, Mr. McKenzie, since I truly do not understand what it is that you find so blessed amusing, perhaps you'd care to enlighten me?"

He crossed his arms perfunctorily. "Don't think so."

"Well then!" There were many unpleasant things in Elizabeth's life that she was forced to endure, but Cutter McKenzie was not one of them. "If you will please excuse me! I've no time for this cockamamie nonsense!" In spite of her blasphemy, she rose gracefully from the chair, her expression undaunted, and started for the door, only to find her skirt firmly snagged by a jagged corner of the desk.

Halting abruptly at the sound of rending material, Elizabeth stood stock-still, momentarily paralyzed, too terrified at the thought of turning to face Cutter's smug expression to even survey the damage.

She was even less thrilled at the thought of facing Dick Brady. Her eyes wide with indecision, she stared at the door, only two measly feet away, thinking that surely Cutter was snickering at her behind those insolent black eyes of his. The biggest part of her wanted to simply jerk her skirt free, reach for the knob, snatch the door open, and run for her life. But that would accomplish nothing, she knew. Nor did she want Cutter to think she was afraid of him. Suddenly it was very important that she stand up to him, show herself confident and unaffected. She closed her eyes briefly, took a deep breath, and whirled to face him, her chin lifting a notch.

She started to find that he'd already risen and was standing before her, his lips quivering faintly, one brow lifted slightly. Now, how did he do that, she wondered irately—move so quickly without making so much as a scratch of a sound?

With a quick motion, Cutter's hand swept across his lips, as if to wipe the smile from them, then fell away as he stooped to pop her dress from its snare. He didn't rise straightaway, liking the view too much. Stooping at her feet, he glanced up from her ankles, his eyes gleaming as he lifted the dangling end for her to take. "You'll be needin' this, I reckon." In spite of his resolve not to laugh, amusement danced in his eyes.

Exasperated, Elizabeth snatched the torn hem out of his grasp, grateful to find that it was only the flounce she'd added to lengthen her skirt that had ripped. His fingers closed about hers, not really detaining them—though she didn't realize that fact until she removed them quite easily a few stunned seconds later.

The shock of that discovery left her dumbstruck. What was wrong with her that a brief touch from him should leave her weak-minded?

She was ready to bolt. Cutter could tell by the look in her eyes, so he stood cautiously, retreating a bit. He sat back upon the desk, arms linked lazily across his chest, as he scrutinized her. He wasn't ready for her to leave, but knew better than to ask her not to go. The ready defiance in her expression told him that she would do so just to spite him.

"Think Brady's gone yet?" he asked conversationally, knowing full well that it would both divert her attention and deter her from leaving the room until he could manage to smooth her ruffled feathers.

Surprise touched her features first, then consternation as she recalled the reason Jo had dragged her into the office to begin with. With a dainty finger, she pushed her spectacles firmly up the bridge of her nose, seeming to consider his question carefully. Lifting himself from the desk, Cutter retreated further, moving behind the desk to give her a greater sense of security.

"Listen," he said before she could reply. He lifted a brow. "You have my apologies if I offended you somehow . . . Never meant to. It's just that I can tell Jo cares for you." Her emotions were so transparent that he could tell the very second she began to relax. "I'd really like t' help you if you'll allow it."

Cutter held her gaze, never releasing it, even as he poured himself another shot of whiskey. He sat, stretching his legs, as he tossed down a potent swallow, then shook his head, muttering something to the effect that the stuff was enough to blow a man's lamp out . . . though obviously not rank enough to keep him from lifting the tumbler for another swig.

Somehow Elizabeth didn't think he was all that repentant. Piqued by that thought, she watched as he took a painfully slow sip, and felt a fluttering in her breast as his tongue swept down across his lower lip, lapping up the lingering taste of whiskey. She had to remind herself to exhale. Then, by God, his eyes crinkled at the corners, hinting at that rude smile he'd only just apologized for.

Refusing to allow him to run her out of the room, she raised her chin, returning his impertinent stare. At the moment, he was still the better choice over Brady. She had no wish to leave the sanctuary of the office until Josephine had the chance to rid the bar of him. She came forward, placing both hands upon the desk, hem still in hand. "All right," she asked before she could stop herself, "how is it that you think you are able to help me, Mr. McKenzie?"

Cutter's gaze swept down, studying the long, lean fingers that were spread so boldly upon the desk, taking in the swatch of material she held pinned beneath her right hand, and then back up to her tawny eyes. It took all of his resolve to keep from bustin' his guts. Most folks didn't like to meet his gaze a'tall, much less stare him in the eye, yet here this little filly was giving him equal measure, challenging him. For that matter, she looked as if she were wishing him an early tour into the Happy Hunting Grounds.

Brows uplifted, he motioned for her to sit. She gave him a doubtful look, then did, reluctantly, moving her hand to the edge of the desk as if she were prepared to shove its weight at him the instant he made a wrong move. A move she obviously expected him to make any moment.

Again, he raised his glass to his lips, holding her gaze as he tipped another swallow. "You have no cause to be frightened of me, Doc."

Elizabeth's heart lurched at the sensuality in his tone. "Frightened?" she reflected aloud. That wasn't quite the word for what she was feeling just now. Taking great pains to seem composed, she took a deep, calming breath, then reached out for her own tumbler—not to drink, of course, but to occupy her hands. They were quaking traitorously.

"I don't bite," he assured with an odd glitter to his eyes. He grinned engagingly. "Not usually anyway . . . and not too hard, when I do."

Now, why did she think those words held a double meaning? Mercy, she was feeling warm again, though not from embarrassment. Truth to tell, she was feeling quite unusual.

Long minutes passed without a word uttered between them.

The rat wouldn't even take pity on her and look away! she thought testily. Most men, she assured herself, would have been properly chastised and *would* have looked the other way. Well, she was made of sterner stuff, he would soon see!

Her voice was unsteady, yet held an unquestionable note of authority. Years of watching her father deal with people gave her that advantage. She tried for a slightly bored tone, along with a long-suffering sigh. "Perhaps you'd like to explain sometime this century, Mr. McKenzie? How is it you think you can help me?''

His answering grin unnerved her, and she promptly lifted the glass she held in her hands to her lips. Without thinking, she gulped deeply of the firewater, all the while eyeing Cutter over the rim. It burned viciously, choking her, the shock nearly heaving her out of the chair. Holding her throat in desperation, she coughed and sputtered.

In no time, Cutter was at the desk, reaching out to pat her gently upon the back. ''Takes a bit of getting used to,'' he reassured, his tone strangled. ''Next sip should be a mite easier.''

He sounded as though he were laughing at her, but Elizabeth didn't dare look at him to see if it was so. Clearing her throat inelegantly, she nodded. Flustered, she peered down through her lashes at the glass that seemed suddenly bonded with her hands.

Cutter's hand remained upon her back, rubbing soothingly. Unreasonably, Elizabeth didn't even think to protest that intimacy. It seemed perfectly natural. In fact, as the warmth of that callused palm lent her its silent sympathy, she had to fight the urge to jump into his arms and cry her pain away. It made no sense to her at all.

''Better?''

Elizabeth nodded jerkily. ''Fine,'' she replied, much too quickly, glancing up.

''Never thought otherwise,'' he assured with a wink.

Elizabeth could swear he was fondling her hair. Or was he? It was hard to tell, but it felt as though he'd left off the comforting to run his fingers along the length of her braid. And then suddenly the sensation stopped and he brought his hands to his lap, linking them casually. She watched a moment as he drummed his thumbs together, and then glanced up to gauge his thoughts, but his expression was shuttered. Having followed her gaze, he raised his brows suddenly and dropped his hands to his sides. She averted her gaze guiltily, thinking that maybe she'd offended him with her scrutiny. How was it that he seemed so completely unaffected by their proximity, while she, on the other hand, had never felt so agitated? What was wrong with her that she would stare at him so brazenly?

"Tell me something, Doc."

That voice. So deep. So masculine. It sent another quiver down her spine. He was so close that she could smell the warm leather he wore. And his buckskin britches were so snug over his thighs that she found she couldn't tear her gaze away from the muscular delineations. Merciful heaven, in that hypnotic moment she thought she might do or say anything he asked. She nodded, not realizing that she had.

"Just what did you have on Brady to send him scrambling for cover like an old henpecked rooster?"

Elizabeth's mouth curved unconsciously, trembling with the need to smile. And then, as she recalled Brady's alarmed expression, she couldn't control her sudden burst of nervous hysterics. It was as though her emotions had gone haywire. She giggled until on the verge of tears, then looked up at him abashedly, knowing he probably thought her demented after witnessing such an abrupt change in mood.

"I suppose you'd like to know what it is that's so blessed funny?" she asked him.

Her throaty laughter shook through Cutter. It was like a child's in that it was genuine and uninhibited, yet sounded much too earthy to be innocent, and it gave him an immediate physical reaction. "Reckon I might," he allowed with a long-suffering smile.

Unable to wipe the mirth from her lips, Elizabeth shook her head in remembrance and again lifted her glass, sipping from it almost absently, clearing her throat when it threatened to send her into another coughing fit. To her amazement, after the initial sip, the whiskey went down much easier, just as Cutter had said it would.

"Brady's one of those who likes to drink a bit too much," she disclosed, with the slightest curve to her soft lips.

Cutter shifted uncomfortably. For her sake, he hoped she wouldn't get a yen to ogle his leg again. He didn't think he'd be able to hide the effect she had on him. Just remembering the way her eyes had flared slightly in innocent surprise and her pupils had dilated as she'd gawked at him was enough to make him permanently rooty, and the evidence was conspicuous.

She took another sip, clearing her throat daintily, and this time it was Cutter who felt discomfited.

Her lips were her best feature, he decided. Full and pouty, just beggin' to be kissed. ". . . always having accidents," he heard her say. He shook his head to clear it of his lusty thoughts.

"One night," she continued, "he'd come in after catching his thumb in his gun hammer—don't ask me how he managed that! Anyhow, he and his buddies had been shooting at tins, and he came sauntering in, chock-full of brag and fight, and told my father to 'just stitch it up.' But Papa didn't want to do it without giving him whiskey first—Mr. Brady really doesn't seem to like pain very much," she explained quickly. "Anyhow, when my father left the room to look for a jug, Mr. Brady took an immediate liking to one of his shiny new surgical knives." She glanced up to see whether he was following her tale.

Her expression softening suddenly, she gave a little half-hearted chuckle. "Papa and I watched from the doorway as Mr. Brady wrestled with his imaginary bear. You should have seen him, Mr. McKenzie!"

"Wish I had," he said evenly, trying to ignore his growing discomfort as well as he could.

Elizabeth looked up, and this time, instead of being irritated by it, she was warmed by the spark of amusement in the dark eyes that met hers. "Believe it or not, I thought he might even manage to lose that scuffle, too," she said softly, distantly.

Despite the fact that she was still looking at him, Cutter had the notion she was somewhere else entirely. He couldn't keep his eyes from wandering down and assessing her figure through the bulk of her clothes. She was probably much too skinny, he told himself . . . not even a handful.

He raised his brows, his nostrils flaring as he cleared away the sudden tightness from his throat. "So how'd you happen to know it was a bear he was wrestling?" The way Cutter saw it, his best bet was to keep Elizabeth talking . . . keep them both preoccupied. Jo would likely take a shotgun to his ass if she found him rutting over her one and only friend—when the girl was chin-deep in her misery, at that. Come to think of it, he doubted if either of them would appreciate it all that much.

She shook her head faintly, as if to escape the memory. "Because he was talking to the silly thing, is how." Her eyes glazed. "I swear!" she exclaimed. "He stabbed 'n' wrestled with nothing but thin air, and then he reared back to gut it and stabbed himself in the—"

Elizabeth caught herself just in the nick of time, her eyes widening as though startled by what she'd nearly said. Well-bred ladies, she upbraided herself, never spoke of such things in a man's presence. Then again, she was a doctor, wasn't she? Her father had always spoken frankly about the human anatomy. Why, then, shouldn't she?

"Where?" Cutter demanded, inhaling deeply. But it was the wrong thing to do, because he caught her scent in that breath. The sweetest feminine scent. His blood heated, surging like molten lava through his veins.

"His er . . . his . . ." She glanced up at him suddenly, her brows furrowing. "His lower posterior," she disclosed with an exaggerated whisper and a conspiratorial nod.

It seemed to take him a full moment to register what she'd said, but when it finally came, his roar of laughter was genuine, warm and rich, much as her father's had been. It set Elizabeth immediately at ease.

"I'll be," he said, still chuckling as he poured Elizabeth another brimming glassful.

She stared at it numbly, thought briefly to protest, but didn't. She was feeling rather nice suddenly, cozy even. She exhaled languidly, and something seemed to uncoil deep within her. Maybe Cutter was right, she thought dimly. Maybe it would help to forget for just a little while.

"Did you ever meet my father?" Elizabeth asked him on a sigh, looking up solemnly. She was proud of her father. He'd been caring and loving—and never once had he blamed her after her mother and sister had abandoned them . . . despite the fact that she often blamed herself. Maybe if she'd been a little more help. . . ? A better daughter. . . ? More accommodating. . . ? Like Katherine.

He nodded soberly. " 'Bout a year ago—real fine man, Lizbeth."

Something about the way Cutter said her name made her sigh with pleasure. "He was," she agreed. "I miss him." And she would miss her sister, as well, though she hadn't seen Katherine in so many years that it wouldn't be the same. The last she remembered hearing from Katherine was when their mother had died of lung fever four years past. Enclosed along with that letter had been a small photo of Katie at five months: a plump little thing with no hair. Elizabeth had cherished that photo.

Four years? she thought, blinking. Had it been so long? That would mean that it had been seven since her mother had run off with Katherine to St. Louis. So very long ago . . . yet that miserable day was as clear in her memory as ever. Finding the hastily scrawled message her mother had composed on the back of one of her father's notes had been the single most painful moment of her life. Even the words were indelibly etched in the annals of her mind. *With every fiber of my being, I loathe this infernal place. I can't—I just can't suffer it any longer. Forgive me, Angus.* Not a word about her. Not forgive me, Elizabeth. Not farewell. Not anything at all.

Being the elder of the two, and interested in medicine as she was, Elizabeth had been with her father at the time, helping him deliver a baby. For that reason, and because she'd understood how very much her mother had despised the wilderness and feared the Indians, Elizabeth had never entirely blamed her for leaving without her—especially since her mother had been only the first of so many to abandon Sioux Falls. By '62, most of the remaining populace had fled in fear of the Indian raids. At any rate, because she and her father had been so close, she wouldn't have wished to go anyway. Still, it hurt to know that her mother had been so desperate to desert them that she would slip away without bothering even to say goodbye.

Her father had never been the same afterward.

Her stomach plunged abruptly, her head reeling with her next thought. Ironic that her mother had died—in the very place she'd deemed a safe haven—almost a full year before the Indian raids she'd feared so much ever came to pass.

"Where were you?"

"Hmmm?" She opened her eyes, unaware that she had closed them, and looked into Cutter's deep, dark pupils. They were fascinating, the way they seemed to descend forever. But she thought she detected a flicker of pity in his intense gaze, and a knot formed in her throat.

"When I came through . . . don't recall making your acquaintance."

"Oh . . . well . . ." She swallowed convulsively,

clearing her throat of its odd thickness. "No one ever sheems . . . seems to. But I wash here," she assured him. Blinking suddenly, she shook her head discreetly, as if questioning her slurring speech. "Jus—just—like—always," she enunciated slowly. "Ap—p—renticin' with my father." Even as she spoke, she seemed to deflate before his eyes. Folding her arms in front of her, she laid her chin down on top of them, and her eyes took on a faraway look as she spoke again. "I think hish . . . his heart wash weak . . ." Her words trailed off wistfully as she closed her eyes. Cutter thought she might have passed out, but for the hiccup that revived her. "I—I think . . . don't really know . . . didn't complain much . . . just—wish—I—could've helped sh-shomehow." Her head lolled to one side.

She sat there, looking so fragile, so helpless, that Cutter again felt the incredible urge to draw her up into his arms and hold her, protect her from the cold, hard world.

"Lizbeth," he whispered, reaching out to finger an errant lock of her hair.

It felt like silk.

Had she looked up in that moment, she would have seen the naked desire smoldering in his ebony gaze. "I'd've noticed you."

Were her ears playing tricks on her? Elizabeth thought they might be, because her eyes certainly were. Cautiously she opened one eye to find that the room was, in fact, whirling. With a sad smile, she gazed into her empty glass and reached to grab the neck of the bottle. She tried to lift it, but found she didn't have the strength. Warmth touched her fingers. When she glanced up again, it was to find Cutter's hand fitted neatly over her own. Inexplicably that discovery sent a delightful quiver coursing through her. Even knowing she should, she couldn't bring herself to remove it from beneath his anchoring grasp. Her body felt suddenly so blissfully heavy.

"I reckon you've had more'n enough," he murmured thickly. When she didn't respond, only sat, staring at his hand with something akin to bafflement, he asked, "Don't you? The plan was to calm you—your nerves were as taut as an Indian's bow—not get you all hooched up." His thumb lazily caressed the area between her first finger and thumb, sending a delicious chill down her spine.

Closing her eyes, Elizabeth savored the sweet lethargy that closed over her body and soul. She considered telling him that it was much too late, that she suspected she might already be a bit *hooched up*, but was feeling too dozy to bother. Her hand slid from beneath his, down the cool, smooth bottle onto the table.

As Cutter watched her, the thought occurred to him that she was much too innocent-looking for her own good. Likely, whoever she hired to play husband for her would take advantage of that fact. Fool girl. Didn't she understand the dangers she'd be facing? If not from the ruthless land itself, then from those who fought so fiercely to claim it. It wasn't enough that the states had only just ended a bitter war between themselves, but the white and red man both continued to struggle fiercely for control of land. He was sure Elizabeth had no inkling just how risky the trek would be without adding the likes of Dick Brady to her troubles.

The more he thought about it, the more certain he grew. Come hell or high water, he wasn't about to let her put herself into any more danger than she was already courting. But he could see just how much it meant to her to get her sister's child. And it didn't take a shaman to see that Jo felt something special for Elizabeth. As far as he was concerned, that was reason enough for him to step in. Elizabeth had to be a helluva woman to befriend a half-breed barkeep. Most respectable ladies wouldn't even have gotten past the barkeep bit. But then, maybe she didn't know about the other?

"Lizbeth," he whispered before he could stop himself. "Let me help you, gal. Let me be that husband you're aimin' to hire—don't want the money," he told her. "Just let me do it for . . . Jo. I know she'd want me to."

With some effort, she opened one eye to find Cutter's arresting face mere inches from her own. She would have jerked her head away, but felt much too languid to even blink. "Why would you do such a thing?" she mumbled sleepily.

"Don't rightly know," he admitted, lifting his hat and raking his hand back across his dark waves. His eyes glinted, reflecting the lamplight, and his voice was velvet and smooth, reaching into her soul. "Reckon I'd just like t' help, is all."

"I—I don't think so," she told him, shaking her head ungracefully. She wanted to let him, she really did. But she'd had a reason to discount him in the first place.

Now, what was it?

Her eyes closed as she tried to recall—oh yes, because he was an arrogant half-breed. Not that she had anything against half-breeds, mind you, especially this particular one. She suspected she might even like him a bit too much.

And Josephine *was* her best friend.

It was just that if she showed up with Cutter McKenzie as her lawful husband, then it might be worse than showing up alone. Most folks didn't cotton to Indians much. She couldn't take the chance that Katherine's father-in-law was one of 'em. And he had mentioned Indians—not too favorably, either—in the letter. If he was prejudiced . . . then there would be no use in going at all, because Elias Bass would just turn her away empty-handed. She couldn't let that happen, could she?

She yawned suddenly, instinctively sliding her

hand down to cover her mouth, feeling remarkably tranquil. Vaguely she felt her spectacles being lifted from her face, but didn't bother to open her eyes. Really, she didn't know why she still wore the warped old things—should have ordered new ones long before now.

She'd started wearing them at the age of twelve. As proud of her father as she'd always been, she'd wanted nothing more than to be like him . . . and so she'd fished them out of the ash when he'd thrown them away. Course, she'd had to have new lenses cut, because the old ones were cracked, but in spite of the bent frames, they'd looked very authoritative to her, and so she'd worn them anyway. And later she'd found them useful in keeping the men away. It seemed most men just weren't attracted to women in spectacles—it didn't help matters much that the frames were ill formed—but that was just fine with her, because all she'd ever wanted was to be a physician.

Had Cutter really said he would have noticed her? Surely he hadn't.

"Lizbeth, gal, wake up. Look at me," he demanded softly. "I wanna see those brassy eyes of yours."

Now, why would he want to do that? she pondered sleepily. She tried to appease him because he sounded so concerned, lifting her head to gaze at him blankly. She teetered slowly forward. Unable to hold herself up, she slumped against Cutter's solid chest.

So hard.

He was so hard . . . like a dry riverbed. But he was warm, too, like the worn flannel blanket she'd cherished as a child, and so naturally she cuddled against him, rubbing her face cozily against his soft worn buckskin vest.

With a groan and a sigh, Cutter lifted Elizabeth's limp body up into his arms. Sinking back into the chair she'd warmed, he cradled her in his lap with a gentleness that belied his size and strength.

"Chrissakes," he muttered. The woman had only had a few puny swallows. It wouldn't even have affected him, and here she was pie-eyed. Who would've figured? But he reckoned that her small size accounted for some of the difference in side effects— that, and she had guzzled them down right quick . . . aside from having been through quite an emotional strain besides.

He stared at her for the longest moment, studying her pale features in the dim light, thinking that he'd liked to be the one to put roses in those cheeks of hers, to take the pins and ribbon out of her shiny gold hair . . . to run his hands through it. He wanted to show her what she was behind those misleading specs—wasn't a damned thing wrong with her looks, other than the fact that she seemed hell-bent on detracting from them.

She wiggled, making herself more comfortable in his lap, and his physical reaction was instantaneous. Groaning, he closed his eyes to command restraint. Damn him, if he wasn't hotter'n a three-dollar pistol, while she, on the other hand, was feeling no blamed pain a'tall.

He wished she would open her eyes so that he could see their color again. He'd never seen peepers quite like hers before—at least not on a human being. They were like wolf eyes, yellow as fool's gold. His brow furrowing, he shook her softly, to no avail. She didn't even crack a lid. Hell, he thought irritably, she couldn't go to sleep . . . least not yet.

"Lizbeth?"

His hand closed about her soft shoulder, kneading it gently. Unable to help himself, he bent to kiss her sweet, pouty mouth and ended up suckling at her lower lip, enthralled with the taste of her. She sighed groggily but opened for him, and it sent a surge of white-hot desire running through him so fierce that he wanted to shake her awake and take her right there on the desk.

His tongue traced the velvety fullness of her mouth, then dipped between her lips to search out her tongue. He was pleasantly surprised when she met him halfway with her soft little tip.

His heart hammered like a chisel on stone, and his veins pulsed with a primeval heat as his mouth moved over hers, devouring its moist sweetness with an intensity that surprised him.

Chapter 3

~~~~~OO~~~~~

S oft, so soft . . . too soft . . . too easy to lose himself.

It took Cutter a full moment to register the fact that Elizabeth was no longer responding. Groaning, he checked himself, raising his head to look into her face, his mind irrevocably made up.

She seemed too sweet and fragile, too porcelain, her skin too smooth and pure and pale, when most women had tawny complexions from sun exposure. Her brows, so perfectly formed, seemed stark against her face. She needed someone to protect her.

But she'd refused his help.

And he didn't give a mule's squat. She wasn't in any shape to be making decisions. If she was so determined to hire herself a husband . . . then he aimed to be that man. He'd just sit her fanny in the saddle before him and ride. By the time she awoke, they'd be well on their way, and there would be nothing she could do about it.

He didn't bother to ask himself whether she'd be safe in his hands.

He doubted it.

Better him than someone else. At least then, he'd be certain she'd arrive in one piece. Lifting her long, silken braid, he laid it reverently across her bosom. For that matter, he swore he'd send any man who

38

dared so much as look at her wrong to the bone or-chard.

The door creaked opened. Josephine stepped in, completely unprepared for the sight that greeted her. Her eyes went wide with surprise. "Lands!" she exclaimed, squelching a giggle to see Cutter holding Elizabeth with such possessive pride—like a man would his first saddle. Truth to tell, she never thought she'd see the day.

"She fell asleep." His voice was little more than a hoarse whisper.

Josephine moved forward quietly, an odd expression on her pretty face. "She just fell asleep? Just like that? I don't believe it, Cutter—what did you do to her?"

Cutter lifted a brow.

"Let me help you wake her so that I can get her home," Josephine suggested. "You can tend the bar while I'm gone." Her hand arrested in midair as Cutter's eyes flashed her a firm but gentle warning.

"Lay a hand on her, Josie girl, and you'll find yourself swinging facedown over my knee. You're not too old to spank," he cautioned.

Josephine's eyes filled with warmth. "That works two ways," she proposed.

"What?" Cutter drawled, his lips hinting at a belligerent grin. "Think you can manage to haul me over that scrawny knee of yours, sis?" He shook his head doubtfully. "Fact is, the hotheaded little fool's determined to hire herself a husband, and I've a mind to take her up on it. You wouldn't still be hanging on to that wedding band of yours, would ya?"

Momentarily dumbstruck by his disclosure, Josephine simply nodded. It certainly wasn't like her cynical brother to take such an interest in anyone. His lighthearted appearance didn't fool her in the least. She knew the animosity he hid behind that easy facade. Still, he seemed more carefree this time than ever before, and she had a keen suspicion as to why.

Even so, it was only a hunch, because Cutter wasn't easy to read. On the other hand, he seemed to know her only too well.

Something in his sister's eyes flickered and dimmed with her quiet affirmation, and his hackles rose. He knew Josephine wanted a family of her own, but there weren't many choices open to a half-breed woman. Jo was a real looker, but that didn't seem to hold much water when faced with the issue of their parentage. She'd married, sure enough, but the moment her lily white husband had discovered her heritage, he'd left her high and dry, without so much as a fare-thee-well to add to her short supply of memories. Unfortunately, Cutter suspected that not even that kept her from loving the fool man.

"Thought you might," he said without condemnation, though his next words made her want to snap his head off. "You're too sentimental, Jo—should have sold the confounded thing years ago."

Josephine shrugged dismissively, unwilling to discuss the painful topic.

"Mind if we borrow it?"

Josephine choked back a surprised laugh. "We?" she asked.

"We."

She gave him a measuring glance. "Sure," she said after a moment, determining that he was serious. "Just don't you go losin' it."

Cutter lifted his right hand. "Word of honor," he assured. "Now, why don't you run along and fetch it for me."

"You want me to get it now?"

"Isn't that what I just said?" Taking great pains not to wake Elizabeth, Cutter rose to his feet, shifting her over his shoulder.

"Cutter," Josephine cautioned, eyeing Elizabeth's upturned backside with no small measure of apprehension, "you ain't thinking of leaving tonight, are you?'' When Cutter didn't reply, her gaze flew to his. "She's sleeping, for mercy's sake!''

"Try stinking drunk,'' he countered, disgusted with himself for allowing her to get that way. "Just go fetch the band for me, and hobble your lip while you're at it.''

"Lord! She doesn't know, does she? Don't tell me—you offered and she refused?'' Cutter gave her a warning look. She shook her head in bemused wonder. "Lands sakes, you never were one to take no for an answer, but you really ought to consider this . . . You're not just carrying her 'round the bend, you know.''

"Where am I taking her?'' he asked, clutching Elizabeth possessively.

She spun toward him, an astonished expression on her face, hands on hips. "Lord—you don't even know that much? I—I don't know, Cutter; I don't think I should just let you take her—let me talk to her first.''

Cutter shrugged. "Be my guest.''

Josephine's expression remained incredulous as she stepped around Cutter and shook Elizabeth's shoulder gently. "Elizabeth,'' she whispered.

Elizabeth let out a dainty sigh, then settled more snugly against Cutter's back, and Josephine jiggled her shoulder a little harder. "Liz,'' she coaxed, "wake up. Liz?'' She slapped Cutter's shoulder in frustration. "All right, what did you give the poor girl?''

"Not a damned thing,'' Cutter assured her. "The woman just can't hold her liquor, is all. Now, let her be, and go fetch me that ring.''

"Elizabeth!'' Josephine persisted. At last Elizabeth opened one eye with great effort. "Elizabeth . . . Cutter wants to—''

"Cutter?'' Elizabeth sighed, rubbing her cheek against the back of Cutter's vest.

"Yes, yes, Cutter! He wants to—''

"Mmmmmmhhhh,'' she murmured, snuggling contentedly. ". . . izh soooo warm,'' she concluded with a dreamy sigh. Her head lolled to one side and she closed her eye, ending their one-sided conversation once and for all.

Grinning, Cutter pivoted toward his frustrated sister, a gleam in his eyes. "Satisfied?" he asked.

Josephine shrugged.

"Now, how 'bout spittin' out that destination?"

"Why should I tell you?" Josephine retorted. "Seems to me, brother dear, that if Elizabeth had wanted you to know, she'd have told you herself."

His dark, penetrating eyes bored into hers, willing her compliance. "If you don't say, I'll go anyway . . . and probably waste good time riding in the wrong direction. Besides, Jo, I think you care about the gal, and I know you don't want her hiring the likes of Dick Brady—or some other bounder."

"Why don't you just wait until tomorrow?" she asked reasonably. "I'll talk to her. She'll listen to reason if I—"

"Because she's muleheaded, Jo. I can see it in her eyes. She'll say no, and then turn around and hire Brady. Better me than him, don't you think?"

Josephine sighed. "You're right—as usual," she conceded. "But this time I think you're takin' on more than you know."

He chuckled.

Josephine shook her head ominously, snorting in disgust. "You're laughing now," she apprised him. "But she's gonna be real mad, Cutter. You don't know Liz like I do. She *is* stubborn, but aside from that, she's got the damnedest temper I've ever seen. She's had to to survive since her daddy's passin'. *But*," she interjected, "if you're so all-fired determined, then it's St. Louis you're off to—just let me run upstairs and pack a few of my things for her."

She knew better than to ask Cutter for the real reason he was doing this. Cutter wouldn't have told her even if he'd known, but Josephine suspected he didn't. She shook her head again, sighing portentously. "I just hope you know what you're getting yourself into," she said, snatching open the door.

Cutter waited no more than ten minutes before Josephine finally slipped out the back door, her arms laden. Seeing that he was already mounted and had his hands full, she placed her contributions into his saddle pockets, stuffing them full: foodstuffs, an extra canteen, and a few other indispensables.

"Her spectacles are in there." Josephine indicated the saddlebags. "I found them on my desk. But I couldn't find any clothes I thought she would wear, just a blouse—and there's a bit of money, too. I know you don't need it," she said, before he could protest. "But you never can tell. Just give it to Elizabeth. I owe her, anyhow." She looked up with reverence at her brother. "Just for the record . . . I've thought about it, and I'm sure you're doin' the right thing. It just took me by surprise, is all. If you hadn't volunteered, I think I would have asked."

He smiled faintly, giving her a nod. "I suspected as much."

Josephine's eyes misted; she hated the fact that she'd spent so little time with her brother. But Elizabeth needed him more at the moment. She accepted that fact . . . yet it had been so long since she'd seen Cutter last. He was the only family she had, the only one who'd ever cared for her. Their father had left what little he'd earned as a trapper to Cutter, and Cutter had used every penny of it on her. For the Oasis. She loved him fiercely for it.

But he would be back. "Take care, little brother." Unable to help herself, she embraced his leg. Patting his buckskin-covered knee affectionately, she stepped back, relatively composed, her fingers toying with the fringe of his pant leg. She shook her head wistfully. "I wish you wouldn't wear these things. You always have to wear at least one tellin' piece: britches, vest, something, and it just makes you look more . . . well,

Indian." She gave him a pleading look. "I swear, Cutter, if you would only wear normal clothes, no one would ever know—you've got dark hair, true enough, but no Indian has hair that wavy, or—"

"Jo."

It was just one curt word, but it said a multitude. Josephine would have gone on, but it wouldn't have done any good. The discussion was over as far as Cutter was concerned. She knew that he didn't like the fact that she'd turned her back so completely on their heritage, but he respected her decision. She had to respect his—even if it meant he might get a bullet in the back someday. There were just too many folks who didn't deal respectfully with "breeds."

Cutter didn't flaunt his heritage, and he didn't look blatantly Indian either. He just seemed to need that small act of defiance. Well, she consoled herself, at least he didn't look too out of place. Many men of Anglo descent wore buckskin, the difference being, they weren't part "Injun," and didn't take a risk just by wearing it.

"I'll wire St. Louis," she offered. And then her expression was suddenly grave. "And remember . . . don't lose my ring!" She glanced down, almost wistfully, at the shiny silver object she held between her fingers, then thrust it abruptly into his hand.

Without looking at it, Cutter slipped the band into his pocket, his jaw taut. He hadn't counted on the anger he'd feel just seeing the thing again. "See ya soon," he said, adjusting his brim. Then, forcing the harshness from his expression, he gave her a wink of farewell.

"Soon," Josephine agreed as she watched him gently snap the reins. He trotted away, holding Elizabeth protectively against him, and she waved at his back, knowing instinctively that he wouldn't turn.

Though he would never say so, Cutter hated leaving Jo as much as she hated to see him go. But for

the first time, he knew he left her in capable hands—
her own. Jo could take care of herself—always had
been able to, from the looks of it. He'd just never
realized until now. The memory of how she'd handled Brady brought the faintest smile to his lips.
Though he was the younger, he'd thought of her as
the dependent one, but it was no longer so. Had she
ever been? Or was he really just too sheltering?

Jo had said he was.

She'd never openly complain, he knew, though he
suspected she was a mite hurt by his lack of confi-
dence in her. The tone of her voice had all but said
so earlier.

His gaze drifted along the peaceful street. As usual,
the only light came from the few saloons and bawdy
houses that were still in full swing. Most everyone
else was asleep this late in the evening, buildings
darkened, lamps snuffed out.

With a glance upward, he noted that there was less
than a half moon to guide him. But it was enough.
He aimed to follow the Big Sioux River to Sioux City
or thereabouts, and then the Missouri—at least part
of the way—and the smell of the water alone was
enough to keep him on track. In his estimation, St.
Louis was at least a good week's ride with the load
he was carrying, but he reckoned his Palouse could
handle it easily enough.

Question was, could he?

As he reached the edge of town, he touched his
spurs to his Palouse, quickening the pace, eager to
put as much distance between them and Sioux Falls
as possible by the time Elizabeth awakened. There
was no telling how long he had before she did. An
hour? Two? All night? Who knew? The fact that she
was half-crocked would work in his favor, though.
For the most part, a drunken sleep was a dead sleep.
The longer she was out, the better.

As far as he was concerned, she could rail all she
wanted about his presumptuousness once she woke

up, but he didn't aim to make it all that easy for her to go home.

Her hand slid up his ribs suddenly, distracting him, and his heartbeat quickened at the feel of her small, warm palm branding him through his shirt. Lust clenched him as her fingers rubbed him almost imperceptibly, yet enough to make him crazy after only an instant. Emitting a tortured groan, Cutter covered her hand with his, stilling her sleepy movements.

He glanced down at her, thinking that the little light the moon gave off sprinkled silver dust over Elizabeth's fine hair, making it seem lighter than it actually was. And it made her skin seem paler, too. Translucent almost. In sleep, her starchy facade had softened somewhat, giving her a delicate appearance.

But damn him if he could understand how she could stand to have her hair pulled back and braided so tightly. Impulsively he searched out and found the pins, removing them one by one. His fingers gently undid the ribbon that held her braid. Untying it, he stuffed the items into his pocket along with the ring, making a mental note to return them to her later. Slowly, methodically, he unbound her hair, combing through the silk with his fingers until the fine strands blew free with the gentle night breeze.

"That's more like it," he muttered. But he couldn't quite keep himself from running his hand along the length of it, again and again. Nothing had ever felt so good to his callused fingers; they were so coarse that it amazed him something so fine could even stimulate his scarred flesh . . . yet there it was, like feathers over stone.

At the moment her head was resting lightly in the crook of his right arm, and her legs were dangling over his left thigh. He shook his head as he eyed her bulky skirts, thinking that they were gonna be a pain in his ass! He'd swear she was wearing a size three times larger than she needed. Hell, her limbs were all but lost in the folds. Resisting the urge to lift up the torn hem and see for himself, he felt himself growing tense and knew it had nothing to do with her too big clothing.

Looking down into her sleeping face, he let out a sigh, thinking that she seemed peaceful lying there in his arms.

But as the moments passed, there was no peace for Cutter. He felt the wild pounding rhythm in his head, and the blood humming through his veins, the pitch of it ancient and haunting, like the Indian chant that had plagued him since childhood.

Sometimes he could see himself in his mind's eye as a youth, his dark hair long and braided, clad in buckskin britches and moccasins, standing under the moon and listening to the night sounds; his mother's wailing, his father's drunken bellows, his sister's bare feet scampering into the dark woods in fear. And he would once again feel the surging of his blood, hear the anger of his spirit . . . and, yeah, find solace in his *savage* blood.

That incredible feeling sometimes still overwhelmed him. It was something his sister either refused to comprehend or tried desperately to resist in herself. Comfort to her came in denying their mother's legacy; forgetting the language, along with everything else their mother struggled so hard to instill in them. Their father had trained her too well.

But Cutter refused to forget.

You always have to wear at least one tellin' piece . . .

As he glanced down at the fringe of his jacket sleeve, his lips twisted cynically. Guilt, didn't she know. His penance. A reminder that no matter how firmly planted he seemed to be in the white man's world, there would always be that wild song in his soul—that calling he could no more deny than he could his next breath. It was as inexpressible as the sound of a wolf's lonesome howl at the moon—and whether he liked it or not, it felt more right than anything ever could. As right as it felt to crave the woman in his arms, to want to bury himself deep inside her, feed the ruthless hunger, protect her.

Squirming in his lap, Elizabeth sighed groggily, lifting her head slightly. Her fingers curled into the button front of his shirt, and his body reacted accordingly. He closed his eyes, commanding control, but it was the worst thing he could have done, because in his mind he saw her ripping his shirt open, popping his buttons, kissing the whorls of hair on his chest.

He couldn't stop himself. He saw himself letting go of the reins, cradling her head in his big hands, lowering his lips to hers. Almost feverishly, he kissed her, lapping at the flesh of her lips and neck, remembering the taste of her. In his fantasy, her eyes opened to meet his. Throwing her head back like a pagan goddess, she invited him without words. Eagerly he unbuttoned her shirt. His hand kneaded softly at her flesh, then fell to cup one velvety breast.

With a groan, he imagined how it would look against his dark skin, soft white globes illuminated by the pale light of the moon.

"Sooo dark," she moaned, startling Cutter from his fantasy. It sounded almost a child's plaintive voice, and he shuddered, willing the images away. He knew she was dreaming, because her eyes were still closed. But just in case, he slowed the pace to a brisk walk, hoping to lull her back into a deeper slumber with a slower gait.

"Shhh," he murmured, his heart still hammering— an aftereffect of his overactive imagination. "Everything's fine," he whispered hoarsely, withdrawing the ring from his pocket and slipping it onto her finger. "You're with me." As he spoke, he felt the truth of those words, and took in a satisfied breath, feeling more content than he'd felt in a long time.

This was meant to be.

Right as rain.

Elizabeth snuggled against him, burying her face in

the space between his arm and ribs. He could feel the shape of her lips through his shirt, and the pounding in his chest intensified.

"With you?" She sighed, a ghost of a smile touching her lips, and Cutter found himself wondering with a scowl who she thought *you* was.

"But it's dark," she whimpered. "Too dark . . . pleash . . ."

Almost tenderly, as he would with a child, he smoothed the hair from her face. "Please what?" he asked huskily.

She moaned something unintelligible, then whimpered again, the sound mournful. It twisted his gut.

He shook her, though not enough to wake her, just enough to prod her into speaking again, wanting to be sure she was all right. "Lizbeth?"

"Hum—to—me . . ."

Hum? His brow furrowed. She wanted him to hum? Shaking his head in puzzlement, he shrugged, thinking that anything that kept her quiet was worth a try. She settled against him, as if she'd somehow felt that affirmative gesture in her sleep. And for the first time in years, Cutter put sound to that unearthly melody he'd first heard from his mother's lips as a toddler. As he hummed, he looked down every little while to verify she was still asleep.

Jo had warned him that she would be mad.

Just how mad would she be?

An anticipatory smile turned his lips suddenly, as he allowed that he rather liked the brightness of her eyes when she was angry. Actually, he couldn't wait to see her expression when she awoke.

He continued to hum softly, remembering and interjecting Cheyenne words, a phrase here, a phrase there, and Elizabeth was soon completely subdued by the soothing vibrations that came from deep within his chest.

As absorbed as Cutter was with his thoughts of the woman lying loosely over his lap, he never antici-

pated the jab of her elbow to his crotch. It had been
a halfhearted movement, with little enough strength
behind it, but it impacted just right . . .

Or just wrong.

For the briefest second his jaw dropped, as if he
couldn't quite believe what she'd done, then snapped
shut, jarring his teeth into his skull. With lightning-
swift reflex, he jerked his pelvis backward, resisting
the urge to jump from the saddle. Clenching his jaw
over the pain that shot through his jewels, he barely
heard her grumbled words.

"Hafta shcoot over . . . caush thers not 'nough—
room."

Oblivious to the pain she'd caused him, and without waiting to see that he *shcoot*ed, Elizabeth sighed
in her sleep, wiggling to make herself more comfortable.

Somehow Cutter managed to hold on to the reins
as he seized her arm and gently lifted her off his belongings. Even the slightest movement worsened his
predicament. Holding his breath against the pang that
burned at his groin, he crushed the urge to howl out
in agony as he managed to lift himself somewhat in
the stirrups and hunker over, desperately seeking a
tolerable position.

Couldn't wake her—damn, damn, couldn't wake
her—couldn't throw her either!

His hands were otherwise occupied, or he would
have shielded himself at once.

Were Elizabeth not on the horse, he'd have reined
in and hurled himself into the ground—praying for a
swift death.

Hell, he groaned, if the blasted woman hadn't been
in his lap to begin with, he wouldn't have this friggin'
crisis to deal with!

Sweat beaded his brow, his palms turning clammy
as he held Elizabeth steady so she wouldn't slip. Just
before he turned blue from lack of oxygen, he re-

leased the breath he'd held, taking in a gulp of sweet night air to replace it.

Unable to hold his position any longer, he sat again, white-faced, clenching his thigh muscles against the loping movement of his Palouse. And with arms that felt suddenly sapped of strength, he managed to shift Elizabeth so that she was sitting astride, the back of her head nestling cozily against his chest.

Incredibly, she slept on.

In spite of the jerky maneuvers it had taken to sit her upright.

In spite of the knuckle-whitening pain that lingered in his rocks.

At least this way, he reflected sardonically, he couldn't see her—though he could damn well feel her, and he thought it'd be a good idea to get her her own mount as soon as possible!

Every bump and bounce served to urge Elizabeth toward a wretched state of wakefulness. She didn't want to wake up. Deep down, something warned her against it. She prayed for mercy, but the movement continued, rocking her, prodding her, until she could no longer ignore it.

Her head felt as if it had been trampled by a herd of buffalo, she thought sourly. Peeping warily through her lashes, she grimaced at the bright light that stabbed at her pupils, making her head throb all the more.

Just where in creation was she?

No sooner had she asked herself that question when she became aware of the fact that her arms were being squeezed, her calves prodded and poked, her ribs probed.

Was she dead and gone to blazes?

Certainly she felt tortured. She wasn't at home snug in her bed, that much was clear, and that real-ization sent a flash of alarm bolting through her.

The last she recalled, she'd been sitting in Josephine's office . . . with her impossibly arrogant brother. Her eyes flew open to find herself sitting astride a horse in the dewy predawn light, her bulky skirts bunched up around her legs, a firm hand exploring her ribs. Her heartbeat quickened and her breathing arrested, her aches and pains overshadowed for the moment.

Whoever it was, he was giant. That much, she knew because his chin was resting on the crown of her head, and she could tell that he was leaning, to boot.

He stiffened, as if sensing that she'd awakened, and a wave of panic rushed through her.

Elizabeth didn't quite think things through. All she could think was that she was on a strange horse—with a strange man sitting astride behind her.

Drawing in a shaky breath for courage, she elbowed the monster. He grunted, releasing her, and she flung herself from the trotting horse.

But her leg was too slow in coming around, and by the time it did, an arm had caught her firmly about the waist.

But that wasn't going to stop her!

Struggling against his hold, her heartbeat pounding in her ears, she twisted wildly in his arms.

Chapter 4

~~~⌒⟋⟍⟍⌒~~~

The woman was buggy.

What the hell did she think she doing throwing herself from a moving horse? Ignoring the blow to his ribs, Cutter managed to keep his hold on her until she reached back, boxing his right ear with a small, bony fist. With a hoarse cry, he let go of her just enough for her to slip into a precarious suspension.

"Son of a—" She was falling, and there wasn't a thing he could do about it! The least he could do was try to keep her from landing under the horse's hooves. But he'd likely break his neck in the process . . . Still, it was that or nothing. Hurling himself down with her, he propelled them away from the spooked horse, and hit the ground with a groan.

Damn her, anyway—loony female! Like a spitting, clawing wildcat, she was still struggling to get free of him. Didn't the little fool realize that he was trying to help her? That they were in danger of becoming hoofbait? Apparently not, he concluded when she promptly boxed him again.

He rolled to the right, trying to skirt the Palouse's hooves, his arms locked protectively about Elizabeth. Above them, the Palouse reared up on its hind legs and came crashing down mere inches from the back of Cutter's head.

He rolled again, his maneuver more instinctive than

53

design, as the Palouse steadied itself and moved off to the right of them. The force of his thrust sent Elizabeth headlong into the hard-packed earth. The side of her face smacked the ground, and she gave a little yelp of pain.

"Awww sh—" He never finished the expletive. The breath was knocked from his lungs as he rolled, landing atop her.

Elizabeth's head felt as if it would burst. An incredible weight covered her, then the world went black for the briefest second, as if a dark hand had passed over her face. When she opened her eyes, it was to find grass in her mouth and those unsettling obsidian eyes scowling down upon her.

"You?" she snarled. Lands, was he heavy! "Get—off of me!" she cried. "Off, you dog!" Irrationally, her fear melted away, replaced with an immediate sense of outrage. "I—said—get—off!"

Torn between wanting to laugh with relief at the grass blades that were clinging to and moving with her lips, and the anger he felt over her crazy stunt, Cutter settled for lust. For all her friggin' layers of clothing, he'd never been more aware of a woman's body beneath his own, every curve, every soft, tantalizing swell. How had he ever thought her skinny?

And her eyes, they weren't gold a'tall. It had been a trick of the candlelight, no doubt, because they were brown now. Not just any brown, though—a soft brown with flecks of amber gold radiating from dark pupils. Against his will, his breathing became labored as he stared at those eyes . . . those lips, remembering the way they had tasted to his hungry mouth.

Elizabeth suddenly found it difficult to breathe, but it had little to do with Cutter's weight bearing down upon her, because he'd lifted himself up just enough so that it was no longer an issue. She could still feel every inch of his body, however, his broad chest, his solid limbs; one leg resting outside her right thigh, the other just inside her left . . . and *something* in between.

Her face colored brightly; she knew exactly what that *something* was. She was a doctor, after all, and had seen *those things* on rare occasions. Yet it was the intense look on his face that snagged her breath. His jaw was taut, his pupils dilated, his nostrils flaring with the scent of her.

It took all of Cutter's resolve to lift himself off her, but he did, slowly, savoring the feel of her beneath him. When he finally stood, he brushed at his pant legs awkwardly, trying to ignore the insistent rise in his britches. The fact that she seemed to be gawking at that particular quarter didn't help matters much, either. He couldn't keep himself from baiting her.

He raised one brow suggestively. "See anythin' that excites ya, Doc?"

Elizabeth didn't immediately understand his crude question, but once it finally penetrated her fogged brain, her jaw dropped in shock. "Certainly not! Arrogant, foulmouthed cur!" she muttered under her breath.

Cutter chuckled at her choice of words. But his humor faded as the trace of blood on her lip finally registered, and his expression darkened with anger.

Elizabeth scooted backward, giving herself a safe distance from the infuriating man, and sat upright. Glaring at him, she spat the offensive grass out of her mouth. She used her hands to swipe off the pieces that wouldn't quite come loose. Her lip throbbed, and what was worse, she thought she tasted blood!

Examining her hand, she inhaled sharply when she spotted a streak of ruby red across her forefinger. She gave a startled little cry and her gaze flew up to meet Cutter's, but she said nothing because she could tell by his expression that he'd already spotted it, and his black look told her that she didn't want to hear any of what he was thinking.

Standing over her, thumb hooked into his waistband, he shook his head at her, as if she were dim-witted. She hated the way he looked at her. It made her feel so . . . so . . .

"What were you trying to do? Kill yourself?"

"Me?" She snorted inelegantly, squinting her eyes to ward away the pain that shot through her head. Her hand trembled as it moved to her temple in an effort to still the hazy picture her eyes were presenting.

"You!" she accused. "What were you trying to do? And where do you think you are taking me?" She glared up at him again, still slightly disoriented.

In the light of day, he seemed different somehow, more Indian maybe. Ominous, definitely. His clothes were the same ones he'd worn last night, except for the wide blue and white bandanna that was bound about his forehead. It seemed to accentuate the length of his hair, the swarthy tone of his skin. Beads of sweat dotted his brow above it.

That was the difference, she thought dimly. That, and the fact that he was bareheaded besides. It was amazing how that small variation in his apparel changed his entire presence. His hat, his one token of civilization, had obviously tumbled from his head during the fall, because it lay upon the ground not more than three feet from her toes. She eyed it malevolently as she wiggled her foot, then bent her knees cautiously, repeating the ritual for the other foot. Satisfied that nothing was broken below the waist, she tested her arms under his watchful eye, grimacing as a dull pang shot through her shoulder.

Belatedly her gaze slid across the grassland, taking in the wide open space, the fact that there were no buildings, nothing but early morning skies and open land. "Where are we?" she asked abruptly. The landscape looked a little eerie with the dew still hanging heavily in the air.

"Easy now, bright eyes, I'm only trying to help you out here." Delving into a pocket, Cutter removed from it a clean bandanna, using it to gently pat the fleck of blood from her lip. She recoiled at his touch, and he gave her a frown for the effort. "We're on our way to St. Louis," he told her, giving her a worried glance. "Don't you recall anythin' a'tall?"

"St. Louis!" Elizabeth shrieked. Forgetting her aches abruptly, she sprang from the ground, brushing her hands anxiously across her skirts. She resisted the urge to rub her bruised fanny, because that infuriating smile tugged at Cutter's lips suddenly, and she had the notion he'd read her thoughts. Nettled, she dropped her hands at her sides.

Her mind raced, trying to piece together the events that would have brought her to this ungodly predicament, but try as she might, she couldn't remember. Shaking her head in bewilderment, she tried to will away her hysteria.

"St Louis?" she repeated, eyeing him suspiciously. Her panic increased tenfold when Cutter nodded calmly. "But I—I don't remember," she conceded, her gaze narrowing upon him. "That is . . . I—I do recall your offer . . . but I also remember telling you no, Mr. McKenzie!"

His grin swept into his dark eyes, but he said nothing in his defense, and Elizabeth bristled. Like a stubborn weed, his annoying amusement had returned, and she felt in that moment like kicking him with all her might. Only she knew that if her anger had triggered his mirth, then violence might only serve to double him over with laughter—infuriating man! Forcing a calming breath, she looked down at the filth that clung to her dark beige skirts, taking in the dangling hem and her once white blouse, groaning. She sighed and tried again, her nerves fast reaching a breaking point.

She held her hands in front of her as if to ward him away, looking him straight in the eyes. "All right . . . let's say I did request your services, Mr. McKenzie . . . It was very *gracious*—" she spoke the word with barely contained fury''—of you to accept, but I find I don't want you escorting me to St. Louis, after all. You can take me home now.'' His smile deepened, and her anger escalated with it. ''Don't you understand plain English? I don't want you taking me to St. Louis! I want you to carry me right back home this very instant!''

Stifling a chuckle, Cutter shook his head. ''No can do,'' he said implacably. ''We've been in the saddle too long and come too far to turn back. Besides, I was sorta countin' on the *dinero*,'' he lied outright. Walking over to pick up his hat, he tapped it against his leg to rid it of the dust and grass seed that clung to it along with the dew.

Her eyes widened incredulously. ''No?''

''No.''

''I can't believe this! You have to take me back!''

He placed his hat upon his head, adjusting it until it sat comfortably, then made his way toward his horse, which was waiting patiently, nibbling at the high grass only a few feet away. ''Izzatso?'' he remarked without turning.

Lifting her skirts indignantly, Elizabeth marched after him, stopping just before she plowed into his back. ''Yes, it is!'' she declared frantically.

''And why is that?'' he asked, much too calmly for her peace of mind. He didn't bother to turn toward her. Instead, he busied himself with straightening the saddle, tightening the cinches.

Flustered, Elizabeth took a subconscious measure of his shoulders. Good night, they were immense! ''Just because!'' She didn't quite know how to say it. *Because you're a half-breed, Mr. McKenzie? Because there is no way I'll get my sister's child with you posing as my husband? Because I feel uncomfortable in your presence? Because you're an infuriating mule's ass! Because you're much too good-looking for my peace of mind?* No, that would never do.

She looked at him crossly, frustrated, not really

wishing to hurt his feelings—he was Josephine's brother, after all—but she wasn't about to let him take her to St. Louis either. How in blue blazes had she managed to get herself so liquored up that she wouldn't remember hiring him on? "Just because," she snapped again, more irritated with herself suddenly than she was with him.

He made some strangled sound. "You're going to have to come up with a better reason than that," he told her.

"I—I don't have any money to pay you!" she said quickly. *How's that for a reason?* she thought wildly.

He did turn to her then. "Beg pardon, ma'am, but you don't plan on reneging on me, do you?" One brow rose in censure.

"No! Yes—I mean . . . That is to say, I don't have any money with me," she finished sweetly, certain that it was just the thing to sway him.

"Uh-huh," he said, returning his attention to the saddle and trying hard not to laugh. "You know what Johnny Law does to double-dealers, don't you?"

"I don't care what Mr. Law does to double-dealers! I don't know this Johnny Law, and I don't ever—"

"Not Mr. Law—Johnny Law is *the law.*" He glanced back at her to stress the point with an affirming nod.

The high color in her cheeks paled somewhat. "I—I—"

Still fighting his laughter, Cutter decided to put her out of her misery. For the time being. "Look, you can pay me when we get back, Miz Bowcock. I've got a few dimes we can spend until then."

"But I don't have anything!" she protested again, her panic returning. "No clothes! Nothing at all! I can't go to St. Louis!" *Not with you*, she added silently.

"I'll buy you whatever you need. We'll just add the cost to what you already owe me," he told her pleasantly. "How's that for accommodating?"

She grated her teeth. "I don't want a new dress!"

She resisted the infantile urge to stomp her feet like a wayward child. The man enraged her beyond reason! "And I don't want you to be accommodating! I just want to go home!" she told him.

Finished repairing saddle damages, he turned to her with a determined gleam in his eye. "Trouble is, Doc . . . Jo's already wired St. Louis to tell them we're on our way. They'll be expecting us. We have to go." He nodded toward his mount, his jaw set stubbornly. "Now, get on aboard, and let's cut some dust."

He wasn't going to take her home. It took her a full minute to recover from that shocking revelation. She opened her mouth to speak, and then shut it again.

"Josephine?" she asked finally.

"That's right. Where do you think you got that ring on your finger?"

At his declaration, Elizabeth glanced down at the simple silver band that now graced her left hand. Her shock was physical. Try as she might, she still couldn't recall a single thing. Surely she wouldn't have just up and married the man? She didn't even know him, for mercy's sake! She moaned, the sound anguished. "We're not . . . we didn't . . . good night!"

The look that passed over Elizabeth's face was anything but complimentary. She looked downright spooked by the thought, and it struck a raw chord in Cutter. "Don't go getting yourself full of prunes, medicine woman. We're not married, just playing at it," he said curtly.

Shock yielded quickly to fury. "Full of prunes? Oh! You! How dare you speak to me so! You have no right!" She lifted her chin, meeting his hard gaze straight on. "If—if you won't take me home, I'll—I'll simply walk the distance! The good Lord didn't give me two good feet for nothing!" she informed him acidly.

Cutter merely shrugged.

Elizabeth's lungs filled with a long draft of fury.

Heaven help her, but she suddenly wanted nothing more than to give in to the even more childish urge to pound his back as he turned from her abruptly to mount up.

Her body was actually trembling with anger, her eyes blazing amber fire. As much as it galled her . . . as much as she wanted to simply turn around and boldly march away, she was forced to ask, ''Just tell me which way to go!''

Her teeth grating, she watched as he settled in the saddle, taking his sweet time before turning to her. And then he smiled, that odious smile, and she knew, beyond a shadow of doubt, that the next words to come out of his mouth would be pure lies.

''Don't you know?'' he asked, reaching back casually into his saddlebag. He lifted the unbound flap and slipped his hand within, retrieving a shriveled slice of jerky. Ripping it in half, he slid one dark strip into his mouth, holding it firmly between his teeth as one would a toothpick. The other half, he held in his hand, intending to offer it to Elizabeth.

But her indignant expression was too much for him. He chuckled. ''That way,'' he relented, and further obliged her by indicating the correct direction with a brisk wave of the jerky. He was confident in the fact that they were too far for her to cover the distance on foot. As he saw it, she'd grow tired enough to listen to reason before too long. Sore feet had a way of doing that to a body.

Her expression smug, Elizabeth made a big to-do of brushing off her skirts and hands, as if to rid herself of his presence once and for all. Slapping discreetly at her backside, she then turned haughtily in the opposite direction from that which he had indicated.

Cutter's jaw actually dropped a little as he watched her march defiantly in the very direction they were headed. And he almost burst out laughing when he spotted the dusty print of her small hand planted firmly on her left rear, but the laughter died on his lips as he suddenly envisioned himself placing his hand over that curving print . . . thought of how her bottom would feel under his palm. Sweeping off his hat with a frustrated gesture, he shook his head, as if to shift his wayward thoughts.

"You think I'm that gullible, don't you?" he heard her mutter beneath her breath. "Well, you can think again, Mr. McKenzie!"

"I'll be *hanged*," he swore softly. And then he chuckled suddenly, amused that the little she-wolf had actually thought him a liar. Briefly he contemplated whether he should correct her choice of direction.

The answer brought a devilish grin to his lips, because he sure as the dickens wasn't about to. They'd ridden good'n' hard this morning, and his horse was right ready for a breather. As it was, he'd intended to follow her only as long as it took to change her mind, and then turn around and carry her on to St. Louis.

This way, there'd be no wasted time.

Farther along, there was a wide place in the road—just a small town, but one big enough so that they might find a place to hang his hat and hitch his Palouse for the night . . . and maybe, if they were lucky, secure another mount for Elizabeth. Somehow he wasn't too keen on the notion of riding double.

Again, he shook his head and grinned, just thinking of the look of shock she'd wear when they rambled into town.

Deuced little hellcat!

Chapter 5

It had to be that she wasn't wearing her specs, Cutter concluded with a shake of his head. Why else would she set out in the wrong direction? And damn him, if guilt wasn't gnawing at his gut. The thought occurred to him suddenly that she was probably too embarrassed to admit she didn't know which direction he'd pointed out.

A frown crossed his features as he set the slice of her jerky between his lips. He'd tried to give it to her earlier, but she'd refused him outright. After holding on to it awhile, he'd finally decided to eat it himself, out of annoyance. But she needed some kind of sustenance, he knew, so he reached back into the saddlebags, withdrawing another cut. He stepped up his pace, intending to offer it again. Hell, force her if need be. Though he doubted he'd have to, at that, because he was sure the she-wolf was starved by now . . . hopefully enough to overlook her stubborn female pride. He shook his head in fascination.

Women. You couldn't live with 'em, and you couldn't shoot 'em.

Intrigued, he studied her stiff back as she marched, coming to the obvious conclusion. She sure as cuss looked like a woman who thought she knew where she was headed; those feet of hers never faltered once.

Maybe she was just plain contrary, he decided.

"Sure you don't want a lift?" he asked her, watching with ill-concealed amusement as she irritably swatted away the chin-high buffalo grass from her path. They didn't have much further to go, but suddenly he couldn't wait to see her expression.

"Thanks, but no thanks, Mr. McKenzie—I've had quite enough of you, as it is!"

His shoulders shook with mirth. He'd never understood how a woman could nurse her anger for so long. "Cutter," he asserted, his lips curling faintly.

With every hot mile, Elizabeth's temper grew more foul. The morning gray of the sky had quickly turned to a cloudless blue, and the sun now shone down without mercy.

"Mr. McKenzie!" she shot back at him through clenched teeth, turning to pierce him with angry brown eyes.

He shook his head in mock censure, his lips quivering slightly with laughter. "Now, now, Doc, ain't no call to be so rude. Just thought you might like t' ride, is all. You've been on your feet—" scanning the puffy blue heavens, he guessed at the time—"oh . . . a good hour and a half at least."

Didn't she know it! Coupled with the fall she'd had, the walk was nearly killing Elizabeth's poor limbs. Her face flushed with anger as she turned again to glare up at him.

"Now, you just tell me, Mr. McKenzie, why would I get on that horse with you? So you can manhandle me again? Why should I trust you?" she asked without turning. Good night! She'd felt like a chicken being tried for the stewpot with him poking and prodding her as he had! What audacity!

Cutter had the good graces to flush. Hell, he'd forgotten what she'd awakened to, and felt suddenly like the kid who'd gotten caught with his fingers in the proverbial cookie jar. He scowled, completely at a loss for words. He wasn't in the habit of squeezing women's limbs while they slept, but he didn't know how to tell her so. And he hadn't touched anything of any importance—not really, just a leg, and an arm or two, he reasoned. He'd just wanted to be certain that she had enough meat on her bones for the journey. She seemed so scrawny.

The minutes stretched by as he contemplated how to get around her anger, but any way he looked at it, she had a right to it, and so in the end he decided just to drop the subject. "Suit yourself," he relented finally, but his tone gave little hint of contrition.

Turning toward him briefly, Elizabeth gave him a puzzled frown. There had been a long enough stretch of silence between them at this point that she'd somehow managed to forget what they'd been talking about. *Suit herself?* What in creation did the man mean by that remark? she wondered irately. *Suit herself?* Nothing about this miserable outing suited her in the least!

Had she missed something? She'd been so lost in her musings that she'd shut him out completely . . . almost completely. She was only too aware of the fact that he was right behind her, his horse trotting at a snail's pace.

And the way that he watched her unnerved the dickens out of her!

He came up alongside her suddenly, leaning forward in the saddle, his forearm resting upon the saddle horn, his smile knowing and crooked as he offered her the almost forgotten slice of jerky. Elizabeth hadn't realized how hungry she was until that moment, but her mouth began to water in anticipation. Still, she eyed the small strip of meat as though it were a pit viper he were proffering. Her stomach grumbled in protest when she didn't immediately reach out to take his offering, and she glanced up through her lashes, wondering anxiously if he'd heard.

She found him still smiling, curse him to high heaven and back! Oh, she despised him! Heaven help

her, she did! Elizabeth, who had never despised anyone as long as she'd lived—not even her mother for
leaving her—really and truly despised him! Giving
him her most lethal scowl, she kept marching, but he
seemed completely unaffected by her dismissal, and
that made her all the more irate. How dare he be so
nonchalant when she was ready to burst with fury!

And why should she starve herself only to spite
him?

Feeling his presence beside her like a thorn in her
side, she turned, snatching the jerky from his still-
outstretched hand. Shoving it angrily into her mouth,
she ripped a slice from it as though it were his head
and she were snapping it off. Rage as she'd never
known before spiraled through her, making her vision darken at the edges.

If he laughed . . . if he so much as uttered a single
inconsiderate, heartless chuckle at her surrender . . .

A hundred terrible words lay teetering on the tip
of her tongue as she plodded onward, alternately ripping off and chewing her jerky. How she managed to
contain them was beyond her, but she did, though
her breast filled with mute anger. Had she been a
mite bigger, she might have yanked him down from
the saddle to meet her fists. As it was, that notion
seemed so ridiculous that she merely cursed him under her breath.

It wouldn't be long, she told herself firmly, before
she'd be rid of him. And then, as far as she was concerned, she never needed to set eyes on the man
again!

Now, why did that notion seem to bother her? she
chafed. It shouldn't bother her at all! She should be
jumping for joy . . . and she would the moment she
set eyes on Sioux Falls.

She glanced back over her shoulder, catching his
arrogant grin—curse the man! Looking down, she
noted, not for the first time, that her poor clothes were

covered with grass seed and stained with dirt. Her torn hem dragged on the ground behind her.

She supposed she looked a sight. Ignoring the "whys" of her caring over that fact, she pondered what people would think of her, dirty as she was and being followed by a grinning idiot to boot?

Would they think the worst?

To her consternation, Cutter began to whistle, and though it was a fine, clear tune, it didn't even begin to improve her mood. Rather, it grated on her nerves.

Of course they would think the worst!

The odd tune was familiar, but she couldn't place it, and it provoked her. Desperately she tried to ignore him.

She couldn't wait to get home and bathe, and it was that thought with which she consoled herself. A bath . . . How wonderful it would be to sink into a warm, bubbly tub of water.

A great believer in cleanliness, Elizabeth loved her baths and had ordered a tremendous porcelain tub from the catalog, one of the very few luxuries she'd ever afforded herself. There was just something about treating so much infirmity that made one want to soak a lifetime in soap and water. Besides, as much dusty ground as she covered making house calls, a bath was almost always necessary at the end of the day.

And it helped her to forget. Forget that her dear father was no longer around to hum her to sleep at night. For a while, after her mother had gone, she had been afraid of the silence. Not the dark so much, because that in itself was never so terrifying. It was rather soothing, really. Only the silence had terrified her, because in the silence she was alone. So Papa would sit in his own room, one door down, and hum to himself. She'd never asked him to, but he'd done so nonetheless. For her. Because he'd known—to reassure her that he was still there.

Cutter's whistling pierced her thoughts, and again she concentrated on that bath—that warm, cleansing bath. Her father, too, had believed in cleanliness, and she was thoroughly convinced, though there was no real medical evidence to substantiate the claim, that cleanliness was an integral part of any cure. She always cleaned her instruments in strong water. Truth to tell, it was the only thing whiskey was good for—besides getting decent folks into trouble. This morning was a very good example for the record.

She surveyed the landscape, fretting. Nothing! Nothing at all seemed familiar to her! Surely she'd made enough house calls outside of town that she should know the area by now? But to her dismay, she found that she didn't recognize a single thing. Not *one* thing!

Of course, she reminded herself, worrying at her lower lip, it was hard to see much for the tall grass. Grassland was grassland, after all, and there wasn't much different about any one stretch of it to distinguish it from the next. Right?

Yes, of course, that was what it was. She nodded, as if to settle her fears. And so it was a complete shock to find herself suddenly staring at a gathering of blurry, nondescript, and very unfamiliar buildings in the immediate distance. Her first reaction was to reach for her spectacles. Finding them gone was her undoing. Her eyes widened in alarm. How could she have been so absorbed in her thoughts that she wouldn't have noticed her spectacles were missing? Halting abruptly, she whirled to face Cutter, hands on her hips.

"Where are they?"

Cutter came up beside her, his brow lifting in response to her question. "Where's what?"

"My spectacles!"

"Took you long enough to notice they were gone, don't y' think?"

Elizabeth ignored his goading. What business was it of his anyway? She turned her palm up impatiently, certain that Cutter had her spectacles somewhere on his person, and silently pleading with him to give them back.

There was an odd glitter in his eyes as he stared at her hand. Then his gaze flicked up to her eyes, considering her. They were so dark, and fixed on her so intently, that for an interminable moment Elizabeth felt as though he were looking straight into her soul, searching out every dark corner to reveal it.

Feeling unsure of herself, she withdrew her hand slightly. The moment was excruciating. She felt utterly bared to his scrutiny, as though he knew all of her secrets somehow, every fear, every last little ache in her heart. More than that even, she once again had the notion the man pitied her, and a strange pang nearly overcame her outrage. Nearly.

A quiver passed down her spine, breaking the spell. "Well?" she asked. Unnerved, she watched as he turned from her finally and reached into the saddlebag, retrieving her bent frames. Without speaking, she accepted them from him, quickly placed them upon the bridge of her nose, then turned back to the cluster of buildings in the distance, fully expecting them to have reconfigured themselves somehow. The images only became sharper, more distinct, and her shock was audible. She gave a startled little cry.

"*What* is that?" she choked out.

Cutter lifted the brim of his hat slightly, his brows rising as he peered speculatively at the structures in question. "Why," he drawled with distinct mockery, his gaze immediately reverting to hers, "can't be sure, Miz Bowcock, but seems to be a town." His mouth lifted slightly at the corners, yet lift it did, and Elizabeth had suddenly reached her breaking point.

"Not Sioux Falls, it isn't!"

"Never said it was."

"But you . . . you did say . . . and I—I thought . . ." Torn between anger and embarrassment, she groaned, and her cheeks began to heat again. "I can't believe you didn't tell me!" she cried out in frustration. "Why didn't you say something? You knew I was walking in the wrong direction!''

To her alarm, he began to chuckle, and then to laugh outright, and suddenly Elizabeth couldn't help herself. She flung herself at him, snatching him by the arm and yanking downward with all her might.

Never had anyone infuriated her so!

To her discredit, he barely budged from the saddle. Instead, with his free arm he clutched at his side, hooting all the louder as she pulled in vain on his other arm. Crying out in frustration, Elizabeth pounded his thigh.

His laughter slowing to chuckles, Cutter tried to seize Elizabeth's wrists, to save his leg from any more of her sharp blows. But in her fury, Elizabeth was quicker, and he took two stinging cuffs on the hand he'd held out as a buffer.

Without warning, she found herself hoisted from the ground, onto his mount. One arm imprisoned her while he simply sat there and laughed into her flyaway mass of hair—another thing she hadn't noticed! Just how had her hair managed to come loose from its braid? But as soon as she considered it, she knew, and her cheeks burned brighter at the very thought of the liberties Cutter had taken with her. Good night! What else might he have done without her knowledge? And how dare he make fun of her! She wiggled, to no avail, trying for the second time in the same day to free herself from his merciless hold.

''Heathen savage!'' she accused him, mindless with fury now. With her hands trapped by his embrace, she had no alternative but to use her teeth to gain her freedom. She lunged at his neck, like a viper, but the shock of his warm male flesh on her tongue made her suddenly bolt backward in alarm. Or maybe it was Cutter's quick reaction that pulled her away from him. Elizabeth wasn't quite certain. All she knew was that he tasted of salt, smelled purely of man, a scent so mind-jarring that her body quickened wildly in response. It startled her so much that she simply sat, staring at him in utter bewilderment.

As he heard the words Elizabeth flung at him, Cutter's mirth ceased abruptly, and his eyes narrowed upon the mouth that had nearly taken a chunk from his neck. Foremost in his mind was the brief kiss he had stolen the night before. And then his mind focused on that key word.

Stolen.

She'd never have given it freely. He made the mistake of looking up, into her eyes, and a familiar twisting began in his gut. Elizabeth was looking at him, through spectacles aslant, as if he were a two-headed rodent. He'd felt the stab of prejudice many times before, but that she should stoop to flinging insults caused long-buried scars to rip and burn. His anger flared, though only a coolness settled in his eyes.

Why had he thought she would be any different? How could he have allowed himself to forget? Because she was Jo's friend? He damned well should have known better! And it shouldn't bother him. But it did. Because for the first time in a long time, he'd allowed himself to forget, to feel easy with someone. He'd let down his guard.

His mistake, but he wouldn't make it again.

"I wouldn't try that again," Cutter warned. A chill hung on the edge of his words, and his eyes held hers in cool contempt. "As it is, you're damned lucky you're a woman." Despite his outward calm, there was the threat of violence in his expression.

Faced with his anger, Elizabeth felt suddenly ashamed of her childish outburst. Still, she couldn't quite bring herself to apologize. He had harassed her, after all.

Releasing the breath she'd not realized she'd held, she asked grudgingly, straightening her spectacles, "Just how far have we come?"

For the longest moment, Cutter couldn't bring himself to respond to her simple question. He oughta turn back now and take her high-minded self back to Sioux Falls. Yet he couldn't bring himself to do it. In spite of his anger, he just couldn't, and his displeasure over the fact burned in his eyes. "Like I said before, too far to turn back. If I'm not mistaken, that's Indian Creek up ahead. You can come along with me, or run back home with your tail tucked between your pretty little legs. Either way, it's your decision, but if you choose to go home, you go it alone."

The change in his demeanor was frightening. Gone was the imperturbable cad. In his place was someone else entirely. The other provoked her, infuriated her, but she'd never hesitated to respond in kind. This man, she was unsure of. Still, she reminded herself, he *was* Josephine's brother. Josephine wouldn't have let harm come her way—not even by way of her baby brother.

She couldn't keep herself from speaking up. "How do I know what you intend, Mr. McKenzie? You might be a raving lunatic, or bent on murder, for that matter."

His dark, enigmatic eyes revealed nothing. He nodded slowly, lips thin with displeasure. His hand held her arm, squeezing firmly but painlessly. "True enough. But don't you think that if I'd aimed to do you harm, Doc . . . I'd have done it to you long before now?" His silky tone mesmerized her. Unable to tear her gaze away, she swallowed, opening her mouth to speak, but he shook her suddenly, startling the words from her tongue.

"Look," he broke in, before she could gather her thoughts. "You don't know me all that well, that's true, but I'm willing to help you for nothing—Christ knows why!" His intent was to tell her the brutal truth, all of it, even if it spooked her. To his way of thinking, Elizabeth needed a little dose of fear to make her understand that it wasn't a Sunday picnic she was intending. "You can't say the same for someone else," he said bluntly. "You can't even count on help for pay, because who's to stop them from taking your money and tossing up your skirts, just for the hell of it? Maybe even putting a knife between your pretty little shoulder blades, at that—to guarantee your silence?''

Her eyes went wide as his grip tightened convulsively upon her arm. She fidgeted, trying to ease his hold, but he never gave an inch. ''Stop . . . please—stop!'' she cried out. ''You're hurting me!''

His callous, self-satisfied expression raised the hairs on the back of her neck. ''Good. Am I frightening you, too? Sure as hell hope so!'' His free hand found its way into her tousled hair, his fingers curling around the back of her neck to secure her as he finally released her arm. He touched a loose tendril, examining it, then winding it carefully about his finger. His eyes glinted dangerously. ''Because I'd hate to see this—'' he tugged at it softly, bringing her closer, so that their lips were separated only by a whisper ''—dangling from some Indian's scalp belt.''

Forcing her attention away from his lips, she grimaced, meeting his angry gaze, her own eyes flashing. ''And *you* don't take scalps?'' she asked with more calm than she felt, and then she shriveled suddenly as an odd look passed over his features—pain, if she didn't know better—before his jaw turned taut and his eyes grew harsh.

He released her abruptly, and she nearly fell off the horse. She had to reach out and catch his shirt to steady herself, but his gaze never wavered. His expression was cold and proud.

''I'm riding into that town,'' he said, his voice soft but daunting. ''And you're coming with me, Doc. You take tonight to think about whether you're wantin' my services or not.'' His eyes were black, sparkling with fury. ''Then . . . bright 'n' early tomorrow mornin', I'll expect your answer. It's up to you. I don't aim to force you, Lizbeth—or beg you, either. It's purely your decision.'' He leaned back—

ward, reaching into the saddlebags, groping blindly, never taking his eyes from hers as he brought up a small pouch and pressed it into her hand.

No sooner had she accepted it when he lifted her, turning her around to face away from him. Too stunned to speak, she explored the pouch with her fingers without opening it. Coins. He'd given her money.

"I can't accept them," she told him.

"Take it up with Josephine," he said. And then, reaching over her, he gathered up the reins, leaning briefly against her back. She flinched, sensing his anger in every rigid plane of his chest.

"And if in the morning my answer is still no?" she prompted, her shoulders lifting slightly, her expression wary.

He leaned closer, his lips brushing the top of her ear as he spoke, his tone lacking in emotion. "Then I've said all on the matter I aim to. If you don't have the good sense to say yes, Miz Bowcock . . . then I don't care to see you again. Use that money Jo gave you to buy yourself a ticket home." Having said that, he touched his spurs to his horse, and it lunged forward.

Elizabeth's hand swept out to catch her spectacles as she was hurled back into Cutter's chest. She cried out at the impact. Cutter, on the other hand, never so much as grunted as his body absorbed the blow without yielding an inch.

Chapter 6

$\mathbf{I}$t had been hours now since Elizabeth had finished her bathing and put out the lamp, but still she was unable to fall asleep. Her poor eyes felt strained from long hours of trying to keep them shut. With a groan, she pressed her fingers to her lids, massaging them gently.

Why couldn't she go to sleep?

She wanted to . . . desperately. And she'd tried absolutely everything, from regulating her breathing to conjuring dreams, but always her thoughts returned to Cutter. Certainly it wasn't that she was waiting to hear his footsteps pass her door on the way to his room! More like than not, she wouldn't hear them anyway, she chafed. The man was so agile on his feet! Really, he was probably already fast asleep next door, dreaming peacefully, without the least thought for her.

How dare he invade her thoughts so thoroughly!

They'd ridden into town, neither of them having spoken another word, and had gone directly to the only hotel Indian Creek boasted. Cutter had remained merely long enough to procure for them two of the only three rooms available, then had left her completely to herself.

Where he'd gone to, Elizabeth didn't know, but she'd not seen him again, regardless that the town was so small as to be virtually nonexistent. From what she'd been able to tell, Indian Creek consisted of but a small hotel, a bank, three saloons—three, mind you; not one, not two, but three!—a general store, selling everything from boots to bacon, which also doubled as a post office, and a small livery. She'd purchased a pair of men's denims at the general store, only because that was her only choice. But it didn't matter, because nobody but Cutter would see her.

She'd not come across a physician's office, or a drugstore, and she had to wonder what the townspeople did, if anything, for medical aid. All in all, Indian Creek was less than impressive, and it was no wonder she'd never heard of it before now, despite the fact that it wasn't so very far away from Sioux Falls.

She hadn't dared to go out for long, but because it had been so early in the morning when they'd arrived, she couldn't very well have simply shut herself up in the stale-smelling room she now occupied. The first thing she'd done was to ferret out a meal, which she'd then consumed with all the finesse of a ravenous wolf. Once her hunger was appeased, things hadn't seemed quite so bleak, and she'd spent the rest of the day patronizing the meager shop.

She'd purchased the men's britches, justifying it with the fact that her own skirt was torn. Besides that, she told herself, her cumbersome skirt would be too unmanageable on horseback. And then she'd bought a few other necessaries . . . until finally it had dawned on her that she'd already made up her mind, purchasing items for the journey as she was. While her conscious mind had been cursing the man, her unconscious had long since decided to accept him.

Little sense that made!

And that brought her to another question entirely. Why *had* Cutter offered his assistance? What were his motives? He'd said that he'd done so for his sister. But that in itself didn't quite make sense.

Her brow furrowed softly. Cutter McKenzie was all

wrong for the position. Nothing had changed. He still wouldn't do as a husband. *Yet* . . . he'd made plenty of sense this morning. Who else could she trust? And it wasn't a matter of choice; she needed, more than anything else, to get and raise her sister's precious young daughter. She loved helping others. It gave her such a warm feeling inside, and that was why she'd wanted so desperately to become a physician, but something elemental was missing from her life . . . something that left her empty and aching during the lonely hours. What it was, she couldn't say, but like a beacon in the night, her niece drew her.

To her dismay, so did Cutter.

I'd have noticed you.

His silky whisper came back to haunt her. Would he have? she wondered. And did it really matter?

No! she berated herself, shutting out his voice.

With a frustrated jerk of the thin coverlet, she turned to glare at the door. She'd intended to tell Cutter tonight that she'd accepted his proposal . . . so they could get an early start in the morning. But at this rate, she wasn't even going to be able to open her own eyes before noon—blasted man!

At last, footfalls sounded just outside the door, stopping just beyond it, and without thinking, Elizabeth tossed the covers and leapt out of bed, forgetting her spectacles in her haste. Within seconds, she had her ear pressed to the door. The voices were muffled, but she could still make out Cutter's unmistakable drawl.

"Sorry, sweetbritches . . . not up to snuff tonight . . . Here, take this . . ."

Elizabeth bit her lower lip, trying to comprehend what it was that she was hearing.

"Course ya are, Cutter, honey," came a sultry female voice. "And I know just the thing," she purred. "Don't want your money, honey . . . Keep it . . . This one's . . . on me." There was a deep, tortured moan, and a thump, as something or someone fell against the door.

Her door! They didn't even have the decency to fall against Cutter's door! It had to be hers, didn't it?

"There now . . . see how easy that was?" the hussy purred.

"Now, Bess . . . Bess. Aww hell, Bess . . ." Cutter moaned suddenly, the sound low and tortured.

Her heart beating like a tom-tom and her mind reeling, Elizabeth pressed her ear closer to the door. Hearing nothing more, she stooped down frantically to peer through the tiny keyhole. She knew it was wrong to spy, yet she couldn't keep herself from it. In the darkness, she could see nothing, and it frustrated her.

But, oh, she could hear them well enough, scuffling noisily against her door!

It would serve them right, she thought crossly, if she just snatched it open and exposed the two of them in the midst of their . . . of their—whatever it was they were doing! A little voice niggled her, and her temper mounted. Of course, she wasn't jealous! How ridiculous!

She and Cutter were supposed to be traveling as man and wife. Weren't they? If Cutter thought for one moment that she intended to sit back and allow him to bring home women like . . . like . . . like Bess, he'd best think again! How dare he humiliate her like that!

"Come on, now, Bess . . . do you have to do that here?" came Cutter's muffled, flimsy rejection. "Bess . . ."

Bess giggled suddenly, the sound as clear and musical as the tinkling of little bells. "Course not," she replied triumphantly. Listening to Cutter's answering groans, Elizabeth became more agitated with every second that passed.

"Key in this pocket, honey?"

There was a moment of silence, and Elizabeth

imagined that Cutter nodded at the shameless Jezebel. Screams of frustration welled at the back of her
throat.

"Mmmmm . . . nice . . . real nice . . . This here
your room?"

Elizabeth never waited to hear Cutter's response.
She'd heard more than enough! She jerked open the
door.

In fell Cutter, along with the leech in a red dress.
His hat fell off, landing at Elizabeth's feet.

The leech shrieked in surprise, then rolled off Cutter with a curse that should never have found its way
to feminine lips. Huffing angrily, she then rose,
smacking at her dress in indignation. "What in the
blazes?" she exploded.

Cutter, having hit his head on the floor, simply lay
there, cradling it with both hands for an awkward
moment. Closing one eye, he groaned pitifully.

"Cutter!" the woman in red screeched.

Elizabeth refused to be cowed. It wasn't she who
had rolled in clinging so shamelessly to Cutter! With
hands on hips, she confronted them both, her tone
caustic. "Yes, Cutter, dear, do tell!"

Cutter released his head, angling it to look up at
Elizabeth, his eyes gleaming. The harsh lines of his
face were eased now, giving him an almost boyish
appearance. Relief filled her, for she'd been wholly
terrified that he'd never forgive her for her outburst
earlier in the day. Unbelievably, he grinned at her, an
irresistibly devastating grin with no trace of his former animosity.

He'd changed his clothing, and his legs were now
denim-clad in place of the buckskin. His chambray
shirt was a faded forest green, making his skin seem
darker somehow, and his hair was a tousled mess.
One wavy lock fell carelessly across his forehead. He
brushed it back out of his eyes to reveal the narrowed, predatorial gaze. Elizabeth's breath caught at
the intensity revealed there.

"Hiya, Doc," he slurred.

Elizabeth smiled back at him, but there was no humor in her smile. Cutter was sotted. She could tell by his muddled expression that he was. Aside from that, as angry as he'd been at her this morning, there was simply no way that he'd be looking at her as he was now—unless he was inebriated!

"Cutter dear," she said in a honeyed tone, "I'm so glad I waited up for you." It was all she could do to keep her voice congenial. Her anger getting the best of her, she turned to pierce the gaping woman with a scathing glare. "Thank you so much," she said as pleasantly as she was able through clenched teeth, "for bringing my husband to me. But I believe I can take care of him from here."

Bess's ample breasts rose indignantly, and her wrathful gaze snapped downward to Cutter.

Cutter's brow rose abruptly at Elizabeth's declaration, and then a slow grin spread, touching his dark eyes. Tearing his gaze away from Elizabeth, he gave Bess a lopsided smile. " 'Fraid so," he said in confirmation, but there was little contrition in his tone. "Yep, that's my wife, all right." He nodded apologetically.

The woman's gaze jerked upward to examine Elizabeth once more, appraising her shrewdly, then back to Cutter with open ire. "Well, I never!" she exclaimed. With a flourish of her satin skirts, she spun away and stomped down the hall, airing her lungs as she went.

Elizabeth watched until the woman became nothing more than a red blur in the dim hall, then her attention returned to the man sprawled at her feet. Half of him lay within her room, the other half in the hall.

Lifting himself up, Cutter gaped after Bess, whistling softly. "Was that ever close!" he declared. Again, he looked up at Elizabeth, his eyes slitted with exhaustion . . . and something more. "I owe you one, bright eyes. Crazy woman wouldn't take no for an answer." With a grunt and a sigh, he laid his head back onto the floor. "My head hurts," he complained.

Elizabeth gave him a doubting look. "It certainly didn't appear to me as though you were struggling too hard to get away!"

Cutter sighed and closed his eyes, and Elizabeth jabbed him with her bare toe, irritated by his obvious dismissal. "You are despicable! Get up!"

With some effort, Cutter opened his eyes, refocusing his gaze. And then he turned slowly to gawk at Elizabeth's bare foot with new awareness, his mouth creasing with displeasure as his gaze then traveled up her half-clad legs to her chemise.

The color drained from Elizabeth's face as she remembered finally what she was wearing—or rather what she was not—and she gave a startled gasp, her arms crossing automatically to conceal her thinly clad bosom. Her feet, on the other hand, wouldn't move.

"What in damnation are you doing out here dressed like that!" he shouted suddenly, startling her into retreating. He was up and on his feet before Elizabeth could make it into the refuge of the shadows. "What did you think you were doing opening that door? It could have been anyone out here!" He came in, and with his boot he kicked the door shut behind him, scowling fiercely. Catching her arm, he swung her about to face him. "Are you out of your mind, woman?" His vision faded momentarily with the loss of light, then returned more sharply as his keen eyes adjusted to the darkness.

Elizabeth merely stared, wide-eyed and tongue-tied.

Holy hell, Cutter thought, sobering abruptly. How had he ever thought her scrawny? Not even his discovery earlier in the day—when he'd fallen atop her—had prepared him for the reality of the woman before him.

Even in the dim light, he could see that her thin, wash-worn chemise clung enticingly to her bosom, hugging her flesh where it touched. And her bloomers, though a far larger size than she required, were too sheer to conceal much. His gaze fixed upon the shadowy triangle at the apex of her thighs, and he found himself bewitched by it. The hunger that had eluded his body with the whore now returned, slamming into him full force, and he was just tight enough not to fight it.

With a groan, he closed his eyes, knowing instinctively where it would lead them if he didn't avert his gaze. Leaning against the door, he pulled Elizabeth back with him.

Elizabeth's heart jolted, her pulse pounding with the contact of their bodies. She was powerless to resist as he pressed her firmly against him. His head fell back, hitting the door with a thump, and the sound unsettled her.

"M-maybe," she stammered, "y-you should go now?"

There was a moment of strained silence before Cutter's head came up again, his gaze piercing her through the shadows. Noticing that her specs were missing, he wondered again why she wore them if she didn't need them.

"Maybe," he answered softly, enigmatically, his hand stirring at her back. "But don't reckon I will."

"B-But—"

"Shhh," he hissed through clenched teeth, his jaw turning taut. A muscle twitched in his cheek as he fought for control . . . and lost. He brushed a wisp of hair from her face, his eyes slitting languorously. "Do you know how much I've thought about you . . . like this?"

Her body warming with a guilty flush, Elizabeth shook her head in tiny jerks. As his hand moved up her spine, she began to tremble—not in fear, but because her body was suddenly too tense, achingly aware of the man she was pressed to so intimately.

"No?" he whispered gruffly, answering for her. "Then why don't you let me show you, bright eyes." His hand moved up behind her neck, holding her steady as he tilted her head and slowly moved in for the kill.

Their lips brushed lightly at first, sending glorious waves of shock through Elizabeth's entire being. The scents of tobacco and whiskey assailed her and she inhaled deeply, breathing in those scents along with another more elusive . . . and titillating. In response, her insides convulsed faintly. It was as though she were famished, somehow, for what he would give her, all of her senses rejoicing in chorus . . . awakening finally, after an endless slumber.

Then their lips met and she was lost irretrievably to the moment. Merciful Lord, she had never known it could be so divine to kiss a man's mouth. She had at times spied lovers in just such an embrace, but only now, this moment, understood the urgency, the yearning, that drove them.

Cutter suckled gently at her trembling lips, losing himself in the sweetness of the kiss. In his half-sotted state he couldn't bring himself to give a fig what the consequences would be. He could only feel. Though he'd known Elizabeth only twenty-four hours, it seemed he'd waited a lifetime for precisely this moment. Too long.

And she wasn't resisting him.

Sucking a rush of cool, sweet air through his clenched teeth, he slid a hand down to the hollow of her back, crushing her closer, wanting her to feel his arousal, embedding himself deeply into the nest of soft curls he struggled so fiercely not to visualize in his mind's eyes.

Her body was alive, with a will of its own, Elizabeth thought wildly, and then she couldn't think at all as Cutter's tongue slid boldly between her lips.

The shock of it was physical, sending convulsions throughout her body. Momentarily dazed by the intrusion, she stiffened slightly. With a belated gasp, she jerked her head backward, but Cutter's hand held the back of her neck, bracing her for more of his tender assault. She whimpered in protest, but the soft sound only seemed to make his foray into her mouth all the more frenzied.

His tongue swept deeper, seeking out hers, brushing at it softly, almost as though to coax a response from her . . . then again . . . tasting, entwining with hers so erotically that her breath arrested. She felt dizzy! Her knees buckled and she sagged against Cutter as the last broken breath left her lungs. Her will to fight him fled entirely. Before she could think to stop herself, she responded by meeting his tongue with her own, sparring with it timidly, clumsily almost, her heart leaping.

Cutter nearly exploded on the spot. He swept his arms around her waist, pressing her against him as he savored the sweetness of her lips. She might not like the fact that he had Indian blood in his veins, but her body sure didn't know the difference. God, it would be so easy to take her the distance . . . lift her against him . . . carry her to bed. So easy. Her reactions were awkward, but he'd been with enough women to know the signs of her body's awakening.

She wanted this as much as he did.

Though frightened by the intensity of the moment, Elizabeth prayed that it would never end. Never in her life had she felt so heavenly. Her body cried out for more, though more of what, she didn't know. It demanded that she continue, and not even her good sense could keep her from complying. Clinging to Cutter breathlessly, she arched for him as he sank his fingers into her hair, tilting her head backward to give him better access.

"Cutter," she sighed.

As he heard her confusion in the one word, an unwelcome thought emerged from the dark recesses of Cutter's mind, creeping obstinately into his consciousness. Stubbornly ignoring it, he deepened the kiss, only to find that it wouldn't go away.

He had the nagging suspicion that if he bedded her now, it would be over. That it would end here and now. Innocent as Elizabeth evidently was, she wasn't aware of where this was leading, he was sure. Otherwise, the little prudish miss would be clawing his eyes out just now, rather than urging him on with her delightful little body. As angry as she'd been with him, she'd never have submitted so easily. Her prickly pride wouldn't allow it.

Truth was, he could go on . . . and he doubted she'd put up any resistance a'tall . . . but tomorrow, or maybe even seconds afterward, she'd be conscience-stricken over what they'd shared and she'd hightail it home quicker'n a hunted jackrabbit.

And that wasn't what he was after.

But damn, would it feel good!

And—it—still—wouldn't get him what he wanted. Casting a glance over her shoulder, he eyed the small bed pensively, picturing Elizabeth there, lying beneath him in all her glory, her long, silky hair wrapped around his bare thighs. God, he wanted that! Scrutinizing the piece of furniture intently, he forced himself away from her lips, kissing one corner of her mouth regretfully, before he tilted her head to one side in order to better view his coveted destination.

Instinctively, even against his will, his sensual lips were drawn to her exposed neck, like a predator to its prey. Forgetting himself, he nuzzled her hungrily as his fingers twisted in her hair. His teeth grazed her flesh ever so lightly, nibbling, his tongue flicking out to taste her. Finding the fragile pulse that ticked just beneath the pale surface, he groaned at the feel of it. As he feasted, his gaze again returned to the waiting bed, calculating.

So close. So damned close.

And it was by far the longest four feet he'd ever considered crossing. Closing his eyes, he took a deep breath, forcing himself to wrench his mouth away from her warm flesh. His breathing labored and eyes hooded, Cutter again laid his head back upon the door. His hands slipped obediently to her shoulders.

In a state of torment, he watched as Elizabeth's lucidity slowly returned. All the while, he held her away from himself. For the longest moment, she stood as though in a stupor, her head titled seductively, her breasts rising and falling with her quickened breath. Her luscious lips were parted faintly, pursed in anticipation—swollen from his kisses, he noted with deep satisfaction. God, her expression was paradise itself, he thought in that moment, and it took all of his resolve to keep from letting her fall against him and bending slowly forward to reclaim her lips.

He'd fully expected her to turn down his offer. It had surprised him near out of his britches when she'd boldly claimed him as her husband in the hall. But he could still taste the sweet surge of triumph he'd experienced at her declaration . . . and was hungry for more of it. Even as furious as he had been with her, he wanted her . . . and he wanted her willing. Recoiling from the notion of her running from him, he cleared his throat.

The spell broken, Elizabeth opened her eyes with a start.

"You mean to accept my offer, I take it?" he said abruptly.

Chapter 7

Blinking twice, Elizabeth struggled to brush the cobwebs from her addled brain. "Offer? Oh, oh, yes . . . offer! Yes, I do!" she declared soberly. Straightening abruptly, she shrugged out of Cutter's embrace, her face flaming. Once again, she wondered what was wrong with her that she would turn to mush with just a single touch from him. Was she insane? Good night, she was as shameless as Bess! Shivering at the strange look in his eyes, she stepped away from him, retreating into the protective shadows. "That is, I—I thought so," she said peevishly in order to cover her mortification. Her traitorous heart continued to pound frantically. "Until you brought that . . . that . . . *woman*—"

Cutter allowed her withdrawal, never stirring from his negligent stance. Leaning more fully upon the door, he casually shoved a fist into his front pocket. "Just for the record, Doc. I didn't *bring* any *woman* anywhere." His tone was smooth and calm, nothing like the storm simmering in his eyes.

Elizabeth shot him a look that reminded Cutter of the proverbial fishwife, and his lips twisted wryly. Now, why, he thought, shaking his head, did that seem to please him immensely? And why did he feel the need to explain anything a'tall? "The old girl followed me home from the Rushing Bull, that's all."

Annoyance creased Elizabeth's brow. "She didn't

seem so old to me!" she returned petulantly. "In any case, I've thought on it—all day, in fact—and you're right. I can't trust anyone else to take me to St. Louis." Her tone was resigned. "You win, McKenzie."

One brow rose. "I win?" he asked softly. He straightened, drawing his hand out of his pocket, and Elizabeth took another cautious step backward.

"Y-you stay right there!" she exclaimed anxiously. "And . . . and turn around, while you're at it." She made a little circular motion with her hand when he only looked at her. "Please. I need to cover myself."

Sighing, Cutter threw his hands up into the air and turned toward the door, shaking his head over her belated sense of modesty. The moment he turned away, she made a dash across the small room, her bare feet pattering softly across the wood floor, and it sounded to him as though she lifted the bedcovers. His body tensed immediately. "I wouldn't do that if I were you."

All movement behind him ceased. "Do what?" Elizabeth squeaked.

"Hide in the bed," he said, his tone curt. "It wouldn't be a good idea." That was all Cutter needed to try his will, to see her lying beneath those cool sheets.

"That—is—not—what I was about to do, Mr. McKenzie!" Wrapping the coverlet about herself like a protective cape, Elizabeth moved away from the bed, indignant that Cutter would assume she would give such a blatant invitation. *And wounded somehow that he had taken such exception to the notion.* Even so, she didn't dare ponder that last notion of hers too closely. "I'm *not* like your Bess," she exclaimed, "throwing myself into your arms every blessed chance!"

His lips curved meaningfully. "Izzatso?"

The implication was not lost to Elizabeth, and she was at once disconcerted, because she had, in fact, behaved as disgracefully as . . . as Bess. Her best recourse, she decided, was to change the subject, at once. "Yes, it is. Now . . . if I'm going to allow you to escort me to St. Louis, McKenzie, there are a few conditions by which you'll need to abide."

The hairs on the back of Cutter's neck bristled. "Such as?"

Her chin lifted a notch. "Such as," she retorted, "you will never, *ever*, try to—to kiss me again! And you will not touch me. And you will not spend your leisure time with—with women like Bess! You're supposed to be traveling as my husband, after all, and I won't let you humiliate me."

"Whatever."

"And," she continued, "I'll need my own mount. Oh, and my own bedding," she added hastily. "Furthermore, we will never sleep in the same bed—or even room! Not if it can be helped!" After tonight, she wasn't so certain that it was Cutter she should mistrust, but herself.

Cutter was prepared to accept every one of her shrewdly given demands, and hated himself for it; his voice fell to little more than a seething savage whisper. "Anythin' else, Doc?"

"Yes!" Elizabeth said, disregarding his scorn. As horrible as it would sound, she had no choice but to tell him the truth. "I mean to hire someone else once we've arrived safely in St. Louis. For obvious reasons, I cannot present you to my sister's father-in-law as my lawful husband."

Cutter flinched noticeably, as if she'd actually slapped him, then his expression became shuttered. Elizabeth took another step backward, thinking that he looked ready to pounce suddenly, tear her limb from limb.

"Cutter," she appealed, as he turned abruptly and reached for the knob. "Try to understand!" An awful sinking sensation began in the pit of her stomach as he jerked open the door so ferociously that a rush of air whisked by her face.

"It's just that I can't—"

Cutter didn't wait long enough to hear her explanation. The door slammed shut so violently that it jarred the frame. "—chance losing my niece," she finished lamely. Stunned by Cutter's brusque departure, Elizabeth simply stood, gaping at the door, unsure of what to do next. Bewildered, she came forward and leaned upon it, needing the support. Her legs felt oddly insubstantial beneath her.

Surely he didn't mean to refuse her now? Not after all that she'd had to endure? Good night! Was she supposed to hunt him down and beg his assistance now?

It was an agonizingly long moment later when she realized that she'd not heard Cutter's door close—nor open, for that matter—and her heart skipped a beat. Surely he didn't mean to just leave her where she stood . . . without a way back to Sioux Falls?

Good Lord . . . and without any money either. She doubted she had enough to pay for both the room and a horse! Maybe he'd already paid for the room. Had he? Muddled as her mind was, she couldn't remember. Numbly she locked the door and leaned back against it, her mind reeling.

After a long moment, she walked to the bed, nearly tripping over the bedcovers on the way. There she sat, pressing a hand to her temple. The tiniest headache had persisted all day, and now threatened to explode.

Merciful heaven, what was she going to do?

Think, she told herself firmly. Come on now, Elizabeth, don't panic. "It won't help a thing," she whispered to herself. Slipping her thumbnail between her teeth, she chewed it contemplatively.

Somehow she would sneak out of the hotel . . . and if she was able to raise the funds, she'd come back to pay right away. If not, then she could always send restitution later . . . when she was safely away. She simply couldn't take the chance that they might . . . well . . . detain her. Her head began to pound without mercy. Gracious day, she'd never been in trouble with the law before. But . . . they didn't know her identity and wouldn't know where to look for her, she consoled herself. Cutter had not—whether by design or by accident, she didn't know—given her name at the desk.

They did have *his* signature, though, and it would serve him right if they came looking for him, dragged him off to jail, and threw away the key. She grimaced suddenly as a thought occurred to her. She wouldn't put it past McKenzie to have paid for his own room, leaving her bill unsettled.

Well, she determined with a heartfelt sigh, she couldn't worry about that just now. There was too much else to fret over. Her thundering head, for instance. Wearily she lay back upon the small bed, and covered her forehead with her damp palm.

First thing in the morning she would go to the livery and purchase a sturdy mount for herself. Either way—whether it was on to St. Louis or back to Sioux Falls—she'd need a reliable horse for the journey. Calming somewhat with that decision, she took a deep breath. Things would work out; surely they would. They had to.

What if she didn't have any money left over after buying the horse?

Shaking her head resolutely, she thrust away that awful thought with a frown. Just now, she refused to think on that possibility. Tomorrow was soon enough to worry herself sick over it all. Tonight she needed rest. Already she was feeling the aftermath of too much liquor and too little sleep—Cutter's fault again!

With that sober reflection and a wide, unladylike yawn, she curled herself deeper within the coarse wool blanket she'd wrapped around herself, drawing her arms within to shield them against the chill night air. Trying to keep the morose thoughts from her mind, she turned on her side and gazed blankly at the hazy moonlight that filtered in through the window. She watched listlessly as a few dust particles swirled within the stream of soft light, and after a while, she managed to close her eyes and sleep.

Getting out of the room proved easier than Elizabeth expected.

She'd awakened early, just as the sun was beginning to peep into her room. After dressing, she'd contemplated the window a good half hour, considering it as a possible exit. The ground was not but a ten-foot drop, more or less, and there was a short awning that dipped downward, besides, making it a perfectly feasible solution. The thing that kept her from crawling out was the notion of someone catching her in the act.

It seemed more dignified, if just as immoral, for her to simply steal out the front door. And after mustering her courage, she did just that. The fact that nobody had been attending the clerk's desk made it absurdly simple.

Still, her conscience was having a field day with her as she headed for the Hotel d'Horse. Silly name for a stable, she thought peevishly. It sounded garish, even a tad deceitful, for the *hotel* in question was little more than a raggy barn, with boards all askew. Point in fact, it looked near to collapsing. Yet the clerk at the trade store, Mr. Monroe, had assured her that the gentlemen who owned it ran a fair business and would look after her interest. Now all she needed to do was to be sure she had enough cash left over to purchase supplies . . . as well as hire someone new when they reached St. Louis.

That was, assuming Cutter agreed to take her.

Her eyes skimmed the street ahead. Noting the lack of people about, she began searching for movement within each building she passed. She wasn't searching for Cutter, she told herself as she craned her neck to see beyond the Rushing Bull's swinging half door. She hadn't seen him all morning, and finding there was no sign of him within, she had to concede that he had, in fact, left Indian Creek.

"*Drat!* Just you wait until I see Josephine!" she grumbled to herself. Surely Josephine had no idea what a rounder her brother was. Without a doubt, Elizabeth was going to enlighten her good friend as soon as she set eyes on her again. And maybe she'd even give Josephine a piece of her mind. Despite the fact that Jo had meant well, she'd certainly played an enormous part in this ill-fated scheme that had brought Elizabeth absolutely nothing but grief.

It was strange that she'd never allowed herself to dwell in ire before, yet suddenly it seemed a natural state to her. It was as though years of careful control had snapped and she felt on the edge of a chasm filled with animosity, ready to leap in and wallow in it. As though years of anger had somehow built to a crescendo and had finally burst forth, like a volcano gushing after years of dormancy, making the world black beneath its ash. Everything seemed so grim— even the bright blue sky seemed false. And it had all begun with Cutter.

Somehow he had been the catalyst.

The odor of horseflesh and stale hay assaulted her nostrils as she entered the dusky stable.

"Hello," she called out. "Hello . . . anyone here?"

A tall, robust man stood up within the second stall. His face screwed in annoyance, though when he saw her, he smiled brightly, revealing a missing upper tooth. Resisting the urge to finger her own straight teeth, she locked her hands into a fist and held them in front of her. "I'm sorry if I intruded."

"No, no," the man assured, shoving at the stall door and coming toward her. He wiped his soiled hands upon his already filthy denims. "I was cleaning the stall up some . . . Birthed a mare." He gave her a guilty smile, then wiped his forehead with his sleeve. "Anyhow, name's Pete Monroe, ma'am; what can I do fer ya?"

When she heard that his name was Monroe, Elizabeth's brow creased. Suspicious, to say the least. Still, she had no choice but to deal with the man. She proffered her hand, trying to look as fearsome as she was able. "Elizabeth Bowcock, and I need a good mount, Mr. Monroe. I'm willing to purchase it outright." He gave her a skeptical look. "I've got cash," she assured him, thinking that was what he was contemplating. "Mr. *Monroe*—" she emphasized the name "—at the trade store." Mr. Monroe nodded. "He said you would deal fairly with me," she added, just in case he thought to do otherwise.

Pete Monroe acknowledged that fact with a brief nod. "Yeah?" He winked at her. "Well, Miss Bowcock, if ma cousin Will sent ya, then I've just the thing. Haven't really been sellin' ma horses outright, but this once, I'll make you an exception!" He smiled suddenly, his missing tooth conspicuous. "Anythin' fer a pretty li'l gal like you," he told her.

Turning from her, he started into the dusky building, launching into what promised to become a sad sales tale. "Just don't ya breathe a word o' this, or I'll have the townsfolk at my door. You see . . . I haven't had any new blood in stock fer a good while now, and old man Rutherford has been after me ta sell him what I got . . . but he keeps jiggerin' em, and I ain't willin' ta let him do that to anymore o' my horses. They're like family ta me."

Elizabeth rolled her eyes. Family? Not likely! As they went deeper into the stable, the smell of stale hay became rank, almost sour. No man served his family spoiled rations—at least, not if he could help it. But then, maybe he couldn't help it. She considered that a moment. Indian Creek wasn't exactly a prospering town.

Mr. Monroe led her to the very last stall, where a mustang mare stood staring emptily back at her, its liquid dark eyes blinking at her somberly. All thoughts of duplicity fled her at once as she stepped forward, seeing only the reflection of herself in the ebony eyes, her misery, her loneliness, and she was at once in love.

The mare stretched its neck forward to investigate the newest trespasser to its stall. Elizabeth was surprised by the warm welcome; her eyes widened slightly and she turned to smile warmly at the big man beside her.

"She's beautiful!" Reaching out cautiously, she stroked the mare's forehead, brushing its forelock gently with her fingers. Her markings were exquisite: white with scattered spots, ranging from dark gold to deep cocoa.

Elizabeth's hand slid down to its flaring nostrils. There she held it, letting the animal become used to her personal scent, all the while keeping alert for some sign that it would balk. It never did, and finally she moved to caress its fine muzzle.

The mare retreated somewhat at that, but Elizabeth continued to caress the animal reassuringly. Abruptly she withdrew her hand, placing it at her side, waiting to see what the animal would do next. After a long moment, the mare moved forward, as though seeking out her gentle touch, and Elizabeth's heart swelled with pride of accomplishment. She stood without speaking for the longest moment, admiring the animal's beauty, reveling in her good fortune, and thinking that there was something that she ought to be doing with its teeth. Her brow furrowed as she tried to recall, and then she shook her head, unable to. Oh well, all in all, it wasn't a prize horse, she knew, but it would do well enough.

"I'll take her," Elizabeth declared at last, without the least hesitation.

Mr. Monroe smiled shrewdly, giving her a pleased nod. "Thought so," was all he said. "Now, as ta the price, Miss Bowcock."

Chapter 8

Cursing to himself, Cutter rapped sharply upon Elizabeth's door for the third time. Giving it a last whack, he tried the knob and found it securely locked. Every inclination urged him to beat it down, but he doubted it would do any good. If Elizabeth were in her room, she'd have responded by now.

Where else could she be?

Pivoting on one heel, he turned away from the door. He'd come in early this morning, after having spent most of the night drowning his troubles at the Rushing Bull and cursing Elizabeth Bowcock to China and back. Simply put, he'd stayed out carousing too long and had overslept. Hell, he'd had half a mind to just walk away last night, leave the woman stranded, but couldn't bring himself to do it. He'd brought her this far, and he aimed to carry through with it in spite of her contemptuously given demands, her bigotry—and primarily because she didn't consider him worthy enough to play the friggin' part through to the end.

That bit stuck in his craw.

What did she think he'd been playing at his entire life? All he had remaining of his mother's people were a priceless few memories, the recollection of Jack McKenzie's intolerance, and the white man's narrow-minded views of a people with whom they generally refused to empathize.

He felt torn between two worlds that likely would never meet. But that in itself was nothing new. He'd been sittin' on the fence most of his life. Question was, why did he feel obliged to slither off at this point in the game, when he'd never even considered it before?

He was what he was.

To blazes with anyone who couldn't accept him for it!

Images of Sand Creek came back to haunt him suddenly, and he shook them away, thrusting his hand through his dark hair and raking his fingers across his scalp.

In spite of the fact that Chief Black Kettle had been assured that he was under protection of Fort Lyon, and that he'd raised the American flag over his lodge—as well as the white flag of surrender—as a symbol of good faith, Chivington and his men had charged into the sleepy Cheyenne camp, showing no mercy. Many of the slaughtered had been children, yet all Colonel Chivington had had to say over the matter was that "nits make lice."

And they called the Indians heathen bastards?

It made Cutter sick to his guts.

Though he'd proven himself a dependable scout for the U.S. military, he'd also made it crystal-clear that half of him was Cheyenne, and that no matter the cost, he wouldn't track his blood kin. Deserters, fine. And he had no qualms over sniffing out other Indian tribes, either, but he'd gone so far as to refuse his commanding officer outright when he'd been ordered to ferret out a particular Cheyenne winter camp.

After Chivington's butchery at Sand Creek, the government had feared reprisal from neighboring tribes—and rightly so. Little more than a month later, the regular westbound express mail coach, en route to Denver, had been attacked just six miles short of Julesburg.

But hell, he wasn't precisely U.S. military; he was merely under contract to them, and he didn't intend to betray his mother's people—not when there were bastards like John Chivington around to dance on their graves.

In spite of all that, he was about to do what he'd sworn never to. Through the years, he'd had little enough to do with his mother's people; still, he felt it a disloyalty to shed those things that declared him Cheyenne, and he'd not even done so for his own sake.

Yet that was exactly what he aimed to do just now.

He'd show *Miz* Bowcock that he was no different from the next man.

Trouble was, he hated the piss out of it!

So why did he bother?

Taking the stairs two at a time, he made his way down, his gut clenching at the possibility that came suddenly to mind. She wouldn't have gone back to Sioux Falls on her own. Well, hell, now, would she have?

Upon entering the lobby, he spotted her at once, her god-awful skirt and thick blond braid of hair unmistakable, and he heaved a sigh of relief. Turning from the clerk, she met his gaze, and for the briefest moment, he thought he saw that same relief in her glance as well. Then she seemed to compose herself and gave him a glare he was likely never to forget. Despite his anger, he found himself chuckling as he followed her out of the small lobby, his long legs catching her quick strides with little effort.

Resisting the urge to scream out that he "just go away," Elizabeth turned to regard him with ill-concealed ire. As much as it galled her to admit it, she needed him. Even so, she couldn't bring herself to ask for his help again. She'd laid her cards on the table last night, and he'd just walked away. The next move was his, and she refused to humiliate herself further by begging him. He would either accept her offer or not . . . Either way, there was little she could do about it. If he chose not to, she would, for the first time in years, find a nice, quiet place and cry her heart out . . . because there was no one else to whom she could turn.

And he knew it. That's what galled her so much!

Trying her darnedest to ignore him, Elizabeth hurried down the front steps, only to realize Cutter was no longer pursuing her. She turned at once to find him standing upon the top step, leaning with one arm braced casually against the crude wood post that supported the awning. Those obsidian eyes of his glittered devilishly beneath the brim of his hat, and his mouth twisted cynically. In greeting, he touched his hat brim lazily.

His arrogant stance provoked her, for it seemed as though he'd claimed a victory in the simple fact that she'd stopped for him. What he didn't realize was that she'd had to stop anyway, because her horse was tethered little more than three feet away, next to the salina. Good night, she felt like cursing him to high heaven, but doubted she knew any of the words to do it. And she'd have liked to tell him off for leaving her to worry all night, yet she knew it would be wiser not to antagonize him, so she stood there glaring instead.

He was wearing the same clothes he'd worn last night, she noticed, shoving her spectacles up the bridge of her nose—denims and a dark green shirt. And his jaw was still unshaven, making his swarthy face look all the darker for the whiskers. He said nothing, only watched her, and Elizabeth spun toward her horse, unwilling to be the first to speak. The truth was that she had no idea how to go about making amends with all the turmoil that was in her soul.

She'd worried all night. Even in her sleep, she'd been plagued by dreams of him. And this morning— never mind that she'd not been caught—he'd forced her to suffer the humiliation of skulking out of the hotel without settling the bill . . . only to return and find that he'd already paid! What nerve the man had! Her cheeks flushed as she recalled the clerk's words. The man had all but leered as he'd informed her, *"Been settled, ma'am . . . Must have been real satisfied with ya."* And then he'd winked at her. He'd winked! Lord, she'd been mortified! Wrenching open the saddlebag, she dropped her remaining currency into it, glancing quickly about to be certain no one besides Cutter had observed her.

"What is that?" Cutter asked abruptly.

Despite the fact that she'd known he was there, watching her, his voice had that quality about it that easily startled. Her shoulders jerked faintly, but she composed herself at once. "What does it look like, McKenzie? It's a horse," she said evenly, answering her own question without turning to face him. "A mustang, to be precise."

"I know what the damned thing is!" Cutter snarled. "What I'd like to know is what *you're* doing with it."

As she turned to face Cutter, Elizabeth's chin rose determinedly. Her eyes flashed with defiance. "She's mine, of course." But then her gaze returned to the mare, her expression wavering on the brink of pride, and her tone was softer when she spoke again. "She's beautiful, isn't she?"

Seeing her glossy-eyed expression, Cutter immediately came down the steps, skipping the last two and touching down on both feet before her, scattering dust. Some of it settled on Elizabeth's skirt. She glanced down at it, her eyes narrowing.

"Hope you didn't pay much for the damned thing! She's nothing but a sugar-eating Sunday horse. Aside from that, being a cayuse, she's probably as contrary as they come." He arched a dark brow at her. "Like someone else we know."

Since they had no common acquaintances besides his sister, that narrowed the list down considerably.

Choosing to overlook the barb, Elizabeth refastened
the saddlebag and began to stroke the mare's flanks,
more from a need to calm herself than anything else.
The animal's flesh twitched with pleasure where she
caressed it.

"I really don't think it's any of your concern how
much I paid for her, McKenzie!"

He was standing just over her shoulder now, and
though he hadn't touched her, Elizabeth could feel
the heat of his body. Or was it her imagination? Her
flesh prickled, and her heart picked up its tempo,
skipping about erratically. More than anything, she
wanted him to leave her in peace . . . and yet her
brain worked feverishly for a way to keep him with
her. It made no sense at all! How could she want both
things at once—so desperately?

"It is if I'm gonna be your guide, *Miz Bowcock*," he
said softly, mocking her.

His breath was warm against the sensitive skin of
her neck. She had to fight the dizzying desire to lean
back into his broad chest. A shiver passed down
Elizabeth's spine, but she covered it quickly, turning
to Cutter slowly, her emotions rioting.

So he meant to help her?

Though his declaration had been given derisively,
she felt an incredible burst of euphoria. Feeling almost giddy as she faced him, she fought the urge to
cry out in joy and hug him. In spite of her thankful-
ness, she didn't dare touch him again. There was no
telling what might happen if she did. As it was, her
imagination was going haywire. She kept recalling the
way he'd looked at her last night.

The hunger in his eyes.

Lord, she felt warm, and her cheeks were burning.
And it was his fault. Everything was his fault! More
than anything, she yearned to make this difficult for
him. She really liked the image of him kissing her
feet, as she'd once seen an Oriental servant do with
his master. But those thoughts were better squelched,

she knew. Cutter McKenzie would never grovel before anyone. And if she angered him again, he was more like than not just to walk away. She couldn't risk that, so she tucked away her conflicting emotions, and simply nodded acceptance.

Cutter stared at her expectantly, and she realized he was still waiting for an answer to his question. All she needed to do was to respond cordially, she told herself, and they would both come out of this with their dignity intact. If she didn't wish him to escort her, then all she had to do was say nothing and he'd leave. She was certain that this was as close to offering his help as he would ever come again.

She hated the fact that she needed him. "I didn't pay much for it," she conceded grudgingly. "The owner gave me a good price because . . . well, because he said there were a few inconveniences I'd have to overcome."

"Such as. . . ?" Cutter answered acerbically. "Don't tell me—the blamed animal's barefoot?" His glance shot down to the animal's hooves.

Elizabeth gave him an exasperated shake of her head.

"No? Uneducated then?"

"Nothing like that," Elizabeth assured him, her tone carefully subdued, her temper suppressed. "It's just that she's . . . well, she's Indian-broke."

Cutter cocked a brow at her. "Is that all?"

Lord, his tone was patronizing. "Well, not quite," Elizabeth confessed, though very reluctantly. "She's a few years old, as well. Aside from that, however, she's perfectly sound."

"Izzatso? Just a few years?" Cutter remarked baldly. And then he suddenly lost his nonchalance. "Hell, Lizbeth, the fool horse is buzzard bait! You've been buffaloed, don't y' know! Who sold it to you?" He seized her by the elbow. "Come on, we're gonna get your money back!"

Twisting her arm, Elizabeth freed herself from his

grasp, stepping away defensively. "We're not! I wasn't cheated—and his name is none of your concern! For your information, McKenzie," she rushed on without thinking, "this horse was the last Mr. Monroe had in stock! He hasn't had any new blood in for a while, and the only reason he sold this one to me was because Mr. Rutherford kept running his mounts into the ground!"

Cutter's expression remained disbelieving, and Elizabeth bristled.

"He did not cheat me!" she insisted, realizing belatedly how her tale must sound to him. "In fact, he wouldn't even have sold her if his cousin from the trade store hadn't recommended me to him." Good Lord, that, she feared, sounded even worse. Still, she couldn't simply let it lie. He was looking at her as if she were three kinds of fool. "Besides, he commanded a very decent price, and I'm perfectly satisfied with my purchase! It is my money, after all—and if I'm pleased, then it shouldn't concern—"

"How much?"

"It's none of your—"

"Fine," Cutter snapped, cutting off her explanation.

Her heart leapt as he turned from her and headed back up the stairs, back into the hotel lobby. She knew an instant of incredible panic. Heaven help her, she couldn't let him go this time. She just couldn't! "That's it, McKenzie—walk away! Again!" she shouted a little frantically at his back. "Seems to me it's what you're best at—dynamic exits!"

He halted on the top step, his back to her, and stiffened. The powerful set of his shoulders unnerved her. Again, it struck her how tall he was. As she looked up at him from this angle, he towered over her. After a long moment, he whirled to face her, thrusting a hand into his pocket with a sigh of resignation.

"Fact is, Doc, if I had even half a brain, I'd do just that." He seemed to consider that statement earnestly, and then he spoke again, putting her mind at ease. "But seems I mislaid my good sense all of a sudden." He shook his head regretfully. "No, I'm not gonna walk away—just going in to collect my belongings, is all." Removing his hand from his pocket, he adjusted his hat, giving her a harsh look. "I expect you'll be ready to ride by the time I return."

It wasn't a question. It was a command if Elizabeth had ever heard one, but she chose to respond anyway. "I'll be ready," she told him sourly.

"See that you are," he said curtly. And then he turned on his heels and disappeared into the lobby, his muscular body moving with the easy grace of a powerful cat.

Refusing to allow herself the indulgence of misgivings, Elizabeth immediately thrust them all to the back of her mind, telling herself firmly that this was what she'd intended all along. That it was by far the best course of action.

There was no other way.

As it turned out, they didn't leave Indian Creek until well past noon, after having made one last stop at the general store for supplies.

Elizabeth didn't attempt to mount up until then, but opted to lead the mare, instead. Why she felt so reluctant, she didn't know, but at the moment she wished more than anything that she'd not waited to do so in front of Cutter. Or perhaps that was why she'd waited? His presence, for some odd reason, was reassuring, despite the hostilities between them.

To her dismay, her instinct proved correct. Every time she tried to mount the mare, the animal shied away. Granted, she didn't know much about horses, just enough to get her by, but she just couldn't understand what it was that she was doing wrong.

Exasperated, her cheeks flushed with exertion—not to mention the humiliation of chasing her mare all over the dusty street—Elizabeth finally met Cutter's gaze. His eyes, though far from warm, were filled with amusement. As she glared at him, wondering what to do next, how to ask for his help, his smile turned up a notch. She snorted, turning away, determining that if it was the last thing she ever did, she was going to mount the blamed horse by herself!

She nibbled her bottom lip a moment, assessing her chances of mounting from the ground. Certainly she wasn't tall enough to mount just any horse in that manner, but the mare was just short enough to make it possible. More determined than ever, she approached again from the left side, but this time without the slow, predatory movements she'd exercised previously.

If she could catch the animal off guard perhaps. . . ?

With a running leap, she caught the animal by its withers, only instead of remaining still as it was supposed to do, the mare sidestepped with a snort, and Elizabeth lost her nerve. She stumbled over her feet, barely keeping herself from falling flat on her face, and merely stood there, looking thwarted and annoyed.

Cutter chuckled.

Turning to him indignantly, her hands on her hips, she asked him, "I suppose you have a better way?" There was defiance in her tone as well as a note of challenge.

Cutter's mouth twitched. He crossed his arms, leaning with such an infuriating indifference against the awning post behind him that Elizabeth bristled.

"Suppose I might," he said with barely suppressed laughter.

Was she supposed to drag it out of him? "Well?" The expression on his face was so smug that she felt like kicking him in the blasted shin! In the short time since she'd met him, he'd made a complete mockery of her rational nature. She'd exhibited more violence in the last two days than she had in her entire lifetime!

"Lizbeth," Cutter said softly, noting the crowd that was beginning to form around them. As much as he was enjoying the show, he didn't want her to become a spectacle for anyone else. Enough was enough. "Do you happen to know what *Indian-broke* means?" he asked her.

"Well, of course!" Elizabeth replied, but she really wasn't so certain. Her hands full of dust and horsehair, she pressed her forearm across her damp forehead, not caring that the gesture was unladylike. Lord, it was hot! "I assume it means that she was broken in by Indians."

"That's right," Cutter agreed. There was a sparkle in his eyes as he crooked a finger at her. "Come here." His voice was so soft that it could have been a whisper.

Either that, or Elizabeth was going deaf from overexertion and heat exposure. She wasn't even aware that she'd obeyed until she was standing before him, and his lips parted again to speak.

Straightening, he gripped her arm. The shock of it sent her pulses skittering.

He leaned close to whisper in her ear, and Elizabeth thought he might be about to kiss her. She ought to slap him before he even tried. That would show him, wouldn't it?

"Try mounting up from the right side," Cutter advised with a deep chuckle and a playful wink. "That's what Indian-broke means, you see."

Hours later, Elizabeth was still chafing over the patronizing way Cutter had informed her of that particular detail. And to think she'd thought he was about to kiss her! And he'd laughed at her! Good night, had he read her mind? Had he known what she was thinking? She couldn't bear the notion.

Despite the fact that the weather couldn't have been

better for travel, two more stormy countenances couldn't have been found east of the Missouri. Following Cutter's example, Elizabeth rode in sullen silence, keeping her attention on the landscape itself.

For the most part they seemed to be riding the bluffs, though at intervals the river disappeared from view completely. He kept the pace brisk, and Elizabeth surmised that Cutter was trying to show her just how worthless her mount actually was. Only, like its rider, the mustang trotted on without protest. She would have spoken up had the horse seemed winded, but until now, it had not.

Every so often, Cutter changed the pace, walking the horses an interval, but they'd ridden for hours without truly stopping, and her stalwart mare was beginning to show signs of fatigue. Soon, she decided. Soon she would speak up. She thought it might be better if it was Cutter who called the halt, and perhaps he would if she gave him the opportunity. Surely he wouldn't kill her horse just to spite her?

Elizabeth sighed, and again managed to steal a glance at him. In profile his high cheekbones were striking, his jaw strong and taut. His eyes were hidden from view by his hat, which he wore tilted forward to shade his face from the burning sun. That, she thought wistfully, was something she was going to regret forgetting. Already the ruthless sun was toasting her head.

Once more her gaze was drawn to him, prompting her to wonder what it was about the man that drew her to him. And yes, she could deny it to the world, but there was no lying to herself. She *was* intrigued by Cutter McKenzie. There seemed to be a certain magnetism about him that called to her.

Seduced her.

Mesmerized, she stared at the dark hair at his nape that curled into the collar of his shirt, swallowing with difficulty. Her glance was drawn helplessly down, to the damp streak between his shoulder blades.

The heat.

Mercy, was it warm! Almost desperately, she looked forward to evening, when the sun wouldn't be about to blister her skin—even the snappy night breezes seemed preferable. Feeling the heat of the sun on her shoulders, the crown of her head, along with the strange feverish flush that came from within, Elizabeth fidgeted in the saddle, searching out a more tolerable position, but she couldn't find one. Something about the horse's gait made her feel restless.

Unbidden, the memory of the kiss they'd shared popped into Elizabeth's mind, and heat spread into the very core of her being. Her brows flickered faintly. *Shared?* Where had that come from? Stolen! *Stolen* was more like it! She fidgeted again. As far as she was concerned, she had done nothing to encourage him.

Or had she? The kiss, as well as the moments before it, were mostly a blur in her mind, with the only tangible recollection being that of her body's treasonous response to him. Good night, she'd clung to him like . . . like his sweat-soaked shirt was doing just now . . .

Gracious, he had the most distinct muscles.

What's wrong with you? Don't look, she scolded herself.

But she couldn't help herself. She watched the movement in his shoulders and back, the easy posture of his body as he rode, and then, realizing that she was staring again, she forced her gaze away.

Good night, she was as shameless as Bess, she told herself. Had he not walked out on her last night. . . ? Well, she hated to think of what might have happened.

Had he found her wanting?

Well, who cared if he had?

She cared.

Had he?

Her heart skipped a beat at that likelihood. Somehow it seemed terribly important that he not find her lacking. No one had ever looked at her quite like Cutter did at times. No one. And while she tried to be appropriately appalled by the frankness of his gaze, she couldn't quite muster it. To her dismay, she found herself feeling almost . . . well, *grateful* for the way that he had lusted after her. Gracious day, was that it? Did he lust after her? Is that what she saw in his scrutiny? Was *that* why he'd agreed to help her? In answer, she shook her head, disbelieving it. Surely not?

Then again, she had awakened yesterday to his exploring hands. But he'd not touched her besides that, unless, of course, you counted the kiss. And even if you did, he'd left immediately afterward, when he could very well have taken advantage of the situation. Instead, he'd walked away.

The man was a tangle of contradictions—a tangle she intended to unravel.

When Cutter slowed his horse to a trot, Elizabeth took advantage of the opportunity, nudging her mount closer. Cutter spared her only a cursory glance, and a slightly longer one for her mare.

"She's holding up very well, don't you think?"

Turning to her again, Cutter gave her a frown for her effort. As far as he was concerned, she was either goading him . . . or looking for reassurance. He didn't feel like taking up the gauntlet in either case. Wasn't in the mood. Somehow he felt thwarted. She'd accepted him, sure enough, but he'd lost something in the bargain. What it was, he didn't know, but he felt the odd void all the same.

Just how long did he plan to be put out with her? Elizabeth wondered. He'd had his fun at her expense earlier. Shouldn't she be the angry one? The least he could do was stay in character. She wasn't certain how to respond to his brooding.

"Well, I'm mighty proud if I say so myself," she told him. And then, realizing she'd spoken defensively, and that it wasn't likely to help matters between them, she sought to rectify it. "What do you think about Cocoa?" she asked, conversationally.

"Cocoa?" Turning to her abruptly, Cutter gave her a harassed look. "What about it?"

Elizabeth patted her mare's neck affectionately. "I thought I'd call her Cocoa." Her cheeks warmed under his cutting gaze, but she refused to be embarrassed. "My horse," she clarified. Rallying her self-defenses, she smiled pleasantly. "It suits her, don't you think?"

Still he stared, but the only sound to reach Elizabeth's ears was the trotting of hooves against the hard ground. With an almost imperceptible shake of his head, he turned away. Elizabeth was affronted by his rudeness, and her mouth fell slightly open, but she collected herself at once. If they were going to ride the distance together, she decided in that moment, they were going to have to make peace at some point. They couldn't ride on like this much longer!

His own horse was a beautiful Appaloosa, dark everywhere but at the haunches, where it paled to a silvery white and had large black spots. The only blemish it bore was on the right ear; half of it appeared to have been lopped off. Still, as fine an animal as it was, she knew he must be very proud of it. "What about yours?"

"What about it?" Cutter repeated unindulgently, keeping his gaze focused ahead of them. He had no need to look at her at the moment. Her strained tone told him everything he needed to know. He could see her clearly in his mind's eye, her hair braided so tightly that it stretched the pale skin of her cheeks, slanting her eyes—her face pinched in as though she'd been sucking at lemons.

He gave her a quick glimpse—purely out of curiosity—to find that her spectacles had bounced down to a precarious position at the end of her nose, giving the impression that she peered down on him, though in fact she sat a good deal lower than he did. The turmoil in her expression told him that she was ill at ease with her emotions, and he had the sudden suspicion that she'd led such a repressed life that she now had no notion how to handle herself in her pique. Far from being moved by that revelation, he was annoyed by it, because it drew him to her in ways he ought not to be drawn.

Determinedly Elizabeth pushed her spectacles back up the bridge of her nose. "What do you call him?" she inquired a bit too agreeably.

Shaking his head, Cutter gave her that look that suggested she might be out of her gourd.

"Not a damned thing," he replied. "I don't call'm anythin' but just plain horse." To his mind, Elizabeth didn't give him a big enough reaction, prompting him to add, "Only piss-pants 'n' tenderfeet name their animals." His eyes challenged her, never wavering as he awaited her response. No matter how he looked at it, it just didn't sit well that he'd given in to her so easily.

Elizabeth straightened her spine. "I see. So which of the two does that make me—tenderfoot or . . . or . . ."

"Piss-pant," Cutter provided, without compunction. She couldn't even say the word, he thought irascibly. What the hell had he gotten himself into? Damn him anyway, if he was going to let her just up'n hire someone else to play bridegroom for her. Crazy, loony, irritating female—didn't she know what she'd be setting herself up for?

Elizabeth's amber eyes widened in affront. *Piss-pant!* her mind screeched. Piss-pant? Just how was she supposed to respond to that? Her mouth couldn't begin to form the words even if she'd known what to say. So much for conversation, she chafed, and deciding that their discourse was definitely over, she tugged irritably on the reins, drawing back and away.

As she glowered at Cutter's back, she began once again to doubt the wisdom in making this trek with the volatile man before her. Less than forty-eight hours earlier, she'd been sitting, misty-eyed, at her kitchen table, with a letter in hand destined to change her life forever. Yet, even then, if someone had told her she'd be in the saddle today, riding beside the most contrary man she'd ever laid eyes upon, she'd have called them liar . . . Well, maybe she wouldn't have. But here she sat, nevertheless, faced with the dilemma of having to make the best of a situation she'd never have conceived possible.

Alone with a man. A strange man, she clarified to herself. And an obvious rogue, at that. Good night, what would her father have said? He'd never have let himself die if he'd thought, for even one moment, that she'd be so witless! How many times had he warned her to "trust no man unless he's loaded with ether or dead"? He'd never said as much, but she suspected Angus Bowcock preferred the latter if a man was alone with his daughter. It had been her father, after all, who'd encouraged her lamentable state of dress. At least he had in the beginning. Later, in the last months of his life, he'd insisted that she rid herself of the shapeless garments she'd always worn.

Gripping the reins progressively tighter, until they whitened the flesh of her palm, she recalled that he'd even bought her a beautiful printed calico . . . so that she would make herself a dress from it. She'd not understood then. But she did now. He'd known then that he was dying, and he'd wanted her to set about finding a man to care for her. Why hadn't she been able to see it at the time? The sadness in his eyes when he'd come home that day to find the calico neatly quilted, and gracing his own bed. It was all so clear to her . . . but only now.

Oh, Papa, she lamented, *if only you were here.* She sighed wistfully. The fact was that he was not. He was gone. And he wasn't coming back. But she thought he might be proud of her, anyhow.

She'd not even cried when he'd died.

Dauntlessly she'd stepped into his shoes, and even when the townsfolk had balked *because it wasn't fittin' for a woman to tend them*, she'd not relented. If they preferred to die, then that was their concern, she'd informed them boldly when their children were ill, but she'd not let their little ones suffer because of it. And in the end, when a man or his loved ones were ailing, it didn't take much persuasion to make them see things her way. Survival was the name of the game, and if it took a woman to accomplish the task, then so be it.

Gaining their acceptance had taken quite a while, yet it had been well worth it. Now most everyone in or about Sioux Falls came willingly to her, whether their ailments were big or small. And not for the first time, she felt a pang for leaving them without medical aid. Yet, that she could recall, there were none so sick just now that they couldn't survive her brief absence. She'd had no choice in the matter, after all, but even if she had planned *when* she would leave, it was doubtful she could have found someone to replace her in such short time. Still, she would have tried. And then worried when she couldn't—and in the end, would have wasted precious time.

She did have that much to thank Cutter for, she reflected, stealing another glance at his back. He had, at least, taken that weighty decision out of her hands. And that led her to another thought entirely.

How was it that he had gotten her to thinking this was all her idea? And worrying when she thought he'd left her stranded? She wouldn't put it past him to have planned the entire thing! Right down to the last detail!

Lost in thought as she was, she was completely unprepared when a bird swooped down before her, spooking her mare. Instinctively her hands tightened on the reins, startling Cocoa. The mare edged backward, huffing and snorting mutinously. Before Elizabeth could even scream for help, she was tossed headfirst. Landing with a squeal on the ground, she rolled and lay unmoving where she fell.

Chapter 9

Intending to catch her mare before it trampled her to death, Cutter snatched her reins and calmed Cocoa. That done, he leapt off his own mount and rushed to where Elizabeth lay, skidding the last two feet on his knees, and halting at her side.

Her eyes were wide open, but she didn't so much as bat a lash. Anxiously he passed a hand over her eyes. She blinked suddenly and turned to him, her eyes misting, and his heart jolted back to life. Releasing the breath he'd not realized he'd held, he asked softly, "Y' all right, Lizbeth?"

Ignoring the moistness gathering in her eyes, Elizabeth nodded, taking the hand he offered. Using it for support, she hauled herself upright, humiliated.

Seeing that she wasn't injured, Cutter didn't bother to conceal his displeasure. "What is it with you 'n' horses that lands you square on your ass every time?" To his alarm, a solitary tear rolled down her dusty cheek, leaving a dirty, wet trail in its wake. "Well, hell, y' *are* hurt!" he growled. "Show me where!"

With her throat parched and too thick to speak, Elizabeth shook her head helplessly, sniffing back tears. "I'm . . . I'm not," she insisted. But her lip began to tremble traitorously, and then, to her dismay, she broke into sobs. It was as though all the pain she'd been harboring in the months since her father's death surfaced in that miserable moment as

116

Cutter glowered down upon her. Mortified, she hid her face in her hands.

Feeling awkward with her tears, Cutter sat firmly on his backside, and placed a hand to her back, rubbing soothingly. "Come on, now, bright eyes, don't go sheddin' tears on me now," he told her, but even as he said it, he urged her closer, into the space between his legs. She didn't need much prodding. With a smothered sob, she leaned into his arms, burying her wet face against his shirt, and driving him backward with the impact of her delicious little body. Teetering with her weight, Cutter pulled her into his lap as gently as if she were a china doll.

Grateful for the comfort Cutter was giving, but ashamed of her disgraceful outburst, Elizabeth concealed her face against his chest and wept silently, her shoulders quaking softly.

She clutched at his shirt as though it were her salvation, and Cutter could do nothing but sit and soothe her while she unwittingly tugged his shirttails out of his denims. He wasn't quite certain why she was weeping so passionately, and felt a stab of guilt for worrying about his shirt. Thing was, if she pulled any harder, it was like to rip in two, and he didn't have but the two—this one and the one in his saddlebag.

Moving closer, he tried to ease the fatal tension on his favorite shirt. Wrapping his arms around her, he stroked her back reassuringly, and despite his resolve not to yield to his baser instincts, his britches grew snug as his body responded to the woman leaning so intimately into his arms.

Damn him, if she didn't smell good.

Clenching his jaw, he fought the urge to lift her face up, kiss her tears away, because he knew exactly where it would lead if he did. It didn't matter where they were. His body didn't know the difference between a feather-fluffed mattress and the dirt-hard ground. But she would. And somehow, it mattered.

He'd promised her nothing last night, and he sure

as hell didn't harbor any noble sentiments, but he wanted it to be right between them when it happened. And it would happen, without a doubt, but first he wanted her trust.

And her unconditional surrender.

Swallowing with difficulty, he pressed his lips down into her hair, while his hand caressed her. Moving up her arm, his fingers tightened around her shoulders, and then he froze, forbidding himself to go any further.

"Lizbeth," he said hoarsely. "Are y' hurt, gal?"

Her tears continued to flow into his shirt, but she managed to shake her head in answer. Cutter took a deep breath, dismissing the warm female scent of her. "What is it, then?" He glanced over his shoulder, catching sight of their horses a few feet away. Turning back to her, he assured, "There's nothing to be ashamed of, bright eyes. Everyone takes a fall now and again. Hell, I've even done it once or twice." So what if it wasn't true? he argued with himself. She didn't have to know, did she? He stroked the back of her head as he would a child, his fingers sliding down the length of her braid. He'd been disappointed this morning to find her once again withdrawn behind her prudish mask.

She nodded, and he could tell that she'd opened her eyes as well, because he could feel her lashes fluttering through his wet shirt. It was then that he realized she wasn't wearing her specs any longer, and he immediately searched the ground for them. He grimaced when he found them only a few inches away, one lens cracked and the frames bent beyond repair.

"Next time," he apprised her, not knowing how to break the news, "don't keep such a death grip on the reins. If you hadn't been strangling the damned cayuse, she wouldn't have spilled you!"

Still clutching at his shirt, Elizabeth tilted her face up suddenly to look at him with watery eyes. She didn't know what to say to that. "I wasn't strangling my horse!'' But even as she said it, she wasn't certain it was the truth. Her fingers still ached from holding the reins. ''Josephine was right!'' she snapped. ''You are an insensitive oaf!''

Cutter's brows lifted. ''That so?'' he asked dispassionately. Damn her, if her expression didn't make him want to hug her. She looked for all the world like an injured child in that moment, all her fears and self-doubts right there in her expression. She wasn't the type to weep at the drop of a hat, and he suspected that something more than injured pride had spurred the tears that now slid so pitifully down her cheeks. Ignoring her accusatory look, he brought his hand between them, wiping her damp cheek with his thumb.

At once, Elizabeth recoiled from his touch. Catching his hand, she turned it toward her to see what had chafed the sensitive skin beneath her eye. Confusion first, then horror, filled her expression as she examined his severely scarred fingers.

His brows collided violently as he snatched his hand out of her grip. ''Don't ask,'' he warned, before she could.

Elizabeth only stared at him.

A peculiar look stole into his eyes, shuttering his emotions. ''It ain't none of your damned business!'' he told her. ''Chrissakes, you want something to worry over, worry over your specs.'' Reaching out, he scooped them up, and without preamble, dropped them into her hand. ''They're broke.''

''Oh noooo!'' Elizabeth swiped at the wetness on her face with the tips of her fingers. ''Nooooo!'' she moaned. ''Do you realize how long I've had these?'' she cried in panic. Forgetting everything else for the moment, including her chagrin, she squinted while she inspected them anxiously.

Eyeing her skeptically as she labored over the frames, Cutter shrugged, giving her a wry twist of his lips. ''No,'' he said, ''but reckon I could take a wild guess and come damned close.''

Desperately Elizabeth tried to straighten the wire framework, but try as she might, they wouldn't be forced. "They were my father's before me," she explained as she worked.

"No kidding?"

Elizabeth gave him a sharp glance . . . her mistake, because once she looked into his deep, dark eyes, she couldn't look away. She felt snared. Lord, he was handsome. Too handsome for words. Those lips of his . . . those eyes . . . Heaven help her, every time she looked at him, he grew more striking. No man had a right to look that way. Had she hoped for one moment that he would look at her with anything more than pity? Her heart plummeted into her stomach. Her shoulders slumped. She hadn't realized the pressure she was putting on her spectacles until one slender arm came off into her hand. "No!" she cried. "Oh, no . . . What am I supposed to do now?"

Cutter snatched them from her. "I didn't think you needed 'em all that much," he told her.

Elizabeth's brow creased with worry as her gaze reverted to the specs in his hand, and Cutter felt a sudden inexplicable urge to smooth her distress away. But recalling the look of revulsion she'd given him when she'd discovered his fingers, he refrained from touching her again. "Seems to me you see well enough without them," he said curtly.

"Up close I see as well as you," she conceded, watching his efforts with growing concern. "But not distances . . . and I can't read long without getting a headache."

Elizabeth gasped suddenly.

It was as though she suddenly became aware of the impropriety of their position, because she immediately detached herself from him. The fact that she couldn't seem to get away fast enough burned Cutter's gut.

He shoved the spectacles back into her hand, meeting her gaze with turbulent black eyes. "I can't do a blamed thing with them."

She was sitting on her knees, her skirt caught beneath her, hands on her thighs, her expression ashen. For the longest instant their gazes held. She wet her lips nervously, her pink little tongue darting out to moisten her bottom lip, and desire clawed at Cutter from the inside out. Despite his anger.

"You sure you're not hurt?" he asked.

Elizabeth nodded quickly.

"Good."

Her brows drew together at his tone. "You don't have to sound so displeased over the fact," she told him.

"Son of a bitch!" Cutter shouted suddenly, throwing his hands up. "What the hell do you want me to say?"

Elizabeth flinched at his tone, but didn't back down. "And you don't have to curse at me, either!" she shot back, her voice rising.

"Damn me, if you ain't as contrary as that coweyed cayuse of yours!"

"Well!" She couldn't stand it any longer! "Then why do you wanna help me if you hate me so much?" she wanted to know.

"I've been asking myself that same question!" Cutter told her. "Over and over! Hell, I dunno! Maybe I was lamebrained enough to think you'd appreciate it. Maybe I did it for Jo! She seems to care for you so friggin' much that I thought you cared right back! Reckon I was wrong."

"No!" Elizabeth retorted. "No!" And then composing herself, she said more calmly, her expression pained, "You weren't wrong. I do care about Jo. She's my best friend!" A little softer now. "The closest one I've ever had."

A thick silence fell between them. As they stared at each other, something passed between them, a charge that made Elizabeth's heart turn over. A connection neither understood, much less felt at ease with.

Elizabeth was the first to break eye contact. Nervously, catching her lower lip between her teeth, she glanced down at her trembling knees, then back up again to see that Cutter was still watching her intently. His expression was thoughtful, as though he were questioning her somehow, or himself, and didn't like the answers he found.

Well, she didn't care if he didn't like her, she told herself. She didn't like him either! Unsure what to say in that moment, she only knew that she couldn't take his cutting looks and cantankerous disposition any longer. "For Jo's sake," she began sourly, "do you think . . . do you think that perhaps we could call a truce? At least until St. Louis?" Puzzling as it was, she wanted the other Cutter back—the man he'd seemed to be when she'd first met him. "You'll be rid of me then," she appealed when his eyes narrowed slightly.

As she reminded him of the fact that she planned to hire someone else once they reached their destination, Cutter's jaw tensed, but he nodded slightly in response. Rid of her? He doubted he ever would be, but yeah, he could, and needed to, for the sake of the journey, call a truce.

"All right," he agreed, his voice hoarse. "Truce it is. But you're gonna have to carry your weight, Doc, and you can't be fighting me at every turn. When I tell you to do something, you do it. Trust me to know what's right. Agreed?"

Strangely enough, Elizabeth did trust him. She wasn't certain she liked him much . . . but she trusted him. Nodding, she agreed.

Chapter 10

But it was an uneasy truce at best, Elizabeth realized by the following day. Little enough had been said between them as they'd set up camp that first night. Yet that had more than suited her at the time. There had been far too much on her mind for idle chatter.

And despite his charge that she was to carry her own weight, Cutter took care of every last detail, from hunting down a meal to setting up the bedrolls, making her do nothing but sit like a ninny on her backside. She was certain that he'd done so as a consideration to her, because of her fall. But his manner had been brusque the entire evening, never inviting conversation, even had she considered it.

She'd not, however, and had thought little of it until now.

By late afternoon she began to suspect that Cutter was regretting their arrangement, and she felt like sending his brooding self to blazes for making her feel so guilty. This had certainly not been her idea! It had, in fact, been his. And now that he had managed to convince her that it was the best solution, she wasn't about to let him off so easily. How dare he even consider it, anyway? She was not, she assured herself, about to feel guilty!

As of yet, there had been few words spoken between them. And then only out of necessity. Such as when she'd asked to stop so that she could relieve herself—another thing she'd not anticipated. She doubted she'd ever get used to having to share that embarrassing detail with another human being, much less a man—less Cutter McKenzie!

True, she was a doctor, and such things were supposed to be familiar to her, but for some reason, even the thought of Cutter knowing of that very private . . . *act* discomfited her. Especially since he seemed to be particularly amused by it. What he should find so entertaining, Elizabeth was sure she didn't know.

In his defense, he had, upon several occasions, asked after her comfort, and she took heart in that. And then her lips twisted as she recalled the first time he'd inquired. In spite of her sore bottom, she'd promptly assured him that she was just fine, but the crimson stains on her cheeks had given her away. Noting them, Cutter had smiled his very first smile of the day, and then had offered his hat . . . saying with false gravity that the sun was burning her skin even as he watched. The rat! Certainly he was no gentleman for pointing out her blushing, that much was certain.

But then he'd never claimed to be, had he?

Grudgingly she'd accepted his offer, gritting her teeth as she snatched the confounded hat out of his grasp. The only other time she tried to encourage conversation, he practically bit her head off. She merely asked him why his horse only had half a right ear.

"Someone's idea of a practical joke," he snarled.

Elizabeth's face contorted. "Well, I certainly don't think that's very funny," she assured him.

The look Cutter gave her in answer chilled her to the bone. "Neither did I," he replied. "But I don't reckon the man's laughing any longer." Jack Colyer had been one of the most vocal against him. They'd worked together driving cattle for near two years. As one of the older boys, Colyer had made certain Cutter ended up with the worst jobs, the worst supplies, the last of the grub. Hell, he'd actually caught the man bragging over cutting off his horse's ear. Without a word, Cutter had walked into the circle of men, some of whom were twice his age and bigger t' boot, but he'd been too angry to be afraid. No one had moved. He could still feel the silence crawl down his back as they'd watched him move purposely toward Colyer.

His blade had sliced the air so quickly that Colyer had had no idea what had happened until he'd seen the evidence in Cutter's hand. "Ear for an ear," Cutter had whispered. And then he'd smiled, feeling a satisfaction he never should have felt over such a violent act. Yet he'd felt it all the same.

No one had ever crossed him again.

But neither had they accepted him.

"Why would he do such a thing to an innocent horse?" Elizabeth wanted to know, bringing him back from the ugly past.

The look he turned on her was condemning. "Same reason you seem to be so averse to my company," he told her. "He hated half-breeds."

"I don't hate half-breeds!" Elizabeth protested.

Cutter shrugged impassively. "Reckon he just wasn't satisfied with my reaction to his insults," he disclosed. "He just went a little too far in trying to provoke me, is all."

She shouldn't ask, she knew, but she couldn't help herself. "What did you do to him?" Her tone was wary.

One brow lifted as he turned to look at her. There was a long moment of silence. "Scalped him maybe?" he said without emotion.

Elizabeth repressed a shudder. Against her will, she felt a rush of sympathy for the man riding at her side. He seemed so hard, but no one could be so hard that hate wouldn't touch him. She wondered how he'd felt to be persecuted for his race all his life, and then felt another prick of guilt for calling him names. She'd behaved no better than the man who'd cut off his horse's ear.

Still, he had provoked her.

She turned to him, and found him watching her intently.

"You don't want to know," he said enigmatically, deterring her question.

. . . don't reckon the man's laughing any longer.

Elizabeth swallowed. "I suppose not," she relented, shuddering over his cryptic remark. Shaking off her morbid thoughts, she resolved to keep to herself the rest of the day.

As they rode on, the lay of the land changed very little, and she found herself growing weary of the monotony.

And the silence.

And the heat.

Her shirt was growing damp at her back, and tiny rivulets tickled her flesh beneath her breasts, making her feel impossibly sticky. Surreptitiously plucking her blouse away from her bosom, she silently cursed the unusually warm weather.

What was more, in spite of the shade Cutter's hat provided, her face *was* beginning to feel perpetually warm, and she suspected her cheeks and nose were becoming burnt. Instinctively she examined the sensitive bridge of her nose, thinking that on the bright side, she no longer had spectacles to fret over. And then she felt bereft suddenly as she reflected on that loss. Somehow it seemed as though her father had been wrenched away from her all over again . . . and she didn't really understand that at all. They had been mere wire and glass, after all. She sighed, a wealth of emotion betrayed by the dismal sound, and it earned her a discerning glance from Cutter.

Though she didn't notice.

Nor had she caught the many other glances he'd directed her way. Truth was that Cutter's silence had little to do with anger, or even regret. Foremost in his mind was how to prove himself to her. Could he persuade Elizabeth to see him as other than the *heathen savage* she considered him? From the moment he'd awakened this morning to find her sleeping so peacefully, curled like an infant on her side, few thoughts other than those had occupied his mind.

Watching her in those quiet early morning moments, he'd tried to muster up the desire to get up off his hindquarters and shave his whiskers, but he couldn't seem to move. By the time she'd finally gotten round to waking, it had been too late to do anything more than pack—his whiskers go hang.

As he'd watched her, he kept remembering her brief moment of laughter, when she'd told him about Dick Brady's shenanigans, the curve of her lips as she'd smiled on the verge of drunkenness. Somehow he had the impression that she didn't smile much—didn't have much to smile about. And he seemed to crave her smile.

Just couldn't figure why.

Last night she'd quietly hummed herself to sleep, the sound as woebegone as the whine of a lost pup, and it left him feeling her emptiness sharply.

Why was he so drawn to her? he wondered with another glance her way. When she obviously placed so little worth in him? He'd never thought himself a sucker for prudish misses. He dismissed the fact that she turned all dreamy-eyed in his arms. He didn't fool himself a'tall over that. Her response to him was nothing less than he'd've expected from any innocent miss.

He hadn't gotten around to telling her yet that he didn't intend to let her hire on anyone else in St. Louis—wasn't really sure how to make her see things his way. He only knew that she wasn't gonna do it—not if he had anything to say about it. Just the thought of some other man lying next to her in bed—any bed—burned like rotten whiskey at his gut.

Hell, maybe that was all there was to it.

Maybe she just didn't realize that in order to make it look real, she was gonna have to play the part all the way through, right down to the last particulars. And that meant sharing the same room—maybe even the same pillow. Maybe all he needed to do was let her in on that little fact.

Maybe that was all he needed. To satisfy his body's hunger. Maybe once he got her out of his system, he'd quit thinking of those breasts of hers, the way they'd looked barely concealed by her diaphanous camisole.

He felt a stirring in his britches and rolled his eyes. Chrissakes, not again. He glanced at her sharply. Hell, he didn't even have to look at her to get himself all worked up.

By the time they called a halt for the day, the soreness of Elizabeth's bottom had worked its way into her limbs. Even her fingers hurt where she'd clutched the reins, but she didn't dare complain. Flexing them, she determined to be of some help this time, and after deciding just how, she set about gathering firewood while Cutter set off to water the horses at the river.

He returned barely long enough to settle the horses and then remove his carbine from a special attachment to the saddle. He asked her, while unsheathing his army-model Colt from his holster, "Know how to use this?"

Dropping an armload of firewood at her chosen spot, and brushing her hands free of the filth, Elizabeth gave him an exasperated glance. "If I can see it," she muttered, "I can shoot it."

He handed her the gun. "Good," he said, and turned away. "Use it wisely."

Elizabeth stared at it a moment in offense, then at Cutter's retreating back, watching it until it became woolly.

"Trouble is, I can't see," she bemoaned, but she wasn't about to admit that failing to Cutter. By the time her target was in her field of vision, it'd more likely than not be too late. Glaring at the revolver with a measure of anxiety, she decided that she just wouldn't use the blasted thing, is all.

Cutter pivoted toward her suddenly. "What did you say?"

Elizabeth forced a smile. "Nothing," she replied hastily. He didn't look quite convinced, and she gave him an irritated sigh. "I said, I'd be all right! Don't worry about me. Good night," she muttered. She'd been taking care of herself for most of her life. Her father had been too busy, and more oft than not, she'd taken care of him. She didn't need Cutter's concern. If that's what it was. And there was room for doubt.

With a nod and a grin, Cutter turned again. He hadn't missed Elizabeth's squinty-eyed look. "Just don't aim at anythin' standing upright," he told her, "unless it speaks first, and you know for sure it's not me." He heard her indignant gasp and his grin widened, though he didn't look back. "If you need me, fire once—skyward, if you don't mind. Wouldn't want to butt heads with a stray bullet."

He walked away without looking back, and Elizabeth had the sudden urge to point the gun heavenward and squeeze the trigger with all her might, startle him out of his too snug britches—the man was just a little too smug for her liking. They were almost indecent the way they clung to his hips and thighs! She'd tried to ignore those sinewy muscles of his, but it was just impossible. Never had she seen a body quite so hard as his!

Blasted man!

Laying the gun aside, carefully, with a little prayer that she wouldn't need it, Elizabeth finished gathering the firewood. She hoped Cutter would find something a little more edible than jerky to satisfy their hunger. As far as she was concerned, she'd had more than enough of the dehydrated beef already.

By the time Cutter returned, kill in hand, she'd

managed to set up the wood in a fashion, so that air could flow easily between the kindling. That way it would go out quickly, as Cutter seemed to prefer. She was in the process of tindering the fire, and the first tiny flame was licking its way triumphantly into the wooden pyramid she'd built, when Cutter's shouted expletive made her leap up, startled.

Whirling toward the sound, she took in his livid expression and bolted out of his way as he stalked toward her. Astounded, she turned and watched as he stamped out the small flame she'd worked so hard to begin.

"If you don't know how to do something, dammit—ask!"

There was genuine puzzlement in Elizabeth's expression. "I know how to start a fire!" she protested.

Cutter's black eyes speared her, unnerving her with the hostility they revealed. "You're not snug at home, Miz Bowcock," he said through his teeth, "all bundled up beside your cozy little fireplace. Without stones or something of the sort to keep the fire from spreading, we'd start a blaze like nothing you've ever seen this side of hell!"

"There's no need to curse at me! I certainly didn't know!" If possible, Elizabeth's sunburned cheeks became warmer, and her irritation intensified. Just how was she supposed to have known? "And you didn't have to come rushing at me like . . . like . . ."

"Like a savage out of the wild?" Cutter offered.

Elizabeth's chin rose a notch, and she took in a breath, releasing it slowly in an effort to keep her composure. "I—wasn't—going—to say that!" Her eyes slitted wrathfully. "Though now that you mention it—"

Cutter's eyes glittered dangerously. "Don't say it," he warned.

"You started this!" Elizabeth felt obliged to point out. "Whatever happened to our truce? Good night, you'd think I was committing the direst of sins, when I was only trying to help!''

No, just wheedling her way into his every thought, was all. He couldn't even hunt without thinking of her. What the hell did he care what she liked to eat? ''All right, so now you know,'' he said tightly.''Now come on over here and I'll show you how it's done properly.''

Elizabeth didn't budge.

Cutter began by clearing the surrounding area of debris. That done, he knelt, unsheathing his knife from his boot, and dug out a trench two feet long, heaping the soil to one side. Afterward, he gathered stones and arranged them accordingly.

''It's easier to build one above ground,'' he conceded. ''But this way conserves fuel. Aside from that, we don't need anyone aware of us. I've been tracking too long to feel comfortable leaving traces.'' He glanced up, gauging Elizabeth's expression. She'd yet to move forward, though she was watching him, her expression both curious and affronted. ''You wouldn't believe how much can be determined by studying an abandoned camp,'' he said, in an attempt to draw her closer.

At his declaration, Elizabeth scanned the area. Seeing nothing, she returned her attention to Cutter, hands on her hips. ''And just who do you expect is out there?'' she asked abruptly, hating the way her eyes returned not to his face, but to the muscle play in his arms as he worked. His arms, sinewy and bronzed from the sun, gave testimony to a lifetime of strenuous labor. Unable to turn away, she stared, mesmerized.

Quit staring, she admonished herself. *Good night, you'd think you'd never seen a man before!*

Cutter shrugged, never peering up from his work. ''Take your pick.''

Elizabeth shook off a quiver, shaking her head as if to dispel her wayward thoughts. ''Indians?'' she said.

There was horror in her tone, and Cutter winced at hearing her greatest fear. "Could be," he said as dispassionately as he was able. Rising, he slapped at his denims, whisking the dirt from his hands as he flicked her an annoyed look. With a disgusted shake of his head, he proceeded to gather up the buffalo chips he'd found while out hunting.

In an unusual display of clumsiness, he'd dropped them all at the sight of her on her knees by the fire, her pert little fanny clearly defined as she'd bent over her task. It had taken him a full moment to recoup himself after that view. One thing was certain, the woman had one helluva backside.

Once the chips were all recovered, he placed them in the small pit he'd formed, topping them with the smallest bits of deadwood Elizabeth had gathered. The rest, he scattered.

Seeing a chip that he'd missed, Elizabeth bent to retrieve it, dropping it, too, into the pit. "What about the smoke?" she reminded him tersely, thinking that his efforts were pointless. The smoke would be seen for miles.

"It'll last only long enough to cook with," he told her as he removed a scrap of linen and a cartridge from his front pocket. From it, he produced a match and struck it. He put it to the cloth, and for a moment, as he watched it catch, the flame flickered in his mirror-dark eyes. He glanced up at her suddenly, his eyes probing. He didn't understand how she could look at his sister and not see what she was . . . and then she could look at him and see only what he didn't want her to see.

He cursed suddenly as the flame singed his thumb.

"Are you all right? Do you want me to look at that?" she asked him at once.

"No," he told her. "It's just fine!" Muttering another expletive under his breath, he pitched the cloth into the kindling, casting Elizabeth a swift glance as he returned the cartridge to his pocket. Damned woman. She was gonna kill him before it was all over!

"What about warmth?" she asked abruptly, watching as Cutter readjusted several pieces of tinder. "Won't we need the fire tonight?"

"No," Cutter replied. Lifting his head, he gave her a peculiar smile. "We won't—but it isn't as though we're in the middle of winter, Doc. And we've got blankets."

His eyes held promises Elizabeth didn't quite comprehend. Still, she found herself unsettled by them, yet, at the same time, intrigued. "W-what if it's not enough?" she worried aloud. "It was cool last night," she added plaintively.

Cutter's eyes held her spellbound. Had her skirt been on fire, she doubted she could have broken away.

"We've got each other," Cutter said, his lips curving faintly. "We'll be warm enough, I reckon."

There was a sudden wild fluttering in her stomach. "The blankets will keep us warm enough," she assured him much too quickly. "I-I'm certain they will!"

Cutter grinned at her obvious assumption, and her telltale nervousness, then his expression softened considerably. "Ever eat a puddle jumper?" he asked conversationally.

"A what?"

"Rattler."

"Ugghhh! Of course not!" Elizabeth actually took a step backward, waving him off, as if afraid he would force her. "And I *never* plan to," she declared with certainty.

Cutter grinned suddenly. His smile made Elizabeth's toes curl in her shoes.

His eyes darted to the burlap sack that lay forgotten a few feet away. "Never say never, Doc," he advised her solemnly. Elizabeth's gaze followed, then snapped back suspiciously to Cutter, a flicker of alarm in her tawny eyes, and Cutter's grin widened, his teeth flashing white against his swarthy, unshaven complexion. His chuckle was low and rich when it came, bringing back that annoying sparkle to his eyes.

Inexplicably, Elizabeth's heart turned over at the sight of it.

Chapter 11

N ever came much sooner than Elizabeth would
have liked.

With nothing else available, she was forced to at
least taste the despised rattler. And if the truth were
known, it might not have been so bad, had she not
known what it was.

But she did know.

And it was all she could do to get down just enough
to keep her stomach from grumbling. It didn't help
matters much that Cutter seemed to be enjoying her
uneasiness so much. Forcing down the last flame-
singed chunk, she rose and commenced to unpack
her bedroll, knowing they would have no fire to see
by once night fell.

Thinking that she would catch the remaining heat
from the fire as it died, she settled near it. As she
worked, Cutter watched her, his expression preoccupied as he busied his hands with a strip of rawhide
and the rattler's forfeited tail end. After a while, he
set his labors aside and pulled out his own bedroll,
laying it across the fire from Elizabeth.

No sooner were they situated when the sun presented its parting colors, a glorious display of garnet
and indigo.

Unfortunately, unlike the night before, sleep eluded
Elizabeth, even hours later. She'd half expected that
her eyes would close in time with the setting sun. But

it hadn't been so. Miserably, she could feel every lump beneath her, every stone, every stiff blade of grass. Her body was still sore, though not nearly as much as it had been the night before.

Eventually the fire died almost completely, leaving only a few glowing embers, and after a while, even the gentle night sounds conspired against her: the steady trilling of crickets, the distant hoot of an owl. She thought to hum softly to herself, but was too self-conscious to chance that Cutter would hear her; her song sounded more an ungodly squeak on the night breeze than a soothing lullaby.

And Cutter . . . She was only too aware of him—in spite of the fact that his form was barely visible through the shadows. She could feel his presence just as surely as if he were lying smack-dab beside her.

He, on the other hand, seemed not to have any difficulty snoozing at all! He lay like stone. In fact, she thought it might have been a good hour since she'd heard a single rustle from his blankets, and the fact that he could sleep so peacefully when she could not made her feel all the more restless. And offended somehow, though why she should be, she didn't know.

Despite the fact that her eyes felt as heavy as lead, the butterflies in her stomach were wide-awake. Or maybe it was the rattler that churned there? As she was reminded of the rattler, the muscles in Elizabeth's limbs tensed abruptly.

Just where had he found the thing? Not anywhere in the immediate area, she hoped. But . . . he'd not been gone long—he would've had to discover it nearby.

Good night! What if it had little baby rattlers slithering around somewhere? But no . . . she didn't think they traveled that way. They preferred their own company . . . didn't they? Oh, Lord . . .

Something stirred in the immediate darkness.

Elizabeth swallowed back a knob of apprehension. "Cutter?" she croaked.

Cutter didn't so much as move a muscle, but there it was, that sound again.

Now what was she supposed to do?

One thing was certain. She wasn't about to wake Cutter and have him needle her about it in the morning!

But neither was she willing to lie helpless in the dark!

She grabbed her woolen blanket and groped her way around to where Cutter slept, dragging the blanket after her in the dirt.

What harm could there be in resting just a bit nearer to Cutter? For just a while?

She groaned as the blanket caught under her knee. She tugged at it frantically, and belly-flopped to the ground when she jerked it too quickly. Choking and sputtering on an invisible cloud of dust, she scrambled to her knees.

Later, she determined, panic setting in. Later she would move back to her bedroll . . . once she felt certain that whatever had made that sound was gone.

Cutter need never know.

Right?

Right.

Wavering somewhere between sleep and consciousness, Cutter heard her voice. But then, he'd been suffering her all night. Not just that god-awful tune of hers, if it could be called that, but her condemnation. *Indians?* he kept hearing from her lips. *Indians?* He felt like telling her to go straight to hell, but before he could express those powerful sentiments, some sixth sense alerted him to a presence beside him, and his eyes opened, zeroing in on the black form creeping like a thief to his side.

He grinned suddenly. Mischievously. Without a doubt he knew what it was. Or rather who it was.

Elizabeth. As if by cue, his body responded at once to her proximity.

Drawing the covers up, he turned abruptly to lie on his side, watching her alarmed reaction through amused, slitted eyes. Her dark shape froze, then began to sidle quietly away, and he stifled a wicked chuckle. She wasn't gonna get very far—not when he finally had her right where he wanted her.

Abruptly Cutter's arm snaked out, catching her about the middle. She stiffened, and he drowsily pulled her into the circle of his embrace, all the while nuzzling sleepily against the back of her neck. She resisted noiselessly, but she did resist, squirming with increasing strength against the firm hold he had upon her. Instinctively he knew that if he didn't think of something quick, she was going to elbow his crotch again—and empty her lungs right into his ear.

And then a waggish idea popped into his head, and his grin widened.

"Mmmm," he groaned suddenly, his smile unscrupulous as he wrapped his arms sleepily but possessively about her waist. When her struggles ceased for the briefest instant, he took advantage, sliding his hand down boldly to press against her feminine parts.

Her breath caught in shocked protest, but before she could even think to remove his hand from where it sat, he slammed her taut little backside against his thighs.

His hand glided slowly down to her thigh as he wiggled sleepily against her bottom. "Mmmmmmmmm," he murmured, "feels . . . so . . . good." Boy, did it ever! Before she could respond, he added the wild card. "Bess."

As he'd expected, Elizabeth froze in his arms. His lips quivered with suppressed laughter.

Bess? Good night, he thought she was Bess? Wasn't it bad enough that he would dream of the hussy? Did he have to confuse the two of them, as well? How dare he? Elizabeth chafed.

Still, she didn't risk moving, because he obviously didn't know that it was her, and she wasn't about to reveal otherwise. If she woke him now, she'd be forced to explain why she was sleeping so near him to begin with . . . when she'd practically forbade him to sleep within arm's reach of her. How could she possibly explain herself? The truth was, she doubted anything she could say would show her in good light. Even to her own mind, her reasoning sounded lame, at best. She decided it would be best to wait until the scoundrel fell into a deeper sleep, and then she'd slip away—rotten, misbegotten dog that he was!

Burying his nose into the stiff back of her neck, Cutter sighed with the sheer pleasure of it all. She smelled good—no perfumes, nothing, just the fascinating scent of clean skin and hair. He felt like laughing out loud—though why he should feel so pleased with himself suddenly, when he'd been so irritated by her only moments before, was a question he wasn't about to mull over too closely.

What he wouldn't give just now to undo that thick braid of hers, run his fingers through her silky hair. But he didn't want her to know he was awake, so instead, he played a waiting game, a game Elizabeth was fated to lose.

Ruthless as he was, Cutter never loosened his hold upon her. Not even a smidgen. After she waited a long while for him to ease up on his grip, Elizabeth's body began to slacken in his arms.

The instant it did, he began to nibble her neck drowsily, moving his hand to her middle, stroking her belly seductively.

So what was she supposed to do now? Elizabeth knew she should protest, but for the life of her, she couldn't bring herself to do it. Merciful heaven . . . what was he doing to her? With every slow stroke of his hands, her body seemed to stir a little more.

His warm lips found their way into her hair, nibbling, burning her flesh. Unable to bear it, Elizabeth arched, giving him better access.

Cutter stifled a groan at her response. As his mouth leisurely devoured her flesh, his hands moved to her shoulder and then to her back, swiftly undoing the buttons there. With that accomplishment under his belt, he felt a sense of victory, the very same feeling that came over him when he was stalking his prey—animal or man—and forced the final, winning move.

Elizabeth didn't realize she was undone until she felt the crisp air flow down her spine. Cutter's warm lips followed, along with the sleek gliding of his tongue, making her shiver. Her breathing quickened and she stiffened. Was he awake then? Suspicion niggled her. No man could be so seductive in his sleep! Or could he?

She hoped he was still asleep, and didn't pause to wonder why. She told herself that it was because she didn't want him to know she'd allowed him so much liberty. But she knew even as she thought it that it wasn't true. She didn't want this to end, didn't think she could bear it if it did. Still, she shouldn't just . . .

"Mmmm, Bess," he whispered again.

Bess. Elizabeth closed her eyes, shutting out the name, and along with it, her pain at hearing it spoken again from his lips.

Despite the fact that Cutter's denims grew so tight as to be painful, it was worth it, he thought with grim satisfaction. He was only thankful that his britches were snug enough to hide his arousal from her. He hadn't mistaken the look in Elizabeth's eyes when she'd discovered that part of his anatomy the day he'd fallen atop her. She might be an innocent miss, but she knew what it was that went on between men and women, and likely would have leapt out of her skin if she felt it burrowing against her sweet little butt just now.

He smiled faintly against her soft back. What a strange brew she was: naive, yet obviously not totally ignorant. His lips curved into a jaded smile. As far as he was concerned, she had just the right degree of innocence and carnal knowledge in those brassy eyes of hers, making him want to be the first man to bury himself in that delicious body of hers—in spite of the fact that he wasn't comfortable with prudish misses.

But she wasn't that at all, he reflected, despite the front she liked to put up.

Elizabeth moaned low in her throat as Cutter's hands slipped from her back, beneath her open blouse. She gasped as his fingers reached around to touch and cup her breast. With slow, sleepy movements, he caressed her, seducing every thought of protest from her mind. Heaven help her, but she arched for him, daring to ease herself into his palm.

So warm.

So very warm.

He squeezed her gently, and her bottom undulated into his pelvis. There it froze, feeling the hardness there. Her heart burst into her throat. She felt a bittersweet pleasure at the feel of him, even knowing it wasn't for her. He began to move against her, and she squeezed her eyes shut, swallowing, willing her traitorous body to deny itself. But it was in vain. An ache began to build deep within, coiling inside her so tightly that she thought she would die of the pleasure.

The woman was as warm-blooded as they came, Cutter thought with satisfaction as Elizabeth moved unconsciously with him. Thing was, she just didn't know it yet. All she needed was a little shove in that direction. Shuddering with anticipation, he savored the ache in his dungarees, and thought of all the ways he'd make her pay when the time came. He was just arrogant enough to know that if he pursued it, he could get exactly what he craved tonight . . . but he didn't want any regrets in the morning. He wanted her to come to him on her own. He wanted her so ready, she wouldn't be able to deny him if she wanted to. No, he'd just give her something to think about until next time.

Something to crave.

His hand slipped out of her blouse, and drifted across her hips, down to the apex of her thighs. Stroking her over her skirt, he pressed a little deeper each time between her clenched thighs.

Moaning softly, Elizabeth pressed her thighs together more protectively, not understanding why she seemed to need that pressure. Unable to bear it, she whimpered, trying not to be heard. But it was too late; when Cutter pressed his fingers between her thighs one last time, and lifted up, her body shattered.

Cutter told himself that he was satisfied. That he'd gotten what he was after. That for the moment, he was content just to hold her . . . breathe her into his soul. But it wasn't true. Feeling her body's tiny convulsions, her culmination in pleasure, it was all he could do not to let himself go. It was too damned much to bear. One last roll of his hips against her pert little fanny would give him his own release. He didn't move. And it was the most difficult thing he ever didn't do.

God, he hurt.

Coming back to her senses, Elizabeth stiffened in his arms, but Cutter held her tightly, knowing that she was likely as embarrassed as she was confused over what had just happened to her. She was probably waiting for him to release her so she could scurry away. But he wasn't willing to let her go. Somehow, though he didn't understand it, she was beginning to weave herself inextricably into his being. Without trying, she'd managed to wrap her tiny fingers firmly around his rock-solid heart.

Still, he didn't move. He knew she had to suspect he was awake. But he also knew that she was hoping he wasn't, and it was easier to let her keep believing he still slept.

It was a long while later before Elizabeth finally relaxed. When her breathing finally grew smooth and even, he knew instinctively that she had fallen asleep. And only then did he allow himself to drift.

Strangely enough, it was the hush of the morning rather than the glaring sunlight falling across Elizabeth's face that drew her from her dreams first. She stretched lazily, and then froze. Her eyes flew open to find herself facing what had only recently been the campfire. The pit was filled now, and tamped firmly down, the stones disbursed, turned blackened side under so that, to the undiscerning glance, it was impossible to tell that they had once been a part of a blazing fire.

The next thing Elizabeth became aware of was that everything was already packed, including Cutter's bedroll.

Cutter's bedroll.

Somewhere in the back of her mind, something nagged at her. And then it came to her, unwelcome as the memory was. Her heart did a violent somersault as she anxiously reexamined the scene before her, hoping against hope.

Merciful heaven . . . it wasn't Cutter's gear that was neatly rolled and packed away, but hers!

Desperately, nipping at her lower lip until it was in danger of splitting, she tried to recall through her cobwebby thoughts whether she'd crept back to her own bed at some point during the night. But the view was all wrong—obvious even in light of her slightly hazed vision—and she knew without a doubt that she'd not.

Taking in a shuddering breath, Elizabeth mustered the courage to raise herself up from Cutter's bed to face him. She spotted him at once, and thankfully, his back was to her as he readied their horses for the day's travel. At least that was what she imagined he was doing. His movements were somewhat of a blur at this distance. That was the first thing she'd have to do when she got back to Sioux Falls—purchase a new pair of spectacles.

She was still staring when Cutter turned toward her, trying to focus her vision, and her face went crimson with shame.

What must he think of her now? After the shameless way she'd . . .

Oh, God, don't think of that!

It didn't happen.

Besides, he was sleeping at the time, so why should he remember?

What explanation could she give for sleeping in his bed? She grasped at several, but not one seemed fit, so she said nothing.

Recognizing the look on her face, Cutter sauntered toward her, grin slightly awry as he tossed her his hat. After the restless night he'd spent, he wasn't in the mood to show mercy. "Wear it down low over your face," he told her solemnly, shaking his head with mock concern. He barely hid the belligerent smile that lurked behind those sensual lips of his. "Damn me, if you're not getting too much sun." He winked at her.

Elizabeth gasped, catching the hat as it spun through the air toward her. She gnashed her teeth at his smug expression. Had she expected a courteous "good morning" from him? Oh, no, nothing so considerate as that from Cutter McKenzie! He had to slip right into his provoking demeanor first thing. Come to think of it, like his boots, she thought he might never even have bothered to step out of it. It was too much a part of him.

She rose, crushing the hat vengefully onto her head, and stomped her way to the river. It was little more than fifty yards from the campsite, sparkling beautifully in the morning sun, and she mentally scolded herself for not considering a bath after supper last night.

She'd yet to put her shoes on this morning, and was glad of that fact, because she didn't feel like stooping to pull them off. The inside of her thighs were still sore from so many hours of riding.

Not to mention the way she'd clenched her thighs together last night.

Now, why did she have to go and think of that? Jerking her skirt up, she tucked it into her waist, glancing toward camp consideringly. Surely Cutter would know what she was up to and have the good grace not to intrude?

But she couldn't be certain of that fact, and so she abandoned the scandalous notion as quickly as it appeared. The last thing she needed this morning was to be caught in her bloomers again.

As hastily as she was able, she took care of her personal needs and then, with a weary sigh, yanked her skirt back out of her waist. With one hand, she held it out of the water while she waded her feet in the cool river. Stooping, she splashed a handful into her face to refresh herself and then considered her rippling reflection in the water.

Mercy, was she a sight! she thought, aghast, as she ran her tongue along her bottom lip . . . and she had the most god-awful taste in her mouth!

She'd scrubbed her teeth as best she could without asking Cutter for the means. He'd seemed amused enough with her *other* personal duties, as it was. But this morning she was desperate to freshen her mouth. She took in a mouthful of water, swishing it vigorously, cursing herself for the oversight of a toothbrush and powder, but to her dismay, it didn't help all that much. Her mind toiling, she peered around for something of use . . . something grainy enough to scrub her teeth clean.

All at once, a thought occurred to her, and she felt absolutely brilliant. Sand, of course! There was plenty of it about . . . and though it surely wouldn't be pleasant, it couldn't be all that bad either. With the river so low, there were sandbars everywhere. Moving closer to one of the smaller ones, she scraped up a smidgen of the cleanest sand she could find, rubbing her fingers together, testing the consistency of it. Even once she was satisfied with its coarseness, she continued to stare at it a long moment, examining it for little crawly things. There were none. Still she was reluctant.

And she *was* desperate, she reminded herself. Without giving herself another moment to reconsider, she promptly thrust it into her mouth, grimacing at the grainy taste. Though, truthfully, after a moment, it wasn't so bad. Scooping a handful of water, she quickly swished out her mouth, to find that it did feel considerably cleaner . . . though not quite enough.

Again, she scooped up a fingerful, ignoring the little voice inside that told her this was very likely the most foolish thing she'd ever done in her life, and scrubbed her teeth with it, this time more vigorously, reasoning that perhaps she had even discovered some new method of cleansing one's mouth—besides Sanitary, the Perfect Tooth Soap. Who knew? she mused, inordinately pleased with herself suddenly. Perhaps there was even some health benefit to be had here. Wasn't mud good for the skin? Conceivably sand might also be good for the teeth. Her mind raced with the possibilities.

"You just about through here?"

Startled from her contemplations, Elizabeth whirled abruptly, her hand releasing her skirt, and flying to her hat. She was shocked to her toes to find Cutter standing so close behind her. She hadn't even heard him approach.

Cutter stared, nonplussed, at the toffee-colored coating of sand on Elizabeth's teeth and lips, his face contorting with disgust. "What is that?" he asked bluntly, and then wished he hadn't. Hadn't he heard somewhere that women in a family way sometimes craved dirt? Maybe *all* women craved dirt. Maybe, but he couldn't conceive it. Still, who knew what crazy notions went through their minds?

Feeling suddenly three times a ninny, and realizing that her mouth was hanging agape, Elizabeth snapped it shut, covering it immediately with her hands. Her cheeks flamed.

"Jee-zus, Lizbeth!" Cutter muttered, sounding repulsed. "There's plenty o' jerky left over if you're hungry." Then his eyes took in her soiled index finger, and he understood. He lowered her hands slowly from her face, needing another look in order to believe that she was actually brushing her teeth . . . *with sand*. Hell, he'd known she was embarrassed of her personal needs, but this was asinine. Still, he couldn't quite contain the laughter that was brewing.

His lips twisted as his gaze dropped to her hem, which was soaking up the river. He shook his head, clearing his throat. "Never mind," he said abruptly, "don't wanna know. Just don't get any on my hat." He pivoted on his heels, his shoulders shaking suspiciously as he walked away from her.

It wasn't until he was a safe distance away that Elizabeth was able to move again. Coming as close as she ever had to blaspheming, she spat the offensive sand out of her mouth and then swished again with water, spurting it out with a vengeance. It was then that she noticed the rising wet stain on her ruined skirt, and her color rose higher, though out of rage.

How was it that she forgot everything, *everything*, in Cutter's presence?

When she returned to camp, she was slightly more composed, though still tingling with indignity. How dare he make light of her personal hygiene! Surely he had many of the same needs to consider? Avoiding his gaze, she quickly gathered her remaining effects. There was barely enough time to brush the dust from her skirts before Cutter was hoisting her into the saddle.

Hauling himself into his own saddle, he turned to

her suddenly, his grin engaging, his teeth striking against his swarthy complexion. His eyes twinkled with mischief. "By the way," he remarked casually, "next time . . . just ask. You're more'n welcome to use one of my own brushes . . . and powder." And then he had the audacity to chuckle with good humor. Turning, he gently whipped the reins, leaving Elizabeth to stare daggers at his back.

Did he never miss an opportunity to needle her? she wondered. Yet, in spite of her anger, he'd planted a seed, and as irrational as it was, she couldn't quite banish the suggestive image of her using *his* toothbrush. It should have disgusted her, but instead, it gave her a strange quivering sensation deep down.

By midday, she was thoroughly exhausted from having spent such a restless night. Her only consolation was that Cutter didn't seem to have fared any better, though his manner was never more obnoxious. The gleam in his eye when he happened to look her way made her screaming mad. And his winking . . . his winking infuriated her, because she felt as though he were poking fun at her somehow.

Having slept for the second night in her dirty, rumpled clothing, Elizabeth had no delusions over her appearance. For certain, she'd never been much of a beauty, but now she was sure she was just plain unsightly. Her skirt, with its torn hem, looked as though it had seen more years than she had, with all the filth it had accumulated. And the white blouse? Well, she preferred not to think of *it* at all.

At the first opportunity, she planned to change into her new clothes and scrub the ones she was wearing in the river. It didn't matter that she didn't have any soap to launder with. At least then she would *feel* cleaner, even if she wouldn't look it. And it'd be nice to bathe at the same time, but she wasn't sure she'd dare the risk—at least not a full bath, she amended with a distrustful glance at Cutter. Sometimes . . .

sometimes . . . when he looked at her . . . well, she just wasn't certain.

And then there was *that*—whatever it was that he'd done to her last night—that she was trying so desperately to forget. But who could forget? There were moments when she found herself wishing that she were farsighted, and not nearsighted, as she was. She didn't want to be able to see him . . . that strange look he gave her every so often. Yet she couldn't seem to take her eyes off him either.

She gave him another furtive glance, and caught him rubbing his brows tiredly.

In profile, his face was positively striking, his cheekbones high, his jaw thick, darkened considerably by at least a week's worth of stubble. But it was those lips of his that made her feel so vulnerable . . . the way they'd felt on her skin, so warm . . . so mesmerizing. She shivered, and unconsciously ran her hand down the length of her braid, taking note of every loose tendril of hair.

What a sight she must present to him!

She was sure Cutter was used to women's attentions. He could probably choose almost any woman he wished and she would thrill to the opportunity.

How many women had tried to gain his favor?

Now, why did that question seem to bother her?

Why should her appearance matter so much, when it never had before?

And why had he kissed her?

She couldn't even begin to understand what had happened between them last night . . . why she had let it happen. He'd yet to mention the fact that he'd awakened to find her in his bed. Had she disgusted him? Her heart seemed to grow heavy with that thought.

Gliding his hands through his sweat-dampened black bangs, Cutter glanced her way, catching her staring, and a smile curved those arrogant lips of his. Flustered by the devilment in his black eyes, Elizabeth quickly averted her gaze, all the while cursing him to perdition.

Oh, what she wouldn't give for a hot bath, clean clothes . . . those lips . . . No—lands, her mind was running amok! She didn't need . . . or want . . . not *that!* Her face pinkened guiltily, and feeling Cutter's scrutiny upon her still, she turned her head away more fully, hiding the incriminating color on her cheeks.

Cutter chuckled.

Elizabeth chose to ignore him. *He couldn't possibly have known what she was thinking!*

No . . . just the bath, she reaffirmed with a sigh, trying desperately to refocus her thoughts. That was all she wanted—or needed. Course, if the sky grew any darker than it was just now, she considered with a heavenward glance, she might not have to worry over her washing, at that. The rain would likely take care of it for her.

But it didn't rain that day. Nor during the night. Though by late afternoon of the next day, the sky had grown black as pitch, and storm clouds swirled like sinister shadows overhead. Every so oft, a streak of white would flicker against the darkening horizon, and Elizabeth grimaced at the sight of it. To either side of them, the river bluffs butted high against the gloomy sky. As time went on, it grew so dark that it was difficult to distinguish where the bluffs ended and the sky began. As the wind picked up, she squashed Cutter's hat to the top of her head so it wouldn't be swept away.

It came as no surprise when the first drizzles misted the air about them. But they were in the middle of nowhere, Cutter having conscientiously steered clear of the townships, and though the trees were slowly growing in number, Elizabeth doubted they would use them for shelter. She'd heard tales of men being struck by lightning while out during storms. In fact, there'd been a woman last April who'd come in to see her father, claiming that her son had been struck down when a bolt of lightning had split a tree more than twenty feet from where he'd stood. The poor child had never fully recovered the use of his legs.

But there seemed to be no place else to take refuge against the rising tempest, and at this point the bluffs were too steep to climb, so they trekked on, despairing ever to ride out of the storm. Assessing the sky once more, Elizabeth glanced anxiously at Cutter. He seemed deep in thought, surveying the swirling heavens. His long hair snapped behind him in the breeze.

"Looks like we're in for one helluva squall!" Cutter bellowed suddenly, glancing at her.

As if in response, the wind picked up, plastering Elizabeth's wet blouse to her bosom. Her skirt billowed out around her. It fluttered wildly, snapping near as loud as the thunder overhead. Instinctively she lowered the brim of Cutter's hat to shield her face from the buffeting wind. Cocking her head into the bluster, she looked pleadingly at Cutter. "Shouldn't we find shelter or something?" she asked him.

The wind plastered his wet, dark hair to his head. Rainwater dripped from his bangs into his mouth as he spoke. "What do you think I've been doing?" he retorted. "You happen to see someplace I don't?" One brow rose in challenge, channeling rainwater onto his aquiline nose. As he watched her, his hand darted up to swipe at his face, and then tore into his wet hair, removing the offending strands from his forehead. It lingered in his glistening black mane as he stared at her.

In spite of the chaos simmering around them, Cutter was unable to deny himself. His eyes took in the shape of her wet blouse, the way it molded jealously about her breasts—the same way he'd like to wrap himself around her. With some effort, he lifted his gaze to her face. Slitting suddenly, his eyes glittered like the blackest onyx.

As she watched him, a shiver darted down Elizabeth's spine that had little to do with the cold swiftly settling into her bones. Answering his challenge, her own eyes quickly scanned the horizon as she turned the mustang mare in a full circle. And then she whirled Cocoa suddenly, glimpsing something over her shoulder. It was barely visible with her sorry vision and the swirling rain, yet there—a darker shading of rock against the bluff—and she whirled the mare about to examine it more closely, reining in. No matter how hard she squinted, she couldn't see it clearly enough.

"What about that?" she appealed, her tone rising with the wind. Cocoa pranced restlessly beneath her as she indicated the black shadow in the light stone. She couldn't really see much at this distance, but she wasn't about to admit as much to Cutter. She had to trust that his vision was at least slightly better than her own.

Cutter wheeled his mount about, his eyes squinting against the gusts, but to her surprise, he showed no reaction at all.

He shook his head, and then seeing another possibility near it, conceded, "Maybe." His shadowed eyes met hers, then glanced upward as a bolt of electric white lit up the sky. "Might be as good as it gets," he warned her. With a brisk nod, he urged Elizabeth on ahead.

Thunder exploded around them, the sound too loud and too violent for peace of mind.

Elizabeth cringed, her eyes widening fearfully.

Seeing her bloodless expression, Cutter booted the tail end of her mount. "Pull leather!" he shouted, and then spurred his own mount.

Having no choice but to comply, Elizabeth cried out and gripped the saddle horn for dear life.

Chapter 12

Reaching the craggy bluff first, Cutter motioned for Elizabeth to stay put.

"Why'd you hafta kick my horse?" she demanded at once, seeking courage in her wrath, but he ignored her, leaving her to wait in the downpour while he inspected the grotto.

"You could have killed me!" she shouted as he returned to seize her reins. Raindrops sparkled in her lashes, making it difficult to see his face through the haze. Furiously Elizabeth swiped at her wet face, running her fingers upward into her sopping hair, lifting it out of her face.

Without a word, Cutter led her around to where a small opening was discernible. Dismounting, he fell to his knees and crawled into the narrow crevice, backing out almost immediately. Still without speaking, he stood, whisking Elizabeth off her mount and setting her on her unsteady feet. Still without speaking, he urged her down onto her knees. The rain pattered Elizabeth's back without mercy as she obeyed.

But as she began to crawl within, a thought occurred to her, chilling her to the bone, and she hesitated. "What about the river? Won't it rise with the rain?" Drowning was the very last thing she wished to do!

"The river's low!" Cutter shouted over the downpour. "It'll rise, but not nearly enough—now, get in, and get cozy!" He coaxed her under the narrow over-hang and into the wider cavity beyond. Thunder erupted, and though Cutter's lips were moving, she couldn't hear his next words. ". . . stay . . . hold the fort," he finished, backing out almost at once.

As she realized that he was leaving her, Elizabeth's eyes went wide, and she started to follow him out, terrified of being left alone.

Cutter shoved her back with a fierce glare. "Chris-sakes, woman! I said t' stay, and I mean *stay!*" As an afterthought, he seized his hat from her head and began to back out once again.

Again thunder cracked, reverberating clear into the solid rock. Even the ground seemed to tremble be-neath them. Panicking, Elizabeth grasped Cutter's fingers, the last reachable part of him, her eyes plead-ing. "Cutter! P-Please wait!"

He shook off her trembling hands, his black eyes spearing her. "Trust me," was all he said, his tone unyielding, and then he was sliding out again.

Frantic, Elizabeth followed as far as the entrance to watch him go, her heart in her throat. Rain and wind buffeted her face, but fear held her immobile as, be-fore her eyes, his form blurred and was swallowed by the gray mist and rain.

Trust.

There was that word again.

But she did trust him . . . s-she did!

She did trust him.

It seemed to Elizabeth that she lay an eternity on the hard ground, peering out anxiously, waiting for some sign of Cutter's return, all the while repeating those words until they became a litany.

Trust.

The downpour intensified until the echo was a deafening roar beneath the stone shelter.

"Trust," she repeated slowly. *He won't leave you,* she assured herself, her heart racing. *He won't!*

But her mother had . . . and her father had—he'd
left her to face the chaos of her life.

Oh, God . . . alone!

Near hysterics now, Elizabeth began to hum softly.

At first, Cutter was dead certain he was hearing
things. He could swear that above the rain and crack-
ing thunder, he heard . . . humming? but as he
neared the shelter, he knew he wasn't imagining the
sound. It was Elizabeth, her voice terrified and broken . . . and unlike most nights, the melody she
hummed was recognizable and haunting.

"Greensleeves"?

She was humming "Greensleeves."

His chest swelled with some unnamed emotion,
and it struck him suddenly why she would sing that
song every blasted night . . . why she'd had him hum
to her that first night. He could suddenly hear her
voice again.

"*But it's dark,*" she'd whimpered. "*Too dark . . .
please . . .*"

"Please what?" he'd asked. "Lizbeth."

"*Hum—to—me . . .*"

Again, his gut twisted.

She was terrified of being alone . . . as terrified as
he was not to be. Strange thing was, for the first time
he could recall, he didn't mind the comforting . . .
didn't hold against the thought of companionship . . .
didn't mind protecting . . .

As long as it was her.

When Cutter's fuzzy, dark silhouette materialized
from the storm, walking determinedly toward her,
clutching what looked to be their bedrolls and everything else he could carry under his arms, Elizabeth's
heart flew into her throat. His expression, when it
crystallized at last, was as intense as the wind as he
approached, his dark eyes discerning, and she quickly
swiped away the telltale tears she'd not even realized

she'd shed until that moment and moved deeper into the shelter to give him room.

The instant Cutter set eyes on her, he knew that she'd been crying. He could see her dirty handprints where she'd tried to wipe the evidence away. But he didn't know what to say, so he said nothing. With his jaw set, he shoved in their effects, securing them at her feet, then crawled in beside her. He wanted to put his arms about her, soothe away her fears, but had no inkling how to go about it.

Or whether she would even accept his embrace.

Cursing at his own ineptitude, he kicked the rolls down farther into the dugout, shoving them out of his way, cursing again as he turned to pull one of the blankets out of his own fleabag. Somehow he managed to spread it beneath himself. Then he nudged Elizabeth. "Up," he demanded.

Obeying as best she could, Elizabeth twisted so that Cutter could thrust the blanket beneath her, and then she settled back down atop it. Without understanding how it had arisen, she felt the tension between them, and could do nothing but stare, wide-eyed, as Cutter finally turned onto his back beside her.

"Christ," he muttered, striking the low-lying roof with the butt of his hand. And then he looked at her, but it was a mistake. Her eyes seemed to reach out for him. He didn't know what to do. "Ain't enough room in here to swing a cat," he grumbled. Still she said nothing, only watched him, her heart riding in her eyes, and Cutter finally looked away, uneasy with the feelings she'd stirred in him.

After taking measure of the small cavern—if it could be called that—he turned to stare at the stone ceiling a mere foot and a half above his head, and wondered how the hell he'd gotten himself into this coil. In his estimation, they had no more than three feet of headroom in spots, less in others, and the dugout was probably a little over eight feet long, six feet deep. Some of the floor was stone, some dirt, and the only opening was to their right, stretching the length of the shelter, and letting in what little light was accessible. The ceiling was lower closer to the opening, higher toward the back. It was obviously man-made, but for what purpose, he didn't know. Only one thing was certain . . . whoever had made it had obviously not wished to be spotted at first glance—though up close, it was hard to miss.

He took in a deep breath—damn him, if he wasn't feeling stifled already—but the air smelled musty and old, and it didn't help a lick. Determinedly he ignored the sweeter scent that teased his nostrils, and focused on the sound of her shivering breath.

"I had to secure the horses," he explained finally. "Hated to do it . . . but had to tie them to the nearest tree." Rolling to his side to face her, he propped himself up on his elbow. As he scrutinized her, the sound of the rain became no more than a steady drone somewhere beyond them. "You cold?" he asked her, his voice a little huskier than he'd intended. He cleared his throat.

Elizabeth nodded.

He couldn't look away and he couldn't speak at all for the naked emotion still so apparent in Elizabeth's amber eyes. A few strands of her hair had loosened from her braid and were pasted to her dirt-streaked face, one strand to her bottom lip. Gently Cutter plucked it away, smoothing it from her face.

"You should get out of those wet clothes," he suggested, never releasing her gaze. His thumb rubbed at the smudges on her cheeks, without success.

She needed a bath, but in spite of it, she was a feast for his eyes. She blinked, but other than that, there was nothing about her expression that indicated she'd even heard him. He tried again. "You'll dry off faster if you're wearing less. I brought the blankets. They're damp, but they should be a helluva lot more comfortable than your wet clothes."

As if finally hearing him, Elizabeth shook her head

in quick, jerky motions, her lips going dry. "N-No—I—I can't! I'm fine."

Cutter's face contorted. "Chrissakes! I won't touch you," he said almost nastily. "Don't be stupid! You'll catch your death. Hell, you're the doctor—use your good sense!"

Her expression changed suddenly as if his words had injured somehow, instead of reassuring as he'd intended.

"You're—" She swallowed, mortified that he would have guessed her thoughts so easily, hurt that he would so quickly shatter her . . . her what? Hopes? Hopes for what? But he was right, of course. Besides, he'd already seen her in her bloomers and camisole . . . and there was little enough light for him to ogle her by . . . even if he were inclined to. But she wasn't about to feel sorry over that, she determined—not at this point in her life. It was, after all, what she'd set out to accomplish with her baggy skirts and somber appearance. She'd wanted folks to see her as their doctor, not the town belle—not that she could have been, even had she wished it. Had she really expected Cutter to see her differently? She nodded glumly. "You're right . . . How silly of me," she said dully.

Cutter's hand moved to her blouse at once, as if that were all the encouragement he needed, jerking it out of her skirt. Instinctively she recoiled from his ministrations, but the sensation of cool, wet cotton sliding over her warm skin caused a shiver to race down her spine and gooseflesh to erupt.

"Let me help you," he asserted, his dark eyes unrelenting yet tender in some odd way. Still, they'd never seemed so dark, so fathomless, so unprobable, as in that instant. A shiver raced down Elizabeth's spine as his hand slid slowly up her arm to her shoulder, but his squeeze was reassuring. She nodded faintly, unaware that she had.

"You'll need to turn around so that I can unbutton you," he said, his voice turning husky again.

Or was it her imagination?

Realizing that there was no way she could possibly remove her own clothes in the limited space available to them, she turned slightly, willing her wanton thoughts miles away. Inexplicably, she wanted Cutter's arms about her, his touch on her skin.

His movements became slower. The sensation of his warm fingers tugging at her blouse made a slight tremor rush down her spine. Elizabeth closed her eyes, savoring the moment, not realizing all that gesture conveyed to Cutter's knowing gaze.

Her heart hammered against her ribs as she anticipated the warmth of his fingers. And then she felt it, and her heart again leapt into her throat, higher than before. Her lids fluttered closed once more and her head tilted backward slightly as his fingers moved down her back, quickly and adeptly releasing the wooden buttons, one by one.

It was all Cutter could do not to place his lips on her delicate shoulder blades.

In removing the wet blouse from her back, he exposed her to the cool air, but in spite of it, Elizabeth felt suddenly too warm. Incomprehensibly, her shivers intensified, running deep within her. Her back to him still, she helped him remove the sleeves from her arms with quaking hands and then peeled the blouse from her body, leaving only her wet camisole to shield her from his probing eyes.

Despite the storm raging outside, the silence was impenetrable beneath the shelter in that moment, the air intoxicating, as if all time were suspended.

No sooner did Elizabeth release the blouse from her grasp than she felt Cutter's rough fingers on her back, stroking the area between her shoulder blades ever so softly, and her breath caught in her throat. Before she could protest his familiarity with her body, his hands circled her waist, spanning her briefly, as if taking her measure, then slid seductively to the laces in front of her skirt.

Something deep within her thrilled to his touch.

Finding it difficult to breathe in that moment, Elizabeth marveled that even from behind, his fingers were knowing. *That's because he's an experienced rogue,* a little voice screeched, but she refused to acknowledge it.

In the next instant, Cutter was tugging her sopping skirts down, sliding them over her quaking legs. He lingered just a moment too long on the curve of her hips, and her heartbeat quickened.

She meant to tell him to stop, to take his hands off her—she really did—but the words wouldn't come. It was all Elizabeth could do to take her next breath. She felt paralyzed, though not with fear, and her eyes pressed tightly closed, while her breasts suddenly tingled with the need to be touched. Good night—never would she have suspected such sensations were possible . . . such carnal bliss . . . such wanting.

Again, she remembered the way he'd touched her, the yearning it had enkindled, and the pleasure he had given her, and she imagined that he would turn her now . . . put his arms about her, his fingers pressing into her back, and cover her mouth with warm male lips. She actually quivered with the desire for it.

Cutter had to will himself to leave her be.

He'd asked her to trust him, and he didn't aim to betray that trust. Still and all, there wasn't much left between them . . . just her camisole and bloomers . . . nothing more . . . and it would be so simple, he thought. So simple.

But Elizabeth wasn't the kind of woman you could pick clean and then leave to the buzzards. She didn't deserve that. And he couldn't see himself settling down with a homestead and a pack of brats dogging his heels.

He took a deep, fortifying breath, thinking that

somewhere up there, someone oughta be nominating him for sainthood just about now.

A riot began in Cutter's head as Elizabeth turned suddenly to help him remove her massive skirt. He hated the thing. If he got the chance, he thought he might burn it. Watching intently as she turned to lay the obscene thing aside, Cutter cleared his throat.

The spell broken, he turned to fumble with one of the bedrolls at their feet. Unrolling it, he removed another blanket from it, and then struggled to return as he was, drawing the blanket up over Elizabeth as he scooted upward, shielding her from his view—or more likely, himself from the temptation she presented.

"That better?" His voice sounded strange to his ears.

Elizabeth nodded once, her expression still dazed.

"Good." Again, he cleared his throat, trying to refocus his thoughts, and he smiled faintly, almost regretfully. "You had to go 'n' find a gopher hole for us to shelter in," he told her mildly. Actually it was beginning to feel more like his own private hell, but he didn't say so.

The concern in his tone overshadowed his accusation, and Elizabeth shrugged, averting her gaze in . . . disappointment? Turning on her side, she faced away from him. She couldn't quite look him in the eye after what had just passed between them, because she didn't understand what it was, and somehow, knew that he did.

Cutter's sigh was ragged, as if it took great effort to release the tension from his body. Immediately he took in another deep breath, needing the cleansing air.

At least they were dry, he told himself.

And the shelter wasn't really all that bad. Little enough rain blew in at them on account of the roof being so low. The only thing he could see to be concerned over was the fact that water was beginning to trickle in. But it was a slow stream, and he doubted it would do much harm . . . unless the rain didn't let up. But if he knew anything about late summer storms, and he fancied he did, then it would be over before much longer. It was likely to end as swiftly as it came.

And if worst came to worst, he'd just scoot closer to Elizabeth. He glanced at her suddenly, feeling the tension he'd just alleviated return with full force as he contemplated scooting nearer to her.

Like a pesky gnat, that thought badgered him.

His lips twisted cynically.

Hell, it wasn't as though there were a wall between them—though he'd be damned if it didn't feel like it.

Besides, sainthood never had appealed to him much.

Damn her, anyway—his brows collided violently—if she thought for a minute he was gonna lie here and freeze to death just to protect some squeamish female's tender sensibilities!

With a savage curse, he unsheathed his knife from his left boot, setting it aside, and then he kicked it off. As he undid his shirt buttons, he struggled with the other boot, prodding it with his bare toes, unable to get it off fast enough. It wouldn't come, and he cursed again.

A glance in Elizabeth's direction told him that she was busy ignoring him. But that suited him just fine. Jerking his shirt out of his britches, leaving it wide open, he moved to unfasten his soggy denims—just the thought of being free of the restrictive fabric lightened his mood considerably.

It had nothing to do with the fact that with his own clothes off, there'd be one less barrier to overcome. Hell no, his motives were purely honorable . . . or, at least, not dishonorable.

Well, not really.

Elizabeth heard the pops as he released the buttons of his wet denims, and she tensed. Having ignored the previous warnings—his boot sliding off of his foot, the crinkling of his shirt as he fumbled with it—she was afraid to turn and look Cutter's way. Pulling the blanket a fraction higher, she asked, though she knew better than to do so, "All right, McKenzie. Just what do you think you're doing?"

Chapter 13

❦❧

"What do you think I'm doing?" he returned smoothly, not a trace of misgiving in his tone.

Actually, he sounded more as though he were . . . grinning? "Not undressing, I hope?"

Cutter chuckled richly.

"You can't!" she shrieked, taking his laughter as confirmation. "You can't just lie there with nothing on—not beside me! You do at least have your . . ." Good night, she couldn't even think the word—much less say it!

Guessing at the cause of her hysteria, Cutter chuckled again. "Reckon you'll just have to turn around and find out," he told her, his voice liberally tinged with laughter as he twisted to remove his other boot. His britches were now wrapped about his ankles, their removal hampered by his stubborn-as-hell boot.

Wrenching the blanket over her head, Elizabeth burrowed herself deeper into the wool as his husky laughter rang in her ears . . . along with another sound that seemed strangely like . . . like . . .

A horse's whinny? And it sounded so near . . . yet it couldn't be—but it was—and there it was again!

Cutter, too, had heard and was no longer so amused.

Her curiosity getting the best of her, Elizabeth bur-

164

rowed out of the blanket and turned to stare out into the downpour.

Cutter's body was still twisted, his hands frozen in a death grip upon his right boot, but he was peering out as best he could from under the overhang. In the meantime, Elizabeth stole into his spot, so that when he leaned back for a better view—thinking that it was probably the horses, and that they'd somehow gotten loose—his back touched Elizabeth's damp camisole.

Staring out in horror, Elizabeth never felt the shocking contact, but Cutter did. All thoughts of horses flew out of his mind at once.

"Good night! Cutter, do you see that?"

The proud but blurry silhouette of an Indian materialized from the rain and mist, his horse treading along at a tired pace. Elizabeth crawled forward to better see. Squinting, she could see that he held his head upright, proudly, though it teetered suspiciously before her eyes. What appeared to be two large feathers were outlined in his hair, tilted downward on one side, and his hair seemed to be free, falling just below his broad shoulders. Blinking from the strain of her scrutiny, she refocused and could barely make out a bare chest, painted with what appeared to be red streaks on one side. On his legs, he wore buckskin trousers. The features themselves never sharpened.

Still, she couldn't tear her gaze away.

"What is it?" Cutter fidgeted in order to get a better look.

Suddenly the Indian lurched forward in the saddle, and Elizabeth cried out. "No—oh, no! He's hurt!"

The hairs on the back of Cutter's neck stood in alarm. He quickly tugged his denims back up. "Who's hurt?" he demanded.

But Elizabeth never answered; she was already crawling out of the shelter, into the storm, her fear forgotten suddenly, her modesty dismissed, instinct taking over.

She'd slid past him before Cutter's mind had even had time to register her intent.

"Lizbeth!"

Damn. She was actually going out into the storm? In her friggin' bloomers! Great! Just great! It was just his luck to be saddled with a closet exhibitionist! Fumbling for her legs, Cutter tried to stop her, but Elizabeth was too quick. Bucking upward, he yanked the denims over his rear, and immediately shifted to his stomach, slamming his head into the stone ceiling in the turn. His vision swung to black for an instant. Cursing violently, he clutched at his throbbing head, and started to crawl out after her.

Why the hell had he agreed to this? he wondered irately. Was he a glutton for punishment? Fool woman was determined to get herself killed—him, too, in the process!

And then he saw what had gotten her so distressed, and he cursed a blue streak.

"Lizbeth!"

In slow motion, he saw her running through the downpour, her bloomers and camisole pasted to her body. Her sturdy black shoes splattering mud. "Nooo!" he howled. Damn him, if the little fool wasn't really gonna get herself killed! His stomach lurched. "Elizabeth! No!" It was a ploy—he had to stop her.

His heart hammering in fear, Cutter bolted from his knees, sprinting after her, racing like a man possessed, one boot on, one off. His bare foot lit on something sharp, slicing into his sole, but he didn't feel the pain. In his mind he could see the bastard rising up with a war cry and putting his knife to Elizabeth's lily white throat.

In her panic, Elizabeth never even considered how the horse would view her reckless approach, and she halted abruptly as it snorted, sidling away from her in fear. With the force of that movement, the Indian toppled to one side, sliding listlessly off the horse's back. Acting purely out of instinct, she moved to catch him, and floundered under his incredible weight. The horse moved away immediately, calming with the distance put between them. She clutched the Indian to her breast as her knees buckled, and then tumbled to the soggy ground, falling atop him.

In that instant, Cutter reached her. With a savage cry, he wrenched her off and flung her away. Stumbling, Elizabeth landed on the ground on her backside, her hands flying out behind her to break her fall.

"*God*—damn you!" Cutter snarled, glaring at her furiously.

The barely leashed violence and anger left Elizabeth speechless. She stared back at him as though he were deranged.

Doubling over to catch his breath, legs spread, hands on his knees, shirt hanging open, Cutter stared down at the unconscious man at his feet. Beads of rain dripped from the end of his nose.

Streaks of red flowed from a wound in the brave's chest, running down in watery rivulets to stain his soiled buckskins. Despite that proof of the man's injury, Cutter's anger was far from diminished. *It could very well have been a ruse!* The fact that it wasn't didn't lessen the risk Elizabeth had taken one shred in his mind.

He glowered at her. "Damn me if you even have the brains God gave a snake, woman! Just what did you think you were doing?"

Grating her teeth, Elizabeth glared at Cutter with burning, reproachful eyes. "Can't you see the man is hurt?" she countered, still shaken by his crude handling.

Cutter only gaped at her, his disapproval evident in every rigid plane of his face. Droplets of rain sparkled in his thickening beard as his lips tightened in fury. All he could think of in that moment was that he'd come too close to losing her, and he couldn't bear the thought of it.

It tore at his gut.

Like nothing before.

Stooping over the unconscious brave, Cutter plucked open the man's lids and then felt for a pulse at his neck. Satisfied with the results, he turned again to glare at Elizbeth. "What if he hadn't been? What if it had been an act—a trick to sniff us out? What then, *Doc?*"

He mocked her, she realized, with the use of her title, but knowing instinctively that there was no time for his rebuke, regardless of the sense it made, Elizabeth stood abruptly, swiping her palms over her wet bloomers. "But it wasn't!" she returned. "He *is* hurt—and *I am a doctor.* He needs me, McKenzie, so if you don't plan on assisting, then just get out of my way!"

Her unexpected voice of authority took Cutter aback, but he never let the surprise show on his face. In spite of his anger, he couldn't argue with the facts; the man *did* need immediate medical attention. He gave her a curt nod, yielding, though grudgingly.

Above them, a watery sun appeared through the drizzle as Elizabeth rushed to aid the unconscious Indian. Brushing past Cutter, she determined to ignore the brief contact of their bodies, but couldn't. Even in her fury, his touch made her heart react strangely.

But her body's reaction to him was completely forgotten when she looked down into the young brave's face. The cast of his skin was a sickly blue, and she knew what that signified. Automatically she felt for a pulse on his neck. Feeling it, though faintly, she blew a sigh of relief. Her heart raced with hope. "He's in shock," she explained as Cutter stood behind, watching, a little in awe of her calm proficiency.

The wound was deep, gaping, and ragged—almost as if he had been cut repeatedly in the same spot. There was so much blood that it was difficult to tell whether or not there was some foreign object still lodged within. Gulping down her uncertainty, she fingered the wound, and finding nothing, determined there was not. Whatever had been there had been removed already.

As if by some sixth sense, her gaze fell on the small knife he had sheathed at his side. The handle was bloody . . . and she knew instinctively what had happened. Evidently he'd attempted to remove whatever had been lodged there on his own . . . and had nicked an artery? Or worse, had he severed one? How much blood had he lost? How long had he been bleeding?

Biting down on her bottom lip, she glowered up at Cutter. "Well! Don't just stand there, McKenzie—help me get him inside!" The rain had slowed considerably, and in that moment, ceased entirely. "Never mind," she said abruptly. "Just move him closer to the shelter." Knowing Cutter was perfectly capable of carrying the man by himself, she hurried to retrieve her discarded skirt, along with her bedroll.

The roll, she quickly unfurled, and then motioned for Cutter to place the brave upon it while she fumbled with her skirt. No sooner had he set the man down when she began tearing the sagging hem from her old skirt, inspecting it as it came into her hands.

She hadn't recalled her state of dress until she'd spotted her skirt lying across the floor of the dugout, and though she was disconcerted to be caught undressed in the broad light of day, there had been no time to worry over it . . . nor was there now.

The first foot of the hem was incredibly filthy from having dragged the ground, and she ripped it away completely. The rest she deemed perfectly suitable and divided it into strips. Immediately she began forming compresses for the wound, pressing the first one into place while she formed another.

Cutter watched her work in silence, admiring her stoicism.

"Start a fire," she demanded suddenly, without turning. Taking a deep, shuddering breath, she tried desperately to forget the hungry look she'd spied in

Cutter's eyes when she'd crawled back out of the dugout, clenching her skirt in her teeth, and shoving her bedroll out before her. There was no time to be exhilarated at the desire she'd spied there, she reminded herself firmly. But somewhere in the back of her mind . . . she thrilled to it, despite herself.

It took Cutter a full moment to grasp what Elizabeth had demanded of him, but when he did, his face contorted as though he thought she were mentally unbalanced. "Hell no!"

Elizabeth glared up at him, all the while applying increasing pressure to stanch the rapid flow of blood. "I have to cauterize his wound," she ground out. "He's losing too much blood!"

Cutter's gaze never faltered. "No." His tone remained unyielding.

"Why not?" Elizabeth retorted. Then, seeing the set of his jaw, she appealed, her voice breaking suddenly, "He'll die!" She couldn't believe Cutter could be so cold.

"We can't be sure he's alone," Cutter stated matter-of-factly. "If he's got friends out there, then we're better off not drawing attention to ourselves. Besides, Lizbeth, the man's already dead—I've seen that look too many times not to know. You can't save him," he said bluntly.

Her eyes pleaded with him. "How can you be so heartless?" she asked him. "Certainly they would understand that I mean to help him?"

Cutter's expression remained shuttered as he shook his head, his jaw setting all the more stubbornly. "Can't take that chance," he said evenly. If it were only himself he had to worry over, he'd have done so without a second thought. But he wasn't alone. And he wasn't about to risk Elizabeth.

Furiously Elizabeth turned on him. "I *don't* think you understand, McKenzie. *I* don't intend to let this man die! Fact is, if you don't start that blasted fire, then I will!" Again, she added a compress, giving a concerned shake of her head. "He's lost so much blood already . . . can't lose much more." She glanced back up at Cutter, her heart in her eyes. "Please, Cutter," she appealed. As he watched, her eyes glazed with unshed tears, startling him with their heart-wrenching intensity. "Please."

When she put it like that, Cutter couldn't begin to deny her. Disgusted with himself, he spun away. Cursing to himself, he buttoned up his shirt and hastily tucked one side into his denims.

As he'd feared, the fire took quite a while to kindle with the wood so wet, and sent up a considerable amount of smoke in the process. Shaking his head, he watched it curl upward with no small measure of concern.

In the meantime, Elizabeth had cleaned the wound area as best she could without removing the bandages. She could only hope that the rain had managed to clean the laceration itself sufficiently, because she didn't dare remove the bandage and start the bleeding all over again. At least not until she was ready to cauterize. He'd lost too much blood already. As it was, it was still flowing, only much slower than before. And all the while, the Indian brave lay without moving, not even a twitch of his brow. He seemed completely unaware that anyone was tending him at all.

When the fire was lit to his satisfaction, Cutter retrieved his knife from the dugout, where he'd tossed it, and held it over the flames, trying in vain not to gawk at Elizabeth's dusky areolas through her threadbare camisole. It was a good thing the brave was unconscious, he thought viciously, because he might have to kill the bastard if he so much as set eyes on Elizabeth at the moment. Her breasts were so close to the Indian's face . . . and for a moment he imagined himself lying there instead, his lips so close . . .

His face contorted suddenly.

What the hell was wrong with him?

A man lay dying before him—a man whom, at any another time, Cutter would have likely killed for, all for the blood they shared—and here he was with murder on his mind, for the sake of a woman.

But not just any woman.

As much as he hated to admit the fact . . . Elizabeth Bowcock had gotten under his skin. The spine-tingling fear he'd felt when he'd spied her running headlong into danger was something he'd never forget . . . not if he lived a hundred lifetimes.

She'd somehow become as vital to him . . . as nothing ever had been before. And though he hesitated to put a name to the emotion, he suspected it nonetheless.

And it made him sick to his gut.

Because it made him susceptible, and he didn't like that one damned bit.

Chapter 14

O nce the blade was hot enough, Cutter handed it
to Elizabeth, hilt-first, and watched in disbelief
as his little mouse did her dirty work, never flinching,
or even hesitating in her duty. The transformation in
her was startling. He'd been well aware of the sparks
beneath her surface, but the woman before him
seemed wholly different from the one he'd thought
he knew. He'd have offered to help had he not been
so stunned by her proficiency. As it was, he couldn't
tear his gaze away, even when the stench of burning
flesh reached his nostrils.

For the briefest moment, the brave opened his eyes,
catching Elizabeth's gaze, and she immediately
wrenched the burning knife away, not wanting to
hurt him, but his lids fell again without his ever having acknowledged her.

Squaring her shoulders, Elizabeth finished with the
wound, and then again began tearing strips from the
length of her skirt. With it, she bound the man's
chest. And then very quickly—unable to stand her
state of dress any longer—she slipped the much-
shortened skirt on, deliberately avoiding Cutter's gaze
as she laced up the front. Finally, kneeling again, her
cheeks as warm as the Indian's appeared, she drew a
blanket up to his chin in order to conserve his body
heat.

Shaking her head gravely, she contemplated the

173

bright flush in his face, determining that he would
need an infusion for the fever before long. Liquids,
too—she was certain that they had a little salt in Cutter's satchel. She'd add that, as well—to help replace
his body fluids. Of course, there was no way she
could administer any of it while he was unconscious,
but she could certainly have it prepared for him when
he did wake.

Instinctively she examined the man's forehead for
fever, sliding her hand down his face to his scalding
neck. There she turned the back of her hand against
his skin.

"Cutter," she began, thinking that surely there was
something . . . some herb growing in the area that
she could use for an infusion. There had to be. She
glanced about, quickly surveying the area. White wil-
low bark would be perfect, but as far as she could
see, there were only pine and oak . . . as well as a
few birch.

Unable to help himself, Cutter stared at Elizabeth's
dignified profile as she, in turn, perused the landscape, her lashes so dark, her eyes slitted slightly as
she concentrated on the view. Inadvertently meeting
his gaze, she looked quickly away, sliding her hand
beneath the woolen blanket to probe at the Indian's
bare flesh. Against his will, Cutter's own body jolted
in response, reacting purely out of instinct, feeling
the heat of her hand as though it were upon his own
flesh.

Damn him, anyhow, he groused—he'd never have
believed the passion with which she was treating the
Indian. It didn't seem to matter to her at the moment
that he was nothing more than a *heathen savage*—her
own words—only that he was a man, and that he
needed her. And that knowledge crumpled the last
of his armor.

And damn her, too, because without even trying,
she'd managed to reach in and fill that part of him
he'd once thought would never see the light of day

again. The farthest reaches of his hard-as-hell heart.
Uneasy with the intensity of emotion he was feeling
suddenly, he cleared his throat, and Elizabeth finally
looked up at him, her expression as troubled as his
own.

If she could feel so much for a stranger, he found
himself wondering, how much more could she give
to the man she loved? Cursing himself roundly, he
shook off the thought, turning away.

"Cutter?"

He stopped, though reluctantly, and turned back
toward her.

"Would you watch over him? Please . . . while I
see what herbs I can locate?"

Her tawny eyes pleaded with him, though they
needn't have, because it was suddenly as important
to Cutter that she save the man as it seemed to be to
her.

As he saw it, it didn't pay much to get sentimental
over anything, not people, not horses, not even life
itself. He'd learned long ago that in this world, things
came, and then they simply went—just like that. And
there wasn't a damned thing anybody could do about
it. Uncharitable as it may have been, he hadn't felt
much for the Indian brave, except maybe an odd sense
of futility—hell, he could have sworn the man was
dead in the saddle. But maybe, just maybe, Elizabeth
could save him. Her desire for it sure was infectious.
Maybe sheer will alone could do it.

"He's already much too warm," she entreated
again, mistaking his hesitation for reluctance.

His throat too thick to speak, Cutter nodded, and
Elizabeth smiled gratefully, leaping up to hug him
quickly before he could think to change his mind.

With his booted foot, he kicked at a clump of wet
sod, and then sank down upon the corner end of the
bedroll. "Just stay within sight," he muttered after
her.

Nearly an hour later, to Elizabeth's dismay, she had

found nothing of use. There were coneflowers, gay-feathers, fameflower, even some larkspur—the former all worthless, and the latter? Well, her intent was to cure the poor man, not kill him. When finally she gave up and returned to camp, she returned empty-handed.

Watching her approach, Cutter stood, shaking his head at the unspoken question in her eyes. Slapping his hat—which he'd retrieved in her absence, along with his other boot—upon his knee, he gave her a grim twist of his lips, and then replaced the hat to his head with a deep sigh.

At his unspoken revelation, Elizabeth's shoulders wilted a little further. With a weary sigh of her own, she dropped herself into the very spot Cutter had warmed, nodding dejectedly as her gaze returned to the unconscious Indian.

Considering her, Cutter watched a moment longer, before turning away. Without a doubt, he knew he couldn't leave her to go off hunting—not while she was so distracted. He was sure the man wasn't alone. Even if he had been, the fire was smoking so much—probably sending off signals for miles. He stared at it with disgust, following the smoke into the sky a moment as he contemplated that thought.

The river was within sight, so he found himself a sturdy stick, along with a thick tree to set his back against while he worked. Sprawling backward and raising a knee, he unsheathed his blade and began whittling a spear to fish with, all the while watching Elizabeth from a distance and admiring her professional dedication to the Indian. She worked diligently, never abandoning hope. It wasn't until she'd examined the man's face and skin for fever the umpteenth time, without a single sign of recovery, that he shook his head over the futility of it all.

He was almost finished with the lance when the throbbing of his foot began to bother him. Rising, he made his way down to the river. Sitting, he jerked off his boot and sighed as he examined the clean slice in the arch of his left foot. He had no idea what he'd stepped on, only that it smarted like the dickens. But he'd had worse, so he washed it out as well as he could in the river, and then headed back to camp, spotting a bramble bush on the way. They hadn't eaten anything but jerky all day long, and he knew Elizabeth was sure to be famished by now, so he gathered up a handful and carried them to her, dumping the blackberries unceremoniously into her lap.

It didn't surprise him much when she didn't stir at first. What concerned him, though, was that even after a long moment, she still didn't seem to realize he was standing there watching her. Like a gloomy statuette, she continued to watch over the unconscious brave. And when she did finally acknowledge him, it took her another long moment to ascertain that he'd placed something in the folds of her ragged skirt. But seeing it finally, her eyes lit up.

Her eyes widened ever so slightly. "Blackberries?" she whispered with a note of enthusiasm.

Cutter tilted his brows, looking at her a little uncertainly.

"Where'd you get them?" she demanded at once, snatching one up, inspecting it with a strange shimmer in her eyes.

Cutter opened his mouth to reply, but she cut him off.

"Merciful Lord!" she exclaimed suddenly. "Please tell me there are more!"

Hell, Cutter thought, he'd known she'd be hungry, but for the life of him, he couldn't see her reaction to the berries as normal. Frowning at her in earnest, he rubbed at his beard with concern.

"Oh, Cutter!" Elizabeth exclaimed happily, glancing up at him briefly, then back to the berry in question. "Do you know what these are?" She laughed infectiously. "*Do you know what these are?*" she re-

peated with glee, still staring, wild-eyed now, at the
berry poised like a precious gold nugget between her
delicate fingers.

Stooping to look her straight in the eye, Cutter
grasped Elizabeth by the shoulder, forcing her attention on him. Capturing it finally, he nodded slowly.
"Yeah. Blackberries." He wondered if her wits had
finally gone beggin'. "Lizbeth, gal, you all right?"

Without warning, Elizabeth's arms flew out and
caught him about the neck, squeezing joyfully—
choking him. Reflexively he pried at her arms, loos-
ening her grip.

"More than all right!" Elizabeth replied joyfully.
"The leaves will do wonders for fever!" The warmth
of her lips moved like liquid heat against his face. As
she drew back to look at him, her gaze transformed
before his eyes, from hopelessness to something akin
to adoration, and it took him momentarily aback. He
had to fight the urge to pull her back and cover her
mouth with his own.

"An infusion of the leaves would be perfect," she
explained, but Cutter wasn't listening, he couldn't
quite tear his eyes away from her mouth.

"Just perfect!" he heard her repeat gleefully, and
then she suddenly kissed him—in the eye. With a
heartening smile, she turned again to her patient.

"Now, don't you worry," she said, a note of gaiety
shining through. She lifted one knee, preparing to
rise. "I'll have you well in no time! You'll see!" She
patted his arm reassuringly.

As if in response, the Indian abruptly lifted his lids,
and Elizabeth rocked forward onto both knees at once,
as though, with that small effort, he had somehow
jerked her back to him. She gave a startled little cry.

The dark stare was vacant, the pupils dilated and
huge. Noting it, Elizabeth felt suddenly ill. *Too late*
was her first thought, but she shoved it resolutely
away.

He was *not* going to die!

She wouldn't let him!

This was the first time since her father's death that a patient's life was at stake . . . the first time *ever* anyone had depended solely on *her* skills to survive. She couldn't fail—her father wouldn't have, and neither could she.

Ignoring the implications of what she saw in the young Indian's eyes, she thrust her palm boldly over his brow, her own brows slanting dejectedly at the feel of his flesh. He'd been as hot as an iron over a fire only moments before, but his skin was swiftly losing its rosy tint, turning as pale as if he were already dead.

A knot formed in her throat. "If only . . . if only I could make . . . the infusion," she began, her voice painfully soft, catching abruptly on the last word as if it were suddenly too difficult to speak.

As if by cue, a soft drizzle began. Cutter watched as Elizabeth caught the brave's hand into her own, clutching it stubbornly. A lone tear trickled down her cheek and she took a shuddering breath as the jet black pupils constricted before her eyes.

"No," she whispered dismally. "No—don't die. I'm not finished yet . . ." Her plea sounded pitiful, like a forsaken child calling out for comfort. When, an instant later, the brave's last breath passed with a slight tremor of his limbs, her shoulders immediately began to quake.

Even knowing there was nothing more she could do, Elizabeth couldn't tear her gaze away, couldn't release his hand. To let him go was to let him slip away forever. Her lips began to quiver as his pupils became little more than pinpricks, his stare as empty as black glass. "Oh, Papa," she cried softly, still unable to release the young brave's hand. Nor could she look away. "Oh, no . . . no . . . no . . ."

She looked up, pleading. "Oh, Cutter," she sobbed, swallowing the thickening lump in her throat. Against the back of her hand, the mist continued to fall in cool sprinkles, while against her palm, the Indian's flesh turned as cold as the mist. And she knew, as surely as she breathed, that he was irretrievably gone.

"Not fair!" she cried out suddenly, and with a choking sob, she laid the cold hand reverently upon the unmoving chest. Vaguely she was aware of Cutter reaching out for her. Turning to him, she thrust herself into his arms.

Chapter 15

"Life ain't fair," Cutter whispered. Comforting in the only way he knew how, he stroked Elizabeth's back and shoulders soothingly, profoundly moved by her compassion for the Indian. He lifted her chin so that he could see her tearstained face, but she stubbornly avoided his gaze and kept her eyes downcast as another tear slid past her dark lashes. His own eyes stinging against his volition, he wiped her cheek with his thumb. This time she didn't protest his callused touch. "Your first?" he whispered hoarsely.

Elizabeth nodded jerkily, restraining her sobs.

"Thought so," he said gruffly. "Listen to me, bright eyes, there wasn't a damned thing more you could have done to save him. Nothing." His tone was gentle, soothing, though his blood was beginning to heat with the feel of her in his arms. Whether he wanted to or not, in that moment he felt more drawn to her than he'd ever thought possible. More than he had ever been to any woman.

At last Elizabeth peered up at him through dampened lashes, but her eyes seemed darker somehow, deeper than before, as though this single death had in some way shaken her deep, deep down.

"I should have known what to do!" she cried mournfully. Her palm splayed upon his chest, her fingers toying nervously with his button.

As he felt the timid gesture, Cutter's blood began a slow simmer. Damn him, if she wasn't making this hard on him. He forced his gaze away from her budding nipples. Her body's innocent reaction to him both thrilled and tormented him simultaneously.

"I should have saved him. I could have—my father would have!" For this alone she had lived her life, driven herself, even. If she was incompetent at this, her one ambition, then everything had been in vain—her life without purpose! "There must have been something I missed . . . something I didn't do right . . . something . . ." she broke off miserably, glancing up at Cutter with pleading eyes. Tears sparkled on her lashes.

With a will of their own, his hands slid to her waist, then inched to her back as he kissed her forehead once, firmly, feeling his body tense. Then again, his control slipping with every second she lingered in his arms.

He took a deep, mind-cleansing breath, but it was the worst thing he could have done, because with it, the scent of her filled his nostrils. He groaned, and thought with self-disgust that at the moment, he didn't feel much more than aggravation at the Indian for dying so inconveniently.

Hell, he felt for the man, but not as much as he *felt* for Elizabeth. Unfitting as it was, his body didn't seem to have grasped the seriousness of the situation. Thankfully, his mind still clung to a shred of sanity.

His voice sounded gruff, tortured. "You did all you could for the man, Doc." His fingers brushed aside a damp tendril from her face.

"Don't call me that!" Elizabeth protested weakly, jerking away from his touch, smacking at his hand when he brought it back to her face.

Misunderstanding her reaction, Cutter sighed and gently drew her away from him.

"They were right to doubt me," she murmured unhappily, ''all of them! It's just that . . . that . . . I—I tried so hard . . . so very hard . . .''

Cutter could imagine her suddenly, fighting tirelessly to win the townsfolk's approval. In spite of the fact that she had practically stepped into her daddy's shoes, it wouldn't have been a simple task to win their respect. Yet clearly she had, because he'd heard them refer to her as Doc, and without any reservation at all. He couldn't let her begin doubting herself now.

And he couldn't help himself suddenly.

Driven by the need to soothe away her pain—not to mention the influence of his nether regions—his lips touched her salty lashes, pressing them softly against her moist lids, then moved down to the bridge of her nose to plant another tender kiss there.

At last the sprinkling ceased altogether, though neither of them were aware of it, so lost were they in the intensity of the moment; Elizabeth in her self-doubt and grief, and Cutter in his physical torment.

His throat thickened with emotion. ''Shhh, bright eyes.'' His lips brushed against hers as he spoke. ''Don't cry.''

Suddenly his mouth covered hers hungrily, coaxing with savage intensity, crushing her to him, sending waves of shock spiraling through her. She was astounded at her eager response; unable to deny him, Elizabeth opened for him willingly. He gripped her shoulders roughly, and the shock of his tongue delving gently between her trembling lips quieted her sobs at once. Her breathing stopped entirely as one hand moved to grip the back of her neck, restraining her so that she couldn't have withdrawn from the soul-searing kiss had she wanted to. His other hand splayed at her back, forcing her into full contact with the hard planes of his body.

Helpless to contain it, Elizabeth whimpered deep in her throat, unable to bear the intense pleasure of it . . . yet feeling conscience-stricken that she could

experience such overwhelming joy over a *kiss* . . .
when a man lay lifeless at their feet!

But Lord, she wanted this . . . more than anything
. . . wanted the comfort he could give her. Merciful
heaven, what was wrong with her?

With a tortured cry, Elizabeth suddenly shoved
Cutter away, repulsed by her actions, and knowing
that if she didn't stop him now, she'd soon be begging him to continue.

"How could you?" she demanded breathlessly.
How could she? her mind shouted in rebuttal. Cutter's
eyes were so black that she had the momentary sensation of toppling headfirst into their murky depths.
She felt divested completely of her will.

Only Cutter's self-restraint kept her from shaming
herself further.

The lift of his brow sent a curious chill down her
spine. "Easy, Doc," he answered huskily, and her
body tingled where his eyes touched her so boldly.
"The hard part was keeping myself from it." His lips
twisted wryly.

Mesmerized by his disclosure, Elizabeth could only
gape at him stupidly, disbelieving his callousness, yet
secretly thrilling to his words. "I asked you not to call
me that!" she said, averting her eyes. More than a
little discomfited by his piercing stare, she sought refuge in outrage—before she could be tempted to throw
herself on his mercy. Ruthless as Cutter was, he
wouldn't turn her away, she was certain. Fighting
back tears, she tried to rise, but Cutter kept her from
it with one hand to her shoulder.

Knowing full well that the moment was over, Cutter sighed regretfully. Aware of the fact that Elizabeth
seemed to take strength in her anger, he told her with
a slow lift of his brow, "Maybe you're right, *Doc*.
Maybe you don't have what it takes, after all. Maybe
the man *was* better off without you. Y' think—*Doc?*"

It took a befuddled moment for his unfeeling words
to register, and then Elizabeth's eyes widened in of-

fense. She slapped him. "No!" she cried. "I don't! I
did everything I knew to do! Everything! Everything!"

At his nod of agreement, Elizabeth hushed
abruptly, her shoulders slumping and her face contorting with grief. "I'm sorry!" Tears swam in her
eyes, choking her voice. "Oh, Cutter," she whimpered. "I did—I swear, I did. And still . . . it wasn't
enough!"

Cutter rubbed his jaw belatedly, where the imprint
of her small hand was beginning to form, and Elizabeth looked at him sorrowfully, her lips quivering pitifully.

"I've seen so many die—men, women, brothers,
babies. It's not the dying itself that hurts so much . . . .
just that this time—" she tapped softly at her breast,
once again beginning to cry, calling his attention back
to the diaphanous camisole "—I was the only thing
standing between life and death . . . and I failed—
miserably!"

With a muttered oath, Cutter caught her by the
shoulders, gripping her firmly. "No you didn't, Lizbeth," he said bluntly. "That's what I've been trying
to tell you! The man was already six feet under when
he fell off that horse! I tried to tell you as much—
remember? But you wouldn't listen. There was nothing
more you could have done." He softened his voice
abruptly, wanting her to understand. "As my mother's people would have said, The Shadow had long left
him, he only breathed. Chrissakes, woman, don't you
know how proud of you I am?"

Elizabeth was startled by his declaration; her gaze
flew to his. The heat in his eyes was overpowering.
"P-Proud?" she asked hesitantly. Somehow she
needed so much for it to be true.

Cutter nodded, wiping away the glowing moistness from her eyes. "Proud," he repeated with a
slow, firm nod. Then, with a tormented groan, he
brushed the back of his hand across her cheek, rev-

eling in her sweet softness. Now was not the time, he knew, this not the place.

But soon . . . real soon. He couldn't wait much longer. His body was literally in pain with need of her.

"Damn proud," he whispered again, almost reverently this time. And then, with a wink, he touched her bottom lip with his scarred finger, rolling it gently to reveal the soft inner flesh.

The coarseness of his touch sent a shiver through Elizabeth.

For a long moment, neither of them could look away, so strong was the pull between them.

Then, rising abruptly with a rueful sigh, Cutter hauled Elizabeth up with him. "Come on, Doc, let's give the man a proper resting place and then move on downriver." He didn't want her to dwell on what had happened here, and knew that she wouldn't begin to forget until they were away from the place.

Having no shovels available to bury the Indian, Cutter decided to enclose him within the dugout. The opening was just slim enough that it was possible to close it off with a few large boulders and some dirt. After removing their belongings from the grotto, they moved the Indian within. And while Cutter worked to seal up the tomb, Elizabeth quickly assumed her damp shirt, and then set to packing the horses as she'd seen Cutter do so many times now.

When Cutter was finished at last, it was all but impossible to tell that there had ever been an opening in the stone structure. To the undiscerning glance, it appeared to be no more than a mass of odd-sized boulders, all clumped together.

Finally he spoke a few words over the makeshift crypt, and Elizabeth placed an impromptu bouquet of white sage and fameflower atop it, feeling somehow accountable for the Indian's death—even knowing it was ridiculous to feel that way. Still, she didn't think she'd ever forget him. And it was difficult to leave him all alone in his final resting place. Despite the fact that she knew absolutely nothing at all about the poor man, she felt some queer bond with him . . . and knew deep down that she always would.

Always.

Filled with sorrow, her eyes took in the precipitous cliffs in the distance, the river flowing heedlessly by, and the blooming meadow interspersed with trees. Ahead of them, the Missouri seemed eternal, the bluffs unreachable.

All in all, it was a very lonely place.

"No one will ever know that he's here," she lamented, her eyes shimmering.

Tapping his hat briskly on his thigh, Cutter scanned the bluff top. "Oh, I don't know," he replied shortly. Placing his hat on his head, he tapped it low over his eyes. "I expect someone will."

Elizabeth's eyes immediately followed the path his had taken, finding absolutely nothing. Swallowing the lump in her throat, she turned away and mounted up.

With a last narrow-eyed glance at the bluff, Cutter did the same.

They didn't go far, just out of sight of the tomb. And while Elizabeth hadn't thought she could eat anything after the ordeal they'd gone through, by the time they made camp once more, and Cutter fished up dinner, she was so ravenous that she was certain she could eat an entire river full of trout.

After supper, to her surprise, instead of putting out the cooking fire, Cutter added more kindling, and then settled on a half-rotted log near it. Keeping herself occupied so as not to think of the Indian, Elizabeth unfurled her bedroll, and Cutter's, as well, wondering how she would bear the thought of sleeping where a man had died. She didn't think she could.

For all that he'd seemed preoccupied, Cutter hadn't missed the look of bewilderment Elizabeth had given him over the fire, but he didn't comment. The only explanation he could have given was that he sure as cuss *was* going to make love to her tonight, and he wanted to see every exquisite inch of her while he was doing it. His foot hurt like hell, but something else ached a whole lot worse. And he was tired of being chivalrous, tired of not sleeping nights because she was lying so close that he couldn't get her scent out of his system, tired of burning. If he had his druthers, he'd be anything but gentlemanly.

It went against his grain.

Besides, it seemed they had a few guardian angels on their trail, and he doubted anyone would approach tonight without him knowing it.

He'd spotted the trio of Indians just after he'd finished burying the brave. He just wasn't certain why they'd remained hidden from view, instead of coming forward to help bury their own—unless they hadn't trusted him?

Still, if there were only three of them, it was likely they hadn't approached because they weren't packin' iron. And that was another reason he'd decided to get the hell away from the tomb. Totin' or not, Cutter was sure they intended to reclaim their friend—or, at the very least, check out his handiwork. In either case, he had no desire to get in their way.

As he saw it, there wasn't too much cause to be concerned about them stealing into camp tonight, because he'd purposely left the dead Indian's horse for them as a token of good faith. He was glad Elizabeth hadn't asked over it. Luckily, she'd been so distraught that she hadn't even noticed the horse grazing in the meadow when they'd left. But he was certain the Indians *had*, even if she hadn't.

With a quick glance at the darkening bluff, he slid down to sit on the ground, setting his back against the log. It had been at least an hour since he'd last spotted the Indians, and unless he missed his guess, they were likely at the tomb, even now.

And that suited him perfectly.

His gaze was immediately drawn to Elizabeth. Walking into his hands, like a butterfly to a spider's web, she approached him, a fair amount of her slim calves showing below the tattered hem of her skirt. Her sturdy black shoes were grimy as hell, and he focused on them as she sat primly on the log beside him. Smoothing her fingers across the deep-set wrinkles in her skirt, she looked a lot like a dirty little waif sitting there, trying to impress him with her self-control—when he knew deep down she wasn't finished with her cry. She was holding it back stoically, and he had to admire her for that.

"That certainly was satisfying," she remarked conversationally, alluding to the fish. "Much better than jerky or . . ." She glanced at him coyly, admiring his lean, dark-skinned profile, the fine lines that crinkled at the corners of his eyes. "What did you call it? Puddle leaper?"

Cutter chuckled at her ascetic tone. "Jumper," he corrected, with a twinkling glance upward. *"Puddle jumper."* Her tawny eyes still held a certain sheen to them, seeming to glow in the fading light. Without being asked to, Cutter rose and sat beside her on the log, leaning forward to rest his forearms on his knees, his legs spread till they were just shy of hers. There he remained, staring at the ground a sober moment, before turning to look her in the eye.

Elizabeth's pulse quickened as his smoldering black eyes met hers. He was sitting so very close. So close that if she only moved her leg a fraction to the right, they'd touch. Did she dare? Lord, give her strength. They were so close that his body heat made her burn. Like a wick to fuel, she felt his intoxicating warmth seeping into her, feeding her in some unknown way, making her restless.

Swallowing tightly, she stared at his powerful-looking hands, which were now threaded loosely in front of him, and closed her eyes with the sudden undeniable need to reach out and touch them. She was sitting so close, it seemed impossible not to. And before she could think to deny herself, she did exactly that.

More so than she'd imagined, his flesh burned where her fingers touched his forearm, sending lightning bolts shivering through her, clear to the tips of her breasts. She thrilled to the texture of his skin—so masculine, so warm—unaware that every emotion was apparent in her expression. She resisted the urge to smooth her fingers along the springy hairs of his arm.

Mesmerized by the feel of him, it took every ounce of her will to emerge from the haze of pleasure enveloping her, and she tried desperately to seem casual. But her voice didn't quite sound normal, even to her own ears. "Thank you, Cutter, for understanding . . . when I needed it most." Her golden eyes beckoned him, even without her realizing they did. She swallowed convulsively, clearing away the raw ache from her throat. "And . . . and for your kind words."

Cutter's gaze met hers briefly, softening. "No kindness intended, I assure you." Seeing her brows draw together in confusion, he added, "Just the truth. You did real good back there, Doc."

"Did you think I'd won my title by default?" she asked, without offense. Too many had wondered the same about her to fault Cutter for his misgivings.

He gave her a guilty twist of his lips. "Reckon I'd be lying if I said no. The thought had crossed my mind a time or two." Deliberately his eyes returned to her hand on his arm, her trembling fingers, then back to her face, as if to caution her somehow.

She sighed a little tremulously. "And you wouldn't be all wrong. I didn't take instruction in some fancy school back east." She looked up into his eyes. "But I made an eager pupil to my father—and he *had* earned his degree. Besides that, I devoured every book on healing and herbs I could get my hands on."

Her eyes moved down to where Cutter's were still focused. Her fingers. But, try as she might, she couldn't remove them from his arm, even knowing she must appear appallingly brazen. Somewhere, deep down, she knew what she was inviting . . . and couldn't stop herself.

Her lashes fluttered closed with that revelation, and she willed her breath to slow. When she opened her eyes again, her heart turned over violently. The unmistakable heat flickering in Cutter's black eyes startled her.

Was it possible? she dared to hope. That he could desire her, too? Suddenly she felt giddy. With all the terrible things Elizabeth had heard of men's self-control, it had been impossible to believe that Cutter had done nothing more than kiss her now and again, when they'd spent so much time alone together. Yet it was true. And though she'd told herself it was what was right . . . that she was glad of it . . . it also stung.

Now her heart danced with the possibility. He'd looked at her just so a number of times, but it had seemed inconceivable that he could—that anyone would. Yet the proof was right there in his eyes. A slow burn, a hunger, smoldering there, sparking an answering flame deep within her. Absurdly, with nothing more than his naked gaze, he stoked her own budding passion to an exhilarating peak.

Before she could stop herself, her fingers slid boldly down to his hand, turning it gently to her scrutiny, and exposing his disfigurement. Once again, their gazes met and held, neither of them able to break away from whatever force held them snared. Cutter said absolutely nothing.

But then, Elizabeth hadn't expected him to. He wasn't the sort of man who would reveal anything easily. Yet she sensed that the moment was right. And she needed to know. "How—"

The shadows deepened in his eyes, making them appear fathomless, as though one could topple into the depths of them and never, ever, find her way back into the light . . . as though they'd seen more than a man should have. "Leave it be, Doc. You don't wanna know."

Elizabeth's gaze never wavered. Despite his closed expression, she sensed his vulnerability. "Yes, I do," she insisted, her voice soft but determined.

Cutter sighed ruefully, shaking his head, as though he begrudged himself the comfort she was offering, yet couldn't turn it away. His voice sounded gruff. "It's not anything worth digging up, Liz . . . too long ago now."

Acting out of impulse, as well as the need to return the comfort he'd given earlier, Elizabeth lifted his hand to her lips, squeezing with compassion. And then, before she could stop herself, she was kissing each scalding fingertip, lingering on each, as though to kiss them were to heal them.

As he watched her through heavy-lidded eyes, growing heavier, Cutter's insides vaulted. His throat constricted. "Lizbeth," he said thickly. "I don't think you know what you're doing, gal."

Elizabeth chose that moment to meet his gaze, and what was revealed in the depths of them made Cutter's pulses leap to life.

Damn him, if the little harridan wasn't trying to seduce him!

Why he suddenly felt compelled to warn her off, he didn't know. But he did. He had the feeling that she was riding on instinct, that too many days on the trail with a man had made her vulnerable, and he didn't want her that way.

She kissed another finger compassionately, her eyes closing with the intensity of her feeling. "Lizbeth," he groaned. But further words failed him—to hell with good intentions!

With a tortured moan, he lifted her up, into the spot between his legs. Weakened by the quivering of her limbs, Elizabeth couldn't help but sink to her

knees with a gasp of surprise. With a grunt of satisfaction, he wrapped his arms about her, hauling her
up against himself. His hand went to her throat, his
thumb beneath her chin, raising it up.

Elizabeth never even thought to protest. She knew
he was going to kiss her . . . prayed that he would,
even . . . wanted it so badly. His gaze grew heavier
as he drew her closer, as if he would pull her inside
of himself, and then, very slowly, his mouth slanted
over hers, warm, hard, and unyielding, and Elizabeth
swore she'd suddenly died and gone to heaven.

Chapter 16

He kissed her deeply, feverishly, as though he were losing himself with every second that passed, and Elizabeth found herself clinging, arching toward him desperately, her body seeking out his instinctively.

It felt so good. So right . . . the yearning so deep. Warmth began a slow coil deep within her, creeping out into her limbs, making them languid with desire. More than anything, she wanted to give herself to Cutter. It really didn't matter that nothing could come of it later. Nothing mattered. Only this—the moment. And she intended to seize it. She'd had so few in her life . . . so very few . . . and this was one she couldn't deny herself. Lord help her, but she couldn't.

So intent was she on the interplay of their mouths that she hadn't even felt Cutter undo the braid from her hair. But suddenly she was aware that he was threading his hand through the length of it, separating the long, rain-thickened strands with great care as if it were rare silk, freshly washed, instead of damp and unkempt. Like a man consumed, he brought a lock to his nostrils, and they flared with the scent of it. The look of intense pleasure on his face sent a warm quickening through her.

His lips were scalding against her ear. "Sooo long," he hissed. "I've wanted to do that for so long." He kissed her lobe, nibbling it gently, all the while combing his fingers through the length of her hair. Tilting her head just so, he brushed the side of her face, sighing into her hair. The tenderness of his touch was almost unbearable.

With her hair down, Elizabeth looked so soft . . . so soft. He couldn't fathom why she'd wear it any other way. "Lizbeth," he whispered, "don't you ever just wanna let down your hair . . . be free?"

She did. Sometimes the feeling fairly overwhelmed her. Sometimes . . . sometimes she craved nothing more than to kick off the heavy high-button shoes she wore and run barefoot through the fields . . . to laugh . . . How long had it been since she had laughed? Truly laughed? Without realizing it, Elizabeth nodded, her body going limp in his arms. Whatever Cutter wished of her, she wanted to give him in that moment.

Anything at all.

Reverently he spread her hair about her shoulders. Without a will of her own, Elizabeth clung to him wantonly, her head tilted seductively, her eyes closed in delight.

"If you'll let me," he began huskily, his voice whispering promises, his lips worshipping her face, "I can show you how easy it is to cut your wolf loose . . . how good it can be between us." His knuckles swept across her nipples, and they budded instantly as he stroked them deliberately.

"Feel it?" he whispered as she whimpered. All the while, he stroked the tip of her breast with the back of his hand. Stopping suddenly, he gently tweaked the nipple, rolling it between the roughened pads of his fingers.

The sweetest ache pulled at Elizabeth's core. Lost in the sensual bliss, she nodded, her voice having fled entirely. Though her eyes were opened, she could see nothing through the sweet haze of pleasure.

"Just say the word," Cutter coaxed, a ruthless gleam in his eye.

Elizabeth didn't know what to say. How to say it. Some part of her still understood that to acquiesce was to go against everything decent ever taught her. And though she wanted to, more than anything, she couldn't step over that line. She arched again, begging without words, and Cutter understood. He didn't need to be asked again. With a grunt of satisfaction, he lowered his mouth to the breast she offered so willingly, nibbling at it feverishly. Nipping at it through her cotton shirt, he sensed the hardening and craved her sweet, bare flesh between his lips. Very reluctantly, he tore himself away, only long enough to fumble with her blouse.

Drinking her fill of him, Elizabeth's eyes never left his as his free hand undid her buttons. One by one, quickly, deftly. Her breath coming in small gasps, she let him support her with a firm hand behind her back, while once again, the feel of cotton sliding out of her skirt sent quivers down her spine. With his rugged fingers, he laid her blouse open, lifting her camisole, exposing her breasts to the cool air. He dipped his head to suckle one nipple eagerly, while he fondled the other. The coarse texture of his fingers against her soft skin sent a quiver of pleasure rippling through her.

Unable to contain it, Elizabeth moaned with the sheer joy of him. Her hand slid instinctively around his neck. Nothing in all her life could have prepared her for the sweeping sensations that shivered through her body in that moment. As he suckled, a thread burned from her breast to her most secret reaches, and she wanted insanely that he should touch her . . . *there*.

Again.

She cried out suddenly. Wicked as the notion was, it scandalized her an instant, but just as swiftly, desire overwhelmed her, removing all coherent thought from her mind. Her fingers curled into his hair.

"Cutter," she sighed. "Oh, Cutter . . ."

His answering murmur burned her flesh. "Come with me, Lizbeth. Don't hold back," he told her, his whisper savage. Never pausing in his feasting, he peered up at her through his thick, dark lashes, watching her expression intently, reveling in it, his dark eyes smoldering.

Well beyond words now, Elizabeth shook her head no, that she wouldn't, and lest Cutter misunderstand her, she clutched his head possessively to her heart. Her hands threaded more deeply into his hair, tugging gently in desperation.

That was all the encouragement Cutter needed. Without a word, he swept her up, carrying her to his bedroll. He placed her down upon it reverently, kneeling over her, his lips curving at the sight of her. Her eyes remained closed, as though she couldn't bear to watch what he was about to do. He kissed her lips reassuringly, coming away with the beguiling taste of her on his lips.

"Lizbeth," he whispered huskily, his breath hot against her mouth. "Open those beautiful eyes for me, gal." She did, taking his breath away with the emotion nestled in the depths of them. His breath quickened, sounding as though he'd run a country mile. "Say no now . . ." He kissed her softly, hoping like hell she was too far gone to hear or comprehend his advice. "If you've any doubts at all . . . it'll be too late once I . . ."

Groaning as she brushed his face with her velvety soft fingers, he surged forward, thrusting one hand beneath her bottom and lifting her up against his hardness. "Damn me, if it ain't already too late," he muttered without regret. His other hand covered her breast as he buried his face into her soft neck. "Much too late," he whispered.

His fingers skipped down her body worshipfully, then glided the length of her leg, her thigh, lifting her skirt, searing her flesh where he touched her. Like a man possessed, he slid down to kiss the inner length of her thighs, sending delightful shudders coursing through her. While he kissed and caressed her there, his hands worked at the laces of her skirt. Freeing it, he moved up again to nibble her lips as he tugged her skirt down. Almost eagerly, Elizabeth helped him in the endeavor, lifting herself at his will, not realizing she did.

Then came her blouse, her camisole . . . her bloomers—all shed before she could even think to protest. All the while he kissed her lips so masterfully, so wickedly, his tongue dipping in, then out, the sensation so intoxicating that she never even realized her nakedness until the cool night air kissed her burning skin.

Mesmerized, she watched as he straightened momentarily to unbutton his own shirt. Peeling it off, he cast it aside. Bare-chested now, he knelt over her, examining every inch of her with his eyes as he'd craved to for so long, not touching, yet increasing her desire with his lusty gaze.

Never had anyone looked at her just so, with so much heat, as if she were beautiful. Never. And to Elizabeth's shame, she rejoiced in it.

By now it had grown dark, the firelight casting a rosy tint over Elizabeth's flesh, her breasts, even the darker areolas. Remembering the sweet taste of her, Cutter imagined his children suckling there, and felt white-hot desire knot his gut. Impatient to be inside her suddenly, he brought his hands to his buckle, unfastening it deftly. Removing his gun belt, he placed it gently aside while Elizabeth watched, her eyes wide.

The harsh sound of his buttons popping sent a momentary shiver of alarm rushing through her, but she willed it away. She wanted this, she told herself. So much. And it felt so right. More right than anything ever had before. Still, a lump of fear rose in her throat, nearly strangling her.

As quickly as he could, Cutter removed his boots,

then his denims, and suddenly he was free, the night air gliding over his sweat-dampened skin, heightening his pleasure. This, he thought triumphantly, was the way man was meant to be. Free.

His hands touched her knees, urging her legs apart. Elizabeth swallowed convulsively, resisting instinctively. "I—I can't!"

"Don't fight it," he whispered. "You want this as much as I do."

Elizabeth shook her head.

Cutter's eyes devoured her. His hand slipped between her legs, and he grinned suddenly. "The hell you don't!" he hissed.

Elizabeth willed her fear away, remembering only the pleasure she'd felt under his touch the first time.

He eased between her thighs, covering her suddenly, his flesh burning her clear to her soul. And his hardness nudged shamelessly at her private places. Taking her face into his big hands, Cutter kissed her lips feverishly, tiny pecks, then with a tortured groan, filled her mouth with the heat of his tongue.

His body nearly exploded on the spot when she instinctively lifted her knees, tilting herself to give him perfect access.

"So sweet," he groaned. "So good."

In response to his words, Elizabeth careened her hips even more. "That's it," he coaxed, trembling with restraint, his whisper tormented. Sweat beaded on his brow. "Open for me, bright eyes."

He was poised at the barrier, his arms straining with the effort of constraint, not wanting to hurt her, torturing himself with the wait. Had to check himself . . . had to make this good . . . for her.

Again she tilted, moaning with the ecstacy of his promised intrusion. "Please, Cutter," she breathed. "Please . . ."

Still Cutter didn't move, only shuddered violently somewhere above her, within her.

Without warning, Elizabeth lifted her hips forcefully, urging him inside, filling herself with his heat. The pain was minimal—too much a part of the pleasure to even be called pain.

With an oblivious groan, Cutter began to rock into her, out of her, filling her and then withdrawing again. Crying out, Elizabeth willed him deeper still, and with her fingers, clawed at his back, silently pleading for the release she knew he could give her. Instinctively her hands slid down to his buttocks.

Following his lead, she moved her hips along with his, whimpering with the exquisite rhythm he'd created, following him desperately. Suddenly, without warning, her body convulsed, fragmenting somewhere deep within. Just as it had the first time. Only the degree so much more. So, so much more. She cried out, kissing his shoulder reflexively, again, and again, grateful in a way she'd never been before.

Feeling her body tighten around him, and hearing her soft cries of release, Cutter gave himself up. Drawing back with a primitive cry, he drove into her with a ferocity that would have startled Elizabeth had she been the least bit aware. With a last grunt, he collapsed atop her with a deeper satisfaction than he'd ever experienced.

Kissing her temple long and hard, he rolled to the side so as not to crush her beneath him, and then hauled her up against himself, hugging her fiercely. He said nothing for the longest time, only stroked her hip and thigh absently. It seemed obscene to tarnish what they'd just shared with mere words. His body glistening with well-earned sweat, he turned a deaf ear to all sound, focusing instead on the ruthless pounding in his chest. It was only when Elizabeth seized his hand and raised it to her face to hold against her cheek that he felt compelled to speak.

His blood pounded through his temples. He swallowed the salty burn in his throat. "Did it branding cattle," he said gruffly, swallowing again. "I was fifteen . . . and too stupid to know better when they told me I wasn't a man unless I could fire the branding iron bare-handed.''

Listening quietly, Elizabeth crushed his hand to her cheek, willing the awful images away. She felt a bond with him this moment unlike anything she'd ever known before.

For the briefest moment, Cutter could see again the curl of the men's lips as they jeered him on. In their eyes, he'd been no more than a useless half-breed kid, fit only as a distraction for their boredom. And hell, he'd been too green and too desperate to prove himself to see the contempt in their eyes. He'd learned the game quickly enough, though.

Hugging Elizabeth jealously, he allowed himself to feel again the scorch of the metal rod boring into his palm, searing his fingers, smell the stink of his own burning flesh. And then, with a fierce shuddering, he thrust the memory back again into the graveyard of his mind . . . where it belonged.

''Anyhow, so now you know,'' he said matter-of-factly, without emotion, ''and you owe me one.'' He brushed her hair gently away from her face, kissing her temple. ''Tell me about 'Greensleeves,' '' he whispered, squeezing her gently for encouragement.

''Greensleeves?''

For a befuddled moment, Elizabeth couldn't fathom what he was talking about, and then it came to her, and she felt as though her heart constricted. How had he known? It didn't matter. She wasn't ready to bare herself to anyone. Too long she'd kept herself apart from everything but her work, and despite the cherished moment they'd just shared, she couldn't open herself up for his scrutiny—didn't know if she ever could. Her eyes misted. Her throat burned. ''I-It was my mother's favorite song,'' she said with difficulty, stiffening a little in his arms. ''She used to sing it to me as a child. That's all.''

That *wasn't* all there was to it, and Cutter knew it, but he didn't push it. He gave her a little reassuring squeeze, letting her know that, and then kissed the back of her head with a sigh. Hearing a smothered sniffle, he asked, ''You're not gonna start regrettin' already, are ya?''

Elizabeth shook her head, cursing herself for a sniveling idiot. Why, she wondered, were her emotions so near the surface lately when they never had been before? She'd always prided herself on being so clear headed, so strong. What had happened to her since meeting Cutter?

''Good,'' he whispered, turning her suddenly, and planting a kiss on the tip of her breast. '' 'Cause I'm not through with you yet.'' Positioning himself over her once more, he suckled her gently, and with a whimper, Elizabeth arched toward him, amazed that he could so quickly stir her body to life, awed that his could recover so quickly when her own felt so bone-deep sated.

Almost reverently, he ran his rough hands along the length of her, chasing chills up her spine as his fingers moved up her arms. He pinned her hands to the blanket, and stroked the inside of her palm with his scarred thumb.

The last coherent thought Elizabeth had was that Cutter McKenzie was very, *very* good at driving away demons, while ironically, Cutter wondered whether he was actually seeking to drive away hers . . . or his own.

Cutter wasn't certain what sound it was that roused him. Normally he was a very light sleeper and came awake fairly alert, but not this time. His mind was still cobwebbed from an exhausted sleep. His ears strained to pick up sounds, but nothing was immediately discernible.

Still, his instinct told him someone was there.

He could smell the intruder's scent in the rain-cleansed air. Despite the fact that he sensed the presence, knew it was there, when his eyes adjusted finally to the darkness, he was jolted to make out the expressionless face hovering so close above his and Elizabeth's huddled forms.

Silver flickered in the moonlight, and he held himself still.

He knew at once that it was one of the three Indians he'd spotted along the bluff-top, and his eyes quickly scanned the area. He could make out the other two still mounted. They'd remained at least ten yards away, along with the dead Indian's horse—silent watchers.

Though his adrenaline surged, Cutter resisted the urge to leap to his feet. He cursed himself for his recklessness. Hell, he'd forgotten the Indians were even there. And because of that fact, the advantage was theirs.

And they both knew it.

His gun wasn't but a foot above his head, but if he dove for it now, he'd be wearing the Indian's blade through his windpipe before the thought ever finished crossing his mind. Very slowly, Cutter removed his hand from under Elizabeth's back, trying not to wake her in the process. It'd be better if he didn't.

"Your woman makes you careless," the Indian said matter-of-factly, in his thick Cheyenne tongue, admonishing Cutter with a careless wave of his knife.

"But she has fire in her spirit, and in her hands," Cutter returned just as coolly, "and that is worth a dozen deaths to any man." His gaze never left the Indian's. He met the man eye to eye, leaving his thoughts open for the Indian to know.

The Indian nodded sagely, sheathing his knife suddenly. "I had a woman with fire once, but she was slain by the *Ooetane*." Elizabeth stretched lazily beside him, and the Indian jutted his chin at her. "She knows the ways of our people," he said, but it was more an astonished question than a statement of fact.

Inopportunely, before Cutter could reply, Elizabeth chose that moment to open her eyes. Seeing the strange Indian hovering above them, she choked back a terrified scream, but it remained to be seen in her eyes. The Indian's face contorted.

Elizabeth understood nothing of the exchange between Cutter and the Indian. All she knew was that the Indian sounded irate. And suddenly Cutter turned to her, his look accusing.

"You put white sage on the tomb?"

"I—I what?" she stammered. Instinctively she gathered up the blanket to hide her nakedness. Cutter, on the other hand, sat facing the Indian, as naked as the day he was born. Elizabeth doubted he spared it so much as a thought. He appeared so calm, and it seemed incredible that he could remain so utterly composed when she herself was suppressing a blood-curdling scream. Clutching her end of the blanket to her bosom protectively, she inched her way to Cutter's back, taking refuge there.

"He wants to know about the sage," Cutter repeated brusquely, without turning. "Did you put it there?"

A thousand tortures visited Elizabeth's mind, every horrible tale she'd ever heard in reference to the Indians—ridiculous as they may have seemed when she'd first heard them. They cut out tongues, shaved scalps, kidnapped women and children, stole away their souls!

"Oh, God have mercy—not on purpose, Cutter!" Her fingers dug into his bare shoulders as the Indian gave her a skeptical look. "I swear it! I really meant no harm!" she declared to the Indian, panicking. "I—I just gathered a handful of blossoms without thinking!" His expression didn't soften. "I—I didn't know!" she insisted.

Cutter sighed impatiently, shaking his head. "Lizbeth."

"What!"

"*Shut up.*" The command was no less convincing for the soft way it was spoken. Nor was it unkind. His cockeyed smile returned as he turned to speak to the Indian in his own tongue. The Indian nodded once, and responded briskly, then grinned broadly as Cutter added something more. Suddenly the Indian burst out laughing, and stood to walk away.

"What did you say to him?" Elizabeth demanded at once.

"Nothing you care to know," Cutter told her honestly, giving her a quick once-over. Satisfied that all her choice parts were well covered, he turned again to watch the Indian mount up and listen to his bantering with the others. At once all three burst out laughing, and glanced again at Elizabeth, all of them nodding appreciatively.

Cutter smiled, sharing a rare moment with his mother's people—not his mother's tribe, but it didn't matter. The connection was still there. He watched their easy camaraderie with a mixture of envy and pride—felt their unspoken grief for their friend. Not one of them looked back to the travois where the dead man lay, but their body movement told Cutter that they were more than aware of him, and their voices were subdued, as if in deference to his eternal sleep. Even their laughter held a note of sorrow.

As they turned away, Elizabeth started to see the crudely constructed cradle hitched up behind the riderless horse. A dark form lay there unmoving, swaddled in rags, and her heart wrenched painfully. She clasped the blanket more tightly to her bosom. It was the dead Indian, she knew without being told.

They'd come to claim him.

"You did them an honor," Cutter told her, seeing her stricken expression. "The white sage purifies. By placing it upon the tomb, you have kept the wicked shades at bay until they could prepare him for his journey to *Sèyǎñ*.'' His gaze held hers briefly, then skittered back to the Indians. "They separated in the storm." His Adam's apple bobbed, and then his eyes, glittering strangely, returned to meet hers. "They know you tried to save him, when you didn't have to."

Elizabeth didn't know what to say. She could sense the profound emotion bottled so deeply within him. Though she felt compelled to, she didn't look away. "*Sèyǎñ?*" she asked huskily, her voice sounding strange.

"The place of the dead," Cutter replied softly. "Those who die follow the Hanging Road above to *Heammawihio.*"

Not about to attempt a pronunciation of that one, Elizabeth nodded. Shuddering, she watched as Cutter threw his head back and scanned the heavens, reminding her of a lone wolf baying at the moon. And the moon—she couldn't help but follow his gaze upward—it was so big in the sky tonight, yet appeared so solitary. Like Cutter. Bigger than life, yet despite his infuriating nonchalance, there was an inherent loneliness about him that struck at her heart. "Hanging Road?" she asked in a whisper.

"The Milky Way," Cutter clarified with another quick glance her way.

Elizabeth's brow furrowed, and she nodded. "Oh." In silence they watched the trio make their way to the bluff, their horses picking their way expertly in the darkness. "And where are they taking him now?"

"Home," Cutter answered gruffly. "They're taking him home." And a part of him grieved over that place he'd never know. That he'd never known.

"Did they explain how it was that he was wounded?" Elizabeth ventured again.

"No." Cutter's eyes never shifted, though by now the trio was no longer visible through the blackness. "Didn't ask."

"Well, what *did* they say?" Recalling their strange words, the length of their conversation, she was dying of curiosity over them.

As Cutter turned to her, the shadows disappeared from his eyes. He grinned slowly, his teeth gleaming white in the night. "He wanted to know why you spoke so sharply in their presence—did you hate them for the color of their skin?"

Elizabeth's face contorted. "Of course not!" She choked on her shock. "W-What did you tell them?" To her mind, it was certainly nothing to grin about!

Cutter chuckled. "I told them no—that you didn't." His glittering eyes gave him away.

"That's not all you told them," she accused him, slapping at the back of his head wrathfully. "What else, McKenzie?"

"Damn, woman, if you ain't heavy-handed!" he said with mock aggravation. And then he held out his hands to ward her off, remembering the way she'd battered his leg in the heat of her anger, laughing. "I told them you always spoke so sharply," he said quickly, "and that you made love like a yellow-eyed she-wolf . . . and that if they didn't believe me, they could check out the mile-long marks on my back—stings like the devil!"

Gasping with outrage, Elizabeth mustered enough indignity to smack Cutter again, this time a bit harder. He caught her wrist effortlessly. "You didn't!" she protested breathlessly, her face heating fiercely. A reluctant smile trembled on her lips.

Cutter's shoulders began to quake, and then he laughed outright.

"Oh, you couldn't have!" she cried. "Tell me you didn't!"

Cutter's laughter bowled him over, and he fell back on the bedroll. Hooting hysterically, he peered up at Elizabeth's ashen face, made more so by the pale light of the moon. " 'Fraid so," he told her, barely able to speak without breaking into chuckles—the look on her face worth an entire gold mine.

Elizabeth shook her hands free and would have smacked Cutter yet again had the voice not startled her from it.

From somewhere along the bluff-top, the Indian's disembodied voice resounded clearly in the night.

"Ne-a'éše!" he said with passion, and as he continued to speak, his voice sounded almost an eerie echo to her ears. It sent chill after chill racing down Elizabeth's spine, though she had not an inkling what was being said. At the end of the pronunciation, all three Indians began to whoop. She searched for them frantically along the bluff-top, but could see nothing, could only guess at their actions.

They seemed agitated over something.

Cutter's laughter stopped abruptly, and he, too, shuddered as their sounds faded in the night— only, not out of fear. Without warning he reached up, seizing Elizabeth passionately into his arms, feeling never more connected to someone in his life.

"What did they say?" she whispered anxiously, her lips so close to his that they could have been sharing the same breath.

For the longest moment, Cutter couldn't respond, could only lie there feeling her heart throb against the beat of his own, his chest feeling near to bursting with pride. Taking a deep breath, he stroked her back reassuringly, and gazed into her expectant face, his own expression achingly tender. There was still the slightest twinge of laughter in his tone when he spoke again; though his words were murmured, his eyes fairly twinkled with mirth.

"He said, *Ne-a'éše;* it means thank you."

"And?" Elizabeth prodded, knowing all those words couldn't possibly have amounted to one simple phrase.

Cutter smiled, holding her tightly, anticipating her

outraged reaction. ''Yeah, well . . . he also said . . . Black Wolf, who is gone from among us, was my brother, but—'' a quiver sped through him, raising the hairs on his arms ''—she who claws at man's back shall forever be called my friend.''

Chapter 17

For long hours afterward, Elizabeth was unable to erase the sound of the Indian's voice from her thoughts. Nor could she forget the tenderness in Cutter's eyes as he'd loved her again afterward, the feel of his warm hands wandering possessively over her body.

Never had she felt more alive.

In the early hours of the morning, knowing that sleep was hopeless with the sun beginning to rise on the horizon, they dressed. She traded her blouse for one Cutter handed her: a white one with buttons down the front and frothy lace at the sleeves and collar. As distinct as it was, she recognized it at once as one of Josephine's. But despite Cutter's disapproving look, she again donned her trusty old skirt with the tattered hem. She didn't have the nerve yet to wear the men's britches she'd bought, though soon she wouldn't have much choice. Her skirt was literally wearing away!

The packing went swiftly, because they'd unpacked so little to begin with. At last Elizabeth mounted up, with Cutter's help. But as Cutter turned to mount his own horse, the sound of riders approaching kept him from swinging his leg over his Palouse's rump. Sliding down once more, he turned to see who it was.

Two men dressed in Union blue reined in. The lead

man wore a full beard, along with his filthy blues. His shoulder-length hair was wild and unkempt, though he might still have passed as handsome, with his well-chiseled features, if it hadn't been for the coldness in his gray eyes. They were icy and unresponsive, lacking any emotion but for the flicker of malice he didn't bother to disguise.

"McKenzie," the man said in greeting, surprise evident in his tone. In spite of it, the word managed to sound profane coming from his severe lips.

If Cutter was surprised by their unexpected appearance, it didn't show. He nodded, giving Elizabeth a quick glance, urging her without words to be silent. As if he'd not heard the man speak, he turned his back to the duo and mounted up. Once he was settled in his saddle, he turned to them again, tipping his hat. "Sulzberger," he replied acerbically. He nodded to the other, not recalling the face. "What blood you lookin' to shed this far east, boys? War's over, y'know?"

The man, Magnus Sulzberger, sprayed tobacco-yellowed spittle on the ground. "Always were a smart-ass, McKenzie . . . and you're *dead* right . . . *that* war is over." He'd emphasized the word "dead," and now his grin widened, his lips tightening over the lump of tobacco beneath. And then his eyes narrowed again, gleaming with open hostility. "But there's still a war goin' on. Reckon you ain't heard 'bout Platte Bridge?"

"No," Cutter affirmed. "And don't reckon I care to either."

Magnus carried on as if Cutter had never spoken. "Three, maybe four thousand of them redskin bastards drove in a cavalry detachment and wiped out a military supply train there."

Cutter shrugged dismissively. "Ain't my concern anymore."

"Well, now, McKenzie . . . the way I hear it told . . . *never was*. At any rate, you ought to be remem-

bering, when you go running your mouth and siding
with them *savages*, that you no longer have government protection. These days, I reckon I might just
watch who I was rilin' if I were you." Both of his
brows rose abruptly. "You think?" His beard split
and a demonic smile spread across his almost nonexistent lips.

Cutter grinned in return, but there was no benev-
olence in his expression. His eyes narrowed to dark,
predatory slits. "*If you were me,*" he said pointedly,
his tone low but carrying clearly. "But then, we both
know you're not."

To Cutter's way of thinking, any man who would
run down a toddler in cold blood, spearing him with
his bayonet as if he were a cold-blooded trout, was a
coward of the worst kind, and Magnus had done that
and worse at Sand Creek. Much worse. Had it been
up to Cutter, the man wouldn't be wearing his stripes
at the moment, much less the cocksure smile he wore
like a badge of honor. But it wasn't up to Cutter, and
there wasn't a chance they'd take a half-breed's word
over a full-blooded white's, not any day. And so he
kept his damned mouth shut and watched his back.

Magnus's smile vanished, and there was suddenly
cold fury in his eyes.

Cutter's expression remained a mask of stone. He
tapped his hat out of his eyes with a finger and, in
one smooth movement, reached down to flick open
the leather thong that kept his revolver holstered. The
fluidity of his gesture was a warning in itself. "State
your business, boys, and move on," he told them.
"Oh, and Sulzberger . . . you'd do well to remember
that that protection you're talking about works two
ways." His dark eyes turned sinister, and the softness of his voice sent a shiver of apprehension down
Elizabeth's spine. The faintest smile touched his lips,
crept into his eyes. "Means I no longer have anyone
to answer to."

Magnus's mouth took on a mocking twist. "I hear

you," he drawled, readjusting his wad of tobacco before spitting it out. "I hear you, McKenzie." He gave Elizabeth a bone-chilling sidewise glance. "Hafta wonder, miss, if you know who it is you're keepin' company with?" His gray eyes glittered with unconcealed malice as he took in her lamentable state of dress.

Elizabeth averted her gaze, and Magnus laughed harshly, the sound obscene. "Well, hell, darlin', maybe you do," he said cryptically.

There was no doubt in Elizabeth's mind that the man was trouble, and she suddenly couldn't wait to be away from him.

"Anyhow," he carried on, "ain't lookin' for trouble with you, McKenzie. Happens we're out hunting a pack of renegades. Raided a camp about thirty miles east of Fort Riley. Swiped some food and supplies." He glanced again at Elizabeth, and the look he gave her raised the tiny hairs on the back of her neck. "Stuck one of my men as they were leaving," he continued with loathing, tipping his head in the direction of the youth beside him. "O'Neill here spotted your smoke last night and . . . Well, anyhow, you ain't them. Ain't happen to've seen 'em, have you?" There was unconcealed suspicion in his question, as though it really didn't matter what Cutter said. He already clearly disbelieved him.

Cutter was silent a long moment, resisting the urge to glance over at Elizabeth. Would she give them away? It didn't matter; Magnus wasn't stupid. Vicious, maybe. Yellowbellied, maybe. But not stupid. "And what if I have?" Cutter asked casually, one brow lifting in challenge.

Magnus responded with a slow sneer. "Well then . . . I reckon you ought to say so."

One side of Cutter's lips lifted contemptuously. "Yeah?" His wintry smile crept into his eyes. "And you say they stuck an officer?" He hoped it was one of Magnus's colleagues, and he found himself feeling sorry for the kid at Magnus's side. Sulzberger knew the art of intimidation only too well. Likely he'd have the whelp dancing over bullets for his kicks and believing it was his lucky day for being able to do so.

"That's right," Magnus drawled.

Cutter gave him a nod. "Well, now, seems I do recall they went that way." He pointed halfheartedly in the direction the Indians had, in fact, gone. "Came through yesterday, late afternoon. Four of 'em."

Elizabeth's breath snagged, and her eyes widened. She couldn't believe Cutter had actually given them away! Didn't he realize what these vile men would do if they caught up with them? She didn't find it so difficult to believe that the Indians had perhaps killed a man. They'd seemed perfectly capable, but for some strange reason, she felt connected to them, even grateful. And some little voice in the back of her mind told her that they wouldn't have killed for sport, that it was perhaps hunger . . . or even revenge that had driven them, for even in Sioux Falls she had heard tales of Sand Creek. Still, she refrained from saying anything to refute Cutter, only because she knew it wouldn't help matters even if she did.

Once again Magnus glanced her way, appraising her thoroughly, and his answering grin was malignant. "Much obliged," he said curtly, never taking his scrutiny from Elizabeth. Then he turned his mount away, and back again. "Oh, and, McKenzie . . ."

Cutter didn't respond, only sat back in the saddle and crossed his arms, watching the men before him with keen eyes.

"Reckon you ought to know . . . General Sully is looking for you."

Cutter shrugged apathetically. "So let him look," he replied tersely. "It ought to make you pretty happy when he doesn't find me, Sulzberger." And with that, he touched his hat brim in dismissal, spurring his mount closer to Elizabeth's. Snatching her reins out of her hands, he turned his back to the gawking pair, and led her away without another word.

"Be seeing ya, now," Magnus called after them, staring.

"If y' say so," Cutter responded without turning.

Elizabeth, on the other hand, for all that she tried, couldn't tear her gaze away from the duo behind them. When the younger man touched the smooth butt of his revolver, she tensed, and started to scream out a warning, but Cutter eyed her sternly.

Seeing Elizabeth stiffen, Cutter called out his own warning, again without turning. "Draw that gun up out of there, Blue-boy . . . and you'd better be prepared to use it."

Astonished that he had known, and dazed by the peculiar exchange she had witnessed, Elizabeth lagged behind and turned to look at his back with something akin to awe and then again to the disgruntled pair behind them. Magnus gave the younger man a vigorous shake of his head, and the youth immediately abandoned his revolver, muttering an inaudible curse.

"How'd the bloody son of a bitch know?" Elizabeth heard him ask.

"Savage in him," Magnus replied sourly, spurring his mount in the exact opposite direction Cutter had indicated. "Last man to underestimate him ended up with a .44 between his baby blues—but don't you worry none, O'Neill, he'll come into his own someday. Real soon—damned redskin-lovin' deserter!" With that declaration, he cast them a backward glance, smiling with promise at Elizabeth. Tipping his hat, he gaffed his mare.

When they finally disappeared from view, Elizabeth urged Cocoa up beside Cutter's mount. "How did you know, Cutter?"

"With that look on your face?" Cutter shrugged. "It was evident someone was going after their gun. Sulzberger's been round long enough to know bet-

ter . . . That left little Blue-boy back there." He shook
his head. "Kid like that's always rarin' to show off
his gun hand. Thing is, he's like t' end up six feet
under before he ever shaves his first whiskers."

He led her up the bluff, following the same path
the Indians had taken, leaving the river at their backs.
Again, Elizabeth lagged behind, musing about what
he'd just revealed.

"No," she said at last, catching up with him once
more. "Not that. How did you know that those men
would search in the opposite direction?"

Cutter adjusted his hat and sat back in the saddle
to better see her. There was wonder in her eyes. He
grinned engagingly. "Didn't," he admitted with a
gleam in his eyes. "Never thought anyone could be
so contrary that they wouldn't believe God's truth
when they heard it . . . till I met you. Just took a
gamble, and it paid off."

Elizabeth gasped, her eyes widening at the affront.
"Contrary! You are . . . are just . . . just . . ." She
couldn't find the words to describe him. What kind
of man could make love to a woman and then insult
her in the next breath? "The worst!"

Chuckling, Cutter responded, "That bad, huh?"
And with that, he winked at her, turning his attention to the steep trail before them.

They reached the bluff-top to find rolling hills as far
as the eye could see, white oak and cottonwood trees
flecking the view. Having abandoned the riverbed and
bluffs, Cutter made use of every last watering hole
they encountered. While the horses fed late in the
afternoon, they lunched, then set out again and didn't
stop until they reached the Grand River. By then,
Elizabeth had fallen asleep in the saddle.

Seeing her waver, Cutter snatched her up into his
own saddle with no small measure of concern. The
last time she'd slept in his arms, she'd given him a
healthy fear of doubling up on one horse, but he
couldn't very well just let her drop from exhaustion—

sure was tempting, though. As they rode, *that* part of him was never very far from his thoughts. And because of it, he was as cagey as a stallion in a brood mare's stall by the time they made camp.

It had been dark for over an hour when they stopped for the night. With sleepy murmurs Elizabeth allowed Cutter to tuck her into her bedroll. He placed his own next to hers, and having satisfied his hunger earlier in the day, gnawed on a tough slice of jerky as he contemplated the night before.

Lizbeth had grit—had to give her that much. With a grin that crinkled the corners of his eyes, he thought about her temperament, deciding that she must have had a full-blooded Scot hanging somewhere on her family tree.

He closed his eyes and ruminated, thinking that they'd made real good time all day. But time was something he was swiftly running short on. He shifted uneasily, his eyes seeking out her huddled form in the darkness. He swallowed the last bite of jerky. Remembering the rattler necklace he'd made for her, he pulled it out of his denim pocket, staring at it a long moment. Scooting closer to Elizabeth, he carefully placed it over her head, tucking it reverently into the space between two of her buttons.

He had to make her see things his way—just couldn't let her hire on someone else. He just wasn't sure how to convince her of it.

Trying not to think about the ache in his foot, as well as the one in his britches, he jerked up his own blanket and drew it over Elizabeth—two blankets wouldn't hurt her none—and then he threw a protective arm over her for good measure, and willed himself to sleep.

The next morning he was still thinking over some way to convince Elizabeth to let him stand in as her husband while he prepared to shave. After breakfast, he hung his mirror from a tree and then filled his bowl with water. He'd scrubbed his face and then lathered his whiskers, and was about to draw the folding razor across his chin when Elizabeth walked up to him, a bundle of dirty clothes squashed in her arms. He watched her approach in the mirror, admiring the soft sway of her hips—if not the bulky, ugly, ragged fabric that covered them.

"Cutter?"

With his hand still in midair, he glanced at her.

Cutter was bare-chested, his skin taut and dark, and it was difficult to remain coherent at the sight of him. Elizabeth had thought, when she'd felt the light mat of hair on his chest and arms, along with the tightness of the skin across his ribs and belly, that nothing could be so incredible. But seeing him was. It fair took her breath away.

"I—I wanted to thank you for the necklace," she said hesitantly, her hands trembling as she clutched the bundle of clothes. She yearned to reach out and touch him, the necklace at least, but couldn't because her hands were full. With the necklace, he'd given her a keepsake, something tangible that she could hold on to and remember . . . after he was gone. Something that would prove it had all been real and not a wonderful, magical dream—the most beautiful night of her life. She didn't fool herself; she'd been available, and he in need. He just wasn't the marrying kind, she knew, nor would it have worked out for her . . . not when she wanted her niece so desperately. She couldn't take that chance.

He was still staring at her, his eyes probing, as if he were trying to read her soul. And then he gave her a nod and returned to his mirror, his thoughts obviously preoccupied. As she watched, he lifted the razor.

"Did you make it from the rattler we ate?" Elizabeth asked, her brows furrowing as she peered into the bowl, then at his beard, and again at the razor in his hand.

"Yeah," Cutter replied, and then turned to look at

her again, thinking that she'd come a long way—from not being able to even mention her body's inborn callings to feeling at ease gawking at his own rites. There was something inherently satisfying in that, Cutter mused, and then he realized that she was scrutinizing his face a little too intently.

"I thought Indians didn't have to shave," she said abruptly, obviously befuddled by the fact that he was about to do just that, and surprised that it hadn't occurred to her to notice before now. "I'd always heard, you see . . . and the others . . . well, they didn't seem to have any—so why do you?"

Her question, so innocently asked, took Cutter by surprise, and he didn't immediately reply. Elizabeth looked so interested in his response that he didn't have the heart to tell her that it was likely the most asinine question he'd ever heard. With a confounded look, he scratched his temple with his thumb. "Hell, Lizbeth, how should I know? Maybe it's the white in me," he added caustically.

Averting her eyes, Elizabeth nodded, shrugging, immediately embarrassed that she'd asked such a personal question. "Just wondered, is all." Pulling her bundle more closely against her breasts, she walked away, and for a moment Cutter just stared at her, dumbfounded, as she headed toward the river. And then it struck him suddenly, and he wondered why he hadn't thought of it sooner.

Seeing himself suddenly in a different light, he studied his reflection in the hazy mirror. Hell, he thought, Jo had been right . . . he really didn't look like much of an Indian—less so with a beard. If it weren't for his dark coloring, and the way he wore his clothes, most folks would probably never suspect. His Irish blood was just as prominent as the Indian, showing itself in the wavy texture of his hair, for one . . . and his body hair—didn't have lots, but . . . more than he should have had.

He wasn't sure how long he stood there gawking

at himself, his expression incredulous, but his dark
eyes turned suddenly cunning. A slow smile lifted his
lips as he washed the caking lather from his face, and
dried himself briskly with a small towel. Then he me-
ticulously trimmed his beard and, once satisfied with
his appearance, went in search of Elizabeth.

He found her scrubbing laundry in the river, her
sleeves rolled up to her elbows, her ragged skirt sopping up the water. She was washing his favorite green
shirt, putting heart and soul into it, and he smiled at
the image she made. The sight of her, her clothes
damp and clinging to her delicate curves, at once
shifted the nature of his thoughts, and his smile
turned devious.

"Mind scrubbing something else for me?"

Startled by his husky baritone, Elizabeth leapt,
nearly losing the shirt she was laundering in the slow
but steady current of the river. Cutter stood on the
bank, his arms crossed, his eyes dancing with mischief. For some reason, his imperious manner pricked
at her. "No, I don't, but must you always sneak
up—" Her protest ended abruptly with a gasp of surprise. "You can't—Cutter!"

He chuckled at her stricken expression, but his
hands never ceased unbuttoning his denims. "Ain't
nothing here you haven't already seen, Doc," he told
her coolly.

Or felt, Elizabeth wanted to add, her face heating
fiercely. Still, it wasn't the least bit proper. "Cutter,"
she protested weakly. But her gaze never wavered as
he began to shuck off his pants . . . and then his underwear, stepping out of both. Finally he stood before
her as naked as the day he was born—unashamed
and even a bit arrogant in his stance. To her dismay,
she remained transfixed, her heart pummeling her
ribs.

"If there's anything needs washing, it's these," he
revealed huskily, dropping the clothing in question
into the pile of laundry she'd left on the bank. As

Elizabeth gaped, he waded into the cool river, and dove under the rippling surface.

To her dismay, she didn't even realize that she was still gawking, her fingers clutching at his wet shirt in her hands, until he surfaced near her, shaking his head like a wet puppy, flinging droplets of water everywhere. Yet even as the cool droplets pattered her face, she stared.

His eyes crinkled at the corners. "Need help?" he asked.

The water had come to midchest where he'd first surfaced, but as he stalked toward her, it dipped to his waist, his thighs . . . his . . .

"H-Help?" Elizabeth stammered, when he stood before her at last. "I—I—" With some difficulty, her eyes lifted to his face as he began to pry the soaked cloth from her hands. With a nod, he tossed it upon the bank and then turned to face her, his eyes smoldering with that same hunger she recalled so vividly. And then a tremor passed through her as they darkened before her eyes.

"Help," he repeated, his fingers touching her shoulders, gripping them firmly and then kneading them for a moment.

Elizabeth's legs went as limp as the water she was standing in. His fingers went to her braid, untwisting it, while she stood, like a ninny, staring up at him.

"I like it down," Cutter revealed, his voice so warm and masculine that it sent shiver after shiver down her spine. Still, she couldn't move. His eyes twinkled as he spread her hair about her shoulders, smoothing it with his fingers. His hand moved from her hair to her face, his fingers caressing at first and then cupping her face as though it were his greatest treasure. He made her feel so very beautiful, made her believe . . .

"Y-You do?" she whispered, her eyes slanting with remembered passion.

"I do," he said with a nod, and then he slowly dipped his head to her mouth.

Elizabeth's knees went weak as he descended. His lips touched her briefly, then withdrew, and reclaimed them in a soul-searing kiss. His mouth moved with slow finesse, coaxing a response from her. Instinctively Elizabeth opened for him, shivering when his tongue slid deep like velvet heat over hers.

"Cutter."

"Yes?"

"The laundry . . ." Reaching out instinctively, Elizabeth threaded her fingers into the thick waves of his hair.

"It'll wait."

Elizabeth nodded in profound agreement, her mind becoming more hazed with every moment he held her. His arms swept about her waist, lifting her up against himself, until she could feel every wet, solid inch of him through her own clothing. He was aroused . . . she could feel him, and her breath quickened in awakened response. She threw her head back, offering him everything he would take of her . . . anything.

Like a man drunk with desire, Cutter allowed his lips to feast on the flesh of her neck. "I'll even help when we're through," he promised huskily, his breath tickling the hollow of her throat.

But not his breath, Elizabeth realized suddenly . . . his beard. "You didn't shave?" she asked dreamily.

"No, I didn't," Cutter agreed, trying not to chuckle at the airy quality of her voice. Her lids were falling, and he lifted her face, kissing them closed, reveling in her artless reaction to him. "Thought it might be best."

"Mmmmmmhhh," Elizabeth agreed, arching into him instinctively, and then it seemed as though her lips continued speaking of their own accord, because Elizabeth was no longer the least bit interested in conversation. He gave her lips small, cherishing pecks, and she sighed as ripples of pleasure washed over her. "Best . . . for what?" she asked breathlessly.

Cutter winced and considered not answering her question—at least not until afterward—but it was what he'd come to the river for, he reminded himself. With a sigh of resignation, he forced himself to speak, knowing it would be too easy to refrain. "You're not hiring on someone else," he said bluntly, bracing himself for her anger.

For the longest moment Elizabeth remained in her dreamy state, her eyes closed in pleasure, and then it dawned on her what he'd said and her eyes flew open.

Chapter 18

❦❦**W**hat do you mean, I'm not hiring on anybody else?''

Cutter released her suddenly. Elizabeth nearly fell
backside-first into the river. She stumbled and then
steadied herself, her hands going to her hips.

There was no yield in his expression, only a hard,
cold-eyed determination. ''Just what I said.''

''You know I can't let you be my husband, Cutter!''
Her expression was wistful, but resolved, and he
countered with a slow smile that left her grating her
teeth.

''I wasn't asking, Elizabeth. I'm telling you how it's
gonna be.''

Her full name on his lips gave her a start, and his
implacable expression was unnerving, but left her no
more disconcerted than did the fact that she was ar-
guing with a naked man. ''It's just not possible!'' Nor
was it possible to make a reasonable case with his
nudity staring her so insolently in the face!

She shook her head, trying desperately not to look
at any one part of him for too long—most especially
not *that* part! A moment ago she hadn't felt so awkward, but a moment ago she'd been wrapped in his
warmth, and hadn't recalled his state of undress.

''Why?'' he asked much too softly, daring Elizabeth to voice her objections.

"Don't make me say it, McKenzie," she pleaded, not wishing to offend him.

"Why, damn you?"

She flinched at his harsh tone, but eyed him wrathfully, infuriated that he would put her in such a position. "You *know* precisely why!" she shouted back.

A shudder went through him as he said quietly, "Take a good look at me, Liz—a real good look!"

Lord have mercy, but she was trying not to! Elizabeth shook her head adamantly.

"Look at me!"

"No! I don't need to!" He grabbed her chin, but Elizabeth jerked it away, swiping at his hand. "I remember only too well!" Cutter gripped her shoulders and tried to force her gaze upon him. "No!" she shrieked. "Let go of me, McKenzie!" She shoved at his chest, but he didn't seem to budge.

Near hysterics now, Elizabeth shook herself free. Lifting up her skirts, she made a mad rush for the bank, but moving against the current was difficult, and she stumbled. Seizing the back of her skirt, Cutter swept her toward him, ripping it from her waist.

"Damned thing is too big for you, anyhow!" he groused. With another vicious jerk, he rent the material completely free of her.

Shrieking in protest, Elizabeth made a desperate grasp for her skirt, but Cutter was too quick. He hurled it downriver. Horrified, Elizabeth simply stood there in her wet bloomers, gawking helplessly as the current carried her skirt away. She turned to him suddenly, her expression as stormy as his own. "You—had *no* right to do that!"

"Yeah? Well, why don't you ask me if I give a damn!"

Before Elizabeth could recover from the shock of Cutter's actions and words, he'd lifted her by her waist and was marching toward the bank. She struggled, flailing her arms and kicking wildly, but to no avail—his hold was too strong.

''Rules were made to be broken,'' he taunted. ''Didn't ya know?'' And then he cursed a storm as his bad foot ground onto something spiny. Jerking his leg up in pain, he lurched forward, dumping Elizabeth unceremoniously onto the bank.

Elizabeth didn't notice his jerk of pain and mistook his curses for simple rage. She winced as her head slammed into the ground, but didn't waste time weeping over it. She tried to rise, but Cutter held her down with one firm hand to her breast. Angrily she shoved it away, glaring at him.

''Don't touch me!'' she spat. ''Just don't you touch me! You don't understand—and you won't even try! I've already lost my mother *and* my sister because of *your people.* If it weren't for *your murdering kinsmen* raiding and slaughtering, they would never have abandoned us in the first place! And maybe—just maybe—they'd still be alive! *I will not lose my niece because of you too!''*

Your people.

The way it was flung from her lips, with so much resentment, gave Cutter a momentary jolt.

Your murdering kinsmen.

It didn't matter that, for all practical purposes, he wasn't raised Cheyenne. His mother had died of his father's abuse long before he had been able to even ask of his culture. Hell no! And it didn't matter that all he knew was his father's way of life—that his father had tamped down in him all that was Indian. Elizabeth saw only the Cheyenne in him.

''I won't!'' she sobbed, mistaking his expression.

Suddenly Cutter's eyes narrowed, transfixing her, and he bent forward very slowly, like a predatory animal stalking his prey. He trapped her beneath him, between his arms. ''So you'd rather take your chances, would ya?'' he said with lethal softness.

Elizabeth's mind screamed that he leave her be, but the words never emerged on her tongue. The calculating look in his eyes completely paralyzed her.

Feeling no mercy, Cutter slid his right hand boldly into her bodice. Feeling the warmth of it, Elizabeth instinctively tilted her head back, closing her eyes, fighting her traitorous body. Before she could gather her thoughts to protest, he popped her buttons with a clean slice of his open fist, sending them whizzing into the air. Several of them plunked ominously into the water. And in that moment, she lost all trace of uncertainty. At once she tried to roll free of him, but his hand came down swiftly to halt her escape.

"Beast!" she cried out, resisting the urge to pummel his chest.

"Savage?" Cutter returned with a frosty smile, his tone no less frightening for its husky softness.

"I didn't say that!" Elizabeth protested, suddenly understanding his vehemence.

"Not this time," he agreed, "but you damn well thought it—didn't you? You want savage, Lizbeth? *This,*" he said through clenched teeth, a muscle ticking at his jaw, "*is savage!*" At once his knee dropped between her legs, prying them open. He seized her by the hair, tugging until she cried out.

She didn't want him this way, didn't know him! Didn't want to know him! Though his eyes were cold, they burned clear into her soul. "Please, Cutter," she whimpered. "You're frightening me!"

His mouth lowered to her nipple, nibbling it softly through her camisole, but his hand in her hair tightened and she cried out again, more startled than anything else. His fury was barely leashed. She could feel it in his grip, see it in every rigid plane of his body and face. It was as tangible as the anguish in her heart.

"Please—"

Again he wrenched her hair, his knee burrowing itself more firmly between her legs.

"Cutter, please, please—don't!" Her eyes misted as his mouth moved to her other breast, feasting on it almost brutally. He tugged on her hair again, si-

lencing her once and for all. Her eyes implored him
to stop, but she didn't dare speak again. Hot tears
began to pool in her eyes, trickle down her cheeks.

Despising himself for the brutality he'd just dis-
played, Cutter cursed under his breath. But his point
was made, and in this case he was convinced that the
end more than justified the means. He couldn't—*no,
wouldn't*—let her set herself up for the same thing
from someone else.

Someone else wouldn't care for her as he did.

Someone else wouldn't . . .

Love her?

Her face was ashen, and her lips trembled. He
wanted so badly to lower his mouth and cover them,
heal her pain—make her see him differently. He
couldn't help himself. With a tortured groan, he covered her mouth, but his kiss was painfully tender,
belying his anger.

Elizabeth moaned in protest, but yielded to him,
sobbing as his tongue stabbed into the warmth of her
mouth, tasting and relishing.

His arousal had never diminished. Even in his anger, he was hard as a brick, and growing more so by
the second. He was losing his reason.

Elizabeth shoved him away abruptly, her eyes
spearing him, and he released her, though his arms
still caged her beneath him. "Understand now?" he
asked hoarsely, his voice harsh but unsteady, a wintry glitter to his eyes.

Elizabeth shook her head. "N-N-No," she sobbed.

Cutter pinned her hands at her sides, and with a
muttered curse over his failure, he shook his head at
her, fury spilling from his black eyes. "*Think* about it,
Liz. That's exactly what you'd be inviting if you hired
on some stranger—chances are slim to none that you'll
find someone to play the part who won't expect all
that goes along with it! And if you turn him down,
he'll just take it! Is it sinking in yet?" A bleakness

settled into her eyes, mirroring her emotions, and he said with no small measure of relief, "I see that it is."

Her tears kept flowing, and guilt twisted Cutter's gut like a dull blade. "To make it look genuine," he tried to explain, his voice losing some of its harshness, "you're gonna have to share a room—ain't a man on this earth who wouldn't be tempted to take what's so easily accessible. And what would you do then? Scream? And lose your niece? Reckon that would be rather pointless—even more asinine than taking a chance on a useless half-breed! Y' think?"

With a whimper, Elizabeth turned away, hating that he would use her conscience against her, hating the truth of his words, and feeling a loss as if she'd already been stripped of everything that was dear to her.

Cutter gripped her by the chin, forcing her to acknowledge him. "Chrissakes, Lizbeth! You'd think I'd taken every chance I could to rape and batter you!" His voice was soft and entreating when he spoke again, and his eyes compelled her to understand. "Think about it—haven't I gone out of my way to prove to you that you can trust me? Damn you . . . have a little faith!" Her eyes appeared haunted, without hope. "I can do it," he hissed, his voice strained and his breathing becoming difficult.

Swallowing abruptly, Elizabeth turned from him again, unable to meet his gaze. The fact that his words rang true didn't ease her heartache any. She squeezed her eyelids tightly closed, cutting off the flow of her tears, nodding hopelessly.

For certain now, she would lose Katie. It was too much to hope for that Elias Bass would overlook the fact that her husband was a half-breed. Why, oh, why, had she ever, *ever*, dared to hope? Why? She nearly cried out the question, but couldn't speak for the trembling of her lips.

Why did Cutter have to be right?

She turned to meet his eyes, her own eyes shimmering, her voice weak with defeat. "All right," she said with a despairing softness, "we'll do it your way, McKenzie."

Relief washed through Cutter at once, making him shudder with the incredible release of tension.

Seeing the gesture, Elizabeth despised him for it. A sob escaped her tightening throat, and anger surged through her, but she didn't move at all. She was too numb to attempt it. "Only know this," she added brokenly, a single tear escaping and rolling down her ashen cheek. "If I lose my niece because of you, Cutter McKenzie, I swear to heaven above that I will despise you until my dying day! I swear it!" she cried out with more emotion, swallowing the salt of her tears.

"And what if you're wrong, Elizabeth? What if Elias does accept me? Why! Why are you so sure he won't?"

His question jolted her momentarily. *Why did she think Elias would persecute Cutter? Because she did? Could it be true? Did she?* She shook her head in denial . . . yet somewhere deep down, she knew that it was so.

And then hope surged within her.

Maybe Elias wouldn't hold it against him.

Maybe Elias wouldn't even know.

Wouldn't care.

And maybe he would. And it was that possibility that made her heart wrench.

Cutter must have read her thoughts, because something in his expression darkened abruptly. His jaw grew taut, and his countenance twisted with a look of pain that turned quickly to fury. "Reckon you're the one with the problem, Elizabeth, and not Elias?" By the answering look in her eyes, he knew that he'd struck a chord, and his teeth clenched so tightly that he thought his jaw might split. His gut twisted. "God—damn you, you're no better'n—" He turned his face away in disgust. When the hell would he learn?

"No!" Elizabeth shouted. It couldn't be true. His gaze snapped back to hers, and her voice broke. "K-Katie is *all* I have left in this world . . . If . . . if you take her away . . ." Tears began to course down her cheeks unchecked. She sensed Cutter stiffen above her, but she couldn't hold back the impassioned words. "If I lose the chance to raise her because of you . . . I'll never, *ever*, forgive you for it!"

With a furious oath, Cutter jerked away from her, as if stung by her words. He hauled himself onto the bank. Still cursing, he tugged his denims up over his wet legs, not bothering with his underwear, and snatching up his boots, he limped back to camp, not able to face the anger, or the hurt, in her eyes.

Nor that within his soul.

At the moment, he detested himself for the way he'd left her. And her, for the lack of faith she had in him. Above all, he was afraid she was right—that he would cost her the child. And that she'd follow through with her promise.

That she'd hate him until her dying day.

Still, it was a risk he felt compelled to take. The mere thought of someone else in her bed burned like acid in his gut.

Chapter 19

Crossing the Grand River proved easy enough. As shallow and narrow as it was, the spot in which Elizabeth had laundered and bathed could have easily been forded on foot. Both horses crossed without hesitation, though Cocoa seemed less inclined to the task.

Suffering Cutter's surliness and her own keen sense of loss, on the other hand, was the greater trial.

It seemed to Elizabeth that ever since their argument, Cutter never spoke to her unless absolutely necessary.

He seemed to hate her.

And he hadn't been too pleased to see her dressed in men's britches, either, though he still hadn't uttered a word against them. Yet she could tell by the way he stared at them. When she caught him looking, he would shake his head and turn away in disgust.

"I wouldn't have to wear them if you hadn't thrown away my skirt!" she told him defensively.

Still, he didn't respond. Only his eyes gave away his disapproval.

And whereas he'd made it a point to avoid civilization in the past, he led them directly into Fayette late the next day, securing a single room.

When Elizabeth started to protest, he narrowed his eyes at her and said sharply, "What makes you think I plan to sleep here with you tonight, Doc?" Near black circles had appeared beneath his eyes almost overnight, making them appear sunken above the high contours of his swarthy cheeks. The look in his jet-dark eyes was unmistakably hostile and kept Elizabeth from uttering another word.

And keeping to his promise, Cutter did not share her room, nor did he attempt to when they rode into Fulton City the next day. He left her that night, as he had before, and she didn't see him again until morning.

The knock came early. Elizabeth opened the door to find Cutter leaning against the frame, his shoulders set stubbornly even in his casual stance. In spite of himself, her heart quickened at the sight of him.

He was dressed in his denims, but the black shirt he wore was new and crisp. His beard, though not quite full, had grown considerably, making his face appear lean beneath, while the shadows under his eyes had deepened.

"Henry Elias Bass the man you're looking for?" He swept his hat from his head, raking his sweat-dampened bangs from his face. "Had a son by the name of John?"

In spite of his haggard appearance, it seemed to Elizabeth that Cutter grew more startlingly handsome every time she set eyes on him. She nodded, acknowledging the facts as those she'd already given him, her heart aching.

Cutter eyed her britches, and then, with a shake of his head, he leaned harder against the doorframe, reached into a pocket, setting his jaw against the pain in his foot, and withdrew a handful of bills. "Then I suggest you get out today and buy yourself a new getup. Seems he's not in St. Louis, after all. Lives just another thirty miles east of here, though I hear he has business in St. Louis."

He nudged the door open a bit to get a better look at her. Those damned pants she was wearing swallowed the hell out of her. He couldn't honestly say which was worse, the pants or the skirt he'd thrown away. Still, there was no mistaking her sex. Not with hair like hers. She wore it down, the soft cascades flowing about her shoulders like liquid gold, and her cheeks were sun-flushed. The outdoors and sunshine suited her, he decided as he pressed the money into her hand.

"We'll stay here in town tonight . . . head out tomorrow. If that suits you?"

Elizabeth nodded, wishing so much that there were not such an awkwardness between them suddenly.

"If we leave early and ride hard, we should get there by early afternoon at the latest."

"Fine," Elizabeth replied softly. An impenetrable silence followed as they simply stared at each other. At last Elizabeth averted her gaze.

"Well," Cutter said, shifting abruptly, "reckon I'll see you in the morning, then."

Again, Elizabeth nodded, at a loss as to what to say to make things right between them. Something was missing, she knew, but she had no idea exactly what it was. He'd been angry with her before, but not like this.

"See y', Doc," Cutter said tersely, and then he willfully pulled the door closed between them, as if he couldn't stand to see her face any longer.

With a sigh, Elizabeth leaned her cheek against the inside of the doorframe. Seizing the rattle suspended from her neck into her fist, she shook it once, and then listened to the echo of Cutter's boots against the wooden floor. When they faded finally, she moved away from the door.

Despondently she fell back onto the bed and contemplated weeping. Not since her father's death had she felt so empty. But weeping would accomplish absolutely nothing, she knew. And there was too much to be done before tomorrow.

With a weary sigh, she rose and began to plait her hair, studying her reflection in the mirror. The woman who faced her now was so different from the one she remembered. Her head tilted suddenly and her expression turned wistful as she recalled Cutter's whisper. *I like it down.*

Almost absently, she began to arrange her hair loosely about her shoulders. Would it be so wrong to pretend—while she could—that she was his wife?

Cutter's wife.

How wonderful that sounded.

She made a sound that was part sigh, part groan, and then, shaking her head at her own foolishness, she recommenced braiding her hair. It did sound wonderful, but she couldn't afford to dream. Not since she had been a child in her mother's arms had she dared. And her mother was long gone . . . her sister . . . her father . . .

Only Katie remained, and she wouldn't lose her, too, she determined. Not if she could help it.

Haven't I gone out of my way to prove to you that you can trust me? Damn you . . . have a little faith . . .

Elizabeth started at the little voice in her head, and for a moment, instead of her own reflection in the mirror, she saw Cutter's, the earnest appeal in his shadowed eyes.

Reckon you're the one with the problem, Elizabeth, and not Elias?

Elizabeth stared at the mirror a long moment, horrified by the pain she saw in those accusing eyes, and cried out suddenly, tearing the braid free. It just couldn't be!

This, she resolved, her expression determined, was going to be the most convincing performance she could muster. If Cutter thought he could do it . . . then by God, she would stand by him while he tried. He knew how much this meant to her, and she felt instinctively that he wouldn't let her down.

It *was*, after all, a matter of trust.

As Cutter had predicted, the ride to the Bass spread took most of the morning and into early afternoon.

During the ride out, Cutter's manner was less abrupt than it had been, though he still appeared jaded somehow, and the dark circles remained. But at least he was speaking to her, Elizabeth reflected.

"And so Katherine's husband was killed in the war?" Elizabeth asked, trying to ignore the ache that was growing in her rear. Cocoa, in her weariness, had fallen into a gait that was absolutely brutal upon the posterior.

Tapping his hat up out of his eyes, Cutter nodded, and uncharacteristically refrained from remarking over her grimace of pain.

"Seems so," he said, raking his fingers through his beard. Had he been in the mood to smile, the sight of her sweet little butt bouncing off the saddle would have had him grinning from ear to ear. As it was, he was amused, but didn't show it. "As far as I can tell, Elias had only one son."

"When?"

"Petersburg," Cutter replied. His eyes met hers, then traveled the length of her admiringly. She was wearing her new outfit, a turquoise-colored riding skirt and matching shirtwaist. Her hair was loose and shone like yellow sunshine down her back. A few shorter tendrils curled appealingly around her face, framing it beautifully.

Elizabeth nibbled her bottom lip a moment in thought and then announced, "I can't believe Mr. Bass would worry me as he did. In his letter he wrote that they'd both been killed—*killed,*" she stressed, her tawny eyes seeking out Cutter's. There was a peculiar sheen in them, as she asked, "Can you imagine how that made me feel? He had me thinking that both Katherine and her husband had been in an accident—or that they had been murdered, even!" Elias Bass had quite a lot to learn about the phrasing of his words. She shook her head with disgust, her expression growing gloomier by the second.

She couldn't help but speculate that her sister might

still be alive today . . . that her little daughter might not be orphaned . . . if only their mother hadn't taken Katherine away . . . if she hadn't been so terrified of being scalped alive that she'd run off to St. Louis without so much as a good-bye. She glanced up at Cutter suddenly to find that he was watching her. How right he was; *life wasn't fair!* "How did you happen to discover so much in such a short time, anyhow?"

He lifted a brow. "Ain't much a few drinks and the right questions can't ferret out."

Elizabeth's brows knitted as she remembered the night they'd first met, and the drinks he'd plied her with. It seemed to be a favorite ploy of his—this getting people lushed so he could have his way with them. Against her will, she suddenly found herself wondering whether he'd gleaned his information from some jezebel like Bess, and she couldn't help but give him a wounded glance. "While you were at it . . . you didn't happen to discover how it was that Katherine died, did you?"

Cutter sighed, hating the pain in her eyes. "Nope," he said, "but it won't be long before you can ask Bass yourself. Looks like we're here." He tipped his head.

Turning, Elizabeth caught the dazzling reflection of the afternoon sun on the distant windowpanes. They glittered like jewels.

The ranch and its accompanying buildings were surrounded by cottonwoods and oaks. As they neared, the big house began to take shape, and Elizabeth thought it was the most beautiful place she had ever seen in her life.

So this, she marveled, was the place Katherine had called home.

With its double stories and whitewashed brick facade, it was also the grandest place she had ever laid eyes upon. Yet there was a lonesome beauty about it, too, emphasized by the fact that there was no one bustling about with chores, no one rushing out to greet them. The lawn, with its tall, unkept grasses, hinted of defection, and was infiltrated with wildflowers of every color. To Elizabeth it looked more like a meadow than the manicured lawn it was supposed to be.

Two cottonwoods sat, one on either side of the walkway, the lush green of the leaves contrasting with the white of the house. The effect was striking. Adding to it were the white-painted trellises built high against the brick. Red roses in full bloom climbed askew. Some of the branches grew free of the trellis and fell forward untrained, the leaves spotted and yellow, while other branches were completely bare but for the thorns, and a cluster of red blooms at the extremity. The thought that came immediately to mind was that the war had taken its toll here, as well. It was obvious that someone had once cared very much for the place . . . and that now no one seemed to bother.

Nor were there servants about to work the small vegetable garden off to the right of the house—or to paint the small picket fence that surrounded it. The whitewash was chipped and peeling. At their approach a small black and white spotted dog perked its ears and then barked succinctly, as if the effort were more than he should have been expected to give. Again it barked, swaying on its feet, as if battling the urge to flop lazily to its belly.

"Dat's Shifless," a child's voice called out as they neared. "But don' worry . . . he won't hurt you none!"

As if in affirmation, the dog squatted, keeping its ears perked and its eyes fixed on the trespassers.

Startled by the voice, Elizabeth felt her heart vault. She reined in, her eyes searching frantically, desperate for a glimpse of the child who had spoken. It would have to be Katie, she knew intuitively. And it seemed as though she'd waited and waited and thought of this moment for an eternity.

What would she look like now?

Who would she look like?

What was she like?

Where was she?

"We call him Shifless 'cause my papa said so," the voice revealed sweetly.

Again, Elizabeth whirled about on her mare, searching. At last she spotted the small girl perched precariously upon a windowsill on the second story, and her heart leapt within her breast.

As tiny as she was, the tree limbs had completely concealed her from view until now. As Elizabeth stared, bewitched, her heartbeat accelerated, beating into her throat. In that instant she felt near to bursting with pride . . . and so many other emotions, she couldn't begin to understand them all. As she watched, the child rocked forward, coming alarmingly close to losing her balance, and Elizabeth's breath snagged. She froze in the saddle, wholly terrified that the child would fall to her death right before her eyes.

"Well . . . you seeee . . ." The girl shrugged matter-of-factly. "He usa be called Smiley," she said smartly, "but my papa said he was too shifless to smile." She proffered a dainty upturned hand, pausing, as if remembering, and then her expression screwed pitifully. "My papa's gone now," she revealed, with the innocent bluntness only a child could possess. "He went to heaven in the war."

Elizabeth was too shaken by the child's near fall, and too taken aback by her revelation, to reply. She wasn't even aware that Cutter was no longer beside her on his horse until she spotted him on the trellis, climbing swiftly upward as though he were born to it.

"Who are you?" the little girl asked bravely, tilting forward a little to see better.

Elizabeth cried out in panic, finally discovering her voice. "Please—sit back for me!" she instructed, on the brink of hysteria. Immediately she slid from Cocoa's back to the ground, hurrying forward, until she stood just below the child's window, looking up. She struggled to focus her vision.

All at once she was stricken dumb, blinded to everything but the child above her. The most beautiful, if somewhat blurry, little face looked down at her where she stood . . . small, pert nose, it seemed—like Katherine's, she thought with melancholy. Dark hair, a mass of ringlets—perhaps her father's? And the eyes? At this distance, she couldn't tell.

As Elizabeth stared, transfixed, hot tears pricked at her own eyes. Her throat constricted.

"My name is Katie Lizabeth," the child declared impulsively, her voice precious.

And again Elizabeth's heart leapt. A sob escaped her tightening throat as she whispered the name reverently. Katie Elizabeth. Katherine hadn't forgotten her, after all. Against her will, her vision began to cloud. It had never bothered her much that her vision wasn't perfect, but at the moment, she loathed that fault in herself.

Elizabeth gulped down the knot that rose in her throat. "Katie Elizabeth?" Elizabeth repeated hoarsely.

The child nodded once, with fervor, smiling. "What's your name?" she asked boldly.

"My name?" Elizabeth's voice broke with emotion. "My name . . . is . . . is Elizabeth, too," she answered slowly, her eyes stinging and raw.

"Oh," Katie replied thoughtfully. She wrinkled her nose prettily, considering that fact a moment. "Well . . ." She wagged a finger down at Elizabeth brashly. "But I bet you din't know I hadda aunt named Lizabeth, and she's coming to get me—my grandpapa says so." Suddenly her eyes widened. "Oh! Are you my aunt?" she asked hopefully. And then, with a bit of skepticism, she added, "You're not my aunt, are you?"

Elizabeth's heart welled with emotion. *Yes!* she wanted to shout. *Yes! Oh, yes!* "Well," she began slowly, her stomach fluttering wildly. She attempted a tremulous smile. "Yes," she said, at last, choking back her tears. And then, with more force, she repeated, "Yes, Katie, I am."

With a shriek of delight, Katie surged forward, clapping her hands, and kicking the brick at her feet.

"No, Katie! Sit back before you fall! Where's your grandfather?"

"Don' worry," she boasted to Elizabeth, "I never fall!" But in that moment, Cutter caught her attention. She peered down at him curiously, teetering further.

Elizabeth bit her lip as she watched Cutter quicken his pace, only to slip when a rotten slat gave way. Feeling blindly with the toe of his boot, he regained his footing and began the climb once more. Silently Elizabeth urged him to hurry.

"Is that my uncle climbin' up the house?" Katie wanted to know. "I climbed up and up, before, but my mama spanked my butt," she said gravely, nodding. And then her eyes widened in speculation. "I bet you're gonna spank his! Aren't ya?"

Elizabeth heard Cutter's soft chuckle, but had no idea how to respond, even had she been able to. Her thoughts were focused only on Cutter's ascent. The higher he climbed, the slower he seemed to move, the more the trellis swayed.

"I bet you din't know that I was this many!" Katie exclaimed suddenly, meeting Elizabeth's gaze once more. She held up what appeared to be five fingers, and then struggled to get down the fifth. Failing miserably in the endeavor, she thrust her thumb down forcefully with her other hand, releasing the sill in the process . . . losing her balance.

"Katie!" Elizabeth shrieked, but just as the child toppled forward, Cutter reached her, placing a steadying hand to her small chest.

"Easy there, little gal," Elizabeth heard him say.

"Oh, but I never fall!" Katie exclaimed indignantly. "I never do!" she insisted at the rise of Cutter's brow.

"Well, I do," Cutter imparted. "Fell out of a tree once when I was just a mite bigger'n you. Been scared of heights ever since," he swore with so much emphasis that Elizabeth found herself smiling.

Katie gasped. *"You're* not scareda heights?" Cutter nodded slowly, and Katie giggled, as though it were a ridiculous notion. "Not me!" she boasted, her hands going to her hips. "I bet you're scared now. Aren't ya?"

"Reckon so," Cutter admitted soberly.

"Ohhhh, you pooooor thing," Katie said with so much parental concern that Elizabeth had to giggle. Nodding gravely, Katie added, "Do ya want me to pull ya in? Do ya? I can save ya!" she declared solemnly.

"Can you really?"

"Oh, yes!" Katie swore with vigor, her eyes sparkling. "You just watch me and see! Give me your hand," she demanded.

"Oh . . . I dunno," Cutter said, resisting the urge to do just that. His foot was hurting like hell, and standing out on the trellis wasn't helping any. "Maybe you should get in and pull? I believe I'm too afraid to give you my hand unless you're safe inside your room. That is your room, isn't it?"

"Uh-huh . . . but why?"

" 'Cause we might both fall," he explained, "and I sure wouldn't wanna break my arm again."

"Oh!" Katie exclaimed. "Dat mussa hurt! Good idea!" She scrambled down from the sill. "And know what? I think I will be stronger in my room. But why did ya climb up if you're so darned scared?" she wanted to know.

"Darned?" Cutter reproved.

"Uh-huh. My granpapa says it all the time," she

explained somberly. "Din't ya never hear that word a'fore? People say darned when they're reeeeal mad, you see, and sometimes they even say . . ." She whispered a word, but Elizabeth couldn't make it out.

"You don't say," Cutter remarked, managing to sound only mildly amused. He glanced down at Elizabeth and sent her what appeared to be a wink.

"Oh, sure," Katie said matter-of-factly. "Din't ya never hear that one, neither?"

" 'Fraid not," Cutter lied.

Katie chatted incessantly, but with Cutter's help, she was soon standing safely within her room. Once inside, she thrust out her hand.

Astounded at the scene unfolding before her, Elizabeth watched as Katie held out her little wiggling fingers for Cutter to grasp. And she couldn't help but giggle as Cutter pretended to let Katie pull him within, grunting and moaning. Feeling a sense of wonder, she stared at the pair in the window. When Cutter was on his feet inside, he spoke to Katie softly, patting her head. And still Elizabeth stared, feeling an affection in her heart that startled her in its intensity.

From what she could tell, Katie looked much as she remembered Katherine had looked at that age. And Katherine had been a beautiful child. The only difference she could discern in them was the hair. Katherine's had been as rich a gold as wheat before the harvest, and as straight as her own.

It wasn't until Cutter had been inside a full moment that she began to wonder if he didn't intend to come back out. Her expression turned suddenly disbelieving.

"Cutter?" No reply. There was only the blur of an open window. "Cutter!" she hissed. The dog barked behind her, but Cutter never reappeared.

"Cutter!"

Chapter 20

❝You can't just leave me here!" Elizabeth shouted up to the empty window. "Cutter McKenzie! You come back out here this instant! You can't—"

Abruptly the front door flew open and a woman's unfamiliar round face peered out, looking first bothered, and then stunned. As she stared, her chin dropped and her eyes widened. Suddenly she cocked her head, as though in question.

"Uhh . . . uh . . . h-hello," Elizabeth stammered. "I—I—"

"Lands!" the woman declared suddenly, so loudly that Elizabeth leapt back a step. Her face was pale, as though she were looking at a specter. "But no! It couldn't be!" she continued, as she slowly came forward and did a half circle around Elizabeth.

Elizabeth watched her warily, following her steps with question, turning as she turned.

"My, what an uncanny resemblance!" the woman said at last. "You *must* be Elizabeth!"

Elizabeth nodded slowly.

The woman nodded, too. And with an abrupt shriek of delight, she seized Elizabeth by the hand. "Oh! But isn't that always the way!" she exclaimed. "We've been expecting you, but Mr. Bass isn't here just now! He was called away on business, wouldn't you know." She patted Elizabeth's hand reassuringly, then released it. "But do come in, and don't mind me! Lands sakes, I just can't believe my eyes! Katie will be so glad to see you, finally. And goodness, if you don't look so very much like her mother!"

Elizabeth's brows furrowed. She did? Katherine? But she didn't recall that as so! At a complete loss for words, she followed the woman inside, and was led into a large foyer. From it, two pillared doorways led, one right, one left, and a double stairwell curved upward from its center, joining above them to form a loft of sorts. Beyond the stairwell, there was what appeared to be a small parlor.

The woman stopped at the foot of the right stairwell, calling upward, her voice shrill but warm, "Katie, dear . . . please come down!" She then turned to Elizabeth.

Elizabeth merely stared, her thoughts whirling. Folding her hands in front of her nervously, she smiled, and the woman tittered happily, coming forward to take and pat her hand once more.

"I should tell you that that child upstairs has wanted to know, every single day since your telegram came, just when it was that you were arriving. She just couldn't wait!" And then, with a catch to her voice, she added, "You'll have your hands full with that one, I fear." Her eyes sad, she averted her gaze. "Katie!" she called again, glancing upward uncomfortably.

Elizabeth looked about anxiously, silently cursing Cutter for leaving her alone. He was sure to come down the trellis and find her gone. And then what? Surely he would realize that she was inside? He would knock, wouldn't he? He wouldn't just leave her? She grimaced at the thought. With the mood he was in lately, she wouldn't put it past him. Her gaze was drawn helplessly to the stairwell. What on earth could he be doing up there for so long? she wondered peevishly.

"You're so quiet," the woman marveled, watching

her. "Your sister was so chatty—bless her soul—like her daughter, I'm afraid."

Elizabeth remained speechless, nodding mutely, remembering that her sister had, in fact, been very talkative as a child.

"Goodness!" the woman said suddenly, frowning as if recalling something at last and chiding herself for not remembering sooner. "How remiss of me." She left Elizabeth abruptly and went to the door, snatching it open.

Peering out over her shoulder, Elizabeth searched for a glimpse of Cutter. Finding none, she frowned.

The woman turned to Elizabeth, nonplussed. "Well, now, I thought there were two horses out there. Where's your husband?" she asked with genuine puzzlement.

Elizabeth's brows lifted in surprise. "H-Husband?" she repeated stupidly. "Oh, yes! my husband!" Looking about uneasily, she wished Cutter a dozen ways to perdition. "Well!" she began, her mind racing wildly. Impulsively she extended her hand. "I—I am Elizabeth B-B—McKenzie," she amended quickly. She nodded uncomfortably, having no idea what else to say.

The woman appeared amused, her smile enduring. "Yes," she said, her eyes alight with kindness. "Yes, I know. And I am Mimi," she returned, proferring her own hand in welcome. Elizabeth grasped her fingers, shaking them absently, all the while heaping blasphemies on Cutter's head. She gritted her teeth.

Mimi continued to smile benignly. "He did come with you, didn't he?"

Elizabeth smiled back, though she felt like crying and screaming. "Oh, yes," she conceded nodding absently. Miss Mimi began to nod, as well, her brows lifting. She waited patiently for an answer Elizabeth didn't have, and Elizabeth despised Cutter in that moment. Elizabeth continued to nod, her mind racing.

"Your husband?" Miss Mimi prompted.

"Oh! Well, you see," Elizabeth continued uneasily, "he's . . . he . . . well, you see, he—"

"I saved him! I saved him, Miss Mimi!" Katie's voice called out above them.

Both Elizabeth's and Miss Mimi's gazes were drawn up at once—Miss Mimi's to find Katie bouncing with glee on a dark stranger's shoulders, her hand tucked neatly under his chin, throttling him.

It was another moment before Elizabeth could actually see the faces, and it felt as though her eyes crossed before they focused. "Cutter!" she gasped with horror.

"I saved him!" Katie exclaimed happily, hugging Cutter's neck.

Miss Mimi gasped in surprise, her gaze skidding back to Elizabeth's, her expression clearly shocked and a little distrustful.

Recovering quickly, Elizabeth offered a meek smile of apology, a warm stain rising high upon her cheeks. "Uhhh . . . m-my—" she tried not to think of the lie as she spoke the word, and closed her eyes briefly "—h-husband," she stammered, nodding grimly as she opened her eyes. "He's . . . he's . . . well . . . he's already in . . . inside," she said as brightly as she could. Still, Miss Mimi said nothing. "As . . . as you can see." Elizabeth's face burned, but she managed to meet Cutter's dark eyes, and he reassured her with nothing more than a wink.

And then her gaze was drawn upward, to the child sitting wide-eyed on his shoulders. The child stared back, releasing Cutter's chin in surprise.

To Elizabeth's shock, Katie's eyes were as dark as . . . as Cutter's. They were eyes that could seize you, reach into your soul. Eyes that were sad and gleeful, all at once . . . eyes that, aside from their difference in color, were so familiar, it made her heart ache. "K-Katie?" she choked out.

Seeing Elizabeth's expression, Miss Mimi stood by

in silence, watching the scene unfold, her demands for an explanation cast aside as Katie squirmed excitedly, trying to find a way down from Cutter's broad shoulders.

Obligingly Cutter swung her down, holding her upright when her feet wouldn't quite work, and still the child gaped at Elizabeth. "We've gotten to be pals," Cutter assured them both, winking at Elizabeth.

Her heart skipping beats, Elizabeth dropped to her knees at once, opening her arms in welcome, but Katie stood transfixed. At last, after an excruciating moment, Katie took a step forward, and when Elizabeth thought she would rush into her arms, she dashed past her, leaving Elizabeth kneeling empty-handed. Her eyes closed and she swallowed convulsively as she listened to the child's feet racing away. It was to be expected, she told herself. Katie didn't know her, after all. She opened her eyes to meet Cutter's.

There was strength in his gaze, and she drew from it.

Miss Mimi. There were tears in her eyes, and the tip of her nose was growing pink.

Suddenly she was aware that those same little feet raced back toward her, skidding to a halt in front of her. And before Elizabeth could speak, a small picture frame was thrust before her, so close that the three figures depicted were no more than a dark blur. Reaching for it, she drew it away from her face to see it better, then close again, unable to focus at the distance she had held it. She held her breath as the shapes began to take form.

Katie rocked forward on the balls of her feet, her hands locked behind her back. "You look jus like my mommy," she whispered reverently, a touch of sorrow in her quiet tone. Her little eyes glazed over as Elizabeth watched, but her tender smile negated her grief. "She went to heaven, too. But not in the war," she confided in a whisper, glancing up suddenly to Miss Mimi for assistance.

Miss Mimi came forward, placing a reassuring hand on Katie's little shoulder, squeezing gently, her own eyes hazing.

Her heart aching, Elizabeth drew Katie's tiny fingers into her own. To her joy, Katie didn't recoil from her touch, but instead stepped closer.

Miss Mimi cleared her throat. "Katherine, you see . . ." she began, only to stop short, overwhelmed by emotion. She dabbed at her eyes.

Knowing instinctively what Miss Mimi was about to say, Elizabeth drew Katie toward her, hoping to shield her, or at the very least, lend her her own strength. To her surprise, Katie hurled herself into Elizabeth's embrace, as though she were starved for the warmth offered.

"You see," Miss Mimi continued, "your sister passed away during the birth of her second child . . . a little boy. Joshua Elias," she choked out. "We buried him next to his mother."

As though her life depended on it, Katie clung to Elizabeth while Miss Mimi spoke, and Elizabeth gave her a little reassuring hug.

"Near six months ago," Miss Mimi continued, her voice breaking. She shrugged her plump shoulders, silently asking that Elizabeth understand, because she couldn't bear to go on. "News of John's death took so much of her strength, I'm afraid—" She choked suddenly on her words.

Elizabeth held tightly to the child in her arms, hot tears pricking at her eyes, and then she gazed down over Katie's shoulder, to the picture in her hand.

Three smiling figures stared back at her: Katie, perhaps at two, her hair shorter, but just as curly, her face just as sweet; a man she assumed would be Katherine's husband, John, his dark, wavy hair sweeping proudly to his shoulders, his brass buttons gleaming; and Katherine, looking so much as Elizabeth recalled.

Beautiful, beautiful Katherine.

Elizabeth laid the frame gently against Katie's back as a tear trickled down her cheek. "I only need to know . . ." She faltered over her words, glancing up at Miss Mimi. "Was my sister happy?"

Dabbing again at her eyes, Miss Mimi nodded. "Oh, dear, yes!" she exclaimed. "Very happy!"

Elizabeth nodded, closing her eyes, further words failing her. That was all that mattered, wasn't it? That Katherine had been happy? That her life had been good? And now it was her duty to step into Katherine's shoes as mother to the priceless child in her arms. It was, she thought, in a moment of revelation, what she was born to do.

It felt so right. Her free hand slid into Katie's curls, rubbing soothingly. "Don't cry," she soothed.

Katie held tighter, burying her face into Elizabeth's hair. "I never cry!" came a muffled exclamation, but the child held tighter, and then she sniffled, belying her claim.

Elizabeth smiled with understanding. "Of course you don't," she agreed, remembering vividly another time, another place: Katherine had fallen, and had skinned her knees and her elbows. Elizabeth had wiped the dirt from her sister's dress, and then from her knees. *"Look! Lookee here, it's mostly dirt!"*

"My dress!" Katherine had wailed pitifully.

"Don't worry, Katie, Mother will understand. Look, it's all gone! Don't cry!"

With her sweet face upturned, and the blue of the sky reflecting in the sheen of her eyes, Katherine had sworn vehemently, *"I'm not crying. I never, ever cry!"* But tears had shimmered in her eyes.

Heaven help her . . . if it was the only thing Elizabeth ever did in her life, she would make her sister proud. Never let Katie forget. For the first time ever, something aside from her role as healer moved her to her very soul, ranked just as important—more so, perhaps, because there was something so inherently fulfilling about cradling the child in her arms. Her little body felt so very precious. A lone tear trickled down her cheek.

Miss Mimi gave them a moment longer, and then, unable to keep herself from it, joined their embrace, weeping joyfully and without restraint, telling Elizabeth how much she'd been spoken of—how well she'd been praised. And again, how much she looked like her sister.

And then, while Cutter hauled in their belongings, Elizabeth listened in silence as Miss Mimi expressed Katherine's profound regret that they'd lost touch with each other. But she could find absolutely nothing to say in response as Miss Mimi led them up the stairs to the room they would be occupying during their stay. There was little that could be said that would fill the loss of her sister—a loss that, though it had occurred years before with her parting, only now waxed complete.

Still, there was comfort in that Katherine *had* thought of her—if not enough to correspond, then at least on occasion. Yet it would always pain her that through the years their separation had become so absolute, that had it not been for Elias Bass's letter, she might never even have known her only niece.

A vision came to her abruptly, of the three of them together—she and Katie . . . and Cutter. Shaking her head to dispel it, she forced her thoughts to Elias Bass.

What kind of man would he be? How could anyone not want adorable Katie? Her gaze was drawn to the child darting ahead of them. Opening a door, Katie dashed into the far room, and by the time the three of them had reached the doorway, she was romping on the large four-poster bed.

"Hope this will do," Miss Mimi said. She wagged a warning finger at Katie, but Katie disregarded the reprimand, never ceasing in her play. Without missing a beat, Miss Mimi turned to Elizabeth, as if she'd never expected the child to mind her anyway, and said, "The wardrobe is empty. Use it, if you wish. Oh, and I thought you might like a bath?"

Elizabeth smiled with appreciation, her eyes skimming the room. "Yes. Thank you. That's very kind of you." She placed her load upon the bed, flexing her arms. Without a word, Cutter set his yannigan bag next to hers, and then went to the window, thrusting his hands into his pockets. "The room is beautiful," Elizabeth assured her as she watched him. "I'm certain it will do wonderfully."

A large birch wardrobe occupied the left wall, while the headboard sat flush against the right. The door was behind her, and a small window was set in the far wall, with another dresser made of birch before it. Beside the bed sat a commode, and upon it, a washbasin and ewer of ivory porcelain. A stiff-backed wooden chair sat in the corner next to the wardrobe, kitty-corner to the bed.

"Mr. Bass's late wife ordered everything from back east," Miss Mimi revealed. "Bless her soul—she's been gone near to ten years now."

Elizabeth nodded, and having no idea what to say in response, began to unpack. "She had wonderful taste," she said belatedly, looking up in time to see that Miss Mimi wore a fond smile, and was nodding in profound agreement. Staring down at her belongings, Elizabeth sighed. There were so few of her own items that she lingered over each one, hoping that Miss Mimi wouldn't notice the telltale lack. "Did Katherine live here, too?" she asked conversationally, trying to avert Miss Mimi's attention.

Miss Mimi threw up a hand. "Oh, goodness, no—but they didn't live far," she said. "If you'd like, I'm certain Mr. Bass will take you there tomorrow."

"I can go, too," Katie said, rather than asked, falling upon the bed. She barely missed falling upon Cutter's bag. And then belatedly, her face screwed uncertainly. "Can't I, Miss Mimi?"

"Of course, Katie," Miss Mimi assured her with a

wink. "That is . . . if it's all right with your aunt Elizabeth."

"Of course," Elizabeth agreed, smiling anxiously as she hesitated over her very last item. Her eyes fell at once to Cutter's bag. She debated whether to unpack it, as well.

Glancing up, she saw that Cutter was no longer at the window, he was leaning against the right wall, his left foot braced casually behind him, his arms crossed. And then her gaze reverted to Miss Mimi, who was scrutinizing her curiously. She glanced anxiously down at Cutter's things.

What was wrong with her? she wondered peevishly. They were just clothes, weren't they? Along with his toothbrush, powder, and razor, she added mentally. Her face heated at the memory of Cutter finding her at the river with sand in her mouth.

It didn't matter that it made her feel strange inside to . . . to touch his things. It didn't matter that they brought back shameful memories, because if they had, in fact, been married, then it would have been expected of her as his wife to unpack for him, and that was exactly what she was going to do!

Besides, she reminded herself, she *had* already seen, as well as touched, his clothing—when she'd washed it in the river. Still, she hesitated, glancing briefly to Cutter. He was grinning his lopsided grin again, and her eyes narrowed in censure.

Swallowing, Elizabeth forced herself to reach out and touch Cutter's green shirt, and heard him chuckle beneath his breath. While Miss Mimi prattled on about there not being enough hours in a day, Elizabeth lifted it up, scrunching it, her fingers recalling the wash-worn texture of it. And then, without thinking, in the most intimate of gestures, she brought it to her nostrils, breathing deeply of the soap she'd used to cleanse it . . . and the more elusive male scent that was as much a part of it as the fibers that bound it.

Desire shot through Cutter like a lightning bolt as he watched her. No longer aware of Miss Mimi, he heard her voice as no more than a distant drone. In that moment he craved Elizabeth more than he'd ever thought possible.

But it was more than the intense heat in his lower anatomy that roused him, unsettled him, made him restless. It was the satisfaction he'd attained in that one simple gesture of hers—an intimacy to be shared only by a man . . . and his woman.

His woman.

The phrase hounded him like a raving wolf at his heels. Fascinated, he watched as Elizabeth folded his shirt, placing it neatly within the drawer. His gaze smoldered, narrowing with the gratifying memory of her washing that same shirt in the river. He wanted her to do those things for him always. Not that he couldn't fend for himself, but it gave him a deeprooted pleasure to see her touch him in that way . . . without touching him at all.

It made him burn.

Even absorbed as he was, Cutter immediately sensed the new presence, and the hairs on the back of his neck bristled. His deliberations ended abruptly as he glanced up to see that an older man now stood behind a chattering Miss Mimi in the doorway, observing them without speaking, his stance nonthreatening. Yet the man's expression was unmistakably guarded. Cutter stiffened. No one else seemed to have noticed his appearance, and he said nothing to alert them. He stepped away from the wall abruptly, dropping his hands to his sides.

For a long moment their gazes met and held, each man assessing, and he knew instinctively that it was Elias Bass taking his measure. The man who would decide his and Elizabeth's fate. For sure as hell was hot, if Bass denied Elizabeth the child . . .

She *would* hate him.

It was obvious that she was already in love with

the kid. But then, it didn't take much. It would be real easy to get attached himself . . . if he allowed it. But he couldn't afford to . . . and didn't aim to.

"Lookee here, Aunt Lizabeth!" Katie flipped on the bed, and then froze abruptly on her head when she saw her grandfather in the doorway. "Granpapa!" she shrieked, peering at him through her little legs. She leapt upright and off the bed, racing like a small bolt of lightning into his arms.

Chapter 21

E lias Bass was a tall, lanky man, with silver hair
and blue eyes that crinkled heavily at the corners. The laugh lines at his mouth were just as prominent, though at the moment they were drawn into
an uneasy smile.

Straining upward, Katie snuggled her cheek against
her grandfather's silver-flecked beard. She popped
upright suddenly. "Oh, Granpapa!" she cooed happily, running her little fingers through his beard. "My
aunt Lizabeth is here with my uncle Cutter! An' ya
know what?" she said soberly. "He climbed up the
house! An' ya wanna know what else? She's not even
gonna spank him!"

Elias Bass chuckled at his granddaughter's incredulous expression and, with his free hand, nudged her
under the chin. "That so?" he asked jovially. He
flipped Cutter another quick glance through his
lashes, and then, adjusting Katie in his arms, he
stepped into the room, proffering his hand to Cutter
in welcome.

At the same time, Cutter moved away from the wall
and came forward, around the end of the bed,
squeezing Elizabeth's shoulder on the way. "Cutter
McKenzie," he offered formally, leaning forward to
grip the man's hand.

Elias grasped it, shaking it as firmly as he was able.
Then, with an overburdened grunt, he set Katie on

256

her feet, never taking his eyes from Cutter. At once she returned to the bed, hurling herself upon it. "Glad to see you made it," Elias said, releasing Cutter's hand finally.

Cutter returned a nod, and then pivoted, catching Elizabeth by the wrist, drawing her forward. *"My wife,"* he stated, with so much pride that Elizabeth's heart jolted violently at the sound of it.

It sounded so genuine.

Her eyes met Cutter's briefly, and then skittered guiltily to Elias's. She swallowed nervously, but Cutter's hand on the small of her back gave her courage. "I . . . I . . . I-It's good to meet you . . . er, finally," she finished lamely, her legs faltering.

Elias smiled, nodding in agreement, and though he didn't offer her a hug as Miss Mimi had done, the look in his eyes was in that instant just as welcoming.

Still, Elizabeth felt ill at ease in his presence, aware of the lie as though it were a tangible being among them.

"It's been a rough trip for Liz," Cutter explained, sensing her unease. He rubbed her back soothingly, the gesture affectionate.

"Imagine so," Elias returned, scraping his beard with his long fingers. He coughed abruptly, glancing quickly at Miss Mimi, and then cleared his throat, looking directly at Elizabeth. "You folks take the train at all?"

Elizabeth tried in vain to tamp down the panic she felt. His look penetrated so deeply that she was certain he could see the lie. Her thoughts and voice fled. She tried to speak, to tell him no . . . but her voice wouldn't materialize. Good night! She'd lose Katie for certain! It just wasn't possible to fool Elias Bass! She couldn't! How had she ever considered it?

Cutter gave her a gentle shove at her back, urging her without words to speak up. When that didn't work, his hand slipped down to cup her rear, squeezing softly.

"No!" she gasped, leaping away, her hand going behind her to swat Cutter's away. Unobligingly, he didn't release her, but when she would have leapt inadvertently into Elias, his firm grip on her skirt kept her from it, and so she let it pass without another word.

Elias took a wary step backward, but his old eyes didn't miss the position of Cutter's arm, nor had he missed Elizabeth's indignant little slap of surprise. Still, what he saw was a couple clearly familiar with each other. Again he coughed and cleared his throat, glancing with raised brows at his housekeeper.

Miss Mimi looked guiltily away, obviously having seen the gesture as well, and Elizabeth felt flooded with shame for shocking the woman so.

"Well," Elias began with a slow-spreading grin, "I reckon you two are pretty tuckered." He and Cutter shared a knowing look, and Cutter returned his lopsided smile, along with a nod.

Elizabeth plainly understood what Elias hadn't asked aloud. *Need time alone?* But before she could utter a protest, he was ordering Katie off the bed and shooing her out the door. "Out, Katie," he said gently, and then, looking to Cutter, still grinning, he added, "We'll let you folks be for now. Reckon there'll be plenty of time to get acquainted later."

Cutter nodded once more. "Reckon so."

"But I wanna stay!" Katie objected with a single stamp of her foot.

"You can come back later," Elias promised. "Now, go on."

Elizabeth opened her mouth to say that there was no reason Katie shouldn't remain with them when Cutter's hand slipped down to her bottom once more. She jolted at his touch, spinning about to pierce him with venom in her eyes. *Just you wait*, she promised silently. *Just you wait.* Turning again, she saw that Elias was already shoving Miss Mimi along before him. And Katie was gone; her lithe little running footsteps were fading down the hall. Her protest died in her throat.

Miss Mimi shook her head. "That child never walks," she complained. "One of these days she's going to kill herself on those steps!" She sighed wearily, and then realizing what she'd said, and the reason for Elizabeth's visit, she looked to Elizabeth, her expression both a little sad and pleased. There was a moment of profound understanding between the two as Miss Mimi handed over the reins to Elizabeth, and then she smiled and turned away. "I'll run the bath for you," she called out, trying to sound cheery.

"No, you won't, Mimi," Elias rebutted, winking at her. "Can't you see these two young people need some time alone? It's been a long trip for them—poor woman's as jumpy as a toad. Give 'em time to breathe, for Pete's sake. Don't worry about the bath, Mrs. McKenzie," he called out from the hall. "We'll warm it when you're ready. Take your time." Their footsteps echoed on the wooden floor, and then suddenly they halted abruptly.

Miss Mimi shrieked. "Elias—stop it!"

Elias wheezed, the sound part laughter, part rasp.

"Don't think I missed that cough in there!" Miss Mimi cried. "You're not well! Didn't I tell you that ride to and from St. Louis would be too much in this heat!"

"I'm fine," Elias assured her.

Miss Mimi snorted in disagreement, and then sighed in resignation. "Don't you think she looks the spitting image of Katherine?" she asked, changing the subject.

"Reckon a little," Elias conceded.

"Oh, Elias," Mimi chided, her voice becoming faint with distance. "You must not have been looking at her face! I say she looks just like Katherine!"

Elias's chuckle was barely audible, and then Miss Mimi squawked again, yielding a final giggle.

When they were gone at last, and there was no

danger of anyone returning, Elizabeth swung to face Cutter, her look indignant. "How could you? They saw you do that!"

His movements as agile and muscular as a mountain cat, Cutter closed the door, turning to lean his thick shoulders against it, his grin clearly predatorial. "Saw what?" he asked, his eyes sparkling with mischief.

"Don't pretend you don't know what I'm talking about, McKenzie! How could you do such a thing?"

"What?" he asked huskily. "Be so familiar with my wife?" He shrugged. "Reckon I couldn't think of a better way to get them the hell outta here. Chrissakes, Liz, given another moment, you might have confessed every sin you ever committed to the man. Couldn't have that, now could we? Besides, I wouldn't worry about shocking those two," he said with a twisted grin. "They could probably teach us a thing or two."

Elizabeth's expression was first appalled and then disbelieving. Not catching his use of the word *us*, she asked, "Elias and Miss Mimi?"

Cutter shrugged noncommittally, raking a hand across his sweat-dampened bangs, sweeping them out of his eyes.

"Oh—how would you know?" Elizabeth snapped. Snatching up the rest of Cutter's clothing into a wadded bundle, she shoved it heedlessly into the open drawer. "She's his housekeeper, for mercy's sake!"

Enjoying her ire, Cutter grinned. "Just do," he replied matter-of-factly. He rather liked the way her eyes lit up in a pique.

Elizabeth snorted. "You couldn't possibly after only a few moments!" she countered, tossing a lock of sun-bleached hair over her shoulder.

Weeks on the trail had turned her dishwater blond hair a sun-kissed gold, with the lightest strands framing her face. And her skin reminded him of peaches and cream; despite the time they'd spent in the sun, it seemed only the slightest bit darker. His lips curved roguishly. "Wanna bet?" he asked. His tone was seductive in its silky softness.

Irritably snatching up a pair of Cutter's socks she'd missed from the bed, Elizabeth threw them, too, into the open drawer, closing it discordantly, wishing that she'd hurled them at Cutter instead. "No, I don't want to bet!" she retorted, grating her teeth. "And that . . ." She turned, wagging a finger at him, her eyes narrowing. "That's another thing! I can't believe you left me standing outside alone, screaming like a banshee up at an empty window! You don't just climb into someone's window and stay, McKenzie! It just isn't done!"

Cutter raised a brow sardonically. "It isn't?" he asked with obvious amusement.

"No! It isn't!"

"In that case—" Cutter lifted his weight from the door abruptly "—I'll have to remember that next time I climb into someone's window. Won't I, *Mrs. Mc-Kenzie*?" He grinned, inordinately pleased with the way that sounded.

Elizabeth took a step backward, but straightened her shoulders, looking as fierce as she was able. "Don't you dare call me that—and you can quit having your fun at my expense! I know what you're doing, McKenzie!"

"You do?"

She held a hand out to ward him away. "Stay back!"

Cutter's grin deepened.

Elizabeth retreated another step, her back coming flush against the wardrobe. "Cutter," she warned. He placed one hand above her head, bracing himself. And then, after an interminable moment, he touched her, his fingers gripping her by the waist—so hot where they touched—and her knees went weak.

"Cutter," she breathed, her legs buckling.

His arm snaked about her waist, catching her,

drawing her to him, and her heart skipped a beat. She went limp in his arms as he slowly savored the feel of her, joining their bodies so close, they could have been one. "You're beautiful," he said softly.

"Please, don't . . . don't lie to me," she begged. "I'm not . . . never have been."

"Beautiful," Cutter stressed, cupping her face gently. "Don't ever let me hear you say otherwise."

The naked hunger in his ebony black eyes made her feel it was the truth he was speaking. That he meant every word. And her heart soared. Her eyes closed. "Cutter . . ."

His fingers wound themselves into her hair, his eyes slitting. "Your hair," he whispered with so much intensity that it sent a quiver down her spine. Like fire, his lips brushed lightly against her own, a whisper searing her clear to her soul. Then again, the velvety heat of them robbing her will. "And your mouth . . ." Again, his lips touched her, but this time he nipped her gently. Her lips parted with a moan. "Especially your mouth." He guided her backward, tilting her head back. Bracing her against the wardrobe, he dipped to kiss the pulsing hollow at the base of her throat, savoring it as though it were the very thing he craved.

But it wasn't.

And they both knew it.

Elizabeth was burning, too. Impossible to bear. Her entire body ached; her breasts for his touch, her lips for his kiss. His lips pressed against hers, then gently covered her mouth, the slow, drugging kiss leaving her breathless. Without warning, his tongue stabbed deeply, leaving her mouth burning with fire, and her breath left her completely. Heat unfurled deep within her, seeping into every part of her, making her tremble with longing.

Heaven help her, she wanted to.

But she couldn't.

She shook her head, denying him, denying herself,

but couldn't speak to say the words. It was one thing out there, alone . . . but here?

The pitter-patter of little feet broke into her consciousness, but before she could recover herself, the door flew open. Shrieking with surprise, Elizabeth shoved at Cutter's chest, her face flushing guiltily. Reluctantly Cutter moved away from her, cursing the kid for her rotten timing.

"Katie?" Elizabeth gasped, her hand flying through her hair, smoothing it nervously away from her face.

Katie smiled. "I jus' wanned to show you somethin'," she whispered loudly, her eyes big and round, as if to emphasize the secrecy of her visit. She came forward slowly. And with her eyes fixed on Elizabeth, she offered her hand, palm-up.

In it, to Elizabeth's shock, was a small locket she immediately recognized. She fingered it reverently, sinking to her knees to put herself at Katie's eye level. She lifted it from Katie's small hand, swallowing the knot that appeared in her throat, and gazed at it dumbly for a long moment. Slowly she opened it to find two small portraits encased within. Katherine . . . and herself. As she gazed at it, bittersweet memories assailed her. Tearing her gaze away from the locket, she found Katie staring at her expectantly.

"Where did you . . ." Elizabeth choked on her words. "Oh, Katie . . ."

"For you," Katie whispered, delighted with her gift, as well as the tender expression she'd gleaned from her new aunt. "My granmommy gave it to my mommy, and then my mommy gave it to me when God tol' her she was gonna go to heaven." She lifted her chin, winking one eye so sweetly that Elizabeth's heart ached for the loss she was accepting so bravely.

"Oh, Katie, are you certain? This is so special. Maybe your mommy meant for you to have it."

"Well . . . if you take me home," she suggested in a sweet whisper, "then we could share." She lifted her hands as if to say, *you see how easy it could be?*

"Of course," Elizabeth replied, her heart breaking with every gesture Katie made, every word she uttered. "And we will." Moisture shimmered in her eyes. "We surely will."

"Cause my grandpapa says he's too tired anymore," Katie revealed matter-of-factly, and Elizabeth's heart twisted again. "Right?"

Elizabeth swallowed the lump in her throat. "Yes, and thank you, Katie." She held up the locket. "I'll treasure it always." She searched in vain for the right thing to say, but nothing else came to her. From downstairs, Miss Mimi's voice called out, and Katie's eyes grew instantly wide.

"Don' tell!" she urged in an anxious whisper. "Granpapa says you was tired an' that you was gonna sleep . . . and he tol' me not to bother." She lifted a hand up and shook it daintily. "But I didn't bother . . . so don' tell . . . all right?" She looked so unsure of herself that Elizabeth had to smile.

"All right," Elizabeth agreed, closing her fist against the cool silver of the locket. "I won't tell."

Katie's dark eyes sparkled, and with an enormous grin, she suddenly turned and scampered from the room, forgetting to close the door in her haste.

Slowly, cherishing the moment, Elizabeth turned to find Cutter watching her intently. He was leaning casually, one shoulder on the wardrobe, his stance easy. But he said nothing, and his narrow-eyed look sent a tingle down her spine. What must he think of her? As he continued to scrutinize her, she felt a deep sense of shame for the predicament they'd been caught in. By Katie nonetheless!

Not for the first time, she wondered what was wrong with her that she forgot everything, including to breathe, in his presence? What had happened to all the caution and good sense her father had instilled in her? Cutter made her so weak with only a look, and she shuddered inwardly at the thought of his lips on her own. And then her gaze was drawn to the bed, the only bed in the room, and she nibbled nervously at her bottom lip.

"That certainly was close," she said abruptly. Cutter didn't reply beyond lifting a dark brow, and her embarrassment turned quickly to annoyance. "About tonight, Cutter . . . I don't think we should . . . we should . . ." Lord help her, but she couldn't say it. She watched as Cutter's jaw set, and felt a quivering run the length of her.

She tried again. "I wouldn't expect—well, that because I'm a woman, I should have the bed . . ." Her gaze was drawn to the wooden chair, and she winced, thinking of how uncomfortable it would be to sleep there. But then, the only other recourse . . . would be pure heaven, she admitted, if only to herself. Still, it wasn't right, and she wouldn't shame herself, or her sister's family, by sleeping with a man she wasn't wed to. "I'll sleep on the chair," she concluded, nibbling gently at her lip. "You can have the bed."

With a curt nod, Cutter lifted himself off the wardrobe. "I see," he said, his eyes smoldering as he came forward. "It's all right to share the half-breed's roll, but not his bed?" Shaking his head in disgust, Cutter stalked past her, giving her a narrow-eyed glance as he passed by. He jerked open the door and stopped. Without turning back to her, he said, "Don't bother with the chair. You're welcome to the bed!" He wanted to add that he wouldn't be back, but the words wouldn't come. And in his frustration he realized that that was the crux of it all; he knew he would return. He slammed the door as he walked out, leaving her standing in stunned silence behind him.

Chapter 22

There wasn't a muscle in his body that wasn't
tightly coiled with fury as Cutter leaned forward
upon the fence, clutching it wrathfully, yet he managed to look casual as he gazed out into the endless
fields. Wheat, he thought. Acres and acres of it. He
squeezed the wood until it made raw imprints in his
palm. The sun was just beginning to set, and the
grasses swayed gently with the breeze, the golden-
brown tips blending against the golden light of the
sky . . . The scene was as quietly seductive as she
was.

Hell, he should have seen it coming.

So why hadn't he? He shook his head in self-
disgust.

"Get yourself in trouble with the little missus?"

Hearing Elias's voice, Cutter stiffened abruptly, the
tiny hairs upon the back of his neck standing on end.
Willing the tension out of his body, he straightened
and turned his back to the fence to find Elias Bass
sauntering toward him, grinning knowingly. He
leaned back and crossed his ankles, assuming a negligent stance, glancing briefly at the house, then back.
"You might say that," he conceded ruefully.

Elias chuckled and halted before him, crossing his
arms.

Again Cutter broke eye contact—long enough to
tuck his volcanic emotions away—and then returned

it. He couldn't afford for Elias to see his anger—
Elizabeth couldn't afford it, he corrected himself.
Since when had he taken a personal stake in this? "I
believe she's afraid we made a poor first impression,"
he said.

"And you?" Elias prompted.

Cutter shrugged. "I think she's already half in love
with your granddaughter," he said bluntly. "And
she's scared to death you're gonna change your
mind—that you're gonna disapprove of us for some
odd reason." He watched Elias's expression meticu-
lously, taking in the guilty color that immediately suf-
fused the man's face, and swore silently.

Elias nodded, using the moment of silence to digest
that bit of information. "You're real direct, Mc-
Kenzie, aren't ya?" He glanced down at his boots
abruptly and kicked the ground, then again met Cutter's gaze. "Well, I like that," he announced.

Cutter only nodded. Sure he did . . . He liked it—
but! Damn, he could almost feel the word as though
it were suspended between them. A tangible thing.
He braced himself for the sound of it.

"About that reason, McKenzie . . . I'm glad you
came down." Elias turned his back to the fence and
dragged himself atop it, settling down upon the top
slat next to Cutter and hooking the heel of his boots
over the bottom rung. He sighed heavily, looking
weary. "There's something we need to talk about."

Once again the hair at the back of Cutter's neck
bristled. At his right side, his hand curled into a fist.
There it was—he could sense it coming. It was all in
the tone of Elias's voice, and he swore again; at himself for believing it could be otherwise, at Elias Bass
for proving Elizabeth right—and at Elizabeth for walking into his damned life to begin with! His gaze
shifted abruptly to Elias, his eyes narrowing, his heart
hammering, his gut twisting violently. Elias was
watching him studiously, his old blue eyes missing
nothing. Checking himself, Cutter took a moment to

shut away his emotions, and then asked quietly, "You got a problem with that reason, Bass?"

Again there was silence as both men stared, measuring each other.

"No," Elias replied after a somber moment. His brows rose in question. "Have you got a problem with it, McKenzie? Now, hold on a moment before you go off half-cocked!" he added when Cutter's brows collided fiercely. He held a hand out between them. "I believe I've got a right to that answer! Katie's my only granddaughter! Honest to God, McKenzie, I ain't got no argument with you—don't care what you are!"

Cutter straightened abruptly to his full height. *"What I am—"*

"Just allow me to finish! What you are *does* affect my granddaughter, and we both know it. I care too much about her not to take this up with you! Seems to me you're a decent man. I ain't blind—I know what I saw between you and Elizabeth upstairs, and that's good. It says a lot! But I just need to know that you ain't got a chip on your shoulder—that you know what you're getting yourselves into—what you're getting my granddaughter into!"

Just needed to know? No buts? Shutting out the tiny jolt of elation he felt at what he *wasn't* hearing, Cutter forced himself to settle back against the fence and cross his arms. He could hear the plea in the old man's voice. Never releasing Elias's gaze, his jaw remaining taut, he was afraid that he was mistaking Elias's meaning.

Elias shook his head gravely, choosing his words cautiously. "I gotta know she's gonna be all right, McKenzie—that you're gonna take care of her . . . that you ain't gonna let them get to her."

There was no need to clarify who *them* was. Both knew. Still Cutter didn't reply. A muscle ticked at his jaw, though he wasn't certain it wasn't out of simple giddy relief. *No buts.*

"You see, I know," Elias began carefully, meeting

Cutter's gaze unflinchingly. "I know how vicious folks can be."

Cutter relented with a nod, acknowledging Elias's right to be concerned. He glanced at the house and disclosed quietly, "It's been a long time, Bass, since anyone's done any name calling . . ." His gaze returned to Elias. "To my face or otherwise. Still, I can't promise you how other folks are gonna be. Though I *can* assure you I *will* handle it. And . . ." He glanced away abruptly, unable to look Elias in the eye as he spoke the rest. "She'll have a good and loving home." It was the truth, he knew—with or without him in the picture.

"Well," Elias replied, "I—"

"Granpapa! Granpapa—wait for me! I gotta tell you somethin'!"

The front door slammed discordantly in the distance. Both Cutter's and Elias's gazes jerked toward the sound of Katie's exuberant voice. Each watched her enthusiastic approach with an odd mixture of relief and frustration.

Cutter was the first to tear his gaze from her. He shook his head, suddenly recalling her earlier interruption. "She always have such rotten timing?" he asked bluntly, though his lips were on the verge of a smile.

The dry humor in Cutter's tone—as well as the tiny note of dread—didn't pass Elias by. His face broke into a wide, lip-splitting grin as he turned to face Cutter, mischief sparkling in his eyes. "Always," he swore emphatically.

Just then, Katie reached them. She glanced up at them, scrunching her nose in disgust. "Aunt Lizabeth's gotta get a bath!" she exclaimed in disgust. "Why does Miss Mimi *always* wanna give *everyone* a bath? Me—Shifless!" she enumerated. "*Now* Aunt Lizabeth!"

Elizabeth was taking a bath.

An involuntary shudder coursed through Cutter at

the declaration, and his gaze was drawn at once to the house.

What he wouldn't give . . .

"And we haven't even played yet!" Katie exclaimed.

Cutter shook free of his carnal thoughts, and despite himself, he chuckled at Katie's disgruntled expression. He stooped to her eye level and ruffled her hair. Still chuckling, he asked, "Whattaya say, partner? Think we oughta go find ourselves a hidey-hole before Miss Mimi comes out scrubbing for us, too?"

Behind him, Elias stroked his beard, having missed nothing, and his grin widened as Katie giggled and nodded vigorously.

The bath Miss Mimi had promised was wonderfully soothing, and for the first time in over a week, Elizabeth felt refreshed. In spite of the fact that the house boasted more luxuries than Elizabeth had ever known could exist under one roof, the ritual of bathing was carried on little differently than it was in her own small three-room home—in the kitchen, with water heated from the stove. Only, if the truth be known, her own tub was much nicer, and much more comfortable.

The tub she found herself scrunched into just now was little bigger than the small basin she used to launder her clothing at home. Still, it was a bath, with clean, warm water, and Elizabeth would never think to complain. It was amazing how quickly one became immune to the aches and pains of the trail—as a matter of necessity—and how quickly they returned at the end of the journey. Truthfully, she was afraid to look, but she could swear that her bottom was bruised until it was blue. And the back of her thighs? She grimaced inwardly. If they weren't, as well, then it would be a miracle.

Miss Mimi, bless her soul, remained to wash her hair, knowing that it would be an impossible task to do herself in the body-squashing bowl she was sitting in.

"I just can't get over how much you resemble Katherine!" Miss Mimi swore as she scrubbed.

Elizabeth winced as Miss Mimi's nails raked over her scalp so vigorously. "It's strange to hear you say so," she admitted, grimacing. "Because I've never thought so. Katherine was always so beautiful."

"Yes, she was," Miss Mimi agreed soberly. "But have you ever looked in a mirror, Elizabeth? You're certainly nothing to scoff at yourself! Why, I bet every man in Sioux Falls cried the day you were wed!"

Elizabeth smiled at the ridiculous statement, overlooking the reminder of her lie. "I'm afraid not," she admitted, hating to disappoint Miss Mimi. "But then, I never felt too badly over it," she rationalized, "because I never really knew many men who weren't already married. Sioux Falls isn't exactly swarming with people these days."

"What a shame," Miss Mimi said lamentably. "But it turned out all right for you, didn't it, dear?" Finished with the scrubbing of Elizabeth's scalp, she dipped a ewer into the tub. "Close your eyes," she demanded, and Elizabeth immediately complied, bracing herself for the downpour. "That man of yours is really something to look at," Miss Mimi remarked casually, dipping the ewer once more. "I can certainly see why you settled on him. Why," she declared, with a girlish giggle, "if I weren't already—" She blinked, and continued in another vein, a little more soberly. "Well, if I weren't so darned old, and he weren't already your husband . . ."

Elizabeth stiffened guiltily as Miss Mimi poured water over her head—this time without warning Elizabeth to close her eyes . . . and her mouth, which was hanging agape.

Elizabeth sputtered, spewing water.

With a last strangled cough, she composed herself. Certainly she couldn't continue to feel so ill at ease every time Cutter was mentioned . . . or the word *husband*. There wasn't a more certain way to lose Katie.

Still, she had to admit that Miss Mimi was right. Cutter was as handsome a devil as they came. He was certainly the most fascinating man she had ever met.

Recalling the way that he'd spoken to her only hours before, she couldn't contain the breathy sigh that rushed past her lips. What was he doing just now? she wondered. And then she recalled the irate look he'd given her before leaving their room, and her brow furrowed. How long did he intend to stay angry with her *this* time?

". . . Anyhow, I do hope you don't make *that* same mistake in your marriage," Miss Mimi was saying.

Realizing that her thoughts had drifted while Miss Mimi had chattered on, and that she'd missed the last of what had been said, Elizabeth nodded absently, trying to ascertain what it was that they were speaking of.

"No! Tell me you don't!" Miss Mimi rebuked, seeing her nod. "Oh, Elizabeth! Forgive me for speaking so plainly, but it pains me to see such a lovely couple lose so much in their relationship for the sake of modesty!" She sighed portentously. "But . . . as I said, Katherine was that way, too." Frowning, she came around the front of the tub, dragging a stool. She settled it before the tub. "You, at least, have an excuse—though not after today, you won't!"

Her expression grave, Miss Mimi sat facing Elizabeth. "Now," she began. "I realize that your father would never have said such things to you, but I do not have such a disinclination. Frank speech bothers me not at all."

Elizabeth nodded dumbly, having absolutely no idea whatsoever what it was that had gotten Miss Mimi so riled. She stared blankly, trying not to look as confused as she felt.

"That poor sister of yours had the mistaken impression—and I won't say who it was that gave it, though I'm certain you know . . . Anyway, it's just not true that you should just lie back and simply do your duty.''

Elizabeth was more confused than ever; her brow furrowed more deeply, and then suddenly her eyes widened and she sank into the tub in humiliation. To her dismay, she was beginning to grasp the topic finally. Appalled, she averted her eyes.

Seeing her guilty reaction, Miss Mimi sounded all the more riled. ''Where such a ridiculous notion began, I'll never know! But that, my dear—and you know what I mean by *that*, I'm certain—is just as special to a woman as it is to a man. And that's God's truth—I do swear!''

Too disconcerted to respond, Elizabeth simply stared at the dispersing soap bubbles, watching them burst, one by one, wishing she were anywhere at all but in this tub, in this kitchen—listening to Miss Mimi. Never had anyone spoken to her of such things, and she wasn't certain how to respond. Obviously she'd mistaken Miss Mimi's look of shock earlier. Nothing could shock the woman! Elizabeth was certain.

''Now, Katherine,'' Miss Mimi continued somberly, ''I know she loved her John very much, but that poor child believed everything your mother told her—every last little bit of drivel! And I'll tell you now precisely what I told her then. There is absolutely nothing wrong with loving your man. It's the most natural thing in the world to want him back—and don't think that carrying a baby changes any of that either. Don't you dare be ashamed if you happen to want to lie with him even more during that time. That's the way it's supposed to be! You'll see,'' she promised, waving a finger in reproach. ''I know what I see in that man of yours' eyes—he's a lusty one. Just don't you fight it. Promise me that much.''

Her cheeks staining crimson, Elizabeth sank lower into the tub.

"Do you understand what I'm telling you?"

Forcing herself to look up into Miss Mimi's knowing face, Elizabeth nodded quickly, her face flaming.

"Oh, for Pete's sake, Elizabeth, you stop that blushing this minute!" Miss Mimi rebuked. "There's absolutely nothing to be embarrassed about. We're both grown women, aren't we?"

Elizabeth nodded again, the stain on her cheek darkening considerably, and Miss Mimi smiled down benignly at her. Then suddenly she slapped at her knees. "Well that's all I have to say over the matter. Honestly, I just didn't want you to feel guilty . . . and then make your man guilty over something God intended just as surely as He made rain!" To Elizabeth's immense relief, Miss Mimi rose, lifting a towel from the table and handing it to her. "Now, come on out of there," she asserted. "Elias is sure to have put your husband to work—he's been so long without his son. There's so much he can't do on his own anymore," she lamented with a sigh. "It really bothers him, you know? Anyhow, they're sure to return famished—so out! Out!"

Throughout dinner, Elizabeth could hold no one's gaze for very long. If Miss Mimi smiled at her, she'd recall their discussion of earlier in the day, and would die of humiliation. Even now, her face warmed as she poked at her stewed carrots.

When Cutter so much as glanced at her, she blushed all the way to her roots, mortified to look at Miss Mimi for fear that Miss Mimi might be watching them watch each other.

When Elias Bass looked her way a moment too long, she felt guilty to her toes over the lie. Thank goodness it appeared Cutter was right about the two of them, because for the most part, Elias and Miss Mimi seemed too preoccupied with each other to give her much notice.

The only safe haven seemed to be Katie. Katie had

been out with Cutter and her grandfather during Elizabeth's bath, watching them work, and seemed to have really taken to Cutter. Her eyes never strayed from him long.

When conversation shifted to talk of Petersburg, Katie suddenly scraped her chair backward, slipping off quickly to the floor.

"Katie?" Elias admonished.

She froze with only one foot on the floor. "Oh!" she replied with a frown. "I forgot. Can I may I please be 'scused? I wanna go feed Shifless," she explained, her eyes cheerless.

Elias settled his fork on the table, adjusting it as he cast a glance at Elizabeth. "All right," he allowed finally, his gaze reverting to Katie. He coughed discreetly. "Go on."

Katie immediately snatched her plate from the table and turned to flee.

"Katie." She stopped abruptly, turning again to face her grandfather.

"Take this, too."

Katie made her way around to where Elias sat, smiling when he placed a large pork bone in her plate. "Shifless'll like that one!" she informed everyone, her cheer returning. Her gaze was drawn to Elizabeth as she explained. " 'Cause he likes the big ones." And then she turned abruptly and scurried from the room, clutching her plate of bones and scraps protectively.

Elias sighed wearily. "Doesn't seem to like to hear about her father," he said with sorrow in his voice.

For the first time since their arrival, Elizabeth met Elias's gaze without wavering. "Sometimes it's too painful," she disclosed. "When my mother left, neither my father nor I would speak of it . . . not ever." Her eyes were distant a moment, before focusing again on Elias. She shrugged. "It just hurt much too much, I suppose."

Elias gave a nod of agreement, glancing automatically at the door through which Katie had vanished.

"Katherine and John were good to her, you know. The best. It's been real hard for her without them. For a long time she wouldn't let them go . . . especially her ma."

Elizabeth nodded, understanding perfectly. "Katherine . . . she died of childbed fever, didn't she?" Her eyes turned sad, wistful, as she wondered whether there might not have been something she could have done to prevent it.

Miss Mimi nodded, her eyes melancholy. "Yes, she did. I was with her, you know. Actually, it was in those last moments that she spoke of you raising her daughter. I think she knew—" She glanced at Elias for rescue. "Well . . ."

Elias cleared his throat. "You see . . . well, she knew that Miss Mimi and I . . . well, we're getting on in years . . . and it ain't so easy to . . . well, jeez— don't really know how to say this . . ."

"Don't have to," Cutter broke in. "We understand, don't we, Elizabeth?" He peered across the table at her.

Elizabeth stopped chewing and nodded hastily.

Cutter's scrutiny shifted to Elias, his dark eyes definitive. "Liz here and I'll take real good care of your granddaughter, Mr. Bass. She's a good kid." To Cutter's surprise, he found that he meant every word. He glanced at Elizabeth to find that she appeared as shocked by the intensity of his declaration as he felt. Their gazes held, neither of them able to break away.

"I know you will," Elias replied after a moment of silence. "If I'd had any doubts before . . . I don't now. I can see you two love each other very much, and it takes a helluva load off my shoulders." Again, Elizabeth's and Cutter's gazes were drawn to each other, and the dark intensity of Cutter's expression sent a quiver down Elizabeth's spine.

"You finished?" Elias asked Cutter.

Cutter didn't respond. He was still staring at Elizabeth, his eyes searching.

''McKenzie?''

Raising his brows, Cutter sat back finally, taking in a deep breath as he tore his gaze away from Elizabeth to acknowledge Elias. He nodded, clearing his throat.

Elias rose abruptly, scraping his seat backward. ''Good,'' he replied. ''Thought we might just go butt heads awhile.''

Cutter rose, as well, tossing down his napkin. He winked at Elizabeth, chuckling when she blushed, letting her know that he was no longer angry, but amused. ''Lead the way,'' he told Elias.

As if sensing her sparkling smile, Elizabeth let her gaze skip to Miss Mimi. When Cutter turned his back to the table, Miss Mimi waved a spoon, her smile deepening, as if to say, *I told you so, dear.*

Chapter 23

Elizabeth did what she could to help Miss Mimi with the dishes and then she climbed the stairs to her room, thoroughly exhausted. Though once there, she told herself that she didn't want to be caught undressed, so she didn't remove her clothing right away.

And it was a good thing, because after a while, Katie tiptoed in to say good night, again without bothering to knock. Smiling, Elizabeth hugged her, and then escorted her back to her own room, tucking her in and pulling the blankets up to her chin. Without thinking, she began to sing:

"Alas, my love, you do me wrong to cast me off discourteously,
And I have loved you so long, delighting in your company.
Greensleeves was all my joy, Greensleeves was my—"

She halted abruptly, as though suddenly realizing what it was she was doing, her brow furrowing, the beat of her heart erratic.

"That's a real pretty song, Aunt Lizabeth."

Elizabeth nodded absently. "Yes. Yes, it is." She glanced down at Katie. "Your grandmother used to sing it to your mommy and me when we were children," she found herself explaining. "And her mommy used to sing it to her.'' She smiled in remembrance, gazing up at the window wistfully, into the night, seeing the soft spun gold of a distant lamplight, and two little girls with shimmering hair, their faces together under the blankets. Katherine had clung to her so many nights, running tiny fingers through her hair. *"Sing it again, Beth,''* she could hear a little voice say again in her mind. And then a sigh. *"One more time, Katie. Just one more time.''* Her eyes hazing over the memory, Elizabeth again looked down at the child her sister had brought into this world. Another Katie to love. "Sometimes even,'' she disclosed in an aching, misty-eyed whisper, "I would sing it to your mommy. She loved it even more than I did.''

Katie's eyes were wide. "Did you get to sleep together always?'' she asked with awe. "I never did have nobody to sleep with me—'cept maybe sometimes my mommy.''

Elizabeth smiled, holding back the tears. "Yes, Katie, we did.'' Gently she swept the curls from Katie's forehead. "We only had one room, you see—'' Her voice broke, her emotions too near the surface. "And . . . and we had to share it. But then your mommy moved away and I had to sleep alone. Just like you. It's very, very hard to do,'' she admitted. "Isn't it?'' Silently she acknowledged the fact that she never really had gotten used to it. And it dawned on her suddenly that even though she'd not spent the last few nights with Cutter, neither had she sung herself to sleep—not since the night Cutter had asked about "Greensleeves.'' For the first time in years, she'd forgotten her nightly fear: that she would wake up to an empty house, an empty heart. But the truth was that her house had long been empty, yet her heart had never been so full.

Katie nodded. "Yeah—but did ya never see a ghost when you was alone? I did !'' she swore emphatically, shifting Elizabeth's thoughts.

Elizabeth chuckled at her tone. "No," she replied as soberly as possible, shaking her head thoughtfully. "I don't believe I ever did. I wonder what your ghost looked like," she pondered aloud, gently tousling Katie's soft hair.

"Like my mommy," Katie responded at once, sending a quiver down Elizabeth's spine. "And I wasn't even scared," Katie said, "but my granpapa said it was a dream ghost, anyhow, and I shouldn'ta been ascared, anyway. Do ya wanna know what the dream ghost tol' me?" she asked, with just the right hint of intrigue.

Elizabeth stroked the back of her fingers against Katie's cheek, smiling fondly at her. Without even trying, Katie had somehow become so much a part of her. And it had happened so easily, and so swiftly. "What did the dream ghost tell you?"

Katie's eyes were wide and haunting in the darkness. The lamplight falling across her face made her skin pale, her features ethereal. "She tol' me you was gonna be my mommy now."

At the unexpected declaration, Elizabeth's heart twisted violently.

"I asked my granpapa, and he said you was. Are ya?" she wanted to know, her dark eyes round and hopeful.

Again, Elizabeth's chest constricted. "Do you want me to be your mommy?" she asked with a catch in her voice. The sweetest smile touched Katie's lips, and she nodded slowly. Smiling faintly, her heart as full as it had ever been, Elizabeth bent to kiss the child on the forehead, tucking the blanket higher about her little chin. "Then I would like that, too—very, very much!" she assured her. She rose, but her fingers continued to caress Katie's cheek. "Good night, sweetheart."

Like a satisfied kitten, Katie stretched, and Elizabeth could almost feel the tension leave her. "Night, Aunt Lizabeth," she replied.

Elizabeth dimmed the lamp slowly, waiting for a protest. When it didn't come, she snuffed it completely, and then bent again to kiss Katie's soft little cheek, thinking, with a sigh, that this day had easily been one of the most emotional she'd ever endured. Katie's sparkling eyes followed her as she went to the door, opening it.

"Sweet dreams," Elizabeth whispered, feeling suddenly as drained as she'd ever felt. Stepping out, she drew the door closed behind her, touching it briefly, her eyes closing as she turned away.

On the way back to her own room, Elizabeth decided with a weary sigh that it would be silly to pace the floor all night waiting for Cutter, fully dressed. Cutter and Elias might very well "butt heads" until late in the night, and it just didn't make sense for her not to go on to bed.

Besides, it wasn't as though there were a reason to wait up.

With that decision made, once she was in her room, she quickly stripped down to her bloomers and camisole, and then she divested the bed of its top cover, placing it upon the chair for Cutter. Savoring the luxury of clean, cool sheets against her flesh, she crawled into bed. As an afterthought, she put out the lamp, snuggling deep into the sheets.

Little more than fifteen minutes had passed when Cutter sauntered in. Closing the door, he immediately began unbuttoning his shirt in the darkness. Elizabeth said nothing, only watched, the tiniest part of her feeling guilty because she was straining through the shadows to catch even the smallest glimpse of him. To her disappointment, she couldn't see a thing, because the curtains were closed and the darkness was impenetrable.

As if he'd read her thoughts, Cutter suddenly stepped toward the window, shrugging off his shirt on the way and dropping it onto the end of the bed. Drawing open the drapes, he let in the silvery moonlight, and Elizabeth squeezed both lids closed, not wanting him to know that she was still awake. A moment later, when the stillness of the room piqued her curiosity, she peered through her lashes.

He was standing, gazing out the window, his face in profile to her. The light that fell across his features made him appear harsh. Made his broad shoulders glisten. As she watched him, he turned abruptly, and she snapped her lids closed, only this time, not all the way.

Through her lashes, she watched him as he released the top button of his trousers, and the sound of it popping loose sent a shiver of remembrance down her spine. In another moment, he'd tugged his denims down just so far, and then sat on the chair facing her to remove them the rest of the way. He tugged off one boot, and then moved to the other, grunting as he loosened it. Finally he jerked it off, but not without issuing what sounded suspiciously like a groan of . . . Was it pain?

With a muttered curse, he threw the offending boot to the floor and then shrugged the rest of the way out of his denims. When those were discarded, he rolled off his socks, sighing long and hard as he dropped them to the floor as well. And then, for the life of her, Elizabeth couldn't tell what he was doing, but it appeared that he was inspecting the sole of his foot in the darkness. For what reason, she didn't know, but she felt like lighting the lamp. Honestly, how did he expect to see anything at all in the dark?

He swiveled toward the window suddenly, lifting his left foot up to probe it by the light of the moon. "Damn," he swore softly.

Forgetting in her concern that she was supposed to be asleep, Elizabeth lifted herself a fraction. She squinted her eyes, trying to get a glimpse of his foot, but saw nothing. She cursed her eyesight.

Hearing the sheets rustle, Cutter dropped his foot abruptly, glancing at the bed.

Elizabeth froze.

"You awake?"

Cutter sighed irritably when there was no response. He'd come in hoping to find her up, but had opened the door to find the lights out, instead, and Elizabeth snuggled in so cozily that he didn't have the heart to wake her. Hell, his foot was aching enough that he'd wanted her to look at it, but he wasn't about to wake her just for that. He'd suffered a helluva lot worse. Besides, he'd downed enough deadshot that it should have been anesthetized by now, and it probably would be soon.

"Cussin' foot," he muttered. The moist heat of his boot hadn't done it much good. But now that the fresh air was soothing it, it felt better. Leaning forward, he rested his forearms upon his lap, letting his hands dangle tiredly between his legs, his fingers linking, while he stared somberly at the bed.

How had she done it? he wondered. Snagged his heart without ever trying? He shook his head in self-disgust. He must be getting soft in his old age, because that chocolate-eyed niece of hers had somehow managed to do the same. He could look into the kid's eyes and almost believe she was his and Elizabeth's.

With that thought, he closed his eyes, and with primeval pleasure, tried to imagine what a child of their own would look like, only to realize the mistake he'd made in following that train of thought. His body responded at the barest hint of their mating, rousing in the space of seconds.

Hell, he'd been walking around in a state of half arousal all day because his pride wouldn't let him make love to her again without her asking him to do so. He'd come too close this afternoon to baring his soul, and it hadn't moved her a'tall. It still galled him that she'd preferred to sleep in the chair than with him.

Lifting the blanket she'd left for him, Cutter shook it out with a scowl, then settled back into the chair.

Propping his feet upon the bed, he covered himself to his chest, and then, as an afterthought, shoved his injured foot out of the blanket. He grunted with self-disgust as the blanket settled over him, forming a tent at his groin. He glared at it as though it were a dirty double-crosser.

If she didn't want to share his bed, he reminded himself, then he didn't want her. Trouble was in convincing his Judas body of that fact, because it didn't seem to have accepted his decision. At this rate, he sure as hell wasn't going to get a wink of sleep.

Laying his head back, he stared at the roving shadows on the ceiling, willing himself to sleep, willing the tent to fold itself up. When that didn't work, and the pain in his crotch intensified, he tried to shift his concentration to the pain in his foot, hoping the one would overpower the other.

It didn't work.

Hell, he could actually hear his breath quickening and his heart hammering . . . pounding? No, more like pattering. His body tensed with awareness, but it was another befuddled second before Cutter realized that the little thumps he heard were not his own . . . that they came from the hall. It was another instant before he determined that it was the sound of Katie's little feet . . . and that Miss Mimi was calling after her . . . and that she was coming closer . . .

"Katie!"

His reflexes kicked in immediately. By the time the handle on the door turned, Cutter had already vaulted into the bed, and was under the bed sheets with Elizabeth, his own telltale blanket left strewn like a trail across the bed.

Her head popping up in surprise, Elizabeth stifled a cry as Cutter's body came flush against her. A firm hand slapped across her mouth, muzzling her.

Finding Elizabeth awake surprised Cutter all of two seconds, and then he regained his senses in time to shove her head down and laid down his own a mere instant before the door flew open and Katie scurried in. She'd gotten no more than two steps into the room when Miss Mimi caught her by the back of her nightgown. "Katie!" she reprimanded. "What in heavens do you think you are doing, child?"

"I tol' ya, Miss Mimi," Katie wailed. "I forgot to say night to my uncle Cutter! Uncle Cutter, are ya wake?" she asked in the same secretive whisper she'd used earlier.

Drowsily Cutter lifted his head, opening one eye. When Elizabeth tried to lift hers, as well, he held her down with a firm hand.

"Goodness!" Miss Mimi declared, seeing the sleepy expression on Cutter's face. "I'm so sorry to wake you, Mr. McKenzie." She shook her head in exasperation. "I went in to say good night to Katie and made the mistake of asking whether she'd kissed both of you good night already."

Katie shrieked in protest when she couldn't get near enough to the bed.

"It's all right," Cutter replied gruffly, spreading his hand across Elizabeth's face. The pad of his little finger settled in the groove of her mouth, while two of his other fingers splayed across her eyes, blocking her vision.

It was all Elizabeth could do not to bite down on his finger. But she understood what Cutter was trying to do, and knew that she was supposed to be appreciative. It was just that he was pressed against her so intimately. Feeling that particular part of him nestling into her bottom so shamelessly, she couldn't stifle a mortified groan. Fortunately for her, Miss Mimi didn't seem to hear it. She was obviously too busy fretting over Katie's unforgivable intrusion to hear Elizabeth's distress.

"She was halfway down the hall before I'd realized where she was off to!" Miss Mimi exclaimed by way of apology.

Again, Elizabeth tried to lift her head, but Cutter

kept her restrained, patting her cheek firmly, instead. "It's all right, sweetheart," he murmured, sounding hoarse with sleep. "It's just Katie . . . and Miss Mimi." Having said that, he removed his hand from her face at last, allowing her to lift her head, but she cringed as it slid to her shoulder, instead, caressing softly. She resisted the urge to elbow his gut and screech in outrage.

"Are you certain it's all right?" Miss Mimi asked.

Cutter feigned a yawn, his hand leaving her shoulder for the briefest second, and then returning to squeeze it gently. Elizabeth shivered over the tenderness of that gesture.

"Sure," he said with good humor and a wink for Katie. Katie beamed. The moment Miss Mimi released her, she flung herself into the bed, scrambled across it, and stretched her neck over Elizabeth to peck at Cutter's cheek.

"Couldn't sleep myself thinking that I'd missed my good night kiss," Cutter assured her.

With a smile as wide as the Missouri, Katie slid back off the bed, landing nimbly on her feet.

"I take it your aunt Lizbeth's already gotten hers?" he asked, all the while stroking Elizabeth's shoulder and upper arm as though it were the most natural thing for him to do.

And it might have been . . . had they been man and wife. But they weren't. And it wasn't. Elizabeth's heart cried out with that reminder, and her eyes stung.

"Yes, sir," Katie replied as she scrambled out the door. "Night!" she called from the hall.

"Night," both Elizabeth and Cutter replied simultaneously.

Miss Mimi's expression was abashed. "Thank you," she said fervently, "a-and good night to you, too." Tossing her gaze heavenward, she shook her head and closed the door.

"That was close," Elizabeth sighed with relief, when they were alone.

For a long moment there was no answer. And then Cutter agreed, "Yes, it was." He continued to stroke her arm, sending shiver after shiver down her spine. Her head lolled slowly backward, seduced by the gentleness of his touch. She felt his lips move against the back of her head, heard his controlled intake of breath.

"Reckon I oughta get back to the chair," he said regretfully. Elizabeth didn't answer. He dared to hope. "Y' think?"

There seemed to be so much riding on that question that Elizabeth didn't dare respond for fear that the moment would end . . . that everything would end. She didn't want it to be over, not ever. Jolted by that revelation, she felt her heart begin to somersault against her ribs.

As if Cutter had read her thoughts, his caresses lengthened in that instant, drifting seductively over her hip, her thigh—everywhere but where she coveted his touch. Feeling wanton, she shivered at the brazen turn of her thoughts.

And then, when she least expected it, his hand was suddenly splayed over the sheets, over that most feminine part of her, drawing her firmly against his arousal, wanting her to feel him . . . to know what he wanted.

Elizabeth shivered with anticipation.

She wanted it, too.

How could something that felt so right be so wrong? It just couldn't.

Cutter didn't remove his hand, but instead lingered, pressing more provocatively, arousing her by increasing and withdrawing the pressure. Despite the intensity of his passion, he stroked her with controlled slowness, his body shuddering behind her. It sent another shiver through her. Elizabeth was unable to restrain the moan that escaped her constricting throat. With all her heart, she willed him to turn her around, to kiss her now in that same slow, rhythmic way he'd kissed her earlier, but he didn't. His body only tensed behind her, until she could feel every tightly coiled inch of him.

Every tightly coiled inch.

"Lizbeth," he whispered thickly, still stroking her. "Do you want me to go back to the chair?"

A strange panic beset her at the merest thought of his leaving the bed. Her voice failing her, Elizabeth shook her head, wanting him to stay, yet not able to speak the words.

With a forbearance he didn't quite feel, Cutter kissed the back of Elizabeth's head, brushing aside the silky length of her hair with his chin. "Then ask me to stay," he whispered huskily, his lips so close to her neck that they burned, " 'cause I won't stay unless you do."

She couldn't speak to save her life—not until his hand withdrew from her suddenly, and then her voice couldn't return quickly enough. "Stay!" she cried.

Cutter seized her shoulder, shifting as he forced her abruptly onto her back to stare down into her face. Sweat beaded upon his brow as he wove the golden strands of her hair through his fingers.

"Say it again," he demanded softly, his eyes slitting, penetrating her defenses. A fine sheen of moisture glistened over his shoulders and chest; one drop trickled slowly down his temple, glistening in the moonlight. "I wanna be sure I heard you right."

Her own eyes slitted as Cutter once again began to stroke her arms so softly, so slowly, so seductively, that it drew the words from her lips, even when she was certain she hadn't the courage for them. She sighed, her voice trembling with the whispery pleasure he was bringing her. "Stay with me, Cutter. Stay . . ."

For answer, Cutter groaned, lowering his mouth to hers, brushing the smooth heat of his lips against her own, gently at first—more tenderly than he ever had before—and then, when she moaned against his lips, he leisurely deepened the kiss, sliding his tongue, like liquid fire, between her teeth. Her breath broke at the renewed shock of it, her hands going around his neck of their own accord. He tasted and smelled of warm whiskey. Intoxicating.

With an oblivious groan, Cutter swept his tongue into the sweet depths of Elizabeth's mouth, savoring the incredible taste of her. While he kissed her, his hand circled her trembling jaw, taming the trembling. The answering beat of her pulse against his fingertips nearly sent him over the edge. Hissing through his teeth, losing his reason, he slid his hand lower, shoving the blanket way from her precious breasts with an eagerness that surprised him. In that moment, he craved only the fullness of her flesh against his lips.

Slowly his hands raised her camisole, his lips seeking out their reward. But having bared her, he paused to drink in the delicious sight of her beneath him. Unable to deny himself, he reveled in the nipples that budded under the heat of his gaze. And then, most reverently, he positioned the warmth of one palm over one firm mound, inhaling deeply as it was unexpectedly thrust into his hands—an offering more magnificent than any he'd ever been given. With a thick groan of passion, he kneaded it softly, losing control over the satiny feel of it against his rugged skin. Felt so good—so right in his hand.

"So hot," Elizabeth moaned. His touch was so hot—so deliciously hot. Like a cat, she arched against him, giving him everything, everything, and then, suddenly, he was peeling the blankets completely away with an urgency that startled her. In the next instant, he was atop her, but Elizabeth welcomed his weight, rejoiced in it. She moaned with the profound pleasure it gave her. His hands swept like wildfire over her body, scalding where he touched. With a titillating rhythm of his own making, he rocked against her, into her most intimate places, teasing until she thought she would surely lose her sanity.

Unable to keep herself from it any longer, Elizabeth lifted her trembling fingers to Cutter's chest, wanting to touch him in every way that he'd touched her. Following his lead, her hands slid down the length of him, delighting in the male textures of his body.

In response, Cutter deepened the kiss, his tongue stabbing swiftly, and for the first time, Elizabeth understood what it was that gesture meant . . . because she wanted it, too . . . somewhere else . . . with the same fervor and depth that he was giving her mouth . . .

And more.

Emboldened by her own rising passion, she slid her hands down to his buttocks, raking him softly. But he jerked at her touch, hissing through his teeth. Fearful that she'd hurt him, Elizabeth snatched her hand away, but he caught it, drawing it back.

"No," he murmured, "it was good." He shuddered at the feel of her small, cool fingers moving like whispery butterfly wings on his thigh. "Damned good." He released her at once, slipping his hands beneath her back, sliding them down to cup her bottom, and then pressing himself against her, rocking softly against her warmth and shuddering over the intensity of feeling that surged through him.

More than anything, he wanted her naked just now—stripped bare in his arms. Even down to her heart.

He wanted to see right into her soul.

To know if he was there.

As she was in his.

Unaware of his thoughts, Elizabeth moaned, lifting herself against him, seeking him out, telling him without words what she craved.

Cutter smiled, almost savagely, a feral gleam in his eyes. "Tell me what you want," he whispered huskily. If he couldn't have what he wanted of her, then he would at least hear from her own mouth what she wanted of him.

Elizabeth followed him obliviously with her hips, still unable to speak the words. And suddenly he was leaving her, and she cried out at the unanticipated separation. But he didn't go far. He knelt above her, his smile knowing as his fingers caressed her once more, slipping seductively into the waist of her bloomers.

"This?" he asked with a gleam in his eye.

With a slowness that made her breasts ache, and her eyes close with the spellbinding pleasure of it, he drew her bloomers off. She nodded unconsciously as heat coiled through her, savoring every sensation as the soft, worn cotton slid down the length of her leg.

With a victorious growl, Cutter lifted her toe into his mouth, nipping it gently, pressing his thumb into her sole, before slipping her bloomers off entirely. Discarding them, he bent to kiss her calves, her knees, her thighs, making his way slowly back upward. As she writhed helplessly with the incredible need he was rousing, Elizabeth's nails raked the sheets, clutching at them for sanity.

And then suddenly he was at her breast, drawing her nipple firmly into his mouth, sucking it gently, as if it were his greatest joy, his most cherished treasure. To her surprise, waves of ecstasy burst through her, trysting and exploding somewhere deep within.

"Cutter," she cried out. "Oh . . . Cutter—don't stop—don't stop—don't ever stop!"

For answer, Cutter's breath hissed across the wetness he'd lovingly painted upon her nipple, and then he moved to her other breast, lavishing it with just as much care as he'd given the first, leaving Elizabeth breathless with yearning. As Cutter feasted, her heart pounded, leaping with each stimulating suckle into her throat. Moaning with the ecstasy of it all, she curled her fingers through his hair, urging him closer without even realizing.

Vaguely she became aware that his hands were skipping so lightly over her skin, getting so close to that intimate place. Her breath caught and held over his scandalous stroking. Yet, of their own accord, her legs parted to give him better access, trusting him fully . . . wanting him to work his magic.

Magic.

There was no other way to describe what he was doing to her. Knowing exactly how to touch her to elicit pleasure, he cupped her, the full, firm pressure and heat of his palm an aphrodisiac in itself. And then his hand slid up, and ever so slowly he inserted the tip of one finger, making small swirling motions just within, with slow, mesmerizing dips, going deeper each time, as if he were stirring from her and tasting the sweetest nectar. The feeling was exquisite beyond words, and she couldn't bear it.

"Elizabeth," he murmured, barely able to restrain himself with the image of her heat flowing into his hand. "You feel so good . . ." The silky coarseness of his beard caressed her belly as he lowered his head, breathing in the scent of her. "I bet you taste even better." He chuckled wickedly, and shuddered with anticipation, moving down to discover if it was so.

The top of his head receded, until finally Elizabeth grasped his meaning and her heart jolted to a halt. "No!" she cried out, closing her legs before he could reach his intended goal. "I—I can't . . . not . . . not yet."

Yet?

Tilting his head to look up at her with those jet black eyes, he scrutinized her a moment, the hunger in his gaze almost volatile. Then, without warning, he moved up to lie beside her, catching her about the waist and lifting her effortlessly above him for the briefest second.

"Then ride me," he hissed.

In spite of the fact that Elizabeth had no idea what he was asking of her, her heart leapt into her throat, her body thrilling to the demand. Instinctively, still not understanding fully, she parted her legs to sit astride him, and before she could find her tongue to ask, he was impaling her, the tip of him begging entrance.

She whimpered with longing at the feel of him entering so slowly, filling her so completely. Her body accommodated at once, gliding over him with little effort, drawing him into her own with such ease that it seemed they were made to be joined. In spite of her own trembling, she felt him pulse beneath her. Still she didn't quite understand, but feeling the incredible urge to sheathe him fully, she did, tilting her hips instinctively. Again Cutter shuddered. But Elizabeth only sat, confounded as to what to do next. Her heart pounding, she drank in the intensity of his expression. His face was full of strain, his eyes closed, his jaw taut with restraint. The muscles in his arms tensed, and his fingers at her waist were actually . . . trembling?

He touched her more firmly, guided her up the length of him. "Ride me, Lizbeth," he urged, a look of intense pleasure that warred with pain on his face. Again, he shuddered, leading her smoothly down over his erection. And then he opened his dark eyes, piercing her with the heat of his gaze. They were smoldering, slitting—coming as close to pleading as he was able. "Ride," he whispered huskily, his neck arching, thrusting his head back into the bed.

Finally comprehending, Elizabeth nodded, rocking her hips, slowly. With her first stroke, Cutter bucked beneath her.

"Yes," he hissed. "Christ, you feel good!" His jaw clenched.

Now it was Elizabeth's turn to shudder, her eyes widening at the power she wielded over him. She needed no further prodding. With every stroke she made over him, she died a thousand deaths. It was the sweetest torture she had ever endured—ever!

Only, she was the one in control. She reveled in the power it gave her over his body—over her own. The look on his face alone was enough to send her spiraling over the edge—but she wasn't ready to relinquish so soon. Couldn't. It was too good. Too hot. Too . . . too . . . Dear God, it—it was too much!

Crying out at the exquisite feel of it, Elizabeth braced her hands upon his feverish chest. His skin was damp with sweat, the muscles in his neck and shoulders corded with the strain, but he allowed her to ride on at her own rhythm. Then suddenly a muffled cry forced its way through his clenched teeth and he stilled her hips, entrenching himself deeply, firmly, within her body.

Throwing her neck back, her hair spilling like molten gold behind her, Elizabeth moaned with the incredible sensation of him pulsing within her. Her body strained to the feel of it, throbbing for its own release. But Cutter held her too firmly, grunting as if in pain when she moved at all, and so she was afraid to stir. But she couldn't bear not to . . . and then, without warning, her body began to convulse around him. She whimpered, wanting so desperately to twist her hips and thrust herself into the incredible abyss of pleasure that beckoned just beyond her reach . . . so close—so close . . .

"Cutter!" she gasped.

Feeling her pulsate around him, he shifted abruptly atop her, never allowing a separation of their bodies, drawing on the last of his will in order to give her the pleasure he knew she sought. With a last oblivious groan, he drove himself into the depths of her, shuddering with the exquisite pain, spending the last of himself so deep within that he shuddered at the ferocity of the eruption.

Beneath him, Elizabeth cried out, willing him deeper still, driving him deeper, so deep that it would no longer be possible to separate. That was her last coherent thought; *she wished they would never draw apart.* And then she closed her eyes, surrendering with a shuddering breath, her release so consummate that it left her spent.

And still, Cutter moved within her, drawing every last murmur and sigh he could from her lips. He rocked her tenderly, his heart in every stroke, wanting her never to forget. He wanted to brand her, wanted her to cry out his name . . . and only his . . . the rest of her life.

Even when the violence of his release had ebbed at last, and Cutter's tremors ceased, his emotions remained high. His arms enfolded her, not wanting to let go. He fought the urging of his aching body as his eyelids grew heavy, and caressed her hair away from her damp face as she wearily closed her eyes, not wanting to close his own for fear that he would find the sun rising on them when he opened them again. Morning would only bring them all that much closer to Sioux Falls.

And to the end of their charade.

The thought that she would no longer need him then twisted his gut, made him violently ill. But he fought the unanticipated wave of nausea, never more unwilling to release her than he was in that instant.

All his life something had beckoned him on.

All his life he'd wandered in search of it.

And only now, this moment, did he finally and truly understand what it was that had driven him forever onward, with a wanderlust stronger than any he'd ever known. His search was finally over, he sensed, and felt deeply at ease with that knowledge— the only problem was in convincing Elizabeth.

Filling his lungs with the sweet scent of her, he eased his weight off her, then, lured by the temptation of her lush curves, lowered his head to her breast, kissing it reverently, before nestling in to listen to the steady, cajoling beat of her heart. Without looking, he knew that she slept, but he couldn't—not with his heart hammering so ruthlessly . . . not with her arms wrapped so lovingly about his neck, her fingers still entwined in his hair.

It felt too good.

Chapter 24

What had she expected? Elizabeth reproached herself. That he would have demanded they stay and role-play the rest of their lives? Why should he have wished to? Just because she'd never wanted it to end? Besides, the longer they remained, the more difficult it would've been to leave. And she'd been right in pressing Cutter to go. She had obligations to see to in Sioux Falls.

"Nothing lasts forever," she reminded herself petulantly.

Cutter arched his dark brows. "What was that?"

Katie, who was sitting in Cutter's lap—wearing his hat—looked up at her new uncle adoringly, and Elizabeth felt more than a twinge of guilt for deceiving the poor child. How was she going to feel to find that the uncle she was beginning to fall in love with, to trust in, was not her uncle after all, but only a man hired to play the part? Why had she ever thought it a good idea? It was a ridiculous idea! And one that was bound to break hearts—Katie's as well as her own!

Though Katie was obviously excited about the trip to Sioux Falls, she seemed a little blue, as well. Elizabeth thought it was likely she was already missing her grandfather, but there wasn't much she could do about that. Elias had made it clear that, though he loved his granddaughter, he was too old to be raising

296

her. And he was probably right. Besides, he and Miss Mimi deserved time for themselves.

"I think Aunt Lizabeth said that this ride is way too long," Katie told him, with an exasperated sigh. "And I think she's right! I think it's gonna last forever and ever and ever!"

Cutter chuckled, and Elizabeth smiled at the indignant tone of Katie's voice.

"Because I'm sleepy!" Katie added plaintively.

"I know," Cutter sympathized. "Think you can hang on awhile longer?" In the week since he'd met the kid, he'd grown as fond of her as Elizabeth had. When he looked at her sometimes, he could almost believe she was his own, with her dark hair and eyes. Falling into the role of father could be so easy.

"Uh-huh," Katie replied as she began to squirm.

But Cutter didn't notice her desperate gesture, and even if he had, he wouldn't have understood what it meant. As it was, his thoughts were somewhere else entirely. He patted her head in answer, pulling her back to rest against his chest. She'd ridden for the last three hours in his saddle, speaking little but for an interjection here and there to her whiny little dog.

She'd insisted on bringing Shiftless along—swore she couldn't live without the mutt. And Cutter thought he understood. From what he'd gathered, Shiftless had become her living anchor. Shiftless, for his part, seemed a little less loyal. Every so often the dog would stop to whine and wag its tail, then it would dash a few feet to the rear, only to stop again and bark for them to turn around. But because there was nothing Cutter could do about the dog's distress, he ignored it, and Katie usually managed to solve that problem on her own.

With only a gently spoken word or two from her, Shiftless would once again follow blindly, wagging his tail as he dogged the Palouse's hooves. As Cutter saw it, Katie had been raised with the dog, and Shiftless was, more like than not, the one link to her past she couldn't let go of—didn't have to, as far as he was concern ed.

But that was the problem. Unconsciously his hand went about her waist, hugging her fondly as he acknowledged the facts: As it stood, Katie wasn't legally his concern. Nor was Elizabeth. And he was contemplating how to best bring that subject up. And wondering how it would be received when he did.

Did Elizabeth really hold his ancestry against him? She'd said that she'd lost her mother and sister because of *his people*. He could only wonder at the meaning of that. Did she really blame him because Cheyenne blood burned through his veins? It burned for her. With a sigh, he rubbed his jaw, his gaze drawn like a magnet to Elizabeth. Despite the fact that she was exhausted from a night gone without sleep, she sat straight in the saddle; the only sign of fatigue was the fact that her eyes were squinted.

Katie began to rock frantically. "Gotta go!" she whispered urgently, but only an instant later, before Cutter could even blink an eye, a telltale warmth crept under his hindquarters. Katie stiffened. Cutter froze, glancing down warily at the child in his saddle.

Naw, he thought, shaking his head. She couldn't have. Could she? His face screwed with disbelief. Damn him, if it didn't feel like it, though! His nostrils flared and he swore he could smell it, as well. But hell, it couldn't be! Not in his brand-spanking-new saddle? Damned thing was little over two months old!

"Ya know what, Uncle Cutter?" Katie said impetuously, lifting her chin high. But she didn't look up at him as she spoke, and her little shoulders were still tense. Cutter dreaded her next words.

"I'm soooo proud of myself!"

Just as sure as eggs were eggs, the wetness seeped up from his good saddle into his denims. Cutter silently cursed a blue streak. Stunned as he was, he couldn't find his voice to answer the kid. Had he really thought he'd make a good parent? Hell, he hadn't

even considered asking whether she'd needed to relieve herself! Neither had Elizabeth, for that matter.
He turned to give her a cutting glance, and was surprised to find that she returned it.

"Why is that?" Elizabeth asked Katie, when it was
apparent Cutter wasn't going to.

Katie nodded soberly. "Because, Aunt Lizabeth. I
held my pee for sooooooo long!" There was unconcealed pride in her tone.

Elizabeth's eyes went wide at Katie's revelation,
and her first instinct was to laugh, but Cutter's disgusted scowl and Katie's anxious expression kept her
from it. Her hand flew to her mouth.

"Son of a—"

"Cutter!" Elizabeth gasped, stifling her mirth. And
then, unable to restrain herself, she burst into shrieks
of hysteria, doubling over in the saddle with the force
of it.

Cutter only gave her a narrow-eyed look, warning
her without words that she was gonna pay with the
skin of her ass if she didn't quit.

Damn her anyway—Katie hadn't uttered a word
until she was actually pissing in his lap! How was he
supposed to know to keep asking after her personal
needs? In that respect, the kid had everything in common with her blasted aunt; one would rather chew
sand than ask for a toothbrush, while the other would
just as soon pee where she sat than mention the fact
that she had to take a leak. Cussin' females!

Elizabeth, who had been trying so desperately to
control her hilarity in light of Cutter's brooding expression, suddenly burst out laughing again.

Hauling roughly on the reins, and making an immediate turnabout, Cutter gave Elizabeth his most
lethal scowl, though it didn't seem to faze her in the
least. "We're taking the train," he barked.

At that declaration, Elizabeth shrieked all the
louder.

* * *

"So how long you reckon they've been gone?"

Still stunned by all that had been disclosed to him, Elias, his complexion pasty, only shrugged and shook his head feebly. He stared blankly at the half-crumpled dispatch in his hands and read the signature at the bottom of the page for the fourth time: *Brigadier General Alfred Sully*. And then he ground his teeth as his eyes returned to skim the message above one last time. It read simply:

C MCKENZIE TO REPORT TO BRIGADIER GENERAL
A SULLY, ASAP
RE: ABSENTEEISM WITHOUT LEAVE
WILL CONSIDER LENIENCY IN RETURN FOR ASSISTANCE

"Desertion?" Miss Mimi repeated once again, her lips trembling and her hand going to her mouth in alarm. A watery sheen appeared in her eyes as she looked to Elias and then back to the lieutenant seated atop the U.S. Army–earmarked stallion. "I—I don't know—but it couldn't have been more than two hours ago. Are you certain he's dangerous?"

Lieutenant Magnus Sulzberger shook his head in a gesture of frustration that was far from feigned. Colyer had caught up with him a couple of days earlier with the dispatch while he and O'Neill had been hot on the trail of the renegade Indians. Setting eyes on that sweet little document had made his day, and he'd gladly left off the chase for the greater gain. Only, by the time they'd returned to where that half-breed McKenzie had set up camp, he and the woman had already pulled up stakes. From there, he and his men had come straight to the Bass spread, as was Colyer's initial directive, only to find that, once again, they'd been thwarted.

But he wasn't going to let it go.

He might have: if General Sully weren't looking for McKenzie; if Doolittle, the head of the Senate Committee on Indian Affairs, weren't determined to roll some heads; if McKenzie hadn't heaped accusations his way before walking out on his position; and finally, but most auspiciously, if Sully hadn't sent a man who hated this particular breed as much as Magnus did to slap a golden opportunity into his waiting hands.

He might have let it go.

But Sully *had* sent Colyer with the dispatch. And it was just a matter of time before Sully caught up with McKenzie. As far as Magnus was concerned, it wasn't gonna happen. If Sully intended to campaign into the Dakotas, he was gonna require Cutter McKenzie's services. Without it, he wasn't going to find the first hostile. And because of that, there wasn't much of a chance Sully would give up. Sully needed McKenzie, and he'd find him, come hell or high water.

Thing was, as Magnus saw it, Sully's bluff wasn't going to work, anyhow. Furious as McKenzie was about Sand Creek, there was no chance he was gonna give his assist—damned redskin-lovin' breed! The only thing McKenzie was likely to do was nose into ongoing investigations—three of them if the rumors Magnus had heard were correct; two by Congress and one by the military commission. And by damn, if they were looking for someone to court-martial, it sure as hell wasn't going to be him! He'd done nothing more at Sand Creek than the others had . . . and McKenzie wasn't going to live to testify otherwise.

Unknowingly, Sully had seen to that.

Though most folks felt that McKenzie was at least a moral deserter, he, in fact, wasn't a deserter at all. His argument with Sully had been over the fact that, because of the massacre at Sand Creek, McKenzie wouldn't renew his commission. Magnus was aware of that fact—*but* the document in Elias Bass's hand implied otherwise, and that was good enough for Magnus. Wasn't a man alive who wouldn't applaud him for shooting a deserter . . . even if it did happen to be in the back—most especially if he was a breed.

"Ma'am . . ." Magnus sighed for emphasis, while he adjusted the wad of tobacco in his mouth. "Look, I can see why you'd be disinclined to believe me. Your granddaughter's safety is at stake here . . . but I'm more'n sure—I'm damned sure!" Impulsively he looked over his shoulder at the two men waiting silently at his flank. He waved the fairest of the two forward. "Why don't you ask Colyer here about his ear?" Scratching at his beard, he watched the expression on the old woman's face intently as the man he called Colyer nudged his horse forward and raised the hair away from his bad ear, relishing her revulsion at seeing only half an ear where there should have been a whole.

The animosity in Colyer's icy green eyes completely negated his boyish good looks, prompting Miss Mimi to take a step backward. "He slashed m' ear, ma'am," the young man said without emotion. "Without any provocation at all." His eyes narrowed, spilling hate, though he tried to conceal it. "Scariest sight y' ever saw. McKenzie was sane as you or I one minute, and the next—"

Magnus spat the wad of tobacco out of his mouth suddenly. "That's enough, Colyer," he said. "Can't you see the old woman's fainthearted already? Can't take hearing the rest." He made a dismissing motion with his head, and Colyer immediately fell back again to wait with O'Neill.

As was intended, Miss Mimi looked ready to swoon. With a pained expression, she turned, clutching at Elias's arm. "Oh, Elias," she moaned. "What have we done?"

His face turning white, Elias straightened to his full height and took Miss Mimi's hand into his own, bringing it to his lips. His anger was apparent in every taut line of his face. "We did what we thought best, Mimi. There was no reason *not* to trust them," he reminded.

Miss Mimi nodded, her expression pained.

With a nod, Elias released her hand and turned to face the lieutenant, nervous perspiration beading on his upper lip. "If McKenzie's so dangerous," he charged, "Then what the hell took you so long to get here? Dammit—I wired Sully about him as soon as I heard he and his wife were on their way."

Magnus lifted a brow. "Don't know who the woman is," he interjected, "but she ain't his wife."

Miss Mimi choked at his disclosure, her fingers going to her throat, but Elias spared her only a glance in his concern for Katie. "She's Elizabeth Mc—hell, I dunno her blamed name—reckon it's Bowcock if not McKenzie. She's my daughter-in-law's sister!"

Magnus lifted the other brow. "You sure about that, Mr. Bass?"

"Course I'm sure," Elias countered. "Damn you people! Was I informed back then that McKenzie was any army deserter? Hell no! Damn me, too, for not looking into it further! Christ—don't give a hoot about the half-breed part, but that's all you people bothered to reply about!" He waved the paper up at Magnus in outrage.

Magnus nosed his mount closer to the old man and woman, snatching the document from Elias's hand. "Now, now," he said, his tone patronizing. He leaned forward in the saddle with intimidating slowness. "Don't reckon you ought to be takin' that tone with me, Mr. Bass. We came as quick as we were able." He glanced back at his men, then again to Elias. "You're the ones who trusted that roughneck savage with your grandkid," he took great pleasure in reminding them. "Not us." His lip curled suddenly. "And if you already knew *that* much about 'im, Mr. Bass, then you should've considered yourself forewarned. Breeds are breeds are breeds. They ain't no different from the full-blooded bucks! Every one of them savages'll lift your scalp in the blink of an eye."

The veins in Elias's temple stood out as he shook his head in rebuttal. "No, sir, Lieutenant Sulzberger," Elias countered, "I've known my share of half-breeds, and that just ain't true. But it doesn't matter—that's my granddaughter we're talking about. If what you say about McKenzie is the truth, then instead of sitting here jawing, you ought to be out there searching for her."

Magnus's eyes glittered with open contempt now. "Yes, sir, Mr. Bass," he agreed. "We should be. I reckon that's why you ought to be tellin' us where they're headed."

Miss Mimi started to sob in earnest. "Elias," she pleaded, her voice breaking. "We can't risk leaving Katie with them."

Elias gave her a look of intense frustration before glancing back to the lieutenant. He considered himself a good judge of character, and the picture Sulzberger was painting just didn't ring true. Still, he couldn't take chances, couldn't risk his granddaughter. And the man did have his papers—from General Sully, no less. He eyed the document with revulsion. He'd just never figured Cutter McKenzie for a deserter—or, for that matter, Elizabeth for a liar. "Sioux Falls," he snapped out. "But I'm coming with you! Just let me go in and get my gun."

Ignoring his declaration, Magnus surged upward. Standing in his stirrups, he waved his men ahead with an eagerness that sent a chill down Elias's spine. "You heard 'im, boys! Burn the breeze! Fulton City—in case they decided to take the Gulf. And you, sir," he barked, his head snapping back to Elias, "aren't going anywhere." His eyes were intimidating in their brilliance. "This is army business, sir, and you'll just stay put." He tipped his hat in a mock gesture of respect. "We'll get back to you *real* soon." Having imparted that, he slammed himself down into his saddle, driving the full force of his brass heels into his mount's belly.

His expression screwing with suspicion, Elias watched the lieutenant sprint after and catch up to his men. All three suddenly threw victorious punches into the air, and then one of them, the one called Colyer, unsheathed a rifle and held it high, discharging it once while the others whooped.

"Mimi," he said ominously as he continued to watch, "something ain't right here." And there wasn't. All three seemed to take an unnatural enthusiasm in their appointed task. He turned toward the house, springing into a run, intending to get his rifle. "I'm going after 'em," he called out. "Either way, Katie's gonna need me."

Chapter 25

Distracted by the unusually thick crowd milling around the platform, Elizabeth looked around her and reasoned that the throng awaiting to board the train might be a result of the recent end to the war. The station was teeming with Union soldiers who were evidently still trying to get home. A small group of uniformed men caught her eye, as she noticed them laughing at something farther down the track. Following their gazes, Elizabeth spotted a plump man, red in the face, trying desperately to shove his cow into one of the compartments. She smiled and then, turning her attention to Cutter who stood beside her, she found him watching her intently.

Feeling like a ninny, Elizabeth stood, her fingers intertwined with Katie's as she and Cutter simply stared at each other. Strange that, after being together almost every waking moment, this brief separation felt like good-bye.

But it wasn't, she reminded herself.

"So . . . we'll see you on the train?" she said, more for her own benefit than for Katie's. A faint light twinkled in the depths of Cutter's black eyes, as if he knew her thoughts. Flustered by it, she averted her gaze, glancing down at Katie.

As if by cue, Cocoa nickered impatiently, saving Elizabeth from an embarrassing moment.

Cutter chuckled at her look of relief, glancing over his shoulder at the querulous cayuse. "Keep your shirt on, Brownie," he muttered.

Katie burst into giggles at his ridiculous remark, and Elizabeth gave him a narrow-eyed look. He was teasing her, she realized—affectionately, not maliciously—and she found herself smiling against her will. "Cocoa," she corrected. Amazing, she thought, how that causal wit of his had once annoyed her so much, because now she found she enjoyed the sparring immensely—though she'd never actually admit it.

"If you say so," Cutter allowed, reaching down to catch Katie beneath the chin. "Think you can take care of your aunt till I get back?" he asked her with a wink.

Katie rubbed at her eyes tiredly. "Oh, yes!" she assured him.

"That a girl." He shook her head gently, releasing it as his gaze reverted to Elizabeth. "I'll be aboard as soon as I get the animals settled in," he told her, sweeping his hat from his head and swiping his arm across his sweat-dampened forehead. But having said that, he stood, turning the hat in his hands, not quite willing to walk away.

Elizabeth nodded but didn't move, unable to tear her gaze away. At their feet, Shiftless began to yap impatiently, and Katie immediately shook her hand loose from Elizabeth's, bending to give him a pat. "Don' worry, Shifless . . . don' worry," she crooned. "Uncle Cutter will take care of you! Right, Uncle Cutter?"

Reluctantly wrenching his gaze away, Cutter looked down in time to see Katie grin up at him, and the wink she gave him was priceless—the longest, most innocent, wink he'd ever been the recipient of. Charmed by it, he stooped to pat Shiftless's head right along with Katie. "That's right," he told her. Glancing up at Elizabeth, he passed on the wink, feeling more lighthearted than he'd felt in a lifetime. The answering look in her eyes made both his heart turn over, and his body tighten at once. Grimacing, he switched the weight to his right foot, and giving the dog a last pat, he rose to face her.

As she noticed his grimace of pain, and the flush of his skin, Elizabeth's brow furrowed. "Cutter? Are you all right?"

"Fine," he told her with a tight smile. She looked at him a little doubtfully, prompting him to add softly, "Never better." And it was the truth; things had gone so smoothly, so well, that he'd not wanted to spoil it by getting sick on her. The last few days had given him more pleasure than he'd ever thought possible. Reaching out, he smoothed a tendril of hair from her face, his expression softening.

For Elizabeth, every sound seemed to fade away in that moment as Cutter's dark eyes held hers—all sound except for the pounding of her heart. Somehow, as they held each other's gazes . . . somehow, without a word being spoken between them . . . she knew. There would be no more good-byes between them. Not ever. It was time to let go of her fears.

"Cutter," she began, and then losing her nerve, she bit into her lower lip, glancing away. Cutter's fingers gripped her waist in that moment, lightly, so very lightly that her heart jolted at the feel of it. Elizabeth was unable to bear the incredible intimacy of his touch; her eyes fluttered closed and she stood there, her knees going weak, as the world vanished.

They could have been alone, in that instant, or not. It wouldn't have mattered.

Without warning, Cutter swung her into the circle of his embrace, his hat at her back, and bent his head slowly, twisting to fit his mouth over hers. Her heart somersaulted as his lips descended, brushing tenderly over her own, the sensation too heady to bear. Helpless to contain it, she moaned at the velvety caress of his tongue, her heart leaping into her throat as the kiss deepened, reaching clear into her soul.

Suspending time.

With a reluctant groan, Cutter wrested his mouth free. Resisting the urge to sweep her up and carry her away to some secluded spot, he rested his forehead against the top of her head. "Elizabeth," he whispered hoarsely. "You make me lose control, gal." Gripping the back of her neck, he bent to taste her lips once more, closing his eyes, as if drugged by the scent and taste of her. His breath hissing through his teeth, he placed tiny kisses upon her chin, her neck, nibbled her ear . . .

A sudden urgent tug on his pant leg caught his attention.

"Uncle Cutter! Uncle Cutter!" Katie shrieked in panic. "I think . . . I think you hurt Shifless's feelin's!"

As absorbed as he was in the kiss, it took Cutter a long moment to regain his senses, another to digest what Katie had said. He looked down at her with an expression of stunned surprise on his face, having actually forgotten she was even there.

Elizabeth didn't suffer the same disorientation. Startled by Katie's voice, she pulled away from Cutter at once. Bending to take Katie by the hand, she looked up at him guiltily, then back to Katie. "Shiftless?"

"Yes!" Katie wailed, pointing. "See! He's running away! An he won't come back!"

Cutter looked over his shoulder in time to see the dog's wagging tail end disappear into the crowd. "Aww hell!" he exclaimed, sweeping his hat back to his head, adjusting it quickly. "Go on, get aboard!" he told her as he started away. And then he came back suddenly, snatching Elizabeth into his arms to kiss her soundly. Releasing her abruptly, he seized up the reins and sprinted after the dog, both horses at a slow trot behind him.

Elizabeth watched only a moment longer as Cutter

dodged his way through the cram of people, away from the train, noticing his limp for the first time. They'd spent so little time together in the last days, because he and Elias had been busy repairing fences. She'd seen him only briefly during dinner, and then at night, but as far as she could recall, he hadn't complained of any leg pain. Her brow furrowing with concern, she ushered Katie aboard the Gulf Mobile Ohio. "Come on, now, sweetheart," she said. "We'll go find a seat by the window. All right?"

"All right—but what about Shifless?" she wanted to know.

"Don't worry. Cutter will get him," Elizabeth assured her. "Now, up—and watch that next step—careful now."

"I never fall!" Katie exclaimed, her little hand gripping Elizabeth's fingers tighter.

Elizabeth chuckled softly. "Of course you don't," she agreed with a smile. "But you should never say never. Once I said I'd never eat a rattler. you know . . . but guess what?"

"What?" Katie replied automatically, and Elizabeth proceeded to tell her, as they made their way down the aisle, all about the rattler she'd been forced to eat.

Alternating between whistling and cursing, Cutter weaved his way through the depot, away from the train. No matter how loud he called, Shiftless seemed not to hear him—or not to want to. Confounded dog raced like a bullet out of blazes, and kept running, his tail wagging wildly.

Just when he came close enough to catch the dog, Shiftless darted beneath a dozing horse. The animal startled, its ears perking and its nostrils flaring. Knowing it was alarmed and sensing danger, Cutter gave it a wide berth, taking his own two mares through a thick crowd of people in order to dodge it.

When finally he worked his way out of the mob, he spotted at once what it was that Shiftless was after.

Elias Bass. He was coming down one of the side
streets, his rifle under his arm, and was still whistling
through his fingers as the dog leapt up, thrashing its
tail in welcome. Elias ignored the mutt. For some reason, seeing that Shiftless had come alone seemed to
make him all the more agitated.

"Elias!" Cutter shouted in greeting.

Hearing his name, Elias searched the crowd anxiously. The moment he saw Cutter, his face screwed
with anger. He said nothing, just commenced marching in Cutter's direction. When he was within five
feet, he picked up his pace. When he was only two
feet away, he hurled his gun to the ground. Heaving
himself at Cutter, he tossed a punch at Cutter's middle.

Surprised by the attack, Cutter released the reins
he held in his hand, falling backward holding his gut.
His back slammed the ground, knocking the breath
from his lungs. Clutching his chest, he managed to
roll free of the horses.

"You son of a bitch!" Elias snarled, diving at him
again. "You deceiving son of a bitch!" His face scarlet
with anger, Elias threw another unexpected jab that
landed just beneath Cutter's eye.

"What the hell's wrong with you, Bass? You got a
complaint with me, spit it out!" Having spent enough
time with Elias to know that there had to be a good
reason for the man to be behaving so irrationally,
Cutter restrained himself.

Elias threw another right that landed at Cutter's
jaw, the force of it snapping his mouth shut. He shook
it off, telling himself that there was no way he was
going to allow himself to be goaded into thrashing an
old man—especially one who likely felt he had good
reason to be doing what he was doing. "Damn y',
you old codger!"

"Not so old I can't clean your plow!" Elias returned, wheezing as he hurled another. "That's for
lying to me, you son of a bitch!" Cutter ducked it.

Swearing, Elias hurled himself at Cutter, grabbing him by the shirt. "Where's my granddaughter?" He released Cutter's shirt to take another furious jab at his jaw.

Cutter caught it this time, struggling with it in mid-air. "She's fine!" he shot back, beginning to lose his resolve not to fight back. Damn the old man if he didn't have a powerful right for such a feeble-looking fellow. "All right, Bass, you've had your sport. Now, why don't ya tell me what's got y' so riled?"

Elias didn't answer; instead he hurled his left fist. Cutter blocked it, hurling one back, knocking Elias off with one clean blow. Surging to his knees, Cutter rubbed at his jaw, immediately throwing his hands up into the air when Elias came after him again. "You made me do it once, but I'm not gonna trade punches with you, old man, so you can just calm down and tell me what's wrong."

Elias gave him an accusatory glare but held himself in check, his chest puffing with fury.

"Katie's fine!" Cutter repeated. "Now, what the hell's the matter with you that you feel you hafta come at me thowin' punches without explanations?"

His eyes bloodshot with anger, and his lip bleeding from Cutter's blow, Elias rubbed at his own jaw. "You're the one that has explaining to do, Mc-Kenzie—damned four-flushin' deserter!" He began to cough violently.

Cutter lifted one knee to rise and then froze. A chill went down his spine, and his brows collided violently. "What'd you call me?"

At this point the crowd was beginning to thicken around them, and there were startled murmurs.

Elias cleared his throat, his eyes watering. "You're a lying tail-between-the-legs deserter, is what you are!" he spat, wiping the trickle of blood from his lips with the back of his hand.

Black rage shot through Cutter at Elias's accusation, but it was tempered by the knowledge that those words had to have come from someone else. And it was that thought that set his teeth on edge and raised the hairs on the back of his neck. "Who the hell told you I was a deserter?"

It was the lethal calmness in Cutter's voice that gave Elias reason to pause. His brows furrowed in confusion over Cutter's response, and dread trickled down his spine. He met Cutter's gaze without wavering, wanting to see the truth in Cutter's eyes. "Lieutenant Sulzberger," he answered slowly. "He showed us the papers from General Sully and wanted to know where to find you—"

Elias yowled in surprise, closing his eyes instinctively as Cutter shouted unexpectedly, leaping at him. But Cutter never landed.

Elias's eyes flew open and he watched, dumbfounded, as Cutter surged to his feet and bolted away in the direction he'd come. Shouldering his way through the crowd, he left the horses behind, with Shiftless cowering at their feet.

Elias looked from the whining dog to Cutter's retreating back, his eyes widening as he perceived the danger. Snatching up his rifle suddenly, he sprinted after Cutter.

"But I don' see him!" Katie insisted, her nose pressed against the window.

"Don't worry, Katie. Cutter will catch Shiftless. Come away from the window now." Katie moved away from the window, into Elizabeth's lap, and Elizabeth snuggled her closer, thinking that there'd be so much to do once they reached Sioux Falls—in spite of the fact that they'd brought so few of Katie's things: just a few of her dresses, a small doll, and her dog. Just as soon as they arrived, Elizabeth planned to move her own things into her father's room. Katie could have hers. And then Elias had promised to bring the rest of Katie's belongings in the fall, when it would be cooler and would be easier to travel. Her brows knit. What would she say to Elias when he came and found Cutter gone? Well, she'd think of something. In the meantime, she only hoped Cutter would be able to catch Shiftless.

But then her brows furrowed as she considered another matter entirely. How would she manage Katie and continue her practice at the same time? She glanced down at the small child curled so cozily in her lap and resolved that whatever needed to be done, would be done. If it meant bringing Katie along as her father had done with her, then so be it. And if it meant hiring someone to watch Katie when Elizabeth wasn't able to, then that could be arranged, as well. In the meantime, there didn't seem to be much sense in worrying over it. As her father used to say, *everything was certain to work out as it should.*

"Ma'am?"

Startled from her musing by the deep voice at her ear, Elizabeth glanced up to find a pair of intense green eyes looking down at her. Aside from his astounding good looks, the man wore military blue and a smile that easily disarmed.

"Ma'am?" he inquired again, his lips quirking. "You Mrs. McKenzie?"

Elizabeth hesitated a moment over the falsehood, staring at the man as though she'd momentarily lost her wits. But then she glanced down at Katie, and Katie stared back so expectantly that she turned immediately back to the soldier. "Yes," she said firmly. "Yes, I am." She lifted her chin as if to dare him to dispute her. "Is something wrong?"

The soldier smiled. "Well, no, ma'am . . . it's just that . . . well, your husband asked me to tell you that he needed you to join him outside."

Elizabeth's brows knit in confusion. "But I don't understand. He told me to wait aboard the train—that he would join me as soon as he . . . Oh, no, is that it? Has he had trouble securing passage for the horses?"

The soldier cocked a brow at her, and once again Elizabeth was struck by his remarkably good looks. The only thing that detracted was the fact that his hair was too long over his ears, and a bit unkempt. Other than that, his appearance was impeccable.

"Dunno, ma'am," he said. "Your husband just asked me to deliver the message, is all. He did still have the horses. But you can ask him yourself, if you like . . . I'll escort you right to him."

Something about the way the man looked at her sent a shiver of apprehension down Elizabeth's spine. His smile, though warm, didn't seem quite genuine. Tamping down her sense of unease, Elizabeth shook her self out of her daze, irritated with the stifling sense of paranoia she'd recently developed. Why should she suspect the man wished to harm her? Clearly Cutter had asked him to come—otherwise how would he have known they were man and wife? Playing at man and wife, she reminded herself. Besides, he was an officer of the U.S. Army, sworn to protect . . . and they would be stepping off the train in the broad light of day, besides. What harm could possibly come to them? "Yes, of course," she said decisively. "Thank you." She started to rise at once, rousing Katie and lifting her into her arms.

Katie clung to her. "I hope he didn't lose Shifless," she mumbled sleepily.

Elizabeth patted her back reassuringly. "No, sweetheart, I'm certain Shiftless is just fine." Praying to God that it was the truth, she edged out into the aisle, and readjusted Katie's weight on her hip.

"This way," the soldier directed, clearing his throat.

"But I thought the cattle and horses were loaded from the other side," she said.

"They are," he said quickly, "but I don't think he could get them on. Seems everyone decided to ride the rail on the same day." He laughed at his resourceful quip and then stopped her as she shrugged and started in the direction he'd indicated, gripping her by the shoulder. "Maybe you should leave the kid here?" he suggested with a curt motion of his head.

"Leave her? Here?" Elizabeth glanced at the seat she'd occupied and then gave him an incredulous glare. "I'm afraid *not*, Mr. . . . er . . ."

"Colyer," the man replied with an engaging grin. "Jack Colyer."

"Yes, well . . ." Elizabeth gave him another reproachful look, and then turned to make her way down the aisle. "I could never leave Katie to wait alone," she said with certainty.

Katie's head popped upright, her sleepiness shrugged away for the moment. "Yeah! Because I'm only this many," she was quick to inform him. She held up five fingers, glared at them fretfully, and then shoved one down.

Colyer shrugged. "Whatever," he said. Didn't mean anything by it, kid—just thought you might wanna save the seat for your mother, is all."

"She's my new mommy!" Katie proceeded to tell him. "An' you know what? . . . We're going to my new home now. An' my uncle, you seeeee, he scared away my dog, but don' worry, he's gonna get him back," she assured him brightly.

Chapter 26

No sooner had Elizabeth stepped off the train when Colyer lifted Katie out of her hands. "Here," he offered graciously, "let me help. She looks awfully heavy for you."

"No—really!" Elizabeth protested, her hands flying out to bring Katie back.

Colyer gave her a look that sent another shiver of apprehension coursing through her. "I insist," he told her firmly, and then he bent to whisper into her ear so Katie couldn't overhear. "Walk or I slit the kid's throat."

Elizabeth came to an abrupt halt, too stunned to believe that she'd heard him correctly. Her chin fell and she started to ask him to repeat himself, but the look in his eyes as she turned kept her from it. She shook her head.

"Walk," he instructed, shoving his jacket aside to reveal the leather sheath where his knife was buried.

Icy fear gripped Elizabeth at the sight of it. The color drained completely from her face. Her heart racing with terror, she considered screaming for help, but Colyer gave her a look that chilled her to the bone, paralyzing her momentarily, and she wondered how she ever could have thought him handsome. The look transformed him completely.

"Walk," Colyer snarled, when Elizabeth only stared. "And just in case you're thinking to scream,

just remember that we have your *husband* trussed up
like a Thanksgiving turkey ready to be spitted.'' He
snickered maliciously, letting her know that he knew,
without a shadow of doubt, that Cutter was nothing
more to her than her lover. He shoved her forward
abruptly, and she stumbled over her feet. But she
turned and managed to do as she was told, her mind
racing frantically.

"At least let me carry Katie," she said quickly, her
voice wavering slightly.

Colyer chortled, nudging her forward again.
"Think I'm stupid?" he asked viciously. "Get a wig-
gle on it, dove . . . before my fingers get itchy."

Elizabeth needed no further urging. She walked
blindly through the crowd, aware of the fact that Colyer was directly behind her, ready to thrust her forward when she didn't move quickly enough. Aware,
too, that he held Katie's fate at his will. And Cutter's?

What could he want with him? With Katie? She
couldn't fathom. Biting into her lower lip to stifle her
cry of panic, she shook her head in denial, for there
was no reason she could determine.

The buildings Elizabeth passed became a blur, the
people faceless. Her heart hammered with fear. Unexpectedly Colyer thrust a hand on her shoulder,
shoving her abruptly into an alley, where two men
waited, one mounted, the other not. Both she recognized at once. But there was no sign of Cutter, and
she knew at once that Colyer had lied. The knot tightened in her stomach as she looked frantically about
for some means of escape.

There was none—not while Colyer still held Katie.

"She's frightened—please! Let me hold her now!"
Elizabeth said anxiously, and tried to take Katie from
his arms. "We'll do as you say," she swore. "Just let
me hold her!"

Colyer dodged her, boosting Katie up into the arms
of the youth Elizabeth remembered only as O'Neill.

The look on O'Neill's face mirrored the horror in her heart.

"Y' didn't say y' was bringing the kid," O'Neill objected, his Irish brogue coming out with his agitation. "I won't be havin' nothin' ta do with killin' a babe!" Katie began to whimper in his arms. Elizabeth tried to take her from O'Neill, but Colyer snatched her by the waist and dragged her away, lifting her up onto his own bay. He mounted behind her.

Magnus nosed his horse closer to O'Neill's, and the hostile set of his shoulders made Elizabeth's breath snag. "You got a problem with this, Blue-boy?" he asked, borrowing the epithet Cutter had used for him. "If so . . . you can just take off right now." He made a motion with his head for O'Neill to leave, but his hand went to his revolver in a clear warning. "Just turn that yellow tail of yours around and ride."

O'Neill's gaze shifted from Magnus to Colyer to the child in his arms, and then back, narrowing shrewdly on Magnus. "I'm no' stupid, man. I turn this horse about and you shoot me in the back. Is that how it works?"

"Well, now," Magnus said, baring his teeth in some semblance of a smile, his tone taunting. "Why don't you try and see?"

O'Neill shook his head slowly. "No' bloody likely!" And then, as if suddenly realizing his tenuous position, he told them. "I'm with ya now—don't ya doubt it. I just don't ken ta killin' the girl, is all. It's no' right! Besides, you said it would just be the woman— you said she didn't matter because she was a breed-lovin' whore!" He gave Elizabeth a quick, assessing glance, and then his eyes reverted quickly to Magnus, but Elizabeth noted the fact that he was unconsciously petting Katie's back, soothing her. In spite of his comforting, Katie's eyes were wide with fright, and Elizabeth's heart cried out for her.

Magnus noticed, as well, and gave O'Neill a narrow-eyed scowl. "Yeah?" He flicked a look to Col-

yer, then back to O'Neill. "Well, don't shit yourself
over it, kid. Let's just get the hell out of here before
McKenzie finds us. This ain't the place for what we
got in mind." He turned to wink at Elizabeth, and
then motioned for O'Neill to move ahead of him, before he fell back to ride momentarily beside Colyer.

"Thought you said the boy would go along with
anything," Colyer hissed at Magnus. "Thought you
said he had stars in his eyes. All we need is for him
to go causing trouble for us now!"

Magnus gave Colyer a cold-eyed glance that shifted
to include Elizabeth. "We'll take care of it," he said
simply, and then he moved to take the lead.

Elizabeth stiffened with the import of those words,
but Colyer only snickered at her response, nuzzling
his nose into the back of her hair. It sent another chill
down her spine. "You'll never get away with this,"
she hissed, shrugging away in disgust.

Colyer lunged forward abruptly, pressing himself
against her, flattening Elizabeth against the horse's
mane as he dug his heels into the mare. The saddle
horn dug painfully into her stomach, but Elizabeth
resisted the urge to cry out in pain, sensing that it
was what Colyer wanted.

"Already have, dove," he informed her contemptuously. "Already have." His tongue snaked out
suddenly, flicking the back of Elizabeth's neck
through her hair, and she surged forward as far from
him as was possible, cringing against the revolting
feel of it.

Colyer chuckled nastily. "Hafta wonder, dove . . .
if you lay as good as you taste."

With a sense of foreboding wringing his gut, Cutter
vaulted onto the railcar in which Elizabeth and Katie
had boarded. In his recklessness, he cleared the steps
completely. Racing blindly, he tore open the door and
hurried down the aisle, ignoring the stares and curses

flung at him for inspecting each and every occupied seat like a man possessed.

She wasn't there. Christ, she wasn't there—she wasn't anywhere!

"Elizabeth! Katie?" He grabbed a small child who dashed out into the aisle and into the seat directly across, where a woman was drowsing, her face to the window. Blond was all Cutter saw in that instant. The woman in the seat was blond. And the child was dark-haired, but the little girl he swung about to face him definitely wasn't Katie, and she started to squeal in fright.

The blond woman sat up in her seat with a start and began to shriek at him. She lunged forward, her eyes wide with terror, and seized the child from him, clutching her protectively.

Cutter didn't linger to soothe her.

"Did you see that?" the woman shrieked at his back. "He tried to steal my baby!"

"I think he's insane!" yelled another.

Cutter's brows knit as he deliberated his next move. Christ Almighty, he felt insane! The train jerked forward in that moment, taking the decision from his hands. His gut twisted. Having no choice but to examine each and every railcar, he bolted toward the back of the train at a dead run, ignoring the pain that burned through his left leg.

After two exhausting hours of riding before Colyer in the saddle, every muscle in Elizabeth's body screamed from the awkwardness of straining forward.

From the snatches of conversation she'd overheard, she'd been able to conclude that it was Cutter they were after, and not Katie or herself. They clearly despised him; Jack Colyer, for some injury done to his person. What, she didn't know, but she was sure she'd find out soon enough. Magnus's reasons were less a mystery. The simple fact that Cutter inhaled the same air he did seemed to provoke him. Every other word out of his mouth was either ''breed'' or ''half-breed''—or some other less-than-flattering epithet.

Of the three, O'Neill seemed to be the least embittered. He said nothing as they rode, but the care he gave Katie spoke volumes. In him, Elizabeth sensed their greatest chance for escape. But she didn't dare meet his gaze for long to confirm it. Nor did she speak to him for fear of drawing attention to his regard for Katie. Because of his solicitousness, Katie's fear seemed lessened considerably, and Elizabeth was thankful for that. Yet, in spite of it, Katie's eyes seemed perpetually wide and on the verge of tears, and it tormented Elizabeth that she couldn't reach out and take her niece into her arms, couldn't comfort her. Her eyes glazed every time she happened to catch the stoic expression on Katie's beautiful little face.

Still, seeing was better than not.

Every once in a while O'Neill would ride out of her field of vision, and Katie's face would become nothing more than a shadowed blur. It was in those endless moments that Elizabeth's heart cried out the most, for she wanted so desperately to *know* that Katie was holding up. Her ears strained to hear even the slightest whimper, but there never was any, and Elizabeth had to conclude finally that Katie had been right.

She never cried.

They didn't stop until late afternoon, and then only to water the horses. Without explanation, Magnus shoved Elizabeth down onto a fallen log to wait. After a moment, a fitfully sleeping Katie was thrust into her arms.

Watching her abductors with a knot in her throat, Elizabeth sat, rocking Katie and feeling her anger mount with every blasphemy Magnus heaped upon Cutter's head. But she said nothing, only listened, and tried desperately to keep her fragile control. For Katie's sake, she suppressed her anger under the appearance of indifference. But had she been alone, she might have clawed Magnus's eyes out for the insults he hurled at Cutter in his absence. How bold of him to insult a man who wasn't even present to defend himself! The more she heard, the more difficult it became to keep silent in the face of his bigotry.

When Magnus insulted Cutter yet again, saying that he was no man, that he was an animal fit only to be skinned and worn like the buffalo his kind hunted, Elizabeth couldn't keep herself from speaking up any longer—in spite of her resolve not to draw undue attention to themselves for Katie's sake. She flashed Magnus a look of disdain and, as instructed, handed Katie back up into O'Neill's arms before turning to face him again. Her legs wavered slightly, though determination, like contempt, simmered in her amber eyes. "I don't recall you being so vulgar and insulting to Cutter's face," she taunted in a low voice, taut with anger. "Perhaps you aren't so much a man yourself, Mr. Sulzberger?"

Magnus only smiled, his eyes slitting cannily, and then he turned to address Colyer with a belligerent grin. The look they exchanged infuriated her. "She'll ride with me now," he said with relish, and then he turned back to leer at her.

Colyer sniggered. " 'Bout time you showed some emotion, dove. I was beginnin' to worry I'd nabbed the wrong woman."

Her gaze snapped back to Magnus as he spat a wad at her feet, but Elizabeth stood her ground, ignoring his crudeness.

Magnus nodded in agreement. "Ain't seen no sign of that bastard trailing us either," he added. "For a while I was thinking that worthless half-breed might not even care enough to come after her." Excitement flared in his eyes as he turned to face her. He grinned. "Anyhow, you just set my mind at ease, darlin'. He'll come. And when he does . . . I'm gonna take real pleasure in showing you, while he watches, just how much a man I can be. Now," he barked, "you just get that pretty little butt of yours up into my saddle."

His grin widened, his gaze roving up the length of her, lingering at her fully concealed breast, yet making Elizabeth feel stripped before him. She shuddered at his look.

"We're gonna do some powerful riding, you and I," Magnus vowed.

A frisson of panic rippled down Elizabeth's spine and the color drained from her face as she recalled Cutter's passionate plea—*Ride me, Lizbeth, ride*—the rawness of his voice. She closed her eyes momentarily, wishing to God that she'd had no notion what that word meant between men and women, but she did, and by the look on Magnus's florid, self-satisfied face, he knew she understood, as well.

Cold fingers swept over her as he sniggered, and she swallowed convulsively, shuddering inwardly, her stomach turning with revulsion at the merest thought of his touching her. Averting her eyes, she glanced over her shoulder at Katie. She was still sleeping—thank God! She couldn't bear for Katie to hear.

"Well, whattaya know, 'pears that savage trained you real good." His eyes shot her with cold contempt as he gripped her by the upper arm, forcing her into motion. She gave a startled little cry, her throat closing up with fear. "Now," he mocked her, "why don't you just mount up so we can see what kind of moves you learned for us."

Chapter 27

"Bastards want us trailing 'em," Cutter hissed through his teeth. Barely tempering his fury, he swiped at the beads of sweat that dotted his forehead, his mouth set grimly.

Riding silently beside Cutter, Elias glanced up from the rifle he was examining to see that Cutter's face was splotchy and flushed. "How do you know?" he asked, scanning the area ahead before returning his scrutiny to Cutter.

Cutter's slitted gaze was fixed on the horizon, his jaw taut with a rage that had been growing since the moment he'd discovered Elizabeth and Katie missing. He'd checked every last railcar and then had hurled himself off the train and run like hell back into Fulton City to find Elias waiting on him, already set to ride.

Elias had already stabled Cocoa in the nearest livery, and for a few extra dimes, the man in charge had leashed Shiftless to a post outside, promising to feed the mutt until they returned. In the meantime, Cutter had picked up Magnus's trail with a little preliminary backtracking, and they'd been following close on his heels ever since. As of yet, Sulzberger didn't seem to realize it.

"Because we should be tracking a blind trail," Cutter replied finally, "and we're not." He turned to consider Elias, worry deepening the shadows in his eyes. He wasn't certain the old man was up to the trouble they were courtin'—he looked almost as bad as Cutter felt—but there was no choice. Because Sulzberger was a dirty player, Cutter knew he would need all the help he could get.

Aside from that, he wasn't feeling quite right—wasn't exactly sure what it was that was wrong, but knew it had everything to do with his foot. The last man he'd known to snag an infection had had his leg carved off, and he sure as hell wasn't willing to live like that, so it had been easier to let it go, tell himself it would pass.

But it wasn't going to.

The fact that his eyes were burning a hole in his face told him as much. Still, he couldn't risk the time it would take to see to it now. Besides, he'd never known a sawbones to be anything other'n saw-happy, and he fancied himself rather attached to his leg—didn't particularly care to part with it.

"Sulzberger's ridden alongside me enough to know how to trash a trail if he wanted. He's not even trying." He pointed out the wet tracks in the soil as they passed them. "He started out at a dead run, but since late afternoon he's been moving at a snail's pace. Now that we're out in the bush, with no witnesses for what he's planning, he's no longer in a hurry."

He glanced again at Elias, then heavenward, to scrutinize the skyline, recalling with a twist of his gut the way Magnus had ogled Elizabeth. He vowed to himself in that moment that the misbegotten bastard would pay with his life if he so much as lifted a finger to Elizabeth's body—or, for that matter, Katie's. He wouldn't put anything past the man.

"Aside from that," he added, "they seem to go out of their way to dip their heels into water—tracks stay wet for a long time afterward . . . more easily identified that way." He hauled on the reins abruptly, something catching his gaze in the distance.

In the next instant, he'd unsheathed his Spencer carbine and was holding it before him in his lap, inspecting it to be sure it was loaded. The swiftness with which he'd handled his weapon left Elias slack-jawed. When Cutter had completed his inspection, he looked up again, studying the sky in the distance. "Unless I miss my guess," he said, "that's them ahead." Lifting the barrel of his carbine, he pointed out a column of smoke that coiled upward like a wicked serpent into the graying sky.

Elias shook his head. "Don't make sense," he muttered in puzzlement. "Why would they chance a fire? Seems if they're gonna shanghai someone, they'd make real sure not to get caught."

Cutter gave him a swift glance, his black eyes gleaming savagely. "Makes all the sense in the world," he countered. "They didn't count on you riding with me, Elias. There are three of 'em, aren't there? Should have been only one of us. Namely, me." His mouth set in a grim line. "Reckon they figure even *I'm* no match against three—not alone . . . and not in an ambush."

"Think they know we're here?"

Cutter shook his head. "Not yet . . . too busy gloating, I suspect. Don't think they expected us to sniff them out so easily. Judging by the signs they've left for us to follow, they think they're baiting an idiot." He inclined his head toward a small grove of trees that grew to the right of them—a procession of them that marched halfway up the hillock from where the smoke unfurled behind. "You wouldn't happen to know how to climb, would ya?"

Elias nodded, though his expression turned baffled.

"Good. 'Cause I sure as hell don't aim to give those sons a bitches what they're after tonight." A chill black silence surrounded them in that moment, and then he added, "Not till I know what it is."

"Now, McKenzie, hold on." Elias shook his head adamantly, coughing discreetly into his hand. "You can't mean to leave Katie and Elizabeth in their camp all night—ain't no telling what they could do to 'em!"

Cutter gave Elias a look of lethal assurance, beginning to wonder if he should make Elias turn back. The old man had taken great care to keep his fatigue to himself, but it was becoming apparent he wasn't up to snuff. Helluva pair they made. "That's what they're counting on us thinking," he answered finally. "But like I said . . . I don't aim to oblige." He pointed his carbine casually at the hillock in question. "If that were me on the other side, I'd have set up camp so that I could see everything coming over for miles, knowing they wouldn't be able to spot me until they've cleared the hill. Way I see it, you can be damned certain they'll have their barrels trained on us the moment we charge over." He pointed the carbine in turn to the thicket of trees at their right. "Instead, we'll ride up through those, climb the bastards, and then spend the night watching every move they make." He gave Elias a cold, calculating look. "Maybe they'll make a mistake, maybe they won't—but I don't aim to risk either Elizabeth or Katie by getting my eyebrows blown off."

Cutter's glance returned to the hillock, but his expression was unreadable, as though he were searching beyond it. "No, we'll play our own game," he said abruptly. "And if they lay a hand on either of 'em . . . I'll make each and every damned one of them regret they ever took their first breaths." His eyes glittered with grim intensity as he glanced again to Elias.

Sensing Cutter meant every word in the most violent way, Elias shuddered at the promise he saw in Cutter's black expression. In spite of the deep, revealing shadows under Cutter's eyes, and the sweat that rolled from his temples, marking his fatigue, Elias could sense the iron will and determination in him.

As well as the danger.

As he'd decided when he'd first laid eyes upon Cutter McKenzie, half-breed or not, he was one man Elias wanted on his side, not otherwise. He gave a conciliatory nod, not that he felt he'd had much choice in the decision. The tone of Cutter's voice didn't invite question. "All right, McKenzie . . . reckon you know best." Once again, he took in the flush of Cutter's face, a flush that had persisted despite the fact that the sun had long since begun to set and the air had long cooled, and he worried. "You all right?" he asked guardedly, watching Cutter's expression. Something wasn't right about the man. Something he couldn't put his finger on. If he didn't know better, he'd think the man was ailing. But Cutter hadn't said a single word to indicate it was so.

Tipping his head, his eyes gleaming wildly, Cutter swiped the back of the arm that held his carbine against his forehead, soaking up the sweat with his sleeve. "Fine," he replied brusquely, shrugging off the question. He grimaced at the pain that shot through his foot as he removed it from the stirrup to hang free. "You sure you're up to this, old man?"

"Much as you are," Elias countered. "That is my granddaughter out there," he reminded Cutter.

Cutter nodded, knowing they were at an impasse. "All right," he said, "let's just get our butts into that thicket before someone spots us."

Katie clung to Elizabeth's neck, shrieking as Magnus tried to pry them apart. The carnal look in his eyes panicked her, but she didn't intend to be a willing victim. Vowing to make his violation of her person the most difficult conquest he'd ever attempted, Elizabeth twisted her arm out of his grip. And he wasn't going to touch her in front of Katie! That, she swore. "Let go of me, you swine!"

He smiled maliciously. "See you found your tongue finally, huh?"

"Haven't you any conscience at all?" Elizabeth spat, ignoring his taunt. "No heart? You're frightening her!"

Magnus merely laughed. "Don't flatter yourself,

bitch. I don't aim to touch a hair on that head of yours. Pretty as it is . . . turns my gut." He made a motion with his chin, grinning through his beard. "Now, Colyer over there might feel differently. Fact is, he might even like to even the score a bit."

Elizabeth followed his gaze to where Colyer stood, his back against a tree. She couldn't see his face at all, just his obscure silhouette. Still, there was an aura about him that sent a quiver of apprehension down her spine.

Tamping down her hysteria, she turned again to Magnus, her tone as calm as she could manage, for Katie's sake. "If it's his battle, then let *him* fight it for himself. Please . . . let us go . . ."

She gave Colyer a scathing glance, then, feeling herself failing in that tactic, she turned to plead with O'Neill, who was standing faithfully at Magnus's side. "How can you bear to hurt an innocent child? How can you involve us? Have mercy!" She tried to capture his eyes, to communicate with him, but he steadfastly avoided her. "Coward!" she spat. Feeling defeated, she turned again to Magnus, her voice breaking yet full of contempt. "And what do you have to gain in all this?" she spat. "Surely something."

"Dead men don't carry tales," he said cryptically, slanting a glance toward O'Neill. O'Neill flinched visibly.

"My God, what cowards you are—all of you! Are you so afraid to face Cutter McKenzie alone that you would have to use a child for your shield?"

Lunging forward, his face red with fury, Magnus gripped her again by the arm and shoved her down to the ground. Hard. "Bitch! Shut the hell up before you earn yourself and that noisy kid an early grave!"

Clutching a screaming Katie before her with one hand, Elizabeth tried to break their fall to the ground with the other. Her lips trembled as they formed the beginning of the question that had haunted her all day. So many times she'd stifled it, afraid to ask it with Katie in earshot. "Just tell me . . . w-what do you plan to do with us?"

Magnus arched a brow at her. "Well, now, why don't we just wait and see," he taunted.

Elizabeth shook her head slowly, swallowing the lump that rose in her throat. Her eyes grew large and liquid, but she lifted her chin bravely. She had absolute faith Cutter would come for them, but she loathed the man for using Katie as his decoy. "You're nothing but a coward, Mr. Sulzberger."

"I said shut up, ya breed-lovin' bitch! O'Neill, tie her hands and feet! Behind her back. Now!"

Katie's shrieks intensified at his command, and she clutched wildly at Elizabeth. Elizabeth's heart twisted painfully.

"And you," Magnus barked, pointing a finger at Elizabeth, "get that sniveling brat to shut the hell up!"

From his perch in the treetop, Cutter could see almost everything. He kept his carbine trained on Colyer, knowing that until he determined Magnus's motive, Colyer, of the three, had the biggest ax to grind.

It had taken every ounce of his will not to squeeze down on the trigger when Magnus had shoved Elizabeth to the ground. Gutless bastard that he was. He liked using that muscle of his with women and babies. Cutter shook his head suddenly, the image of Sulzberger sweeping down on a small group of Cheyenne children, running his bayonet through the smallest of the band, coming back to his mind with sickening clarity.

The barrel swiveled suddenly to Magnus.

Sweat streamed from Cutter's temples and down the sides of his face as he fought the command of his soul to squeeze. The aftermath of Sand Creek was so vivid in that moment that he tasted the metallic tang of his own blood as he battled his way through the images.

Women. Children. Mutilated. Magnus and his boys coming across a small child, not much older than Katie, buried in the sand. They pulled out their pistols and shot her, then dragged her out and shot her again, leaving her for dead. Christ, he'd never wanted to kill more than he had in that instant . . . as he did now.

The only thing keeping him from it was the knowledge that once he pulled the trigger, there would be hell to pay. Wasn't a breed on American soil who could spill full-white blood and not end up in the skookum-house. If they were lucky they *might* get an unlawful trial before the string-up. If not—hell! He hadn't lived as long as he had by being careless!

His gaze shifted abruptly from his target to Elias Bass, who was perched in a branch slightly above him. If there was business to settle, then the last thing he needed was witnesses. He'd known good men, half-breed men, who were hired by John Law to do their dirty work, and then the minute the deed was done, Johnny washed his hands.

Only this time, it didn't appear as though he was going to have much choice. Again the barrel shifted . . . to Colyer, his vision blurring. Squeezing his eyes shut against the pain in his foot, Cutter blinked hard, turning his head to regard Elias, who was staring a hole through him. Damn, what was wrong with him?

"McKenzie? You all right?"

"Fine," Cutter snarled, his gaze shifting abruptly back to Colyer. Muttering an oath, he watched in silence as all three men picked up their gear and walked away, leaving Elizabeth and Katie alone.

Elias observed Cutter a moment longer, and then, without another word, turned to watch as Magnus and his men set up camp about forty feet away from where Elizabeth remained on the downward slope. The area where she sat was devoid of trees, carpeted only with tall grass, while at Magnus's back there was another thicket, just like the one in which Cutter was concealed.

In spite of the fact that Elizabeth was sandwiched between them, Cutter still had a clear shot at Magnus . . . if only it weren't getting so damned dark . . . if only his eyes weren't playing tricks on him.

What the hell was wrong with him?

He shook his head, ridding himself of the black film that was slowly obscuring his vision.

What puzzled him most was the fact that Magnus wasn't making any attempts to hide his camp at all. It was as though he were using Elizabeth as bait. But why? He turned again to Elias, his eyes narrowing, glinting in the dusky light—the sun was going down fast. Maybe then he could make his move. "You said Magnus had papers?"

Elias nodded, shifting only the briefest glance toward Cutter, noticing that the hands that only moments before had held the carbine steady were now wavering. "That's right."

Cutter shook his head again distractedly. And then his eyes focused once more. "What sort of papers?"

Elias's gaze narrowed, and he suppressed a cough. He knew better than to ask again. Instinct told him that Cutter wasn't about to admit weakness to anybody, not even himself. "A letter from General Sully," he said, clearing his throat. "Accusing you of desertion . . . offering leniency in return for cooperation."

"What kind of cooperation?"

"Didn't say."

"Bastard was bluffing."

Elias shifted a glance toward Elizabeth and Katie. "Didn't appear as though he was bluffing to me." Then back to Cutter. "That's a mighty serious allegation, McKenzie."

Cutter's brows furrowed incredulously; he knew it wasn't possible. He wasn't U.S. military, just under contract, and his contract hadn't been renewed, at that. "The dispatch actually charged me with desertion? To the letter?"

Elias returned his scrutiny to his granddaughter, and then trained his carbine on Lieutenant Magnus Sulzberger. "Well, no . . . not precisely. There were three lines—read something like . . . in reference to absenteeism without leave . . . will consider leniency in exchange for—" his glance returned briefly to Cutter, and he cleared his throat "—assistance, I believe."

Cutter nodded, satisfied. "Like I said, the bastard was bluffing."

"Don't make sense. Why would he do that?"

"Desperate men do desperate things," Cutter answered, shaking his head briskly, blinking again to ward away the haze shutting down like a veil over his eyes. "Sully's career might hinge on his next campaign. Reckon he thought it'd make me mad enough to come lookin' for him. And he was right. I'm sure he figured getting me there was half the battle, 'cause then he could bend my ear, bribe me, whatever. Y' see, he needs something from me I won't give up."

"What's that?"

"My nose."

Elias gave him a skeptical look, and then understanding suddenly, he nodded, his voice rising slightly with the question. "He wants you to scout? Seems a lot of trouble to go through just to get you to scout. Why didn't he just ask?"

"He did," Cutter replied coldly, focusing his sight over the barrel of his carbine.

"And?"

"I told him to go blow himself." His eyes narrowed. "Don't ever aim to be a part of another Sand Creek!" The ensuing silence was thick. "You wouldn't happen to know how Sully knew where to find me?" he asked suddenly.

The silence thickened.

"I do," Elias answered at last.

Cutter gave him a brief glance. "Yeah?"

Elias drew his brows together at Cutter's condemning tone. "I had every right to use my connections to check you out, McKenzie, and that's precisely what I did—as soon as I heard from your sister that you and Elizabeth were on your way. You'da done the same thing!"

"Yeah," Cutter relented after a moment, giving Elias another quick glance. "Reckon so." He turned his attention back to the small group in the distance. With the fading light, his targets were becoming too indistinct. And damn him, if he didn't feel like he was on fire.

He couldn't believe a small cut would take him down. Hell, he had scars from bigger wounds that hadn't bothered him half as much. Sweat beaded on his lip. "What I can't figure is what role Sulzberger has in all of this," he mused aloud. "Unless . . ."

"Unless what?"

"Unless he's got his own plans—'less he aims to use that letter of Sully's to his benefit."

Elias's brows rose. "How's that?"

Cutter's eyes sought Elias's again in the growing darkness. Red-rimmed, they glittered like black glass with the last light of day. "To grease that bullet he'd like to put in my back," he replied without emotion. "That's why." There was silence a moment, and then he added, "Elias . . . I want you to ride back into Fulton City. Bring the law back with you."

"What in damnation are you talking about, McKenzie" he whispered furiously. "I'm an old man, sure enough, but not so useless I can't help out here! My granddaughter needs me!"

"Yeah . . . and that's precisely why you'll go," Cutter replied coolly, giving him a firm nod. "Because your granddaughter needs you." The two faced each other in static silence.

Elias's eyes narrowed. "You trying to tell me something, McKenzie?"

It stung Cutter to have to concede any weakness at all . . . but it was that . . . or lose Elizabeth and Katie out of stubborn pride. He couldn't do that. Wouldn't. And he was losing it fast. He nodded, wincing as he shifted his position slightly. Pain fired through his left leg, and he grunted as it burst into his hip. "Reckon I am," he replied hoarsely. "If you go now, Elias, you can make it back before daybreak. You have my word that I won't go after 'em alone unless I have to."

The indecision was as clear in Elias's blue eyes as the torment was in Cutter's dark ones. He knew Cutter wouldn't be asking if he didn't think it was their only chance. Still, it was hard to leave . . . knowing Cutter wasn't up to scratch.

"My word," Cutter assured through his teeth. Sweat trickled down his temples. "And if they pull out, I'll leave you a trail a blind man could follow." Still Elias didn't reply. "Whatever it takes, I won't let them harm a hair on your granddaughter's head."

Elias cursed under his breath. "I know," he relented, looking away briefly. There was a long stretch of silence, and then he said, "I know about the two of you . . . know you're not married to her."

"Sulzberger tell you that, too?" Cutter snarled.

Elias nodded, and Cutter scrutinized his features when he turned to face him finally, but there was no contempt there. None at all. He nodded back, conceding the fact.

"It don't matter none to me," Elias revealed, glancing again toward Katie and Elizabeth, and then back. "I can tell you love her. If you can give my granddaughter half as much . . . she'll be one lucky girl. It ain't up to me to judge ya, anyhow—not either of ya. You see . . . Miss Mimi and I . . ." He averted his gaze suddenly. "I'm gettin' up in years now . . . and, well . . ."

"You don't have to say it," Cutter yielded. "I know."

Elias nodded. "Yes, I do. You see . . . I want this time with Mimi. I spent too little time with my wife before she died. Too little time with my son. And I don't aim to make that mistake again. I've loved Mimi a lot of years now . . . put off livin' my life the way I saw fit to because . . . well, because I didn't want to offend my son. He was real close to his mother . . . but John's gone now, and I know you'll make a real good father to Katie," he continued, looking down at the ground beneath them. "Anyhow, just wanted you to know before I go." He looked up abruptly, searching Cutter's expression. "You do plan to marry the girl, don't you?" he asked.

Cutter's eyes narrowed slightly. He wanted to assure the old man that he would, *if Elizabeth would have him*, but pride wouldn't let him. "That's between myself and Elizabeth," he said through clenched teeth. "Now . . . you'd best be going."

Elias nodded slowly and began to shimmy down the branch. "Reckon I better," he agreed with a weary sigh, "if I'm gonna get back before sunup . . ."

Almost from the moment Katie had opened her eyes, she'd begun to wail uncontrollably. And despite the fact that her mouth was jammed full with cloth, she continued to shriek, clinging frantically to Elizabeth's neck in the darkness.

Biting her lip until it throbbed, Elizabeth prayed that Magnus and Colyer wouldn't become angered again. On the other hand, she was certain Katie and her shrieking was the only thing keeping Colyer from abusing her. She hadn't mistaken the look he'd given her before stalking off with Magnus.

Muttering about whores and screaming brats, all three of them had moved away from her, toward the warmth and light of the campfire, leaving herself and Katie only the cold, empty darkness.

Giving her fleeting looks of apology, O'Neill had bound her hands behind her back, and then her feet, tightly, so that she couldn't escape. To be certain they were not actually cutting off her circulation, Magnus had inspected them afterward. They were rubbing her raw now, and she gave a desperate little laugh at the notion. Where had they expected her to flee? They were in the middle of nowhere, for mercy's sake!

Because they'd been unable to pry Katie away from her, or even quiet her, they'd tied the poor child's hands around Elizabeth's neck. Her little legs were stretched around Elizabeth's waist and bound as well, and then they'd shoved a dirty sock into her mouth, containing it with a filthy gray neckerchief around her face. It was so big that it covered most of Katie's face, and Elizabeth had had to jerk it down with her teeth so that Katie could see anything at all.

How cruel could people be? Guilt gnawed at her as she acknowledged the fact that if it hadn't been for her own determination to raise the child as her own, Katie wouldn't be suffering at the moment.

Her teeth chattered, though not from the chill night air, but from the stark raw fear she felt for this innocent child. Tears pooled in her eyes, and she began to tremble as she rocked Katie, trying to calm her stifled sobbing.

"Cutter," she whispered, nuzzling her cheek against the velvety wetness of Katie's tiny face. "Where are you?" Did he know what had happened to them? Dear Lord, what if he'd thought she'd left him deliberately?

No matter what Elizabeth did, what she said, nothing seemed to soothe Katie, and the muffled whimpers were beginning to shatter her own composure. God only knew, she understood Katie's fear, understood her hysteria—she actually felt like screaming herself—but Katie's panic made her feel a failure. What would Katherine have done? she asked herself mournfully.

Rocking back and forth, rubbing her cheek against Katie's damp, silky curls, Elizabeth held back her own tears, knowing her own hysteria wasn't likely to help Katie out of hers. "Katie," she pleaded, her whisper broken. "Katie, sweetheart . . ." In spite of herself, a sob escaped, but she bit her lip, holding back the rest. "I won't let them harm you, darling . . . I swear it—oh, Lord! What have I done?" She swallowed another sob before it could manage to escape her throat. "Katherine . . . oh, Katherine, I'm so sorry. Help me."

Helpless to do anything but bring Katie down with her, she lay back wearily upon the grass, thinking of all the dreams she had begun to weave around the child nestled against her. Every one of them included Cutter.

After a moment longer, Katie's tearful sobs finally turned into sleepy whimpers as she went limp with exhaustion. Fighting back her own fatigue, Elizabeth closed her eyes and drifted.

Her thoughts filtered back to the day she'd met Cutter. Hard to believe it had been such a short time ago; it seemed a lifetime had passed. So much had happened since then. So much had happened to her. She was different, regenerated, like a butterfly that had only just burst from its cocoon.

Arrogant and infuriating as the man was, he'd somehow squeezed himself into the heart she'd thought long dead. For so long she'd been careful not to let anyone—not anyone—into her life, because then she wouldn't have to suffer the pain of their leaving.

With Cutter . . . the risk had seemed worth taking. It didn't matter what he was. It never had, she realized in that moment. And if she ever got the chance again, she'd make him see that, too.

Dear God, she loved him!

Her heart began to pound, and she became instantly alert, fully aware of her surroundings, every rustle of grass. She stifled the urge to cry out his name, sensing his presence. She could almost smell him in the slight breeze, but could see nothing.

With no moon, the darkness was impenetrable.

Chapter 28

Elizabeth's heart nearly flew out of her breast when warm fingers brushed her leg unexpectedly. Stifling a cry of panic, she lay as still as she was able, afraid to wake Katie.

Please, oh, please be Cutter, she implored silently. *Dear God, what if it wasn't? What if it was Colyer?*

She couldn't bear it. It had to be Cutter! Why didn't he speak? Well, of course she knew why he didn't speak! she scolded herself hysterically. Sweet heaven above!

Awkwardly the hand groped about her lower legs, feeling for something, and then finding it, halted at the thick rope that lashed her feet together. With bated breath she waited, listening to the sound the knife made as it sawed through the rope.

At last there was a final rent and her legs fell free, numb but liberated.

Her heart pounding without mercy, she watched, her eyes wide, as the shadow crept up to her face . . . so close that she could hear the breath between them . . . but the darkness was too thick.

She couldn't make out the face.

"Ma'am?" the voiced called out softly.

Elizabeth recoiled from it instantly. It wasn't Cutter! her mind shrieked. Oh God—it wasn't! In that moment she felt as close to madness as she had ever been in her life. She must have made some terrified sound, because in the next moment, a hand slipped tightly over her mouth, trapping a scream in her throat.

"Ma'am? It's me, Jacob O'Neill. Don't scream. I won't hurt ya—" O'Neill's words were cut off abruptly as the barrel of a rifle slammed into his back.

"Damned right you won't, Blue-boy!" came a seething whisper.

Hearing Cutter's drawl at last, Elizabeth felt her heart slam against her breast. She swallowed, unable to speak momentarily for the emotions that welled within her. Relief. Joy. Anger! Why had it taken him so long?

"I'd sooner see you in hell," Cutter continued. Despite the fact that his strength was exhausted, and his body was staggering on the brink of hell itself, his voice sounded hard. "Now, get those hands up where I can see 'em," he said through his teeth.

See them? Elizabeth thought hysterically. How could anybody see anything at all?

O'Neill's hand went up slowly, moonlight glinting off the knife as it ascended. "I was gonna let her go, mister—I swear it! If ya'd but come a second later, ya'd have heard me say so. I was aboot to cut her hands free, is all . . . S-Still will . . . if y'll let me?"

A chill silence met his declaration, and he went on without being prompted. "Mister," he advised in a nervous whisper. "If I'm gonna set her free, we're gonna hafta hurry, 'cause my watch'll be over in another twenty minutes." Still, only silence met him. "If ya ain't gonna let me," O'Neill continued, swallowing with difficulty, "then ya might as well put a bullet in ma back now, 'cause Sulzberger will, if you don't. If not him, Colyer then—he don't like you too much on account of you slicing his ear."

"Some folks have no sense of humor at all," Cutter remarked so softly that it sent a chill down Elizabeth's spine. "Pity that. I'd've thought he was chock-full of it."

He don't like you too much on account of you slicing his ear, Elizabeth heard again. She shivered at the subdued violence in Cutter's answer—that and the fact that their exchange triggered a memory—the day she'd asked him why his horse had only half a right ear.

"Someone's idea of a practical joke," his voice echoed in her ear. *". . . Don't reckon the man's laughing any longer. . . . Just went a little too far in trying to provoke me, is all."*

"What did you do to him?"

"You don't want to know."

Her shoulders trembled faintly at the conclusion she drew, while at her breast, Katie began to stir, whimpering softly in her sleep.

"All right," Cutter agreed abruptly, jabbing O'Neill in the back once more. "Cut her loose, then."

"Yes, sir!" Jacob reached for Elizabeth immediately, almost eagerly. "Think ya can sit up for me, ma'am?"

Elizabeth nodded briskly, and then realizing he couldn't see her gesture, she said, "I think so . . ." And she tried, but her lack of arms to use for balance, along with Katie's weight, brought her back down. She rolled slightly atop of Katie, waking her with a start. At once Katie began to whimper behind her gag.

"Shush, sweetheart," Elizabeth whispered frantically. "Cutter's here to take us home now. Don't cry." While she soothed Katie, Jacob helped her sit upright and immediately began to carve into the rope that bound her hands at her back.

"Be real still, now, ma'am . . . wouldn't want ta cut ya . . . Just another—"

From somewhere within the darkness, gunfire erupted without warning. O'Neill's remark ended with a gurgle and a choke as a bullet struck his windpipe. Elizabeth screamed as he slumped forward, into her, bringing her down under his weight. Katie screeched in terror, and Elizabeth reached for her instinctively, snapping the last frazzled thread of rope in her panic. Within seconds, another bullet whizzed by. And then another, striking the ground to her right. Recoiling from it, Elizabeth cried out in panic, trying to free herself and Katie from O'Neill's dead weight. He was too heavy!

"O'Neill—y' double-crossin' bastard!" came Magnus's sleep-hoarse voice.

With a savage war cry, Cutter thrust O'Neill's body off Elizabeth.

Elizabeth automatically fumbled for the boy's body, trying to reach him, to help him—drag him to safety at least. Her duty—the motions so inbred that she didn't immediately think of her own safety, or even Katie's.

Another shot whined overhead, coming from the opposite direction this time, and somewhere she heard feet scattering for cover. "Help me, Cutter— he's hurt!"

"Not hurt!" he snapped. "Dead! Now get a move on, Doc!" Cutter seized her by the hair, jerking her backward without apologies. "Chrissakes, woman," he snarled when she resisted. "Can't fix this one either! Let go!" Coming near to dragging her, he withdrew deeper into the night, pulling Elizabeth up by her waist when he could, trying not to harm Katie as he dragged them both behind a small boulder, barely sufficient for cover. Above them, bullets sang. One struck the stone, ricocheting into the darkness.

Cutter drew his Colt out of his gun belt and pressed it into Elizabeth's hand. "Stay low and shoot straight!" he demanded. "Gotta untie Katie."

"B-But I—I can't see!" Elizabeth gasped, her hand as shaky as her voice. "I can't see to shoot!"

"Chrissakes!" Cutter reached out and pointed the gun in the general direction he intended for Elizabeth to fire, and then, in the same fluid motion, withdrew his knife from his boot, nudging Elizabeth when she didn't immediately obey. "Just squeeze the damned trigger!"

Another volley of shots whizzed overhead, but Elizabeth could no longer tell whether they were coming or going. She froze. "A-Anywhere?" she asked frantically, her fingers shaking violently.

"Anywhere but at me!" Cutter shot back, shoving her head down without warning. "If y' can't see—don't bother looking. Just keep the gun steady and squeeze the trigger." At her back, he quickly found and slashed at the rope between Katie's wrists, freeing her arms from around Elizabeth's neck, then her feet. Jerking her from Elizabeth's hold with a muttered curse, he removed the gag from Katie's mouth and urged the child onto all fours. He shoved Elizabeth down again when her head came up too high, and belatedly it occurred to him that she hadn't yet fired a single shot. He nudged her, hard. "Shoot!"

More out of panic than intent, Elizabeth squeezed the trigger, crying out at the sound and smell of the pistol's discharge.

Having freed Katie, Cutter turned, surging upward against the boulder. Aiming his carbine straight into the night, he fired, reloading at once. His ears straining to pick up the sounds he needed, he fired again, repeating the process with calm proficiency. Then again, reloading as swiftly as he fired. Hampered as he was by his dull-as-ditchwater senses, and the lack of light to see by, Cutter was surprised when a grunt of pain ensued. But he smiled into the darkness and fired again.

Astounded as Elizabeth was that he'd been able to find his mark in the darkness, she recovered her jaw and squeezed her own trigger. As she fired a shot, another bullet struck the boulder, splintering rock and then ricocheting, interring itself into the ground nearby.

"Katie," Cutter said, his voice tortured, turning to catch her by the arm. "You trust me, don't you?"

Things weren't going quite as he'd planned. Hell, he'd hoped Elias would get back before he was forced to go in. But he'd heard Elizabeth whimpering, and had reacted purely on instinct.

Terrified as she was, Katie's head bobbed once in acknowledgment as she responded with the anticipated trust of a child.

Cutter felt the gesture more than he saw it. Relief washed over him, because he sure as hell needed her trust. "Good girl!" he said, while his mind groped for a solution. He'd forgotten Elizabeth couldn't see distances. It only stood to reason she'd be blind as a bat at night. He'd planned to send her along with Katie, covering their backs while they ran for safety, but Elizabeth would likely lead them straight to hell that way. No, Katie was better off without her. Thing was, he wasn't about to leave Elizabeth stranded, either—not knowing which way to run when the time came. If he left her now . . . he wasn't certain he could make it back. He felt trapped between the devil and the deep sea.

He shook his mind clear and gripped Katie's hand firmly. "All right now, Katie. Listen to me . . . I want you to crawl—straight as you can—fast as you can. I . . ." Hell, he had no choice. He couldn't let her go unprotected. "I'll be right behind you," he relented, his gut twisting.

Katie nodded again, but her little body tensed, and Cutter ruffled her curls in reassurance.

"I'll be right behind you," he repeated. Overhead, shots waned momentarily, then stopped for an instant, and Cutter shoved. "Go!" he hissed.

Katie scurried over the ground as quickly as her little hands and feet could carry her, and it was all Cutter could do to keep up.

It took Elizabeth a terrified moment to realize what had happened, that she was alone. But the instant she did, fright struck like cold steel into her heart. Desperately she tried to keep the panic from clutching her by the throat, smothering her breath. Her heart hammered with fear as she squeezed off the last shots in her revolver. But even before the last click, Cutter materialized from the darkness to seize the gun from her hands, as if he'd anticipated it. He resheathed it, and then jerked her down to her knees as another round of lead immediately flew over their heads.

Keeping low to the ground, Cutter led the way, jerking Elizabeth forward each time she lagged behind, the touch of his hand clammy on her arm. Finally, ducking bullets, they reached a much larger boulder. "Katie?" Cutter whispered as he dragged Elizabeth behind it.

Katie mumbled something unintelligible, and Cutter immediately rose against the boulder, leaving Elizabeth to do her part. She searched out Katie in the darkness, calling her name softly. With a frightened little whimper, Katie plunged into her arms, and Elizabeth urged her to keep silent.

The darkness was a mixed blessing—hiding them but shielding the men who fired on them. As the moments lengthened, gunfire became more sporadic, each side thinking to conserve ammo, each side aiming to win.

It was with relief that Elizabeth sensed the coming of daylight. As the first pink streaks of dawn stretched across the brightening sky, she huddled close to Katie, trying to cause the least possible distraction. Watching Cutter intently, she soothed the child, ran fingers through her curls, rocked her.

Her heart lurched as Cutter wavered suddenly on his feet.

Blinking hard, Cutter shook his head to fight away the darkness. In spite of the fact that night was waning, shadows were beginning to converge in his mind, closing in swiftly. There was no doubt about it now. He'd fought it off as long as he could.

The lights were definitely going out.

Again, he blinked and shook his head, staggering

to his knees. He knew better than to panic. Panic would lay them all six feet under. But his strength was fading quickly. He turned abruptly, his back slamming against the boulder as he fell backward, his face sapped of color, his hair and clothing soaked with sweat. Without a word, he lifted his Colt up out of his belt and began to lever bullets into the firing chamber.

"Cutter?"

Seeing his eyes close briefly, Elizabeth startled. Crying out, she slid Katie off her lap and threw herself at him.

"Cutter!"

Chapter 29

❦❦ "**N**o . . ." Immediately Elizabeth began searching for a wound, tears pricking at her eyes, threatening to obscure her vision. With the last of his strength, Cutter thrust her hand away and continued loading, but she returned stubbornly, probing him, holding back her sobs as she searched him.

Sweat trickled from Cutter's brow as he fought to the teeth to stay conscious—at least until he could hand over a fully loaded weapon to Elizabeth.

"Where?" Elizabeth demanded, desperation taking over. She could sense him fading, and still had no notion what it was that was wrong. "I don't see where you were shot!" She was losing hold of her control. Dear God, Cutter couldn't die. He couldn't leave her! She loved him. "Cutter," she moaned.

"Lizbeth, gal . . . we're in a tight . . ." he told her, wavering on the brink of unconsciousness. Shadows flitted before his eyes as he handed her the loaded Colt, butt-first. He swallowed nothing. His mouth was dry as death. "Need your help," he told her hoarsely.

Elizabeth shook her head, shoving the gun away, denying him. She was terrified that if she touched the gun, he would slip away. Desperately she continued to probe his body for the mysterious wound, confounded that she couldn't find it.

His vision reeling, Cutter looked at her blankly, his

eyes narrowed and glassy. "Elizabeth," he said firmly. "Take the confounded gun . . . point it at the bad guys . . . and shoot." he thrust it at her weakly. "Take it," he entreated softly, blinking as his eyes crossed.

Fighting her hysteria, Elizabeth snatched the odious gun from his hands, fully intending to lay it aside while she continued to search him, but the moment she did, Cutter's eyes closed, and he slumped to one side.

"No!" she cried, clutching his shoulders in desperation. "Oh, no—Cutter, no!"

Lead shattered into the boulder, flinging shards of stone. One chip hit Katie in the arm. At once Katie began to shriek, scurrying closer to Elizabeth. Elizabeth shoved her down to lie beside Cutter, her instinct for survival taking over. Saying a short prayer for all their souls, she rose to her trembling knees. The gun wavered in her hands as she peered over the boulder, only to face panic once more.

Oh, God! She could see nothing! Nothing at all! She shook her head, denying the position she was in, and turned, sinking down despondently against the cold stone. But it was no use. Denial would accomplish nothing.

"Dear God, have mercy on our souls," she said with a catch, and resolutely came back to her knees, fully expecting to look death in the face.

She couldn't see anything beyond the swaying grass—not even the boulder she and Katie and Cutter had used for shelter earlier. Everything, everything, beyond her field of vision was a hazy predawn blur of gray and rose. Another bullet whistled past, just missing Elizabeth.

At her feet, Cutter groaned, startling her.

"Just a scratch," he said deliriously, his teeth setting against the pain.

Elizabeth felt torn, wanting to go to him, and knowing she couldn't possibly. Her face as ashen as the pale gray dawn sky, she peered over the boulder again. Another bullet whizzed by, missing her, though barely, and she squeezed one of her own off accidentally. Her hands quivering, she muttered a curse she'd learned from Cutter and glanced back over the boulder, pointing her gun shakily, but not firing.

She couldn't see anything to shoot at and didn't dare waste bullets. Oh, God . . . she couldn't kill what she couldn't see! And she couldn't see anything!

Not true! she told herself. You can see all you need to! Don't panic. "Do not panic," she told herself firmly.

Biting her lower lip almost painfully, she held her breath, and waited. For the longest moment, there was nothing. Nothing at all. The sound of gunfire stopped abruptly, and only the sound of the breeze stirred through the grass.

With every second of silence, her fear mounted.

And then suddenly she tensed, seeing a face . . . oh, God, a face . . . a bearded face! Magnus was on his belly, coming like a snake through the grass!

He was grinning—knowing that she was incapable of staving him off alone. But he was wrong. She *could* do it! Keeping her hand as steady as she was able, she tried with all her might to focus, squinting as he came closer, waiting for the right moment.

Closer.

"Aunt Lizabeth!" Katie squealed in fright.

"Stay down, Katie!" Elizabeth squeezed the trigger, but it merely clicked, the chamber empty. Cutter had missed one. How many bullets had he loaded? She couldn't remember.

"Cutter?" she whimpered.

Magnus's grin widened at seeing her alone. Emboldened by her panic and her empty chamber, he came to his knees, rising swiftly to his feet to rush at her.

Panic threatened to set in. Some part of Elizabeth wanted only to toss down the gun in her hand and throw herself at Magnus's mercy, knowing there was no way possible for her to fire and hit her intended target . . . even if there were bullets . . . but there had to be! She'd watched Cutter load it!

There had to be!

And she had to try. Magnus would kill them all without hesitation. That had been his intent all along, she reminded herself bitterly. Bolstering her courage, she straightened, steadied the gun in her hand, and focused hard on Magnus's beard.

With a hopeless cry, she squeezed the trigger again. Adrenaline sped through her as the gun discharged. Again she fired. And then again. And then again.

And then she blinked, disbelieving her eyes. Before her, as if in slow motion, Magnus wavered a moment, then fell to his knees in the grass, clutching his ribs . . . an *arrow* piercing his heart. Blood gurgled from his mouth.

Oh, God . . . an arrow!

Elizabeth stared at it for a dumbfounded moment. She watched as he dropped the gleaming silver gun to the grass and then collapsed atop it. Shocked, she turned to see that Katie had buried her face into Cutter's side.

And then she looked up . . . and saw another face approaching, a face with eyes as black as Cutter's. But it was familiar and she didn't scream, despite her moment of fear. She swallowed, realizing that it was the very same Indian who had come upon her and Cutter in their sleep. The same one who had spoken to Cutter. Who'd thanked her for the sage she hadn't purposely placed on his brother Black Wolf's grave. She shook her head, as if disbelieving what she saw. The Indian came forward and bent over Magnus's body, placing a hand before his nose and then at his throat.

"É-naaʔe!"

Elizabeth shook her head frantically, not understanding.

"É-naaˀe!" He pointed at Sulzberger and made a quick slicing motion with his hand. "É-naaˀe!"

"D-Dead?" she stammered. "Dead?"

The Indian seemed to understand her, and he suddenly pointed away from them, in the direction Sulzberger had come from. "E-eˀ tóhtahe!"

"C-Colyer?" she asked, pointing timidly in the same direction. "D-Dead, too?" She tried to recall what Cutter had said about death in the Cheyenne tribe. "Sèyăń!" she blurted. She pointed in the same direction the Indian had, once more, hope spiraling in her breast. "Colyer . . . sèyăń?"

The Indian's brows collided, though he appeared amused, not angry. He shook his head and pointed again. Then, turning, he held out his hand. Two of his fingers ran across his palm. "E-eˀ tóhtahe," he repeated.

Elizabeth shook her head, still not understanding.

Suddenly his arms flew wide, and his fingers curled, clawlike. He shouted the word again and lunged at them. Katie screamed, hurling herself into Elizabeth's back, her arms flying about Elizabeth's neck.

Elizabeth didn't dare move.

"E-eˀ tóhtahe!" the Indian said again, pointing at Katie. He mimicked Katie's fear, running in a circle with his hands high in the air. His mouth was agape with a scream that never materialized.

The image was so comical that if Elizabeth hadn't been so dazed, she might have actually laughed. As it was, he stopped suddenly, and she flinched at the suddenness of his movement as he again pointed in the direction Sulzberger had come. Just to be certain she understood, he turned his palm up once more and ran his fingers across it. "E-eˀ tóhtahe!" he repeated.

"Afraid," Elizabeth whispered with a nod. Her

heart pounded fiercely, yet she knew instinctively that he'd meant neither of them any harm. Colyer had run away afraid, she surmised. She made the same running motion with her fingers, and nodded again at the Indian. "Colyer ran away afraid," she concluded, and then she began to pry Katie's arms from around her neck. She brought Katie around to embrace her. "He won't hurt you," Elizabeth assured, knowing in her heart that it was the truth. "He means to help us."

The Indian nodded and smiled, as though he'd again understood. He looked down suddenly and kicked Sulzberger's body violently. Elizabeth winced, but Sulzberger didn't stir.

Satisfied that the Indian had come in peace, Elizabeth wasted no more time in returning her attention to Cutter. With Katie still clutching at her, she turned and began to examine him under the Indian's watchful gaze. Quickly she began to unbutton his shirt, removing his arms from his sleeves. He was much too heavy to remove it completely, so she left it for him to lie upon.

As Elizabeth probed Cutter's arms, she was vaguely aware that the Indian was dragging Sulzberger away from them. When he was gone finally, Katie eased her grip, though she didn't release Elizabeth completely. Her little fist clutched at Elizabeth's skirt.

Katie's whisper was shaky. "I-Is he a Indian, A-Aunt Lizabeth?"

Elizabeth nibbled her lower lip as she met Katie's frightened gaze. "Yes," she replied.

"Is h-he a good Indian?"

Elizabeth couldn't tear her gaze away. There was so much of her own emotions mirrored in Katie's eyes. "Yes, he is," she answered with more certainty than she felt. Swallowing, she returned her attention to Cutter.

"Is Uncle Cutter gonna go to heaven, too, Aunt Lizabeth?"

Elizabeth was startled by the innocent question; her eyes flew to Katie's. Tears stung her own eyes, but she held them back, containing them with anger. "I don't know," she replied honestly, her voice breaking. She averted her eyes to Cutter's chest, laying her hand upon it. She bit into her lower lip to keep from crying out loud. His breath was shallow, too shallow, and his flesh was raging with fever. Fear lodged in her throat as she turned him slightly, peering underneath his back.

Nothing.

His color is good, she told herself. As long as he was still feverish, he was fighting. But how could he be feverish if he'd only just been shot? She shook her head. It wasn't possible. And then she recalled the shots that had killed O'Neill. Had Cutter been hit then, too—all those hours ago—and said nothing of it? It still didn't make sense.

"Katie," she said, trying not to give in to hysteria, "turn around, sweetheart."

"Why?"

Again Elizabeth looked up, beseeching Katie to understand. "Because I have to look somewhere you can't," she said bluntly.

Katie nodded abruptly, seeing something frightening in Elizabeth's eyes. She turned obediently, and Elizabeth immediately began to unbutton Cutter's denims, tugging them down as far as she was able without removing his boots. Nothing. Puzzled, she lifted one leg slightly, then the other, peering beneath.

Still nothing.

Stupefied, she removed his knife from his left boot, set it aside, and began tugging off the right one. It came off without difficulty, but when she came back to remove the left one, it seemed bonded to his foot. Grunting, she hauled on it with all her might, yanking it down, one frustrating inch at a time. At last, when it was nearly off, she caught a glimpse of the angry red streak, and her breath snagged. Her heart pounded as she tugged again, more frantically this time, releasing the boot with a final sucking sound. She toppled backward from the force of her tug. Shaking her head in denial, she righted herself at once, and began to remove his sock. She tossed it aside in disbelief, her heart filling with an unbearable ache.

"Dear God!" she exclaimed.

"Can I look?" Katie asked.

"No, Katie . . . no," Elizabeth sobbed.

The red streak climbed his leg, originating from a gash in his left foot and disappearing into the leg of his denims. She hadn't realized he'd even cut himself! How could she not have known? Why hadn't he mentioned it?

He didn't trust in you, a little voice taunted as she tugged frantically at his denims, removing them.

Cutter didn't believe in her abilities as a doctor any more than anyone else did.

He watched you kill a man with your ignorance, that same voice sneered.

But she could have done something. Anything . . . *anything* would have been better than nothing at all! She swallowed the lump that rose in her throat, for in that moment, it hurt so deeply that he'd preferred to suffer—or die, even—rather than have her tend him!

Perhaps he'd had good reason to doubt her, she mocked herself. She hadn't been able to keep the Indian from dying, had she? But she'd tried. Dear God, with all her heart she'd tried!

He didn't trust her.

The Indian chose that moment to return. "E-haamaʔta," he said, halting dead in his tracks when he saw Cutter's swollen, angry foot.

Katie buried her face into Elizabeth's lap, hiding from him, and Elizabeth never felt more torn; she wanted to soothe Katie, wanted to help Cutter, wanted to cry.

"It's infected," Elizabeth informed him briskly, even

knowing he wouldn't understand. She held back every emotion. Except for the anger that crept into her heart. Anger that Cutter would have let this go so long without having it tended. Anger that he hadn't trusted her. Anger that he might die because of his stubbornness. Anger that she had let herself love him.

Why, oh, why had she allowed herself to love him?

Her hands began to shake uncontrollably. "I'll need you to start a fire," she said, looking up at the Indian, her lips trembling and her eyes shimmering. "Fire!" She set Katie aside and made a desperate motion with her hand, and then, remembering the cartridge Cutter usually kept in his pocket, she searched for it. Not finding it, she mimed building herself a fire, and then cooking, and then eating what she cooked.

The Indian nodded. *"Meséestse!"* he said with a grin, and without another word, set about the task assigned to him.

When he began to build the fire, Elizabeth returned her attention to Cutter, satisfied that she had gotten her message across. Her heart ached as she spied Katie's frightened pose. She was holding her knees to her chest and watching the Indian through her little hands. "Katie," she admonished gently, "don't be afraid, honey. And don't hide your face," she added firmly, her breath catching on a sob. "He won't hurt you, and it will hurt his feelings."

Katie nodded mutely and dropped her hands, looking up at Elizabeth with haunted eyes. Elizabeth's hand went to her mouth as silent sobs wracked her within. Her lips clamped to contain them. Unable to keep them down, she choked suddenly. Glancing over her shoulder, her heart in her eyes, she met the Indian's comprehending gaze.

There was no language barrier between them in that instant. He seemed to see everything that was in her heart. He went back to his task, and Elizabeth turned back to Cutter, her emotions too turbulent to be seen. Too embittered.

"I hate you, Cutter!" she choked out suddenly her hands flying to her mouth, covering the telltale trembling of her lips. *No . . . you don't! You love him,* that same voice countered fiercely. *You love him!*

"Aunt Lizabeth!" Katie sobbed.

The Indian said nothing, only watched her show of emotions from of the corner of his eyes. When the fire was kindled finally, he left without a word.

Her throat seemed to close up as she lifted Cutter's knife to the fire, watching it flare bright red within the glowing blue flames. When it was heated enough, she removed it, swiping the black ash on her skirt, not caring that it singed the material, not caring that she could feel the burn clear to her flesh.

And then, with trembling hands, she began to slice open the inflamed wound on the sole of his foot.

"Aunt Lizabeth!" Katie cried in protest.

"Don't look, Katie!" Elizabeth demanded firmly. "Don't look, honey!" There was little blood and much pus. She swallowed convulsively. But it wasn't the wound that made her ill. It was the lack of tools along with her fear of failure.

There was no pot to boil water with.

No water to boil, even if there had been a pot.

No alcohol to sterilize the wound.

Nothing.

Nothing but the knife in her hands.

Using the best of her skills, she drained the wound, brushing her tears aside when they hindered her vision.

Vaguely she was aware that the Indian had returned. As if he'd anticipated her needs, he set down two canteens full of water beside her, along with a blanket. "*Mahpe,*" he said, pointing to the canteen. "*Mahpe.*"

"Water," Elizabeth returned, her gaze lifting from the canteens.

The Indian nodded, standing. "Wat-er!" he repeated, and then he walked away.

Tears glistened on her pale face as Elizabeth eyed the

canteens blankly, noticing finally that one was made of
tin covered with water-stained leather. The other was
made solely of animal skin, and she determined that it
was the Indian's. With an immediate surge of excitement, she lifted the one made of tin, inspected it quickly,
and then, with her heart hammering, she set it whole
into the fire, watching eagerly as the leather ignited before her eyes and burned away. The moment she felt it
was hot enough, she found a rock and tossed it at the
canteen, nudging it back out. And then another, and
another, until the canteen was completely out of the
fire. Not caring that it charred her dress, she used her
hem to protect her fingers as she lifted up the canteen,
unscrewed the top, and poured a heated droplet onto
the back of her hand. It scalded her, but she merely
smiled with relief and shook it away.

Having little time to waste, she rent a strip from Cutter's shirt and crumpled the cloth, holding it up to the
sole of Cutter's foot as she poured the scalding water
over his newly sliced wound, cleansing it thoroughly.

"Does that hurt?" Katie asked as she watched.

Elizabeth nodded, never looking up. She couldn't
bear to look into Katie's face and see her own fear
mirrored there. "I have to hurt him to help him," she
revealed, setting the canteen aside. She rubbed the
remaining dirt from the wound with the water-soaked
rag, and then again poured over the hot water when
she finished.

When every last speck of dirt was removed from
the wound, Elizabeth once again lifted the blade over
the fire, watching until the metal glowed. She bit
down on her bottom lip for strength, and turned o
set it against Cutter's foot. His foot jerked, the motion
more reflexive, than from pain, because his eyes remained closed, his face pale.

But there was no help for it. Knowing she had to
hurt him to help him, as she'd disclosed to Katie, she
set the sizzling blade to the wound once more, ster-
ilizing and cauterizing it with the heat.

Finally, when she'd done all she could do, she dressed the wound, covering Cutter with a blanket. With the Indian's help, she retrieved Cutter's bedroll and then set Cutter upon it, tucking the blanket lovingly about him.

Worry furrowing her brow, she placed a trembling hand to his forehead. "He's raging," she remarked softly, her voice still shaky with emotion.

"Raging?" Katie asked.

Elizabeth glanced up at Katie, intending to reassure her, but couldn't. "The fever," she explained. "I've done all I can for him," she added dismally. "There's nothing to do now but wait."

Katie stared, confusion screwing her young features. "You don't really hate him?" she wanted to know. "You don't hate my uncle. Do you?"

Dear God, what had she done? The chaos she'd brought to poor Katie's life—how could she ever forgive herself for it! "No, honey," Elizabeth cried. "No . . . I could never hate him." She stared back, but it wasn't Katie's face she saw in that moment . . . it was Cutter's.

You did real good back there, Doc, she heard him whisper. She closed her eyes, almost able to feel the warmth of his breath against her ear. "Oh, Cutter," she sobbed, squeezing her lids tight, blocking out the echo of Cutter's words. She had done the best she could then, too . . . and it hadn't been enough. Black Wolf had died in spite of it.

Dear God, she didn't know what she would do if Cutter died, as well.

She couldn't bear it. Hot, silent tears slipped past her lashes.

Did you think I'd won my title by default? her own voice mocked her.

Well? She scorned herself. Hadn't she, after all?

Chapter 30

$\sim$ ◦ᏠᏅ ◦ $\sim$

Cutter's fever escalated through the day. And though he didn't sink into delirium, he did awaken once, to stare glassy-eyed into the brightness of the late afternoon sun. Holding back tears of frustration and fear, Elizabeth passed a hand over his eyes, closing his lids to protect his pupils from the glare. She couldn't forget Black Wolf's sightless stare, couldn't help comparing . . .

Not even to eat did she leave Cutter's side. Black Wolf's brother hunted for Katie, feeding her, while Elizabeth kept watch. He offered to Elizabeth, but Elizabeth refused.

"*Meséestse!*" he said, bringing the meat to his lips, showing her what he wanted her to do with it. "*Hemèséestse!*" he repeated, thrusting the charred piece of hare at her once more, ordering her to eat it. "*E-peva$^?$e!*"

Elizabeth watched Katie, who was eating silently, sitting surprisingly close to the Indian. And then she turned again to meet his gaze. He was glowering at her, and given the choice she had—to offend him, or not to—Elizabeth took the meat from his hands. There was something to be thankful for, she thought dismally as she chewed. At least Katie seemed less afraid. They'd actually attempted to communicate, and if Elizabeth hadn't been so weary and afraid, she might have been amused by their interaction. The In-

360

dian seemed bent on coaxing Katie with strange items from his person. Only when he offered her a colorful feather did she relent and come nearer to inspect it.

At least, Colyer hadn't returned.

And Katie, having endured such a stressful night, the night before, fell asleep even before the sun descended fully. After tucking her into a blanket, the Indian came to sit beside the fire, keeping Elizabeth company in silence, watching her keenly as she kept vigilance over Cutter, and reviving the fire when it threatened to sputter out. In absolute silence they sat together . . . until late in the night. And still Cutter's fever remained high, though the scarlet streaks on his leg actually receded.

Growing weary, Elizabeth bent over Cutter, laying her head lightly upon his chest, listening to the erratic beat of his heart. Only a few more hours and there would be light to see by. She had to hold out till then . . . couldn't sleep . . . mustn't . . .

"*Ne-tonèševe-he?*"

Blinking when she heard his voice, Elizabeth lifted her chin and met his gaze. "W-What?" she asked, shaking her head in confusion.

"*Ne-tonèševe-he?*" he repeated, pointing at her. He pointed to himself suddenly. "*Na-tšeševehe Hestanováhe,*" he said, pounding his chest with a closed fist. "*Hestanováhe!*" And then he pointed toward Katie's huddled form. "Kay-tee," he said, repeating the word he'd heard Elizabeth use to address her. And again to himself. "*Hestanováhe!*" And then he pointed to Elizabeth. "*Ne-tonèševe-he?*"

She nodded, understanding finally. "Elizabeth," she revealed. "My name is Elizabeth."

"E-lis-ah-bet," he repeated.

Elizabeth nodded, and then glanced down at Cutter. Swallowing the raw ache in her throat, she placed her hand to Cutter's chest as she again met the Indian's gaze.

"*Nà-htsemaʔeme,*" the Indian whispered, before she

could speak. He pointed to Cutter and enunciated slowly. "*Na-htsema⁹eme.*"

Elizabeth had no idea what name he'd given Cutter, but from the solemn way he spoke it, it was obviously one of great respect. She'd thought her tears all used, but another slipped silently from her lashes.

The Indian came closer suddenly. Lifting her golden hair into his hands, he fondled it with awe. "*Véhonéma⁹kaeta,*" he whispered. He nodded and lifted her hair for her to see. At the same time, he dug into a pouch, retrieving a shiny golden object from it. A small medallion, which he then contrasted against her hair. "*Véhoné-ma⁹kaeta,*" he said again.

Elizabeth tried not to appear shocked as she stared at the medallion. Josephine had one similar to it—a token of her father's Catholic upbringing—and she found herself wondering who had owned this one previously. Certainly not the Indian. Vaguely she could see the raised golden image of the Virgin Mary, holding her baby son. Her eyes closed as she whispered a prayer for Cutter. She gulped back a sob, unable to speak for the emotion that assailed her.

Seeing her tears, the Indian restored the medallion into the pouch, and then moved to wipe them away. "*Naáotsèstse!*" he said softly, closing his eyes and cocking his head to one side. When she didn't immediately comply, he again cocked his head and closed his eyes, laying his head upon his hand. "*Naáotsèstse,*" he whispered.

He wanted her to sleep, she realized. Still unable to speak, Elizabeth nodded weakly and laid her head down upon Cutter's chest.

Satisfied, the Indian rose abruptly. "*Na-ase,*" he said, and turned away, and Elizabeth thought he might intend to leave, because he lifted his canteen, studied it an instant, and then set it back down again with a brief glance her way. She was touched by the gesture. That he would leave her something so precious as his waterskin.

"Thank you," Elizabeth whispered hoarsely, her throat raw with the salty burn of tears.

The Indian turned to walk away, and she knew intuitively that he was, in fact, leaving her. "Thank you!" she called out a little louder.

He stopped abruptly and turned to look at her, his brows furrowing slightly.

Elizabeth wanted to ask him why he'd come . . . to beg him not to go . . . not to leave her and Katie alone. But she knew that it wouldn't be in his best interest to stay. He would lose his life if someone came upon them. Too many would hate him for his color. He must have known it as well, and determined that the time had come for him to leave. She sensed it in the wariness that had returned to him. Nevertheless, his coming had been a gift that she would never forget, never question, and would always be grateful for, and her mind searched for the Cheyenne word Cutter had taught her to say thank you. *"Ne-esh!"* she repeated as closely as she remembered.

He raised his brows curiously at her pronunciation of the word; nevertheless, he seemed to understand, because the tiniest smile quirked at his lips as he nodded his farewell. *"Nè-sta-và-hóse-vóomàtse,"* he enunciated slowly. He glanced briefly at Katie, nodding, and then walked beyond the campfire's light, into the night. And despite the fact that she couldn't see him, couldn't hear him, Elizabeth sensed his presence for a long time afterward.

Somewhere, he was watching her.

Grateful for that act of kindness from a stranger, she sank back down over Cutter's still form, repeating the unintelligible words as a listlessness enveloped her. She concentrated on the beat of Cutter's heart, the rhythm of his breath. Tears squeezed from her eyes as she closed them. Seeing Cutter's face, she imagined she heard him call to her, speak to her. Finally she let go, and drifted . . .

"I failed—miserably!"

"No you didn't, Lizbeth. That's what I've been trying to tell you. The man was already six feet under when he fell off that horse. I tried to tell you as much . . . but you wouldn't listen . . . There was nothing more you could have done. As my mother's people would have said, the shadow had long left him, he only breathed—Chrissakes, woman don't you know how proud of you I am?"

"P-Proud?"

". . . Damn proud!"

. . . Don't you know how proud of you I am?
There was nothing more you could have done.
Nothing more.
The shadow had long left him, and he only breathed . . .
he only breathed . . .
only breathed . . .

Sobbing in her sleep, Elizabeth clutched at Cutter's sweat-soaked shirt, holding on to him as though to cleave him to her with that desperate gesture. She couldn't let him slip away, too . . . couldn't live without him. Her eyes flew open suddenly, red-rimmed from so much weeping, to find that the fire had long died, and once again, pink shaded the sky above. Cutter's eyes were closed, but his skin had cooled and his hair and clothes were soaked; a good sign.

Yet he was still. Too still.

The memory of Black Wolf lying so still in death besieged her suddenly, and despite herself, panic found a foothold. Closing her weary eyes in refusal, she began to hum, and when she realized what she was doing, her face contorted and she yielded at last to the convulsive sobs that shook her within.

"You can't leave me," she whispered, grief-stricken. "You can't—I won't let you," she told him, grasping his sweat-soaked shirt firmly. With lips that trembled, she kissed his mouth, tasting the salt of her tears as they slipped onto his wind-chapped lips.

Cutter's eyes opened, but Elizabeth didn't notice. Her own eyes were closed, her lashes glistening with tears, as she pleaded with him, savored his lips. The sight of her bent over him, kissing him with so much tenderness, filled him with exhilaration.

He'd awakened earlier to find her sleeping fitfully atop him, but bushed as he was, he'd let her sleep on. And within minutes, he'd fallen back asleep himself.

"Who will help me raise Katie?" Elizabeth sobbed brokenly. "I can't do it alone . . . I need you, Cutter," she implored. "Come back to me . . . please. Katie deserves a father . . . I need a husband . . ." She gave a choked little laugh suddenly, burying her head against his throat, whispering a kiss there. "Can't raise her out of wedlock, you know . . . What will people say?" she asked a little hysterically.

His Adam's apple bobbed. Elizabeth felt it and stiffened.

His throat thick with emotion, Cutter whispered, "Shhh, bright eyes . . . don't cry." He reached out, touching a lock of her hair, fondling it reverently between his scarred fingers, assuring himself that she was real, that he hadn't died and gone to heaven.

Startled by the sound of his voice, the unexpected touch of his hand, Elizabeth glanced up, tears shimmering in her eyes. A cry of relief broke from her lips. "Cutter?"

"You weren't askin' me to ride the river with you, were you, Doc?"

Confused, Elizabeth shook her head softly, repeating his words. "R-Ride the river?"

"Share a tepee," he said with quiet emphasis.

"Share a tepee?" she echoed over the pounding beat of her heart. A joyous tear slipped over her lashes and slid down her cheek as she began to understand what it was that he was asking. "I-I don't know how to swim," she replied recklessly.

Like the day she'd first laid eyes upon him, his eyes were dark, insolent, teasing her even now. "Blind as a bat, too," he remarked baldly, "and can't shoot to

save your life . . . but I'm willin' t' teach you the one
. . . overlook the other.''

Seeing the flicker of amusement in his eyes, Elizabeth managed a choking laugh, hot tears slipping
down her cheeks. Her fingers brushed reverently over
his beard, her eyes growing dreamy, full of yearning.
''I can shoot,'' she whispered, ''and I believe I see
very clearly, too, Mr. McKenzie—does that mean
you're accepting?'' She smiled tentatively, the beat of
her heart stilling as she awaited his reply.

For a moment he studied her intently. ''Depends,''
he replied huskily, a weak smile tipping the sensuous
corners of his mouth. Everything he'd ever searched
for was right there in her eyes.

''On what?'' she asked breathlessly.

His eyes grew openly amused, challenging her.
''On whether you're asking.''

Elizabeth stared at him, not quite believing what it
was they were speaking of—that *she* was actually asking him to marry her. She was actually asking . . .
She couldn't stop herself. Nothing could have
stopped her in that moment. She felt as brazen as she
likely sounded.

For an instant his eyes turned sober as he reminded
her, ''Won't be easy . . . being a half-breed's wife. Be
more like ridin' the rapids.''

Elizabeth choked on an elated sob. It didn't matter.
Nothing mattered except for the fact that she loved
Cutter McKenzie . . . wanted to spend her life with
him . . . wanted to bear his children. ''I . . . I believe
I'm asking,'' she murmured, half laughing, half cry-
ing. Hot, exultant tears streamed down her cheeks.

''Believe?''

''Am.''

A satisfied gleam came into Cutter's eyes suddenly,
and his husky whisper reached into her soul. ''Then
I reckon I'm acceptin', Miz Bowcock.''

With a joyous cry, Elizabeth surged forward, kissing his mouth passionately, sobbing without re-

straint. "I love you, Cutter McKenzie!" She withdrew suddenly, laying her forehead against his chin. "But you frightened me!" She lifted her anguished gaze to his. "Why didn't you tell me you were hurt?"

"Reckon I thought I was too tough to be brought down by a little-bit scratch," he told her honestly.

Relief washed over her to hear that it wasn't a lack of trust in her. "It wasn't a scratch. Don't ever do that to me again. Promise me you won't!"

He nodded.

"Promise!"

"I swear it," he whispered fervently, urging her back for another silky taste, intending to seal his vow with a kiss.

She sighed breathlessly, whimpering as he kissed her chin and then her lips. "I couldn't bear to lose you," she confessed.

Cutter responded with an oblivious groan, covering her mouth with his own and kissing her with all the emotion he'd locked away for so long, giving it all. Lacing his fingers behind her neck so she couldn't withdraw if she'd wanted to, he thrust his tongue possessively into her mouth, reveling in the sweetness and warmth she offered, his arms going about her . . .

"Are ya gonna make me look away now?" a little voice interjected with dismay, startling them both. "Granpa always makes me look away!"

Elizabeth jerked away in alarm, and Cutter released her promptly. Somehow they'd managed to forget Katie's presence.

Cutter cleared his throat suddenly.

Flushing at Katie's words, Elizabeth stared at Cutter in shock a long moment, not certain she'd understood correctly. And then, as she remembered Miss Mimi's impromptu speech, and Cutter's insight, her jaw slipped and her lips parted to speak.

No words came.

Cutter gave her a long look and arched his right

eyebrow, as if to say, I told you so, and then suddenly let out a peal of laughter at her expression.

Unable to contain it, Elizabeth burst out laughing as well, holding her arms out for Katie.

Katie flew into them, squeezing Elizabeth with all her might. And then her head popped upright as a dog's bark reached her ears. "Look!" she shouted suddenly, pointing over Elizabeth's shoulder. "Look! It's Shifless and Granpa!" She surged to her feet and began to run toward them.

Cutter lifted his head to watch her, along with Elizabeth. And it dawned on him in that instant, as he watched Katie run through the tall grass toward her yapping dog, that Elizabeth had saved his life, as well as Katie's and her own. Without Elias, because Elias was obviously just returning. He turned to look at Elizabeth in amazement.

She was watching Katie, too, her profile beautiful from where he lay. Her eyes sparkled with love, and he thought in that instant that he might be the luckiest man who ever lived.

"Cutter?" she asked suddenly, glancing down at him. "What does *nesta vah hosay voomats* mean?"

Cutter straightened his leg, grimacing at the lingering pain. "The hell you say?"

Elizabeth gave him a narrow-eyed glance and tried again. "*Nesta,*" she began again, "*vah hosay voo mats.*"

His brows lifted suddenly as he realized she was trying to speak Cheyenne. He chuckled. "*Nè-sta-và-hóse-vóomàtse?*"

Elizabeth nodded.

"Cheyenne," he told her. "It's Cheyenne. It mean's 'I'll see you again.' " He reached for a lock of her hair, turning it lazily about his finger. "Why? Did I say that to you in my sleep?"

Elizabeth shook her head, biting down thoughtfully on her lower lip as she glanced back up in time to see two blurry forms tackle each other and fall to the ground. "No," she said as she waved at the approaching riders. They were still too far for her to see them clearly, but one waved back excitedly, and she surmised it was Elias. "He came again," she revealed softly, as she watched the same figure slide off his horse to snatch Katie into his arms. Tears returned to Elizabeth's eyes. Despite the fact that she couldn't really see the touching scene, she could imagine it, and it was no less stirring in her mind.

Cutter's heartbeat quickened. "Who came?" he demanded.

"The Indian. I think he said his name was *Estanovah*," she repeated as best she could. Silence met her declaration, and she looked down into Cutter's face. "What does it mean?"

He would have chuckled at her pronunciation except that a bolt of alarm darted down his spine. "Life-Taker."

"Life-Taker," Elizabeth repeated solemnly, looking back at the hazy scene in the near distance. "It doesn't suit him," she decided with a sad little smile.

There was a sense of peace in her expression that touched Cutter to his soul.

"He took nothing," Elizabeth revealed solemnly. "Only gave." She met his gaze suddenly. "He called you . . . I think it was *'Notsemah-em.'* "

Another ripple went down his spine. "My blood," he translated for her, his voice little more than a hoarse whisper.

Elizabeth understood what a gift those words were, but the look on Cutter's face revealed just how magnificent a gift it truly was. "I never meant to blame you, or your people, for my mother's leaving," she told him, knowing instinctively that he needed to hear it. "My mother left because she wanted to, and for no other reason. Forgive me," she pleaded, her hand reaching out to brush lightly against Cutter's jaw.

Her words brought a jolt to Cutter's heart. They meant more to him than even Life-Taker's recognition of their kinship. "No need to ask," he assured her, pulling her down atop him. He didn't give a damn who saw them, not Elias, the men who rode with him, Katie, or even God Himself. "I forgave it the moment you said it," he told her. And though he hadn't realized until that moment, it was the truth. He knew as soon as he said it that it was.

Still, he wasn't going to let her off so easily . . .

He began to devise ingenious ways for her to make it up to him every day of the rest of their lives. He kissed her earlobe tenderly, nuzzling his head into the crook of her neck, and inadvertently peered over her shoulder . . . Beginning later, he decided with a groan of regret, when they didn't have an audience. He whispered something into Elizabeth's ear, and she bolted upright, her hand flying to straighten her hair.

Together they watched the riders approach; Cutter grinning broadly, and Elizabeth pink-cheeked.

As long as she lived, she didn't think she'd ever understand what happened to her senses when Cutter touched her! Nonetheless, she *was* certain she would enjoy pursuing the answer to that question.

And pursue it, she would.

Diligently.

Epilogue

Elizabeth had had very few customers; with two new physicians in Sioux Falls, the competition was just too great. And it didn't help much that she was in the last days of pregnancy. The women seemed not to be bothered at all by the fact. The men, on the other hand, didn't seem able to look her in the eye without blushing. Most of them seemed hesitant to come to her when either of the other two male doctors suited them better. At least it seemed they thought so.

So when Josephine rushed in, supporting Dick Brady so that he wouldn't fall on his face, Elizabeth was naturally ecstatic. She rose as quickly as she was able from behind her little desk and waddled toward them, her smile enormous. A white-faced Katie scurried in after them.

"He tripped over Shiftless," Josephine exclaimed.

"But he scared 'im, that's why!" Katie added plaintively. "And that's why he bited him, too!"

And it didn't take much to deduce where, Elizabeth thought, her brows furrowing, as she inspected Brady's face. Canine teeth marks ringed his bulbous nose, but only one of the puncture marks was of any consequence, and it was bleeding very little, if at all.

"Snake-headed dog," Brady muttered drunkenly. "Blamed thang yelped 'n' turned on me—made no never mind that I was flat on ma face already. Iffen ya ask me, I say he was bent on bitin' me!" He grinned suddenly and winked. "But I tol' Miss Jo here you'd fix me up right fine, 'n' here I am."

His disclosure thrilled Elizabeth, though she tried not to show it. He'd actually chosen to come to her? She had to remind herself not to be too delighted. The man was suffering, after all. She put on her most solemn expression. "Does it hurt very much?"

Brady shook his head, then nodded.

Elizabeth's brows lifted in confusion. "It does? Doesn't?" He shook his head. "Does?" she tried again, and Brady nodded. "Oh, you poor thing!" she said, giving him her compassion as she glanced down at Katie. There was so much of herself she saw in Katie, more each day; from the way she watched, wide-eyed, while Elizabeth treated patients, to the way she defended those she loved, even when they were in the wrong. Yet, as doting of Katie as Elizabeth was, she forced herself to give her niece a reproachful frown.

"But Aunt Lizabeth!" Katie protested. "Shifless was just taking a nap! That's all!"

Cutter appeared in the doorway, filling the room with his presence. He didn't have to speak for Elizabeth to know he was there. She sensed him and glanced over her shoulder, giving him a welcoming smile as she lifted the lid from a small glass container of gauze pads. He was wearing black trousers and a black shirt, but no guns, and no hat, and the grin he sported as he leaned against the doorframe gave him an almost boyish appearance.

He winked at her, raking a hand through his head. "Wrasslin' bears again, Brady?" he asked casually.

Surprised by the statement, Elizabeth gave Cutter a baffled glance. How had he known about that? And then she recalled, and her gaze flew to Brady. Brady's expression was so comically confounded that she pursed her lips to keep from giggling. He twisted his fingers together as he stared down at the wooden floor, and suddenly Elizabeth couldn't contain her mirth. She envisioned him stabbing and wrestling with nothing but himself, and began to giggle, softly at first and then with hilarity, clutching instinctively at her abdomen. Suddenly she gasped as a searing pain tore through her, doubling her over.

At once both Jo and Cutter hurried to her side. Despite the fact that Cutter was farthest, he reached her first. "Elizabeth!"

Jo's face paled with concern. "Are you all right?"

Katie's face paled, as well.

Together, Cutter and Jo began to lead Elizabeth up the stairs to their apartments above the office.

"No!" Elizabeth gasped, pushing Josephine away as another pang shot through her. "Stay—stay with Mr. Brady! Don't let him near—" she tried to whisper a warning into Jo's ear, but another pain came, making it sound more a shriek "—the knives!"

When Elizabeth doubled over, Cutter swept her into his arms, carrying her up the stairs and straight to the room they shared, leaving Jo downstairs with Katie. He laid her gently upon their bed, and then removed the shiny new spectacles he'd ordered for her.

"The water," Elizabeth groaned, trying to rise.

"Easy now," Cutter told her. "Jo will know what to do! We've gone over it enough!"

Elizabeth closed her eyes. "You're right," she relented. Laying her head back against the pillows, she forced a smile. Cutter's words were reassuring, but his tone was frantic, and she knew that she would need to remain strong to coach him.

All at once, Katie came racing in, with Shiftless barking at her heels. "He's bleedin', Aunt Lizabeth! He's bleedin'!"

Within seconds, Jo appeared as well. "Katie Elizabeth, get that dog out of here!"

"Oh, yes, ma'am!" Katie slapped her little leg, calling Shiftless. "Come on, boy! Come here!" Grasping the dog by the collar when he came close enough,

Katie dragged him from the room. Jo followed her as far as the door, closing it behind Katie, and then she turned to Elizabeth. "That man!" she declared.

Elizabeth's face whitened as dread, along with another contraction, ripped through her. "Good night!" she moaned. "He's stabbed himself!" Again, she tried to rise.

Cutter forced her back down to the bed, glaring at her.

"No. No. Nothing like that," Jo assured her.

"Then what?" Elizabeth asked, giving in to a little hysteria. "He wasn't bleeding when I left him!"

"Dammit, Liz, don't worry about Brady!" Cutter broke in. "You're bringing our baby into this world, and that's all you need to be thinkin' of just now."

Elizabeth's gaze returned to her husband. *"Our baby,"* she whispered reverently, and then another contraction squeezed her, and she gritted her teeth until it ebbed. When it was over, she swallowed and opened her eyes to look into Cutter's. His expression was full of concern.

"Cutter's right," Jo told her. "You don't need to be worrying over Brady. Besides, it's just that I socked him one," she disclosed. "Just an itty-bitty nosebleed is all he's got."

Both Elizabeth's and Cutter's gazes snapped back at Jo. "You socked him?" they asked simultaneously.

"Well, yes! You'd think he'd've learned by now to keep those dirty paws o' his off o' me!" She smiled at Elizabeth, winking.

"You see, I knew you were gonna be a little busy, so I thought I might bandage him myself . . . and the idiot pinched me."

"Where?" Cutter demanded, his gaze jerking up.

"Now, Cutter, he didn't mean any harm," Jo replied. "It's the red-eye that gets him roused. He can be a perfect gentleman when he's sober."

Elizabeth grimaced. "Trouble is, he's rarely—" she grunted as another contraction besieged her "—sober!"

she screamed, clutching desperately at Cutter's arm.

"Lucky man," Cutter said savagely.

Elizabeth blinked, surprised by the remark, and tried to remember to breathe. Her eyes felt as though they were crossing.

"Why is that?" Jo asked.

"Because . . . if I weren't busy playing doc just now, I'd break the son of a bitch's nose! As it is, you'd best get out there and tell the yack to leave before I'm tempted to finish the job you and Shiftless started."

Elizabeth grunted, concentrating on the soothing sound of Katie's voice outside the door. She was speaking gently to Shiftless, and she imagined that Katie was petting the dog, as well—much as Cutter was doing to her just now. She wished he would quit, but didn't have the heart to tell him to get his hands off of her!

"Don' worry!" Katie crooned. "Don' worry! Everything gonna be all right . . . You seeee . . . Aunt Lizabeth don't wanna go to heaven yet! She don' want to!"

Dear Lord, is that what she thought? Did she think her mother had had a choice? Elizabeth vowed to speak to Katie as soon as she was able—make her understand that no one would leave her by choice. She was just too special. She looked beseechingly at Jo.

Jo nodded, understanding Elizabeth's silent plea. "I'll stay with her," she said, "but first I'll fetch water and blankets."

Seven weary hours later, Cain Michael McKenzie was born into his father's hands. Clutching his son protectively, Cutter ran to the door, shouting, "We have a son! A son!" He came back to the bed and dropped to his knees.

Both Jo and Katie rushed in at once to greet the

newest addition, leaving Shiftless to whine and scratch at the door. They cooed over Cain as Cutter took him from his mother to bathe him, and then compared his hands to Katie's while Elizabeth held him.

"Oooh! They're so little!" Katie marveled. "Do you think he'll like Shifless, Aunt Lizbeth?"

Elizabeth nodded dreamily, her eyes drifting shut as she watched the doting scene before her. Glancing up, Jo caught her weary expression and rose from the bed. She ushered Katie out, explaining as she closed the door that Elizabeth and Cain were getting too sleepy.

When they were gone, Elizabeth gazed down at her son, her weary eyes reflecting her pride. The pain had been more than she could ever have imagined, but worth it, she thought as she glanced up adoringly at her husband. She just couldn't believe it. And Cutter had done so well, giving her strength when it seemed she had none of her own. "You saved my life," she whispered worshipfully.

"No," he murmured, lifting her hand and kissing it with so much emotion that Elizabeth thought she would burst into tears. She blinked as moisture pooled in her eyes.

"Much as I'd like to take the credit," Cutter told her, his voice hoarse, "I just followed directions. You did all the work." He gazed at her tenderly, then at his son. Black hair, and blue eyes that appeared more black than blue. "Besides . . ." he whispered as he caressed his son's downy head. He reveled in the feel of the silky hair against his scarred fingers . . . so much softness in his life. "Even if it were true . . . you save my life every day. Before you, Liz, I was dead inside and didn't even know it."

Elizabeth swallowed convulsively, fighting the wave of exhaustion that waited to claim her. "You were?" Tears shimmered on her lashes. Dear God, she'd waited so very long to hear this.

Cutter's eyes lifted, and to Elizabeth's shock, moisture glistened in his black eyes, making them sparkle like jet-colored glass. "I was," he assured her with a wink. His gaze lowered briefly to the child who lay between them, and then back to his wife's face, still disbelieving that she was really his. His. She'd given him so much. Everything he'd ever searched for was right there in her golden eyes. "I'm richer 'n Midas," he told her with a gleam in his eyes, "and aim to be just as greedy. Can't get enough of you . . . never want to."

"I . . . I love you, Cutter."

Cutter smoothed the hair away from Elizabeth's forehead and bent to kiss her eyes closed. "And I love you, Doc," he whispered back.

Elizabeth smiled, her heart filled to brimming, and let her cheek fall against the pillow. As she drifted, she listened to the sounds Cain made as he suckled.

"More than you'll ever know," Cutter whispered. But Elizabeth didn't hear. She'd fallen asleep. It didn't matter. " 'Cause I'm going to prove it to you every day of the rest of our lives," he swore. He didn't stop to mull over the fact that the vow he'd just made seemed vaguely familiar. Instead, he lifted his son up into his arms, his eyes full of warmth and a touch of arrogant pride as he secured the blanket around his baby boy.

"You're gonna hafta take real good care of those little jewels, son. Give me lots of fine grandchildren." He grinned as he looked down into Elizabeth's sleeping face, chuckling richly as he then advised in a husky whisper, "Yep, y' only ride double with the woman you intend to make your wife." He sank back into the nearest chair, propping his boots upon the edge of the bed to settle down for a long man-to-man chat with his firstborn son. Cain gurgled happily and curled his tiny fingers around Cutter's scarred thumb. "Yeah," Cutter agreed, his voice soft as he stared at that flawed thumb with those tiny wriggling fingers holding it in unconditional acceptance. His heart surged with elation. "That's right . . ." He nodded as a lump of pride thickened his throat. "Like your pa, you see . . ."

Unbeknownst to Cutter, Elizabeth's smile deepened.